**Eva** ████████████████ and she now lives in London, where she writes and lectures on creative writing. She likes wine, pop music and holidays, and thinks online dating is like the worst board game ever invented.

# Eva Woods

# THE
# EX FACTOR

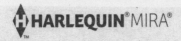
HARLEQUIN®MIRA®

Harlequin MIRA is a registered trademark of Harlequin Enterprises Limited, used under licence.

First Published in Great Britain 2016
By Harlequin Mira, an imprint of HarperCollins*Publishers*
1 London Bridge Street, London, SE1 9GF

The Ex Factor © 2016 Eva Woods

ISBN: 978-1-848-45468-2

0816

Our policy is to use papers that are natural, renewable and recyclable products and made from wood grown in sustainable forests. The logging and manufacturing processes conform to the legal environmental regulations of the country of origin.

Printed and bound by
CPI Group (UK) Ltd, Croydon, CR0 4YY

To Diana Beaumont, who makes me a better writer

# *Prologue*

*Marnie*

'*Will all passengers please fasten their seat belts; the captain has now started our descent...*'

She ignored the announcement for as long as possible. After all, when you were running away—when you had nowhere else to go—there was no hurry to arrive. Only when the air hostess came to tell her off did she grudgingly belt up, and take out her headphones and open her window blind. From above, London was grey. Like something shrivelled, shivering in the January air. She wasn't sure why she was coming back. Not home—she didn't know exactly where home was right now.

The plane banked lower through freezing winter fog. Around her people began to gather their possessions, crumple up their rubbish, stretch their legs and arms. Looking forward to a new city. Buckingham Palace. The Tower of London. Madame Tussauds.

Not her. She was terrified. But if her mother had taught
her anything, it was this: *always get your game face on*.
And so she put on her huge sunglasses, despite the gloom,
and brushed in-flight food from her carefully put-together
outfit, reapplied red lipstick. Was the cape-coat too much?
The dress too bright? No time to change now. She took out
her phone and composed a tweet. Hitting the tarmac! Can't
wait to see you all, London! xx.

She had a moment to think of what she'd left, and feel
the tears push at her eyes for the tenth time that journey.
*Game face*. She pasted on a smile. The tannoy dinged, and
the grey ground came into sight. She was back.

# Chapter 1
## Interrupted Routines

*Helen*

How many texts do you get in an average day? How many emails, Facebook alerts, tweets? Most get instantly forgotten—your friend obsessing about their weight or if their boss spotted them on Facebook (ironically), that marketing newsletter you keep meaning to unsubscribe from, a celebrity's breakfast on Instagram. But sometimes you get a message that's more than this.

This message might not say anything special. At first you might even ignore it, roll over and go back to sleep, slip your phone into your bag, forget about it. But although you won't know it at the time, the message is the start of something that means that your life will never be the same again.

Of course, at least 99.99999 per cent of them are total rubbish, but still. You can never quite be sure.

\* \* \*

Helen was woken by the buzz of her phone, shooting upright in bed, groping on the bedside table among the TV remote, the control for the windows blinds, the tissues, the hand cream, and the framed photo of her cat—her flat was somewhere between NASA launch control and the Pinterest board of a forty-something spinster. She blinked at the phone. Read the message again. Emitted a small 'huh' to the empty space beside her in the bed, then checked the time: 7.45 a.m. Only a person of deep selfishness would text a freelancer at 7.45 a.m.

The message stayed on the screen, burned behind her eyes. Her first thought was: *She's back. Hello, Marnie, goodbye non-interrupted sleep.* Her second thought was: *Bloody hell! She's back!* A flicker of something came and went in her stomach—excitement. Nerves. Something else that she couldn't quite identify. Then she sat up and started Googling bars, restaurants, and detox treatments.

\* \* \*

There's a saying that if knowing someone doesn't change you as a person, then they're not a true friend, just an acquaintance. Helen would have added to this. If knowing someone didn't permanently make you feel like you were about to get on a roller coaster—excited, terrified, and with the slight possibility of serious injury—*then* they weren't a true friend.

She got up on the dot of 8 a.m.—no need to vary the Routine yet—and commenced her morning. It was a Tuesday, so she washed her hair, flossed her teeth, and shaved her legs. She rubbed in a deep conditioning mask, setting her alarm for exactly four minutes, then spent that time looking into the mirror at her flushed face and chanting, 'I am successful. I am happy. I am fine on my own.'

She wasn't convinced by the affirmations—she didn't feel all that successful or happy. But she was most definitely on her own.

She cleaned out the shower and sprayed shine mist, then gave the sink a quick rinse and gathered up the towels and sheets for the wash, as she did every week. Then she made coffee in her cafetière, gleaming beside the sink where she'd washed it last night, and boiled an egg for exactly five minutes, putting the toast in at the three-minute mark. During all this time she didn't glance at her phone once.

Discipline. That was the key.

At 8.46 a.m., Helen judged it was a good time to text back. Hi! Great news. Shall I round up a fun posse? As her finger hovered over the send button, she debated asking where Marnie was staying, then didn't. She probably had something sorted, a squat or a house-sitting job or a boyfriend she'd already picked up in Victoria Coach Station.

The answering text came straight back, which meant Marnie had just arrived, and wasn't sure what she was doing. Yeah! 2nite if poss? Would love to c u all xx.

Helen opened up the Facebook Messenger group she used every day to chat with Rosa and Ani. Guess what! M's back.

She imagined them picking the message up: Rosa at her desk in the newspaper office, Ani on her way to court maybe. Both dressed smartly, with lanyards and coffee and bright work faces. Ani came straight back. Whaaaat? Out of the blue like that? Any word on where she's been all this time?

Dunno. I guess we'll find out. Dinner tonight?

Tonight tonight? As in later on this same day?

Oh come on. Live a little. You can get out at eight surely?

Ani's reply came back. I'm meant to go round to my parents. Crafting ornamental flowers for my cousin's engagement party while answering 10,000 questions about when it's going to be my turn.

Helen typed: Wouldn't you rather come for a lovely dinner instead of that?

Ani: I would literally rather staple my eyes shut instead of that. So—count me in, I guess. What about you, Rosa?

Rosa answered. Am typing from under my desk, guys. Again. Have started keeping tissues down here.

In Rosa's open-plan office, under her desk was one of the few places she could hide to cry. Which was what you needed to do a lot when you'd just split up with your husband, and said former husband worked on the other side of the room.

Would a drink cheer you up? Helen quickly typed. Totally understand if not.

Why not, said Rosa. Career and marriage in tatters, might as well work on social life. Newly single Rosa was prone to such pronouncements. G2G. Need to redo make-up before David comes past.

Take care, sweets, said Helen. Remember you're amazing and we love you and you don't need him.

G2G too, I'm due in court, Ani typed. Acrimonious divorce hearing. At least David didn't sleep with your sister, Rosa.

Probably only because I don't have a sister.

Helen signed off with expressions of sympathy and good luck. Miraculously, she'd managed to gather up all four of them on a weekday night, in London, in January, with just a few hours' notice. That seemed enough of an achievement for one day, but work called.

She clicked on her inbox, taking a deep breath. She loved working from home, couldn't imagine going back to an office, but you had to have rules. Getting dressed was one, even if it was in pyjamas. Another was not letting what she did affect her life—but this was easier said than done.

Her first email said: I think my husband has been meeting someone from your site. Can you give me his details? It's disgusting. I don't know how you can work on something like this.

Helen's heart squeezed. Finding out that the man you loved was seeing someone else, kissing them, holding them, sending flirty messages: it wasn't that she couldn't imagine it. She could, and only too well. But this was her job. She typed out the standard response. We're sorry but we can't give out information about our members. We'd suggest you talk to your husband—it could just be curiosity, or a cry for help. Maybe you can spice things up a bit?

She took another deep breath and added the rest. She hated to, but her boss insisted. PS—you can always sign up with us yourself!

Helen pressed send. Some days, most days, she hated what she did, hated herself for doing it. It certainly wasn't what she'd expected when she'd applied for the in-hindsight-too-good-to-be-true homeworking job two years ago, but by the time she'd found out it was already too late. And here she was, stuck. She glanced at the masthead of the website she ran. *Bit on the Side. The UK's top dating site for people in relationships.*

Another day at the office. Everything was the same as usual, except that Marnie was back.

\* \* \*

*Ani.*

Ani put her phone away as she approached court. Her client was waiting on the steps, smoking into the breeze. Ani tried not to wince as he leaned in to kiss her. She preferred a nice brisk handshake or better still, no physical contact at all. 'Mark, hi. How are you feeling?'

'Can't wait to get it over, like, so I never have to see that bitch again.'

'Well, you will have to see her if Taylor and Ashley end up living with you.' (Which they were asking for. Which she'd advised against.) She kept on her smile.

'Sure, sure. I mean—I just wanna make sure I get my rights, you know? They're my kids too.'

Ani told herself it was not her job to pass judgement. It wasn't her fault if Mark's ex-wife started crying the minute they went into court, or if Mark tried to look down the blouse of their barrister, Louise, or if the opposing barrister was twenty minutes late, causing them all to sit in awkward silence, the judge leafing through the docket with increasing irritation and saying things like 'What is PlayStation?' or 'Mr Smith allowed his daughter to watch *Keeping Up with the Kardashians* for four hours? What is a Kardashian?'

Eventually, Louise started to say, 'Sir, perhaps we should…' and just then someone swept in in a flurry of expensive wool coat.

'So sorry, sir. We had to suspend a hearing, my client fainted.'

*Yeah right*, thought Ani, who was wise to such tricks.

The barrister would be cramming as many cases as possible into the day, trying to bump up his income. She looked up and her irritation grew exponentially. He was about thirty-five, tanned even though it was January, and his green eyes stared out from under expensively cut black hair. Handsome, and entirely aware of it.

'All right, Mr Robins, proceed,' said the judge, mollified. Ani looked at her papers—Adam Robins. He cast her a glance as he glided into his seat, as if to say he could wipe the floor with them without even trying.

And he was right. Louise was good but Adam Robins annihilated her, listing all Mark's transgressions—shagging Denise's sister under the Christmas tree, blowing the kids' present money on *Call of Duty 4*, telling Denise he'd get her a gift subscription to Weight Watchers because 'that's what you really need, love'.

Mark occasionally protested: 'I never!', 'Well, she always said she were fat!', or 'It weren't full sex, just oral', but Ani was surprised when, at the end of it, he still got part-time access to the kids. He trailed out muttering in an unconvincing manner about men's rights. 'This is a disgrace, I'll be getting onto Fathers for Justice.'

'They disbanded,' she said crisply, as they stood on the court steps. 'Well, Mark, it wasn't what you wanted, but it's the best result possible, really.'

Undaunted, he said, 'S'pose. Listen, you busy Saturday?'

She misunderstood at first. 'I don't work weekends, and anyway…'

'Nah, I meant you and me. Curry, pint. You know some good places for a curry I bet. What's it short for, by the way? Ani's not an Indian name?'

She stared at him for a minute, speechless. A voice cut

in. 'Anisha. Sorry, Ms Singh, I mean. I just wanted to say: no hard feelings?'

It was the bloody barrister, Adam Robins, sweeping his dark hair off his face. Mark shook his outstretched hand, seemingly unperturbed by the character assassination Robins had just carried out on him in court. Ani glared at him. How dare he be so handsome and so confident. 'Mr Robins, is it? Maybe you could try not to be late in future? My time is valuable too, you know.'

Adam Robins blinked. His eyes were the exact shade of green Fruit Pastilles. 'I'm sure it is—I know your hourly rates, after all.'

Mark's eyes widened. 'You're saying she…'

'For *law*.' Ani turned her back on the barrister. To Mark she said briskly, 'I'm leaving now. I have other clients.'

'Can I get your email then? Personal, like.'

'Sure. It's ani@notinamillonyearspal.com. Do contact me for the next divorce you will almost inevitably have.'

As she stomped off, she heard Adam Robins make a small noise that could have been a laugh, and Mark asking, 'Is that all lower case, you reckon?' It was unprofessional, but she didn't care. And that was why she was, at thirty-two, more single than a single LP—no B-side—and why when she saw her parents at the weekend she'd have to once again tell them that, no, she wasn't seeing anyone, and no, she still didn't want them to find her a nice boy, thanks all the same. Because how could you believe in love when you spent all day sweeping up the smashed remnants of it?

At least she had dinner tonight to take her mind off things. After all, if there was one person who was more terminally single than Ani, then that was Marnie.

\* \* \*

*Rosa.*

Rosa was sitting at her desk again, running through her mental checklist. Eye make-up smears? Check, she'd stopped wearing it two weeks ago, after she'd interviewed a mid-list actress without realising she had massive smudges all down her cheeks like Dick Van Dyke in *Mary Poppins*. Snot on face, dress, hair? Check, she'd taken to carrying around so many tissues that were she to fall out of an aeroplane she would probably survive without even minor bruising. Her floral dress, cardigan, and thick tights might have caused her fashion-forward boss to visibly wince that morning, but at least she looked respectable. Was she currently making loud gasping sob noises without even noticing? Check, unless she'd gone deaf at that frequency. All was fine, or at least as fine as it could be given her husband had left her two months before.

She looked at the copy on her screen. *Star of TV cop drama* 'Aving a Laugh *Natasha Byrd lived up to her name at our brunch. Picking at a salad, she told me she eats only once a day and...*

Crap. Like jungle drums, she knew when David was approaching. Rosa's desk was right on the route to the main meeting room, and the editorial conference must have ended early—most days she hid in the loos at this time, waiting for him to get safely back to his desk. Only one thing for it. After grabbing her phone, she slid gently to her knees and ducked under the desk again. It was cosy down there, among the trailing leads and decades-old dust. It was fast becoming her new favourite place.

'...So I think let's go big on detox for Jan—more quinoa, more mung—what's the newest grain, anyone?'

*Ow!* The castor of Rosa's chair, pushed aside by unseen hands, rolled over her thumb. 'Holy CRAP,' she yelled, before she could stop herself.

Oh no. 'Bloody hell, are you OK?' She peered up to see Jason Connell, the new whizz-kid editor who'd been poached from clickbait site *Listbuzz*, along with her boss, Suzanne, who was in metal-look leggings and on a two-week Botox cycle.

'What are you doing, Rosa?' demanded Suzanne. 'Aren't you a bit old for hide-and-seek?'

But Rosa could only look at the third person in the group, in his skinny red jeans and clashing yellow T-shirt. The man she'd married five years ago, the man she'd intended to spend her life with. Who she'd never expected to see wearing red jeans, or packing up his collection of vinyl and moving out, or for that matter, sleeping with an intern. She'd advised him against the jeans, but he'd bought them anyway, and in retrospect that should have been a sign.

'Rosa?' David was staring down at her. 'Are you all right?'

'Fine!' She tried to summon every ounce of journalistic *nous* that might be left to her. 'Um, it's a new trend I'm testing. It's called—head-desk-space.'

'Head-desk-space?' Suzanne's over-plucked brows nearly met in the middle of her Botoxed forehead. She had no facial expressions left, so she had to inspire sheer terror through slight flares of her nostrils. It was a closely guarded secret—which meant everyone from the cleaner to the board members knew—that Suzanne had once been caught *in flagrante* with Bill McGregor, the married MD, in the old print rooms of the newspaper, and consequently could never be fired, despite being the personification of pure evil—the impressions on the evening edition had apparently left little to the imagination.

'Yep. It's a new meditation trend,' said Rosa desperately. 'You know, research shows mindfulness can boost performance at work by up to…um…forty-seven per cent.'

'I like it,' said the new editor. He loomed over Rosa—he must have been over six foot tall, and was built like a surfer, his wavy blond hair slightly too long and his tie slightly too loose for London. On a better day, when she wasn't hiding under a desk being watched by her boss, his boss, and her soon-to-be ex-husband, Rosa might have found his Australian accent sexy. 'It's a good angle. Ways to work smarter, not harder. Can we do a feature?'

'Sure!' said Suzanne gamely. 'Whatever you like, Jason. We'll get right on it.' But her nostrils said—*I will kill you, Rosa. I will crush you like I crush fresh lemon for my morning detox.* Rosa, however, could still only look at David. He gave her a quick glance—was that pity?—then turned and walked away. She'd been right. Those jeans really did make him look like a Christmas turkey.

Jason Connell was still watching her curiously. She tried to communicate with a smile that she was a slick, totally professional, valued member of staff—not easy when you were hiding under a desk. He hunkered down to her, and gently flicked her long dark plait. She gaped.

'You had dust in it.' Then he smiled—was that a *wink*?—and went back to his office.

Rosa resumed her seat. Only four hours and twenty-three minutes before she could leave the office, have a drink and, with any luck, obliterate the bit of her brain that would remember this encounter. And Marnie was back! Marnie was sure to have some advice about how to cope with working in the same office as your ex. After all, there was no dating situation on earth she hadn't experienced.

# Chapter 2
## Pickled Eggs and Popcorn

*Helen*

'The reservation was like for seven?' The waiter gave Helen a scowl as he took her to the table (not actually a table but an old school desk, this being a trendy London eatery).

'I know, I'm just early.' Twenty minutes early. Helen-time. She wanted to check it wasn't too noisy or too busy, and that they had a good table, not too close to the door or loos. It had to be nice, since she was dragging Ani and Rosa out on a school night. And things with Marnie might be a little weird, after her disappearing act. She felt another flare of nerves in her stomach.

'Because like I can't hold the table?'

Helen looked around the empty place—it was a Tuesday night in January after all—and tacked on a conciliatory smile. 'Of course. They won't be long, I promise.' The waiter sniffed. He had tattoos up both arms and one of a butterfly on his cheek.

She wondered who should sit where—if only it was acceptable to make out place cards for casual social occasions! But despite it all, Helen was excited. For months now she'd had a slight, a very very slight, third-wheel feeling. Rosa and Ani had met in uni, and even though they'd all been friends for years, Helen was always aware she was the newcomer. But Marnie—well, ever since day one of primary school, Marnie and Helen had come as something of a package deal. 'Like those twins, where one is living inside the other and slowly eating it,' as Marnie had once cheerfully put it. Before Marnie left, the four of them had been a tight-knit group, where no one ever got left out or felt alone. Maybe they could go back to that? Helen's stomach dipped again. So many things had happened since then. It seemed unlikely.

Rosa was the second to arrive, unwinding her long scarf from her plait. 'I couldn't stay another second,' she declared. 'I swear, working with David, it's like—' She mimed a rope around her neck. 'I'm going to have to change jobs. Go back to *Puzzle Weekly* or *Knitting Times*. Oh God. And today I actually had to fabricate a whole trend that helps you chill out at work.'

'I'm sorry. Want some Rescue Remedy?'

'Yes please.' Rosa opened her mouth and Helen squeezed in a few drops from the yellow bottle.

'Berocca?'

'Go on then.'

Helen rooted around in the massive handbag she always carried. Ani called it the Doombag, because it contained solutions for everything that could possibly go wrong in life, short of full-scale nuclear war. Ani herself arrived just then, shouting into her phone. 'Tell them the offer is derisory. Yes, that actual word. *D-e-* Can't you just look it up?' She waved over to them. 'I have to go. Just get it sorted, will you?'

Rosa put a guilty hand over her fizzing orange drink. 'It's, um, a new cocktail?'

Ani raised an eyebrow. 'I don't think caffeine is a good idea for you right now, judging by the manic texts I've been getting all day. How's the fake trend?'

'Booming,' said Rosa glumly. 'How was court?'

Ani took off her jacket, revealing a cream silk shirt and tweed skirt, and fluffed out her neat bob. 'Well, we lost, and the opposing barrister was really hot—'

'Ooh, was he?'

'—yeah, so obviously I was really rude to him and basically called him a twat—'

'Of course.'

'—and then my sleazy client hit on me.'

'Ew.'

'Worse—I realised it was the first time anyone's asked me out in months.' She looked round. 'No Marnie then?'

'It's only twenty past,' said Rosa, checking her watch.

'Will she show?'

'Of course. She texted earlier.' Helen wished she felt as confident as she sounded.

'I bet she's got a lovely tan,' said Rosa, stabbing at the retro pickled eggs the waiter had just brought. 'Maybe I'll move to South America too. Leave behind horrible cold London and my horrible boss and horrible David. Marnie's probably picked up some gorgeous Brazilian beach dude.'

'Or dudess,' Ani reminded them. 'Remember that Dutch girl she went out with?'

'Oh yeah.' Rosa sighed. 'God, I am *such* a dating novice.'

The waiter was eyeballing the empty place. 'Are you expecting the rest of your party soon?'

'Very soon. We'll be happy to move if you fill up.' Ani was pleasant and assertive—Helen resolved to copy her in future. 'So Marnie's been in South America all this time?'

Helen shrugged. 'I think so. It was Argentina last I heard.' Soooo gorgeous, the food is to die for, the kids are beautiful... Marnie's life was like a travelogue, beamed out via Facebook and Twitter. Nothing ever went wrong. Every day was hashtag-blessed. But communication had been sporadic for a while now—Marnie too busy having the time of her life to get in touch, most likely.

Ani was looking at the menu. 'Well, should we order? Oh, surprise, surprise, pulled pork. Tell me this, is there any un-pulled pork in the whole of London right now?'

Helen was starting to feel anxious, checking the time, when she realised—like the night bus you wait for so long you slip into a sort of hallucinatory state—Marnie was there.

\* \* \*

There was something about Marnie. A shimmer in the air around her. Even though Rosa was sad and Helen was worried and Ani was tired, all three of them looked up as she came in, and one by one they smiled.

She was thin, was Helen's first thought. Thin, and incredibly pale given she'd been travelling, and she'd cut her strawberry-blonde-copper-ginger hair into a short crop. It would have made someone else look like a dinner lady, but on Marnie it was cute, child-like yet sexy. She was wearing a vast cape, which again came out more catwalk trend than 'Little Red Riding Hood: the London Years', and a short dress the colour of sunshine. Her big green eyes flicked over them, faltered. 'Guys, I'm late—I'm not used to the tube...'

Helen was on her feet, gathering her up. 'Never mind. You're here!' Marnie smelled like she always did, of exotic spices and airport lounges. For a moment, Helen felt the name hover between them. Would Marnie mention Ed? God, she hoped not.

Marnie's arms met behind Helen's back, and she pulled away, staring. 'Oh my God! Look at you!'

Helen blushed. 'Oh. Yeah.'

'How come you didn't tell me?'

Helen didn't say: *Er, maybe because I haven't heard from you in months.* She said, 'Oh, it's no big deal. I just joined a gym and stuff.'

'Um, hello, you must have lost, what—three stone?'

'Four,' said Ani. 'She looks amazing, doesn't she? Hey, it's great to see you.' Ani was on her feet now too, embracing the other side of Marnie, and Rosa draped herself over them, so the four women were enmeshed in a kind of eight-armed hug monster.

Marnie squeezed Ani: 'God, you look like a grown-up, I love the suit,' then kissed Rosa's wan cheek: 'Sweetie, I'm so sorry about David. I want to hear everything.' Soon they were sitting down, and the waiter, suddenly happy and smiling after the application of Marnie's magic smile and her warm, 'Hi! How's your day been?' was bringing extra pickled eggs and sneaking them popcorn in little tin buckets.

'Pulled pork,' said Marnie, looked at the menu. 'What's that? Sounds like what they used to put in the 'mystery meat' sandwiches at primary school. I'm not paying £17.99 for school dinners, they can do one.'

The others burst out laughing. 'Marnie,' said Ani, raising her jam-jar cocktail. 'London has missed you.'

\* \* \*

It was almost as if Marnie had never been away, Helen thought, trying to manoeuvre her head-sized burger into her mouth. As if she hadn't just left two years ago, without even saying goodbye, only surfacing to email from various exotic locales. Everyone was carefully not mentioning it, though Helen was dying to ask: *Why did you go? Why didn't you tell me?* But then, she was keen to keep the conversation away from the events of two years ago. They'd just been listening to the sorry tale of Rosa and David's break-up, retold for Marnie's benefit.

'…I'd no idea anything was even wrong. I just thought he was a bit stressed at work…'

'Ah love, that must have been horrible.'

'And this girl had started as an intern. Daisy. You know the sort, all cute and helpless and, um…twenty.'

(Cute and helpless was Marnie's thing, and Helen had time to realise this, quickly panic, and then relax in relief. Marnie was not twenty, not even close.)

'Ooooh, tell me he didn't…'

'It came up on his phone. He was too stupid to turn off the messaging…'

'Oh my God, the utter dick.'

'And I asked him and he said they were in love, and he was moving in with her—I mean, Jesus, she lives with four other students in some fleapit…'

'I can't believe it!'

'And Mum and Dad, you know what they're like, they think they're so lefty and hip, then suddenly Mum's crying on the phone to the rabbi and Dad's down the synagogue with David's uncle trying to sort it all out—they're not even *practising*, it's ridiculous…'

By the end of the story Marnie's eyes were jewel-bright with tears, and Rosa was half crying, half laughing. 'At least I kept the flat. And at least I never have to listen to his stupid Bob Dylan B-sides ever again. I guess, if I'm honest, I should have known he wasn't happy. I mean, I actually had to beg him to have sex with me instead of watching *Robson Green's Extreme Fishing*. But now I'm thirty-two, and I'm single again, and I have no idea what to do. How do you date? I don't even know. You're the dating expert—help me!'

Marnie swirled her glass of 'Brigitte Bardot's Knickers' (it being against the law to have non-ironic cocktail names in London), a concoction of Campari, gin, and Fanta, and looked at Ani and Helen. 'Hmmm. What about you two, any romance?'

When Marnie wasn't there, Ani was too pessimistic to discuss her love life, Helen just didn't date (because: reasons), and Rosa had been happily married until a few months ago. So at the question, a silence fell over them. Helen cleared her throat. 'Ani got asked out by her client,' she said.

Ani rolled her eyes. 'Mr "I had sex with my kids' auntie under the Christmas tree", yeah, great. If I'm lucky he still has his Santa suit. Otherwise, no, still nothing that sticks. Mum and Dad are starting to despair of me, I think.'

'And you, Helz?'

She went for an ironic shrug and ended up spattering chipotle mayonnaise on her chin. 'Do Dr Derek Shepherd and Walter White, crack dealer, count as men? Because I've been spending a lot of time with them.'

'No, box sets do not count.'

Helen squirmed. Marnie couldn't know the real reason

Helen hadn't dated in two years. 'Ach, it's such a lot of hassle and heartache—tell her about your last date, Ani.'

'The one where he took out his contacts and said, "You could be anyone now!", then his cat bit me on the foot? I still have the scar.'

'Not him, the other one.'

'The one who took off his trousers and he was wearing Superman pants? Or the one who didn't even have a bedroom? Honestly, he was living in an actual airing cupboard.'

'I was thinking of Blubbing Ben, actually.'

'Oh *God*, yes. Wait till you hear this, Marn.' Ani launched into a story of a date she'd had recently, the punchline of which was 'and then he spent the whole evening crying on my shoulder, and the worst bit was, it was a dry-clean-only top'.

Rosa shook her head over her 'Brighton Rock and Roll'— peach schnapps, vodka, cream soda, a stick of actual rock to stir it. 'I don't know why you can't just date someone nice, Ani.'

'You sound like my mum. I'm *trying* to find someone nice—I date all the time. You guys don't know what it's like. I don't want to put you off, Rosa, but if you decide to jump back into the water, well, online dating is like deliberately swimming into a big shoal of sharks.'

Marnie was nodding. 'My friend Caty, do you remember her? The one who does reiki healing and has that weird little sausage dog? She was seeing this guy she met online, and it was all going really well, except he wouldn't invite her to his place. He said his flatmates were always there, the place was a mess, he needed to clean up, blah blah. Then one day he says, fine, come round. So she goes, and it's lovely. Like a really nice clean grown-up place. And the next morning they're making waffles in the kitchen, and she's in his shirt, just like in a romcom.'

'With yoghurt?' said Helen, transfixed despite herself by the image.

'Yep. They are totally eating yoghurt. Probably he's dabbed some on her chin and licked it off. Anyway, you can see where this is going.'

'Oh no.' Rosa buried her head in her hands.

'Oh yes. So the door goes and it's his wife. That's right, she's home early from her holiday. With the kids. So that's internet dating,' said Marnie grimly. 'Every time you think it can't get worse, you hit another rock bottom. A new low standard every time.'

'It's not all like that,' Helen said. 'I mean, I would know.'

'Of course, I forgot you ran that dating site.' No surprise—Helen never talked about her job. Because: more reasons.

'How come none of us have ever used it? Maybe I should, now my husband's left me for a teenager.' Rosa was attacking her drink as if it had personally offended her.

Helen wished she hadn't said anything. She usually succeeded in making her job sound so dull no one ever wanted to ask about it. 'Um, well, it's sort of a bit…niche.'

'Trust me, Rosa, babe, you don't want to go online,' said Marnie, shaking her head. 'No offence, Helz. I'm sure you do a great job. Rosa just needs to be eased in.'

'None taken,' she said, with huge relief. Mentioning her job, how stupid. That and Ed were two topics that needed to be avoided at all costs.

'She's right,' said Ani, who was on her third 'Why Hasn't He Kahluaed?' (Kahlua, pineapple juice, a dash of paprika.) 'I went on Tinder, and I got chatting to this guy who seemed nice, so I asked him out, and he said could we just meet in a park so in case we didn't like each other we could save money on drinks, and we met up and it was freezing and we walked round in the rain for half an hour and then he tried to shove his hand down my top.'

Helen no longer felt like drinking the rest of her 'Sloe Dirty Orgasm', a sloe-gin martini with an unfortunate splash of Bailey's leaching through it. Across the table, Rosa was also looking crestfallen. 'Sounds awful. Is there any point? I might just stay home and watch *The Great British Bake Off,* like the spinster I'm now inevitably to become.'

'I've got a better idea.' Marnie wiped the remains of her aubergine dip from her plate—as Ani pointed out, London food was more like Milupa every year. 'Ladies—and sorry to lump you in, Rosa, babe—but am I right in thinking that what we have here are four totally single women?'

Helen hadn't known Marnie's romantic situation, was afraid to ask. And there was no need to usually—she would tell you herself, in Technicolor detail. 'I guess so,' she said cautiously, as Rosa slumped into her spicy coleslaw.

'So why is it? Why are we all single? Look at us.' Marnie spread her arms. Helen moved a glass out of her way. 'We're amazing, sassy women.'

'That's the problem,' said Ani. 'They don't want sassy women.'

'No,' said Rosa gloomily. 'They want twenty-year-olds who wear Miffy T-shirts to the office.'

Marnie said, 'I bet that's not true. You must all have one nice ex, who isn't a total moron or douchebag.'

'I've been with David since I was nineteen,' said Rosa sadly. 'I met him in a lecture, and then he showed me how to use the soup dispenser in the canteen. It was so romantic.'

Marnie's gaze turned. 'And you, Ani?'

'Oh, I've dated loads of people, as you know. But I'm considering stopping it all and taking up stabbing myself in the eye with pencils instead.'

'And were any of them nice?'

Ani shrugged. 'A few were fine. Just no spark, you know. Nothing ever seems to get off the ground.'

'Because she's commitment-phobic,' said Rosa, stabbing at her drink.

'I'm not commitment-phobic! I'm just looking for something very specific.'

'Which doesn't exist. No one's perfect, Ani.'

'Well, I'm not giving up just yet. Believe me, when you handle as many divorce cases as I do, you want to get it right.'

Helen knew it was her turn next. She took a large bite of her burger, and a swill of ironic cocktail. 'I don't have any recent exes,' she said, quickly. 'I've sort of been off dating since you—since I last saw you. You know, keeping up with my busy schedule of Netflix and cleaning the bathroom.'

'This whole time?'

That whole time, almost to the day. *Deflect.* 'Well, more or less.'

Marnie wasn't letting her off so easily. 'But you could date if you wanted. You're so pretty—isn't she? And so nice.' Ani and Rosa nodded agreement; Helen blushed into her cocktail. 'See? And loads of boys have liked you. What about…' Helen watched her friend mentally scroll through almost thirty years of history. 'Donny Myers?' she came up with, finally.

'Oh for God's sake. We were six!'

'He asked you to marry him once, remember, with that note in assembly?'

'Aw,' said Rosa, sappily.

Helen held up her hands in disbelief. 'Donnie Darko? You must be kidding me. Don't you remember, he was the prime suspect when Hammy the Hamster went missing that time? And then no one would sit next to him at lunch for the whole rest of school?'

'But *apart* from that, he was all right.'

'Apart from suspected hamstercide? That's like saying apart from those few hours, it was a lovely voyage on the *Titanic*.'

'I'm sure I'm still friends with him on Facebook,' said Marnie stoutly. 'I could look him up. Don't you want to meet someone?'

Ani shook her head. 'We've tried. She doesn't.'

'She's in a rut,' said Rosa.

'Hey, I like my rut,' Helen said. 'I'm thinking of getting it re-upholstered in fact. Maybe in a nice paisley.' And she did like it—as ruts often were, it was very cosy and safe. *Deflect, deflect.* 'What's this all about, Marnie? Are you not dating anyone at the moment?' If so, that was an unusual state of affairs. *And hey, what about Ed? Why did you leave? What's going on in your head?*

Marnie sighed. 'Oh, it's a disaster out there. The last person I dated, Hamish was his name, totally gorgeous, seemed really into me, and then I go to meet him for our fourth date and he doesn't even turn up.'

'Hamish?' Rosa frowned. 'Were there not any hunky Latin lovers out there?'

'Hmm?' Marnie looked puzzled. 'Oh! No, well, you know, there are lots of backpackers and that. Anyway, he won't answer my emails or calls, just totally ghosts me.'

'That sucks,' said Rosa. 'How rude!'

'Par for the course sadly,' said Ani. 'More ghosts in London right now than in the whole of *Ghostbusters*.'

Marnie was nodding. 'Guys. As you know, my love life has been…varied.' There was a tactful silence. Helen ran through some of Marnie's dates—the guy who literally went off to join the circus, the guy who bred guinea pigs in his bedroom, the guy who turned up to meet her high on ketamine… Not to mention Ed, of course. Which she was steadfastly not doing.

'You've certainly given it a good go,' said Ani kindly. 'If dating was a job you'd be in a corner office right now.'

She meant it nicely, but there was another small silence— Marnie's employment history was as long and chequered as her love life. She liked to describe herself as an artist when asked what she did, or sometimes a 'world traveller', which was a bit annoying seeing as it wasn't an actual job, unless you were a Victorian lady of independent means and adventurous spirit, travelling with a feisty lesbian companion or dallying with the porters. Over the years, Marnie had attempted a variety of mad jobs—dog walker, life model, working in an occult bookshop—and even the odd proper one in a call centre or office. But they were thirty-two now. Helen wasn't sure, but she suspected they were approaching the cut-off time between 'charmingly whimsical' and 'forty-year-old still living in their parents' garage'.

'I've had enough,' Marnie was saying. 'I'm sick of moving about, different cities, different countries, meeting guys on Tinder, youth hostels, beaches… I want to find someone *nice*.'

Helen was afraid to say the next thing. 'So what were you…?'

'Guys, I've got the best idea.'

And there it was. The phrase that had prefaced most of the disasters of Helen's life, from the Sun-In green hair incident of 1994, to the vodka and peach-schnapps vomit-off of 2003. But which had also heralded many of the best days, the laughing-till-you-fell-off-your-chair days, the most precious moments, Instagram-bright.

'What?' said Rosa, who was the kindest of them, but who'd also missed out on the most insane Marnie times by virtue of being at home with David cooking Nigella dinners and watching box sets of *The West Wing*.

Marnie said, 'Well, we're all single. I don't think that's ever happened before. Sorry, Rosa. But it's true. And we'd all like to meet someone nice.' Helen opened her mouth to say she didn't want to meet anyone, nice or otherwise, then shut it again. 'But Ani's stories are scary—and me too, I've had some awful times online dating. You can't be sure what you're going to get.' Marnie leaned in eagerly. There was a flush to her pale face, her green eyes glowing. 'What I'm suggesting is this—we each set one of the others up with an ex of ours.'

'That's crazy.' Helen had blurted it out before she could think. She tried to never use the c-word. 'I mean, what? I don't understand.'

'Simple.' Marnie dusted off her hands and pointed round the table. 'Rosa would, say, set Ani up with someone she's dated. Ani'd set you up...'

'What?' said Helen and Ani in unison, but Marnie went on, undeterred: '...and you'd set me up. I'd do Rosa. That's just an example. We could always draw names. And we'd have to have rules. Like, only nice people. The whole point is to get a better option than those online dates. A sort of Freecycle, but for guys. He-cycle, if you will.'

'I really, really will not,' muttered Helen. Dating each other's exes! This was dangerous. *Deflect, deflect!*

'That's mental,' said Ani, and Helen winced at the word. 'Someone would definitely get upset. And how would it even work?'

'Like I just said.' Helen had forgotten that Marnie could be surprisingly organised and persuasive when she put her mind to something. 'Why's it mental? I want to meet someone, don't you?' She looked hard at Ani.

'I mean, I guess, but only if...'

'How many internet dates did you go on in the last year?'

'Um...a few.'

'How many's a few?'

'I don't know.'

'I bet you kept count.' Marnie was staring her out. 'Twenty?'

Ani was turning red. 'Um...a bit more than that, *maaaaaybe*...'

'More than thirty? More than forty?' Marnie was like Jeremy Paxman with eyeliner flicks. 'Come on, tell us.'

'Forty-seven,' Ani whispered.

'Christ on a bike,' shouted Rosa. 'Sorry. Sorry, Christians. I mean—just, wow.'

'I want to find the right person!' said Ani, still red. 'And you know, it's so easy online. You just click, and then if you're free, why not meet up? It's either that or let my parents set me up with Dad's golfing buddy's nephew from Leeds, who has his own mobile disco business.'

'Exactly.' Marnie slapped the table. 'It's too easy. It's like going to Tesco. And it's about as romantic. Whereas this way—well, we can have a man curated for us by our lovely friends, who know us so well.' She beamed at them. 'Think about it. It takes out all the risk—we get pre-screened, pre-dated men.'

'Curated,' muttered Rosa, who seemed to be having trouble with the whole conversation. 'I don't know. This is all new to me. I'm still getting my head around being single.' She bit her lip, and Helen could see her eyes were filling up. Most of their nights out recently had ended with a weeping Rosa. She looked round at her friends—Marnie flushed and determined, Ani scowling, maybe thinking of her forty-seven bad dates, Rosa on the verge of tears. And what if Marnie suddenly suggested someone take on her most dateable ex of all? No way. The subject had to be changed, and fast. And Helen, with conflict-defusing skills that Ban Ki-moon would be proud of, was the Official Difficult Subject Changer of the group.

'Guys, it's a lovely idea, but remember—I don't date. Like, ever. So I'm afraid I'm out. Now, did anyone want dessert? They have an ice-cream sundae made with popping candy!'

# Chapter 3
## The Internet Wizard

*Helen*

Helen woke up the next morning not at 8 a.m, or even 9, but at the unconscionable time of 10.36 a.m. Her tongue felt like the bottom of the bin right before she washed it out with bleach and hot water (second Wednesday of the month). Bloody Marnie.

The night had dissolved somewhere around one, with Helen being poured into an Uber. She never got taxis—she could afford the odd one, but she saw it as a sign you hadn't planned your night properly. And she was always hearing horror stories from Rosa about their shady safety standards. Admittedly, Rosa herself had been fast asleep in the back of one heading north. Helen must have been drunk, because she'd asked if Marnie needed to stay at hers.

'No, no,' she'd said, putting Helen in the cab—she was always mysteriously sober, despite being so tiny. 'I have somewhere sorted. It's fine.' She'd patted the side of the car and stepped back, holding her arms away from her cape to wave.

Sitting up now and groping for her phone, Helen realised she didn't know if Marnie even had the money to get home. Or where home currently was for her. In fact she hadn't managed to find out anything about Marnie's life for the past two years. Some friend she was. But at least, in all this talk of exes, there'd been no mention of Ed. She squinted at her phone. It glowed with message symbols, missed calls and voicemails, emails, texts, even WhatsApps. And her heart stilled.

No. Not now. It couldn't be her mum, after all this time— Oh, thank God! They were all from Logan.

Logan Cassidy: internet mogul, entrepreneur, and owner of a vast network of shady businesses, from the dating/cheating website Helen reluctantly ran, to a cut-every-corner budget airline and a chain of underwear shops for larger ladies, More Than a Handful.

MASSIVE EMERGENCY, the first email read. Helen scrolled down. BIG SECURITY BREACH CALL ME NOW. And the last one—WHERE THE HELL ARE YOU?

Helen closed her eyes for a second. It was going to be one of those days. She called Logan, clearing her throat again and again to try to sound like she hadn't just woken up. 'Hi! Sorry, I had an early doctor's appointment. Er, women's troubles.'

'Whatever, whatever,' he said hastily, in his South London growl. 'Now I need you on this ASAP. I think we've been hacked. Like them that got into the Pentagon.'

'What's happened?' Logan had an overdeveloped sense of the importance of bitontheside.com in global events. It was probably just a server glitch.

'Someone's replaced the profile pics. Instead of all that skiing and raising bloody glasses of wine, they're bloody—well, have a look.'

Helen felt panic bubble into her bloodstream. This wasn't supposed to happen today. She was already behind on dusting the bookcases and brushing Mr Fluffypants, a job that was only slight less dangerous than being a UN weapons inspector. 'They didn't get into the personal data?'

His voice softened. 'No, that's locked up tighter than a nun's chuff. But the rest—the fences are down, the T. rex is out, ya know? So I'm gonna send in the T. rex wrangler.'

'Er, what?'

Logan was a big *Jurassic Park* fan. He reputedly had a life-size model of a dinosaur in the atrium of his mansion in Essex. He saw a lot of John Hammond in himself. 'I'm sending a web guy to you,' he yelled. 'He's meant to be good. Total geek. He'll fix it, OK?'

'OK. But what do you mean, to me?' He didn't mean to her flat, surely?

'You're still in that dump in Peckham, yeah?'

'It's Peckham Rye actually and it's really up and coming—but Logan—Logan!'

'Going into a tunnel. Bloody sort this for me, Helen. I'm counting on ya.' His voice faded.

Helen caught a glimpse of herself in the mirror, eyes bloodshot, blonde curls sticking up, boobs falling out of her *Frozen*-motif pyjamas. Then she heard the cheerful trill of the doorbell. It really was going to be one of those days.

She shuffled to the door of her basement flat, tying up her silk dressing gown—a present from Marnie when she'd worked in a vintage shop, and which for years Helen had felt too big to wear, preferring to hide inside massive towelling robes. A big man stood on her doorstep. Not fat, but very tall, very wide. Strapping. If you could call someone strapping when they wore a T-shirt that said 'No I cannot fix your computer' and combats with more pockets than a snooker table. He had flaming red hair and a red beard, like a Viking, and he glanced pointedly at a Casio watch.

'Yes?' she said, irritably, through the security chain.

'You've got a bug,' he said. Northern accent.

'Um, no, I just—I worked late…'

'In your website, I mean. I'm here to have a look.'

'How do I know that's who you are?'

'Did your boss not say I'd be around?' He scrabbled in one pocket, then another. 'Bollocks,' he muttered. 'OK, here.'

She glanced at what he'd handed her. 'That's a Block-buster video card. Which expired in 2004.'

'It's not my fault the high street could no longer keep up with the increasing ease of pay-to-view websites. Speaking of websites, yours is borked.'

'Borked?'

'Yeah, it's like—a technical computer term for up the swanny. Now let me in or it'll only get worse.'

'OK,' she relented. 'I'm not—this has taken me by surprise.' He looked puzzled. 'I'm not dressed,' she explained.

He looked her over. 'You are dressed, i.e., you're not naked.' Helen stared at him. He stared back. 'Computer… fixey? I'm sorry, you are employed by that dodgy South London geezer, yes?'

'Yes.' Helen snapped into action and held the door open. 'I'm sorry. What do you need me to do?'

'Show me the admin details. Who does the coding?'

'The original design was before my time, but I do the basic maintenance and admin.'

'You know code?'

'Yes,' she said defensively. 'What, because I'm a woman?'

'No, because you wear pyjamas with cartoons on. Actually that's quite a coder-y thing to do, I should have realised.' He sat down in one of her lovely vintage armchairs, making the old springs groan, and whipped out a laptop. It was square, functional and very un-sleek. Like him. 'I'll need your computer too.'

'What? Why?'

'Because, if you have malware or something, it'll be on there. Malware is, how can I put this—totes bad software that will totes corrupt everything.'

'I know what malware is!' People really didn't take you seriously when you wore Disney clothes as an adult, Helen reflected. She set him up with the details, then hovered anxiously in the kitchen as he worked.

'Jesus Christ on a bike,' he said at one point.

'Not good?'

'Let's just say your defences are more lax than *Dad's Army*. A child could get into this.'

'Why would a child want to get into a dating website?' she said, crossly.

'Dating. Is that what you call it?'

'Of course. It's a place to meet new people.'

'New *married* people.'

'You think it's any different from other sites? Half the people on Tinder are married—and so dumb they use their wedding photos as profile pictures. At least this way it's more open, and you know what you're getting.' Helen swelled in righteous anger. 'Anyway, it's none of your business. If you don't like it, don't also work for it by fixing the site.' He stared at her. Helen realised her dressing gown had fallen open in her ire, and hastily closed it. 'Sorry,' she muttered. What was she thinking, shouting at a total stranger?

'Hey, I don't mind either way,' he said. 'I was just curious. The personal details are secure, anyway. But someone's been hacking you. Look, all the profile pictures—well, they're not of *faces* any more, put it that way. Brings a whole new meaning to the term "dickhead".'

Helen looked, then felt a slow blush move over her face. 'Is that…easy to do?'

'No. Do you know of any enemies the site might have?'

Helen thought of Logan and his cut-price empire. The media attention the site had attracted through a series of dubious PR activities. The time he went on *This Morning* and got into a fist-fight with Phil. 'Um…any number, to be honest with you.'

'Right. Well, I've fixed the bug that's replacing the photos, so people can show off their ski holidays and trips to Machu Picchu again. But you need to beef up your security.' He spun her laptop back to her. 'By the way, you've got an email from someone called Marnie. Subject—*amazeballs dating plan*.'

'Give me that.' Blushing, Helen pushed the screen down. 'Thanks for fixing it. But I should get dressed now. I mean, in clothes.' Oh great, now she sounded like she was flirting. 'It doesn't inspire confidence, you know,' she said, in a burst. 'Your T-shirt. I mean, that's your job, isn't it? Fixing computers?'

He squinted down. 'Oh. I didn't realise that's what I was wearing.'

'Do you have another one that says "Have you tried turning it off and on again"?'

'How did you know?'

'Never mind.'

He stood up. 'You didn't tell me your name. Normally people tell me their names and offer me cups of tea and stuff.'

'Sorry. You just took me by surprise.'

'It's OK. I don't understand why people set so much store by drinking hot liquids. Anyway, I'm going to tell you my name, in case you get hacked again.'

'Is that likely?'

'Yep. I've fixed it now but whoever did it was good. The bug also found every instance of the word "snowboarding" and replaced it with "looking like a douche".' He let out a loud laugh. '"I really enjoy jetting off for a spot of looking like a douche." Sorry, but your hacker is hilarious. I'd like to shake them by the hand.'

'But—you're sure this was done on purpose? It wasn't a virus, or a server problem?'

He gave her a withering look. 'A server problem wouldn't replace all the pictures with ones of people's penises. You were hacked.'

'Oh my God, just like in *Jurassic Park*. Logan was right.'

'You like *Jurassic Park*?'

'Duh. I was born in 1982, of course I do.'

'Right. I just thought, you know, the kittens.' He waved a hand at her cushions, which were upholstered in a distinctly feline theme.

'Kittens and dinosaurs are not mutually exclusive.'

'Actually they are, because mammals weren't really around until the Pleistocene.'

'Probably one of the many reasons why opening Jurassic Park was such a bad idea.'

He gave her a long look. Helen held his gaze. He said, 'You're right, as it happens. You can't get Jurassic Park back online without Dennis Nedry. Lucky for you, I am Dennis Nedry.' He paused for a second. 'Except, you know, not really gross and into industrial sabotage and stuff.'

'Good to know.'

He fumbled in one of his many cargo pockets. 'My card. Not a Blockbuster one this time.'

*Karl Olsen, Computer Wizard.* 'Wizard, huh?'

'Yes, I am the Gandalf of online security. They shall not pass. Well, there's no need for you to tell me your name, but contact me if your hacker starts again.' He chuckled. '"Looking like a douche". That's a funny guy.'

'You assume it's a guy.'

'Yes, yes, hashtag–not all hackers, I know. But statistically it most likely is. Bye.'

Abruptly, Karl the computer wizard shouldered his rucksack and headed for the door.

'Wait,' she said suddenly. 'Helen.'

'Helen?'

'Er… That's my name. And I— Look, when I started this job, it was a normal dating site. It just didn't take off, so he changed it without telling me. Always bank on the lowest end of the market, that's Logan's philosophy. I've looked for a new job, but there's not much around.' And she couldn't bear going back to work in an office (because: yet more reasons), and every time she imagined going to interviews it made her throat constrict in anxiety, so she stayed where she was and tried not to think about the harm she was doing every day.

He shrugged. 'It doesn't matter what I think, Helen. I'm just some random computer genius and, as you pointed out,

I'm participating in the evil by fixing the site. So don't worry so much. OK?'

'OK,' she muttered, tying her dressing gown tighter.

'Are you all right?' He looked at her keenly. 'You seem somewhat suboptimal.'

'Yes, I'm just—I was up late, and this is a bit of a shock.'

'It's all fine now. Computer wizard. *Expelliarmus*.' He made a bizarre air-wand gesture. 'You're still upset though?' She shrugged. Of course she was. 'Do you mind if I…' He reached out one large finger and touched her on the forehead, between her eyebrows, pressing hard.

Helen felt an instant relief of tension. 'What are you doing?'

'Pressure points. Helps with the anxiety. Well, bye then. I'd say it was nice to meet you but in all honesty I think it just made you intensely uncomfortable.'

As he left she realised it was the first time a man had been in her flat in two years. Well, a human man, anyway.

'YRRROOOWWL!'

Helen felt an affectionate blood-drawing scratch on her bare leg and bent down to pick up Mr Fluffypants, her sociopathic Persian cat. Green eyes, fluffy white fur, weighing the same as a small Rottweiler. She was very well aware that she was a living stereotype, but when everything kicked off two years ago it had seemed inevitable she'd become a tragic spinster, so she gave in and got a damn cat. And some cushions. And learned to crochet. She had her eye on a foot spa next.

She kissed the cat's fluffy head. 'Who's a good kitty? You're the only man I need, aren't you? You'll never leave me?'

'YROOOOWWWL!' Mr Fluffypants, spotting a bird

in the garden, shot from Helen's arms and right out the cat flap. She sighed. Story of her life.

* * *

*Ani.*

Ani read Marnie's email on her work computer, squinting at the weird fonts and emojis, and immediately dashed off a message to Rosa asking if she'd seen it too. There was no way she was doing it. No. Way. Anyway, she had other fish to fry. Didn't she?

She took a deep breath, flexed her fingers over the keyboard, and called up a different email address. Hi! Hope you had a good Christmas?

Was it too late for that, in January? She changed it to: Hi! Happy New Year!

Too many exclamation marks? She deleted the first one. Still on for tonight then? Where shall we go?

Maybe she should wait for the response before asking where to go—it might seem too forward. But then, maybe it was dangerous to leave the suggestion open that it wouldn't go ahead. She needed this to go ahead.

'Are you OK, Ani?'

She looked across at her colleague, Catherine, who was spooning up quinoa salad from Tupperware and Googling yoga retreats. 'Fine, why?'

'You were sort of…muttering to yourself.'

'Oh. Just…thinking of strategies for the Leyton divorce.'

'The one where she stole all his limited-edition tiepins and had them melted down?'

'Yes. He's suing her for five grand. Who even spends five grand on tiepins?' Ani shook her head. There it was, every single day—the end of love, the terrible things people did to each other when it had all burned away. Sod it. Tonight couldn't go as badly wrong as that—there just wasn't time. She pressed send with a firm click, and then she pushed back her work chair and lifted her Radley bag. Everyone in the office looked up in surprise—Ani was an inveterate desk-luncher. 'Going out,' she said firmly. 'I'll be an hour or so. Or, you know. An hour exactly.'

What Ani had not told any of her friends, largely because she was doing her best not to think about it herself, was that she already had a date that night. Date number forty-eight in the space of a year. Though it was a new year now, so perhaps she could start again from zero. Perhaps this would be the one, and it would all work out, and she wouldn't have to go on any more internet dates, wouldn't have to swipe right and left until her thumb went numb, and definitely wouldn't have to take part in Marnie's ridiculous dating pact idea.

She'd met Will at a birthday party before Christmas—the kind of thing she'd usually avoid, a lot of lawyers, drinks in a chain bar with watered-down cocktails, desultory chats about house prices. One of the couples in the group, Phil and Jemmy—him red cords and coffee breath, her ski tan and tight rictus smile—had got engaged recently and planned to hire a 'lovely little barn' in the Cotswolds for a mere twenty grand. Ani had watched her friend Louise, whose birthday it was, exclaim over the ring, while Jake, her boyfriend, stared uncomfortably into his Peroni.

'Yay! Another wedding.'

She'd looked up at the unexpected sardonic tone—wondering if for a second her thoughts had developed a voice of their own—and saw a man scowling beside her. He was pleasant-looking, with a square-ish face, corduroy jacket, and pink cocktail in his hand, which he was sucking at determinedly through a straw.

She gave him a sideways look. 'It'll be lovely I'm sure. Very original. Dove release, probably.'

'Wishing tree. Pictures of the couple holding up thank-you signs. Japes when the first-dance music starts out romantic then goes into "Smack My Bitch Up".'

Ani looked at him properly. 'Not a wedding fan?' She was already thinking, *But what if he's single and we hit it off and he doesn't want to get married what will I tell my parents maybe it wouldn't work maybe I shouldn't date him.* The part of her brain that could pinpoint potential areas for defence in a heartbeat could also have her married to and divorced from a man in 0.3 seconds.

The man's face fell, but he kept drinking, talking around the glittery straw. 'My fiancée just left me. Sort of put me off.'

Was it a bad idea, dating such a recent dumpee? It was times like this that Ani missed Marnie, despite her flakiness. There was no point in asking long-married Rosa about dating: 'Just be open and tell him how you feel, what could possibly go wrong?' Or Helen, who never dated at all: 'What's the point? Bet the fiancée dumped him for good reason, like he picks his nose or wears her pants.' But Marnie would listen to every last detail, then say he sounded lovely and she was sure it would all work out. Even if he didn't, and it definitely a hundred per cent wouldn't.

As Ani walked aimlessly towards the shops, her phone dinged. Was it him? What if he cancelled, or if his vague suggestion of meeting up hadn't been serious? She'd messaged him after they met, carefully non-committal, so that if he replied 'OMG of course I don't want to date you, YOU

HEARTLESS CRONE' she could claim she was just being polite. Plausible deniability, that was the key in dating. And also in defending people who'd made some pretty serious errors of judgement in life (same thing really). And he'd replied, We should meet up again sometime, but was that just something people said? What if he'd changed his mind over Christmas? Got back with the fiancée?

It was him. Her fingers shook slightly as she scrolled. Hi! Happy New Year. How about a curry maybe—Brick Lane or something? It was an odd choice for a first date—too formal, too pressured—but she let him off, as he was out of practice. She replied Sure OK x, taking care not to be too enthusiastic. She didn't want him to think it was anything better than a solid uninspired choice. Game on.

Nervy and tense, Ani wandered up and down the aisles in Boots, with a vague uneasy sense that she ought to be doing things to herself. Buffing. Moisturising. Plumping up some of her hairs and removing some of the others. She bought a limp prawn sandwich and some Ribena, then found herself staring at the rack of condoms by the till. Uh-uh. Rule number one of dates—you had to trick the universe into letting things go well, and that meant putting in as little preparation as possible. Ideally you wanted to be found with unshaven legs, wearing your least favourite outfit, and perhaps with spinach caught in your teeth. Ani, in every other way a devout rationalist, believed firmly in the powers of the jinx. Unfortunately, she was not very good at being unprepared for things.

'Do you have your Boots Advantage card?' asked the man at the counter.

'Yes,' she sighed, digging it out. Of course she had. She always did everything right. So why couldn't she manage that in her love life?

\* \* \*

*Rosa.*

Amazeballs dating plan!

Rosa received Marnie's email on a painful morning at work, during which she was trying to keep her head, if not actually *under* her desk, then as far down onto it as it was possible to get. Her temples throbbed in steady rhythm with the clacking keys around her. On her desk sat three different types of liquid—a bottle of water, a giant coffee, and a can of Diet Coke. None of them had helped—she should have realised that, as the others had tried to explain over the years, nothing could touch a Marnie hangover.

Unable to face the email at first, she went back to tapping at her feature on 'head-desk-space', the hot new in-work meditation trend that was sweeping the nation. Only trouble was, it didn't exist. So far she had two hundred filler words on January—*Now the last of the mince pies has been eaten and the New Year's resolutions are starting to shake, it's time to reaffirm our goals for the year. A recent study—* here she'd added square brackets and a note to herself saying 'FIND OR MAKE UP LATER'— *says that 67% of us want to be more fulfilled in work. The solution? Meditations and exercises we can do at our desks.*

Her phone beeped and, hoping for the magic inspiration that would finish off her feature, she grabbed it. Ani. Have you seen M's email? She was really serious??

Rosa sent back a surprised emoji and opened her personal email again. She usually kept it closed, as Suzanne was not above snooping: 'So I notice you're having painful periods, I want five hundred words on that by three.' The message from Marnie read Super awesome fourway dating plan!!!!! Five exclamation marks. The points on them seemed to wink at Rosa's hungover brain.

Hi lovely ladies! Rosa groaned out loud. Following last night's totes fun dinner, I have gone and done some further thoughts on our v v sensible plan. 'Totes' had really crept in as a word, Rosa thought. Maybe there was a feature in that... How your thirties are your new twenties. How thirty-something women are pretending to be younger, maybe because their husbands are leaving them for teenagers in cartoon T-shirts.

She read on.

So, I think the best thing to do would be to each pick a friend, then set them up with an ex of our choice. We're bound to at least find someone decent that way. (TripAdvisor for men!) However I think there need to be some rules.

1. Only exes we are over! We don't want broken hearts or unresolved tensions getting between us.

2. They must be nice. No hairy backs or creeps (unless you think your chosen friend will like that).

3. You must tell your friends every single detail! At the very least we can use this as a v v good social experiment. I'm thinking we should call it Project Love—the mission is to find us all a lovely date without the risks of going online.

Rosa groaned for a final time, disturbing the somnambulist occupant of the next desk, Sleepy Si, who did the night shifts. 'Sorry,' she mouthed, as he settled back. She sent another emoji to Ani, this one startled and a little upset. In her current state of mind, the smiley faces seemed to sum things up better than words.

'Rosa?'

She took a deep breath. How did Suzanne manage to move around without making a sound? Did she have some kind of pact with the devil whereby she could defy the laws of physics? 'Yes, hi!'

Rosa's boss was standing over her, tapping one stiletto heel. With her leather trousers and teased blonde hair, she looked like Stevie Nicks with an account at Cos. 'Meeting room. Now.'

Rosa scurried after her, wondering what Suzanne's problem could be. Had the barista put full-fat milk in her latte? Had her childminder allowed the twins to watch *Rastamouse* again? Oh Lord, David was in the meeting room, along with various hacks from different parts of the paper. She slunk into a seat, trying to make herself as small as possible. David looked fresh and youthful, his facial hair shaved into some odd little beard. No doubt it was all the rage with the under-twenty-fives.

Jason Connell, Editorial Whizz-Kid, swept in, buttoning his suit. Rosa caught a whiff of lemon aftershave, masking the unmistakable scent of Alpha Male. 'We're up crap creek,' he said succinctly. 'Five clients have pulled their ads from this week's supplement. We've even lost the underwear chain More Than a Handful, and they've been advertising with us since 1994.' How did he know all this, when he'd only been in post for a month? Rosa supposed she ought to feel alarmed, but such was the horror of her hangover that nothing else could get to her. Not even David, taking notes in the corner like the school swot he was. 'So I need ideas. And fast.'

She was dimly aware that people were saying things. 'How about a piece on ways to save cash?' The Money section. Reviled and mocked for the rest of the year, January was their one chance to shine, and even Jason gave them a brief smile for the effort. 'Maybe. Thanks.'

'What about the rise of mumpreneurs?' That was David, who worked on Business. It wasn't a bad idea. Rosa saw Suzanne's nostrils twitch—he was treading on their turf.

Jason nodded. 'Good. That kind of thing. We need something really snazzy. A big piece that will make people choose us over other papers and magazines.' He pointed to Suzanne and Rosa. 'There's scope for Features to take market share from monthly consumer magazines too, if we come up with something good.'

God, what recycled guff could they peddle this time? Ways to revive your flagging sex life? Top winter sun destinations? Both things Rosa now had no use for.

'Rosa.' Jason's steely eyes were fixed on her, and she felt an odd blush rising up her neck. 'Any ideas?'

'Um…organic veg boxes?'

A terrible idea. She heard Suzanne suck in air through her teeth. But Jason smiled encouragingly. 'That workplace meditation idea—what did you call it? A lifestyle hack?'

'Er, yeah.'

'Right. Well, I want more like that. It's January. Everyone's in a rut, miserable, wanting to change their life. Except they don't want to change their life at all. No one *actually* wants to quit their job and move to Bali.'

Rosa was nodding. She understood exactly what narrative they were selling: change without having to go through any actual change.

Suzanne snapped her fingers in Rosa's face, hissing, 'Come on, ideas, ideas.'

'What, more?'

'Yes, more. This is what we pay you for.'

It wasn't, thought Rosa. They paid her to sub-edit, and she did features for no extra on the side, but her mind had gone blank. 'Um…um…'

'Come on!' Suzanne's face was almost moving—and you really didn't want that. Everyone was staring. Jason, David. All waiting for her to say something decent, anything to prove she was still capable of journalism. 'I want an idea, Rosa!'

Rosa said the first thing that came into her head. 'Um… what about a pact to date your friends' exes?'

\* \* \*

*Helen:*

Helen read Marnie's email with a sinking heart. She was still in her dressing gown, though it was gone midday. The business card of the weird IT guy was in her pocket, poking into her stomach. She reread the line: We don't want broken hearts or unresolved tensions getting between us!

Well, that was one rule that had been broken for years. She wondered if Marnie had thought of Ed when she'd suggested this dating swap. It was her idea to pass on exes. Would she even mind if it was him?

She looked down at her phone. Imagined typing it. Hey, Marnie, sorry I forgot to mention this but I kind of slept with Ed? But no. She couldn't. And she couldn't do this dating pact. Because Helen knew from bitter experience that one of the worst things you could ever do was fall in love with your friend's ex.

# Chapter 4
## The Accidental Proposal

*Ani*

Ani had a terrible habit, almost shameful in modern times—she was incorrigibly on time for everything. She did her best, slowing her walk right down on the way from the tube to the restaurant, but she was still only four minutes late. She ordered a gin and tonic in the almost-empty restaurant, and when she thanked the waiter he said something in reply. 'I'm sorry?' He said it again and she realised—Hindi. 'Er…I only speak English, sorry.'

She'd hoped it would be a cool Brick Lane place, of the type Rosa was always having to do features on, where they served the food in hammocks or only ate cereal or things on toast. She looked at the laminated menu—a bit of curry was stuck on the side. It wasn't a cool place. And Will was late. Despite years of dating, Ani had not been able to reconcile herself to the lax attitude to time most people displayed. On impulse she texted Marnie: Waiting for late date. Many misgivings.

Marnie came back: Might be OK? Give him a chance!

Horrible Indian restaurant. Twenty minutes late. Rebound man.

Hmm. Three strikes already. May as well stay though—a girl has to eat.

That was true, Ani thought. It was nice having Marnie back, rather than off roaming the world somehow. She'd actually missed her. Despite everything. So she stayed, but she'd already eaten her way through five poppadums with lime pickle when Will walked in the door. Twenty-five minutes late. Just inside her threshold for 'no longer pretending it's OK', which was half an hour. 'Hi!' She half rose, wondering if they'd hug, then sat down again when he pulled out a chair. 'How are you? Good Christmas?'

'I— OK, I suppose.' He sighed deeply. 'I'm sorry. It's just—well, I ought to tell you. I had a run-in with Kat last night.'

Kat? Who the…? 'Oh. Your ex?' Ani tried to infuse the syllables with threat, understanding, and indifference all at once. It was hard.

'Yes, she—well, she came around. Said she wanted to get a few things.' Ani braced herself to hear they'd slept together. 'She gave me back the ring,' he said, dolefully. 'Her engagement ring.'

'Oh—well—is that good? Maybe you can sell it?'

'They have almost no resale value. It's worth like a tenth of what I paid.'

'How can that be? The metals at least—'

'The truth is, Ani, jewels have no real value. It's like everything with weddings. It's worth what you'll pay for it. When you still believe you're in love. But take that away and it's just a cake, or a dress, or a bit of metal.'

Ani was thinking through the implications of that. 'It's almost as if you're buying…'

'Hope,' he finished bleakly. 'Yeah.'

Hope, she thought, eyes focused on a smear of pickle on the passing waiter's shirt. Hope was what kept her going on date after date, year after year, thinking, what if this, tonight, was the one, and she cancelled because she was tired and really wanted to watch *The Good Wife*? What if her perfect man, the love of her life, slipped her by because she wasn't paying attention, because she slacked off for a second, because she was too impatient and sharp and scared them away? But she could now see that, despite Marnie's encouragement, tonight's hope was outside the restaurant, setting off sadly down the street. What had Marnie said? *A girl has to eat.* 'I haven't had any dinner,' she said firmly. 'Shall we order?'

'Oh. I guess. I'm not sure I could eat much.'

The waiter came. 'Any ideas?' she said to Will, brusquely. 'I'll have a lamb bhuna and a peshwari naan, please.'

He was staring at the menu. 'It all sounds the same to me. Kat and I used to eat in a lot, salads, healthy stuff. She really kept in shape.'

'So why did you pick this place?'

'I thought you'd prefer it.'

Ani held her breath till her ears popped. 'Look, my parents aren't even from India, they grew up in Uganda. Just pick something.'

'I don't like spicy food,' Will said to the waiter. 'So something mild. A korma?'

Ani and the waiter exchanged a look that needed no translation.

She did her best after that, and they chatted about food, about work, about Louise and Jake and whether they were really as happy as Louise would make out—nothing like a little shared bitch to grease the wheels of social interaction—but at the end of the day it was a cheap Indian restaurant with strip lighting, blaring Indi-pop from a TV in the corner, and only three of the tables occupied—one with a rugby team, who chanted and whooped every time someone took a drink. 'Down it! Down it!' Ani looked at her phone surreptitiously and realised only forty minutes had gone by. Suddenly she didn't care if it was rude—she wanted to go home.

Will clearly had the same idea. He'd taken out his wallet and was staring into it.

'Shall we just…'

'It's here,' he said mournfully.

'What is?'

He held something aloft, winking and glittering in the strip lighting. 'I forgot I put it in here. I—I— How could she? How could she?' He burst into tears.

At that exact moment the waiter clocked the ring, and nudged the others, who started clapping and cheering. 'Congratulations! Wedding bells!' Ani realised, surreally, they were singing an off-key version of 'I'm Getting Married in the Morning'. The rugby boys caught on and started whooping again, and two other miserable-looking couples, insulated in anoraks against the cold January night, joined in with some desultory applause. Ani was still reeling. Will seemed to have frozen in shock.

'Ding dong, the bells are gonna chiiiiime...'

'Get in there, mate! Give her one! A kiss I mean, haaaaaa.'

'No, no, there's been a—no...'

'So do not let them tarry, ding dong...'

'Nice one! Wedding night five!'

Will stood up, knocking the remains of his ultra-mild curry onto his cream trousers. What had she been thinking? She could never love a man in cream trousers. This was what happened when you settled for less than perfect, when you gave people the benefit of the doubt. He shouted, semi-hysterically: 'I don't want to marry her! I just want to marry Kat, and she doesn't love me any more!' And he flung the ring across the room, where it bounced off a framed picture of the Taj Mahal and landed in the insipid rosé wine of a woman in a green anorak.

Later, when she'd dispatched a weeping Will in a taxi, and paid for her meal and his and also the wine of the anorak woman, and explained to the disappointed waiters that no, she wasn't Kat, and fended off two offers to 'give her one instead' from rugby boys, Ani took out her phone to delete his number. She never should have added him in the first place—no contacts in the phone until date two. Stupid.

She found herself trudging along in the cold, the collar of her Reiss coat pulled up against the wind, taking out her phone to text Marnie. Marnie would understand. And that—almost, maybe—made up for everything else. She saw she had a WhatsApp message from Rosa and clicked on it as she walked. Ooohhh noooo may have got commissioned to write a piece on the stupid dating project. Might have to do it now.

Why not? Ani thought. Nothing could be worse than almost getting accidentally engaged in a restaurant with wipe-clean menus. And her friends would do a better job of finding her a man than she was herself. It wouldn't be hard. Me too, she typed, before she could change her mind. What's the worst that could happen?

## Chapter 5
## A Decaf No-Syrup
## Low-Fat Soy Latte

*Helen*

'Great news!' said Marnie down the phone. 'Ani and Rosa are totes in for Project Love.'

Helen's heart sank. 'Ani's in? Are you serious?'

'Apparently she had some really awful date and changed her mind, get her to tell you about it. So you'll do it, won't you?'

No no no no no. 'Ach, I don't know. I haven't dated in years.' Two years, to be exact. She hoped Marnie would never do the maths.

'All the more reason to start!' Helen and Marnie saw the world in very different ways. Marnie kept an ever-growing list of things to try—eating bull testicles, hiking the Inca trail, wakeboarding—while Helen kept a list of 'things I'll quite happily die before I ever do, thanks very much'.

'I don't know, Marn. What if it all goes horribly wrong, or he wears Superman pants like Ani's date, or he's secretly a serial killer? I just read a story exactly like that in *Take a Break*.'

'You don't need to marry the guy! Just have two drinks, then politely leave if you don't like him. That's the minimum— just one is rude, you may as well tell them to their face they're an uggo.'

'See, I don't know any of these rules.'

'It's like a game, Helz. You love those. Imagine you need to get to the top level. Remember when we used to play the Game of Life all the time? It's just like that, only your dearest friends will choose your little blue pin for you.'

'But games make sense. You take action, you get results. People are so—well, let's just say their programming seems to have some serious bugs.'

'But I think it would be good for us. Get us out of our ruts. And it's ages since we did anything fun together.'

What rut was Marnie in? She was living the dream, meeting hot guys on beaches and never paying tax. 'We had dinner literally two nights ago. I still have the hangover.'

'Come on. I'll be your best friend!' It was an ironic yet non-ironic nod to Marnie's stock phrase all the way through their childhood and teenage years. *Aw, Helz, if you don't steal your dad's Drambuie we won't have enough booze! Aw, Helz, have a smoke, everyone else is. Aw, Helz, snog weird Nigel who smells of egg sandwiches!* And Helen was the only one who ever got caught, and then her mum would turn to her with cloudy, hurt eyes, and... 'No,' she said, surprised at her own firmness. 'I really can't. Honestly. Do it without me.'

'But—I'll be your best friend.'

'You already are my best friend,' said Helen, feeling guilty—but not guilty enough to join in with the stupid dating project. 'Look, let's do something just the two of us. How about lunch today?' Before Marnie left, the two of them used to meet up at least twice a week, sometimes even catching the tube together on the way to other things, just so they could chat and catch up. Maybe they could get that back. Never mind that a spontaneous lunch would throw out Helen's food rota and she might not eat all the tomato soup before its use-by date. She could hear voices in the background. 'Are you in a café?'

'Yeah. I'm just…updating my blog about vintage fashion.'

What blog? 'Oh. Well, if you're busy—'

Marnie paused. 'No, no, I'd love to. I'd have an hour, would that be enough?'

'Of course. See you at, say, the Milk Bar? It's this new place. Supposed to be cool.' What if it had stopped being cool in the two days since she'd read about it in *Time Out*? Would Marnie sniff and say, *God, not that place, we should clearly be going to that café in Shoreditch where you eat all your food off of old CDs.*

'Great. Can't wait to see you.'

Helen looked at the latest batch of 'is my partner cheating on me' emails, and pushed her chair away from her desk. Who cared if Thursday was 'clean out the shower and mop the floor' day? Just for once, she was going to do something spontaneous. Marnie was back in town, and that meant things would start to happen. They always did. Though not always in a good way.

* * *

'Hi, hi, sorry, sorry, I'm late. Gosh, it's busy.'

Marnie arrived just after Helen had done the hard work

of finding a table in the hip but hopelessly impractical coffee shop. She was currently staking out a space on a sagging sofa, beside a bearded hipster with arm tattoos and a Mac. They were both compulsory, it seemed. Marnie was soberly dressed for her, in jeans and a plain black T-shirt. She gave Helen a squeeze, then eyed her, shaking her head. 'I just can't get used to you looking so different.'

'Do I look that different?' Helen tugged self-consciously at her skirt, worried she was overdressed beside Marnie's understated look.

'Massively. You look…pretty. Really, really pretty. I mean, not that you didn't before, but…you know.'

Helen dipped her head, embarrassed. 'I was going to order, what would you like?'

'Oh, I'm not very hungry. Just a green tea, please.'

'Not coffee?' Usually Marnie ran on about seventy-five per cent espresso. Did Helen even know her best friend any more?

She shuddered. 'No thanks.'

After the endless order—butter or spread? Gluten-free bread? Soy milk or dairy? Decaf? Sugar?—Helen squeezed back in, knocking against the coffee of the hipster. He took in a hissing breath. Marnie faced him. 'Hey, we're really sorry. It's just so cramped, isn't it? Aren't the suitcases daft?'

Amazingly, the man, who looked as if he hadn't smiled since iOS 6 came out, was responding. 'No problemo. You're right, it's so pretentious here, but the coffee—' he kissed his fingers, non-ironically '—it's really the best.'

'That's great. Enjoy your drink.'

He smiled back. 'Here, I'll move to that table over there. Give you some space.'

Amazing. Helen had forgotten—it was always like this.

Marnie winning people over, blagging things, powering through problems. Helen doing the admin, the clear-up, holding the coats. 'How are you?' she asked. 'I meant to ask—you've got somewhere sorted? To live I mean?' She should have checked this before. Bad friend. But then again: reasons.

'Oh yes. Lovely people, arty types. Cam and Susie and Fred.'

'Did you know them before?'

'No, I just moved in yesterday. It's like guardianship,' she explained. 'You know, like we live in an empty building and the rent's cheap. It's so cool. It's an old school. We use the PE showers!'

Didn't sound cool at all to Helen—no locks and a big draughty building full of dust more like—but what did she know about the latest trends in communal living? She hadn't even had a flatmate in two years. 'Great. Great. And work?'

'Oh, I'm...' Here Marnie paused. 'Well, I'm looking into a few things. Teaching and so on, art, drama...'

Perhaps that explained the all-black and the restricted lunch hour. Maybe she was in the middle of a drama workshop or something cool, and Helen had dragged her out to hear her own 'news', which would consist of Mr Fluffypants catching a mouse and (not unconnected) her plans to re-cover her armchairs. 'So tell me all about the trip! Was it amazing out there?' *It must have been for you to stay away for two years!*

'Where?'

'Brazil. Or was it Argentina?'

'Oh. Well, both, sort of. I moved about a lot. What have you been up to all this time?'

'Um...you know. Working.' *And feeling guilty, and miss-*

*ing you, and generally pining over Ed and staying in a lot.*
Maybe she could work the Mr Fluffypants story up into a
better anecdote if she did some impressions. She didn't tell
Marnie about the website, because she was always afraid
someone would ask the name of it, and also she didn't want
to mention Karl for some reason. Marnie would only suggest Helen ask him out. Which was clearly a ridiculous
idea. Helen tried to think of something cool she'd done in
the past two years. Read every issue of *Take a Break* magazine? Knitted a hat for the cat? Thought seriously about
writing some *Game of Thrones* fan fiction? God, she really
was in a rut. 'Nothing's changed, really.'

'That's not true! You're living on your own, you're working from home now... What made you change jobs?'

'Oh, I just... I felt like something different. Bit more flexibility.' The flexibility to make sure she rarely had to leave
the house, more like.

'How's your mum?' asked Marnie, sipping her tea daintily.

Helen shrugged. 'Oh, she's... I think she's all right. You
can never be sure though. She could go at any time. How's
yours?'

Marnie grimaced. 'Same. On to boyfriend 165, or something.'

'Have you been to see her?'

'And be interrogated by Mr "UKIP just say what we've
all been thinking" about when I'll find a proper job and get
a mortgage? No thanks.'

Helen almost asked about Marnie's dad, then didn't.
Marnie hadn't seen him much since she was thirteen, when
he'd finally made good on his lifelong promises and walked
out. Time to change the subject again. Her mum, Marnie's
dad—both topics to be avoided if possible. 'Soooo...do you

have an ex in mind? You know, for the project.' Again, Ed's name seemed to float between them, and Helen waited for Marnie to bring him up, but she didn't.

'Depends who it's for. It's quite healthy really. I mean why shouldn't we pass on dates we haven't sparked with?'

A millions reasons, Helen thought. Because we're British. Because, ew. Because people are people and not robots and feelings are bound to be hurt and things will get messy. She didn't say any of this. Instead, she said, 'And you think it would be OK?'

'I don't see why not. I wouldn't mind if you dated one of my exes. I'd be happy if you were happy.'

Helen bit her lip. At times she had tried to convince herself of this, but she knew one thing was true: not all exes were the same. Which was why she hadn't, and still couldn't, tell Marnie anything about it. She changed the subject again to safer things. 'Any other plans while you're here?'

'While I'm here? I'm here for good!'

There was a short silence, during which Helen thought of the past two Marnie-less years. What if she just took off again? Of course, she'd always been a wanderer—Spain, Dublin, New York, and Australia were just a few of the places Marnie had lived over the years—but she'd never stayed away for two whole years before. 'I just meant, you know, you said London was so money-obsessed, so cold, so joyless.' This had been the gist of Marnie's first garbled email from the beach, after she'd up and left with no warning.

'Not at all. It's full of theatres and museums and lovely parks and most of all, it's got my favourite people in it.' She gave Helen's arm a little squeeze, then looked at her watch again. 'Crap, I've got five minutes. I better tell you my news—I've been contacting people, seeing who's around.'

Everyone was around. Everyone else they knew had shown a singular lack of imagination when it came to not moving to London, or not staying in Reading, where they'd grown up. Except for Marnie, who had jet fuel in her feet. 'Oh?' Helen was starting to feel as if the majority of the conversation was taking place in her own head. 'Did anyone reply?'

'Oh sure. Anyway I started looking up a few people I've lost contact with, emailing…'

Suddenly, like seeing the mist clear and the cliff top under her feet, Helen realised where this conversation was going. Oh God. Here it was at last.

'So I dropped Ed a line! It's been two years after all, I think it's time we caught up.'

Helen's heart was racing as if she'd downed a quadruple espresso. Did Marnie know? No, she didn't. She couldn't. She heard her own voice try to stay casual. 'And was he about?'

'Well, I haven't heard back yet. He's probably quite busy, you know with his music and stuff.'

*Thank God.* And yet there was something else—a tiny treacherous stab of disappointment.

Marnie and Helen had been close, before. So close they were sworn 'sober death picture friends'. This meant that if one should happen to die suddenly, the other was charged with making sure the officially released photo was one where the deceased looked sober and upstanding, and not one of them clutching tequila shots in a bikini, which would make *Daily Telegraph* readers shake their heads over the marmalade and decide they probably deserved to be horribly murdered anyway. But now, Helen had no idea what her friend was thinking. Was Ed just another guy to her now? After all, she'd broken up with him.

Marnie was saying, 'If he is around, anyway, I think I'll ask him to my welcome-home drinks. It'd be nice to catch up.' She leaned forward to reach her tea, and Helen saw something round her neck. A necklace with a pale green stone. The birthday necklace. Oh God.

She swallowed hard. 'You're having welcome-home drinks?'

'Well, sure. Why not?'

'Um… No reason.' Helen realised she would have to go, and that would mean maybe seeing Ed, after all this time, and being in the same room as him, and talking to him. She couldn't. She wouldn't. She would have to. And then, she also realised, all her defences suddenly caving in like a kid's sandcastle, she was going to join in with the stupid project, and go out with whoever one of her friends picked for her, because anything was better than the way things were after Ed, and nothing was as stupid as what she'd done back then. And anyway, she owed Marnie. Big time.

Marnie was standing up, swallowing the last of her tea. The hipster man paused in frowning at his Mac to watch her. Even in plain black, she was the most striking woman in the place.

'Hey,' said Helen, faux casual. 'That project—you know, if you're all doing it, I guess I will too. Count me in.'

'OMG! Really?'

'Yeah, why not. It'll be fun.' In the same way that gouging out your eyeballs was fun.

'Awesomesauce! We'll find you someone lovely, I promise. Listen, I'll pay for this.'

'Don't be daft, you hardly had anything!' Surely Marnie didn't have a lot of cash right now.

'It's done.' She put some cash down on the counter, then blew a kiss and dashed off. Helen watched her go, off to her cool life, while Helen was heading home to her cat and her box sets. She wondered how it was you could know someone so well, and still not know them at all.

* * *

*Marnie.*

'You're late,' said Barry, tapping on his oversized Casio watch.

'I'm sorry, I just lost track of…'

'No excuses. I'll have to dock you a quarter-hour's pay.' Marnie opened her mouth to say she was only six minutes late, and had he seen how busy the streets were, but she closed it again, tying on her apron. No point in arguing. She needed this job, and as far as Bean Counters was concerned, Barry was the lord and master of all he surveyed—except when the regional manager stopped by once a month. 'And turn your phone off,' Barry hissed. 'We have to give the customers our full attention during their beverage experience.'

*Beverage experience?* Marnie fumbled her phone out of her jeans, spotting a message from Cam, her new flatmate. That was the one who stood too close, rather than the one who peed with the bathroom door open, or the one who she'd already caught 'accidentally' going through her backpack. It said: Party tonite bring ur own stash. She didn't want to go to a party, stash or no stash. She wanted to cosy up in her own nice place and watch TV. Exactly what Helen would be doing, no doubt. A place that was warm, and clean, and didn't contain any sleazy flatmates or recreational drugs, or, for that matter, any bedbugs—she scratched her arm, reflexively. She sighed. Would she ever have that?

'Marie! Get your arse in gear!' Barry was pointing frantically at the counter, where a line of customers was waiting, tapping their feet at the thirty-second delay. She thought about telling him her name was *Marnie,* and that her arse was not and never would be any of his concern, but again, what was the point? With a bit of luck she wouldn't be here long enough for it to matter.

She took her place, pasting on a smile. 'Good afternoon, welcome to Bean Counters. Are you ready to begin your beverage journey?'

# Chapter 6
## The Ex Factor

*Helen*

'Right,' said Marnie, looking round at the other three. 'We're all here. Time to start…Project Love.' They had gathered in Rosa's flat, which she now lived in alone, David having shacked up with The Intern—apparently, a nasty break-up was what it took to get a place to yourself in London, even a tatty new-build on the scruffy end of Willesden Green.

Ani groaned. 'We can't call it that.' She was shoving Kettle Chips into her mouth like letters in a postbox. She waved the bag at Helen, who shook her head. She was prone to anxiety-eating and knew that if she had even one crisp she'd probably end up eating Ani's head, and then it was goodbye four-stone weight loss, hello being lifted out of her house by a crane.

'Are you going to stay here, Rosa?' she said, trying to postpone the inevitable.

Rosa grabbed one of her Moroccan-print cushions and stuck it over her face, her standard response to anything divorce-related. 'I don't know. We'll have to sell, I guess. So enjoy this while you can.' Rosa indicated her tatami matting, her carved Indian table, and all her pretty ornaments. There was a photo of her wedding day over the piano, happy faces pushed together. Rosa in vintage lace, David with a top hat, and, in the background, Ani, Helen, and Marnie—who'd flown in from New York ten minutes before the ceremony—in red bridesmaid dresses, throwing confetti. Helen averted her eyes from it—her dress had been ordered in a size twenty. 'I spent years decorating this place,' said Rosa miserably. 'I thought we'd be here for ever. Or at least until we bought somewhere bigger in the suburbs. He always said I loved Ikea so much, I must have Stockholm syndrome.' Ani met Helen's eyes—they'd have to watch Rosa, or she'd slide into another wine-and-weeping marathon.

'Well,' said Helen brightly, 'I *love* living on my own. Think of all that fun decorating you can do. I'll lend you my fabric swatches!'

Rosa gave what sounded like a stifled scream into the cushion.

'Come on,' said Marnie impatiently. 'We need to get started on Project Love.' She was kneeling at the coffee table with a notebook, like a child playing at school. Today she was wearing a daisy-print dress, her hair in clips. She looked younger than the Intern David had skipped off with. Ani was sitting at Rosa's feet, while she stretched out on the sofa. Helen had the armchair, a fancy grey modular thing David had liked, but which made her nervous she might spill red wine on it.

'Do we have to do this?' she said, hopefully. 'I've brought a DVD of *Mean Girls*.'

'We do,' said Rosa, muffled. 'I'll probably get fired if I don't. And I've already been dumped and my husband's left me for a—'

'We can do it, but we're not calling it Project Love,' said Ani, cutting her off.

Marnie pouted. 'But that's what it is! A new approach to finding happiness.'

'No, no, we can't. It's too optimistic. We might jinx it.'

'Didn't think you believed in that,' said Rosa, from behind her cushion.

Ani blushed a little. 'Trust me. When you date a lot, you start to believe anything. Otherwise you'd have to think it was your fault every time something promising turns into an 18-cert horror show.'

'That's not the spirit.' Marnie frowned. 'Positivity, people!'

'OK, OK. Let's call it Project "Maybe we'll meet a guy who isn't awful and a liar and a cheat, or who won't accidentally propose to you, then burst into tears in an Indian restaurant".'

Rosa removed the cushion and rubbed Ani's shoulder with her stockinged foot. 'That won't happen again. You've definitely taken one for the team there. Hey, why don't we call it the Ex Factor or something? You know, because… exes.'

The others considered it. 'Did you just come up with that right there?' asked Ani suspiciously.

Rosa picked at a thread in the cushion. 'Um… It was Jason's idea actually. For the article, you know.'

Another look from Ani to Helen. Helen said, 'Is it "Jason" now then? Not "Scary Editor Surf Dude"?'

'He's not so scary. He's quite nice actually.'

'Is he hot?' asked Marnie, suddenly interested.

'Oh, I guess,' said Rosa, vaguely. 'I don't really notice other men, you know. Anyway, he can't wait to see the piece.'

Helen's stomach lurched at the thought of the article. This was really going to happen.

'I don't mind what we call it, so long as we do it,' said Marnie. 'Now what we'll do is write down our names, then pull them out of a hat. Do you have a hat, Rosa?'

'I don't know.'

'It's only an expression,' said Ani. 'We can just draw them out of a hand.'

'Oh, OK then, if you want to rob it of all joy and fun and sense of occasion.'

'Put them in that glass thing,' said Rosa soothingly. 'Chuck the tea light out, it's burned down anyway. Like my marriage.'

Ani patted her reflexively. Marnie scribbled down their names and tore the paper up into four.

'And are we picking the name of the person whose ex we're dating, or the one who we're setting up?' Helen had a sense of rising panic. Surely this wasn't going to actually go ahead. She looked around for a candle; maybe she could accidentally-on-purpose set the bits of paper on fire.

Ani looked blank. 'Also what if we pick ourselves?' said Rosa. 'I mean if I picked you…and you picked me…or what if I picked Ani, and then Ani picks Marnie, Helen picks me…'

'God,' said Ani, wrinkling her brow. 'It's harder than I thought.'

'Maybe we shouldn't bother,' said Helen quickly, though she knew it was hopeless. Once Marnie set her mind on something, resistance was futile.

'Honestly, guys,' said Marnie, 'some top professionals you lot are. It's very simple. If you get your own name, put it back in. We're picking the person we're going to set up. Right?'

Oh God, thought Helen. Why had she agreed to this? And which friend would be the worst to set up? Ani, the cynical perfectionist? Rosa, with the weight of her first post-divorce date, or Marnie, who seemed willing to date anyone, from a FTSE-100 exec to a basically homeless busker?

The pot, a stained-glass one Rosa had got in Marrakesh on honeymoon, went solemnly round. 'Choose…wisely,' said Marnie, skittishly. 'Otherwise your face will melt off like that dude in *Last Crusade*. Rosa, you go first, it's your flat.'

Rosa fished, unfolded the square of paper. 'Drum roll, please. So, I'm setting up…you, Marn.'

'Whoop! I bet you'll have a really nice ex for me. Now you, Ani.'

She pulled out a slip. 'I am matchmaking for…Rosa!'

'Hurray!' Rosa clapped. 'You'll get me someone good, I know you will.'

Marnie held out the pot. 'Helz, you choose.'

*Quick, do something set it on fire no there's no candles eat the paper! Eat it!* With trepidation, Helen unfolded her paper and read: 'Ani.'

'Well, here's to my future husband,' said Ani with heavy

irony. Helen bit her lip. The pressure! Who would she even choose?

'OK, my turn.' Marnie unfolded her paper, just as Helen was working out that there was only one name left and it was—

'You, Helz,' said Marnie. 'Great! I've been wanting to set you up for years.'

And Helen had always strenuously avoided it. Because: reasons reasons reasons. Oh God, what if she picked Ed? She wouldn't. No, surely she wouldn't. Was that good or bad? 'Someone nice,' she pleaded. 'Not someone who likes going to clubs or taking drugs or a City banker with a fetish for nipple clamps or a part-time stripper.'

Marnie raised her eyebrows. 'Gary was actually a pretty nice guy, you know. Great abs.'

'Please. Someone normal. Or, you know, normal for me.'

'Just trust me, Helz!' Marnie tapped the table. 'Right, ladies. Now we've got our names, we have to choose a nice ex, then contact them and set them up with our matchmakee.'

'What if they're married? Or say no? Or are gay now?' Helen was still stalling.

'Then choose someone else.'

Oh dear. It was going to be hard enough to find one person, let alone several. Who could she pick? Someone from school? That guy she snogged at an Ocean Colour Scene gig in the first year of university? She couldn't even remember his name—Andy something? Not Peter, her nice-but-dull main ex, who she'd dated between the ages of twenty-one and twenty-five; he was happily married with four kids and working in Kent as a used-car salesman. And thinking over her other thin-on-the-ground exes, and knowing Ani's high standards, she just hoped her friend would forgive her.

* * *

*Ani.*

'You look so beautiful, dar-link!'

'Auntie, I look like a drag queen. That's an insult actually. They'd look much better.'

'What is drag queen?'

'Oh, for God's sake. You know what it means. Like Lily Savage.' (Or Cousin Mehdi, she added to herself.) Her aunt Zhosi still pretended not to speak English properly, even though she'd been in the UK since she was twelve years old, fleeing Uganda with her parents and brother, Ani's dad. And also with her second cousin, Ani's mother. Yes, Ani's parents were second cousins. Not first cousins—though, as she often felt like explaining, that wasn't illegal in the UK—but still a little odd, something that made people look at her twice. It also meant family parties, where everyone was related to everyone else and with grudges that went all the way back to the turn of the last century, could be rather fraught.

Ani's mother came in, glowing in a fuchsia sari and gold jewellery. She blinked at Ani. 'That looks…different.'

'Beautiful, no?' Aunt Zhosi swept a hand to indicate Ani's face.

'Well, maybe we can tone down this eyeshadow a bit. You look like you've been in the boxing ring, Anisha.'

Ani sat glowering as they pawed at her face, her mother removing some of the fifteen layers of foundation, while her aunt defiantly stuck yet more jewels on Ani's face. She just looked daft in traditional clothes. Her short hair clashed with her extravagant make-up and clothes, and the lime-green sari her aunt had picked out made her skin look washed out. She held herself all wrong, used to suits, so the fabric hung awkwardly and had to be fixed by the tutting hordes of aunties and cousins (often both in the same person).

'Mum!' The door flew open and a teenage girl stood there, hands on newly discovered hips, her turquoise sari hanging perfectly. She said breathily, 'Mum, Manisha is well pissed off! She says they've like put the wrong colour flowers on the plates or something.'

Aunty Z threw up her hands and muttered something in Hindi. Ani assumed it translated as, 'I have had it with this damn bridezilla, why didn't I get her to elope?' The girl, Ani's cousin Pria—thirteen going on thirty—glanced at her. 'Um, that colour is like, so not good on you?'

'Who died and made you Gok Wan?' snapped Ani.

'Um, that, like, doesn't even make sense?'

Ani's mother chased Pria. 'Go, go, help your mother. And spit out that chewing gum!' She rested her hand on Ani's head, on the vast concoction of clips Aunt Zhosi had stuck in. 'Are you all right, sweetheart? You don't wish it was you?'

'What, getting trussed up and delivered to a man like a package? No thanks.'

Her mother reattached a failing-off rhinestone. 'You know, I felt the same when my parents suggested I marry Daddy. I was a modern girl, at university—I didn't want to marry my second cousin. How backward. But now look, we have you and your brothers, and we've grown closer each year.' It was true—Ani's parents were still sickeningly in love, even after thirty-five years.

'I just don't want to be someone's Stepford wife, Mum. I'm too independent, it wouldn't work.'

In reply, she got a glare. 'Is that what you think I am?'

Ani's mother was a cardiothoracic surgeon, head of her department.

'No! I just… It's a lot of pressure, you know. Find a man and quick, but make sure it's the right man, so you don't end up with a messy divorce or trapped in a horrible marriage. I don't know how you get it right.'

Her mother watched her in the mirror. 'Do you feel under pressure, sweetheart?'

'Um…a bit. Like, Manisha's three years younger than me and she's getting hitched, and I don't even have a boyfriend.'

'We won't push you into anything, Anisha. We aren't going to take you to India and marry you off. As long as you're happy. But you don't *seem* happy. All this dating and meeting all these boys—do you even like any of them?'

'Some. Now and again.'

'Do you want to share your life with someone?'

Ani thought of her cousin, the year-long extravaganza of family parties, and the boys she'd seen with her parents for six months before, the frantic planning, the beauty regimes, the diets. Manisha, always Ani's chubby cousin, beside whom she could stuff herself with sweets with impunity at family gatherings, had lost three stone and was now an irritating size eight who talked about nothing but 'gluten free, innit'. This was only the engagement party and there were a thousand people coming. Of course, Ani didn't want that. She sighed and said in a small voice: 'Yes. But it has to be the right person. I have to be sure.'

Her mother's hand stroked her forehead. It was cool, and smelled faintly of antiseptic, just like Ani always remembered. 'Well, if you want, Daddy and I can make some enquiries. That's all it would be, you know—we can just introduce you to some boys. No pressure.'

She put her hand over her mother's, stilling it. 'Thanks, Mum. I'm not saying no. Maybe you'd do a better job—I'm not really managing it myself. But not yet, OK? I have a date, anyway,' she said, stretching the truth slightly. 'Not from online. Friend of Helen's.' She didn't know how to explain the Ex Factor. She'd have to find a way to hide Rosa's paper when the article came out. Her parents always read it, wanting to support Ani's friends.

'Oh, good!' Her mother was visibly cheered. 'I'm sure he will be lovely. Helen's such a nice girl. Daddy always calls her when he needs to fix the computer.'

And what kind of exes would she have? Ani hadn't known Helen to even fancy anyone since that guy Ed, who had somehow ended up dating Marnie. She'd always been mystified as to why Helen wasn't more annoyed about that. And who would Ani herself choose for Rosa, so vulnerable and broken? Why had she let herself in for such a mad idea? Ani shook her head, dislodging another three rhinestones.

* * *

The engagement party went by, as parties do. All that planning for a few hours of speeches and glitter. Despite herself, Ani enjoyed it, the music, the clapping, the smiles on the faces of her family, Manisha looking so pretty and so genuinely happy. As Ani sat, her feet aching in the gold heels Aunt Zhosi had forced on her, her grandmother (also her great-aunt, confusingly,) toddled over and pinched her cheek. 'Good and plump! Such a healthy girl.'

Ani winced. 'Hi, Bubs. Here, sit down.' She pulled up a seat for the wiry little woman.

Her grandma shook her head. 'No seats needed, thank you, I'm not dying. How about you, my Anisha? When will it be your turn? When will you meet a nice boy?'

Helen sounded stressed. 'I need help too. This bloody article.'

'Tell me about it. What am I supposed to be saying?'

'Well, just a bit about the guy, how you met, why it didn't work out, that sort of thing. Which one was he again?'

'The one who took me to the most God-awful play I've ever seen. Where the cast came up and threw stuff at you, remember I told you about it?'

'Nope. I'm going to need more than that for the database.' Helen and Rosa kept a mental Rolodex of all Ani's dates over the years. It was well into the hundreds by now, and sometimes Ani couldn't even remember them herself.

'Simon, 2010, receding hair, bought himself a drink at the theatre and didn't ask if I wanted one, stuck to soda water all night while I accidentally got drunk, theatre critic?'

'Oh yes, got it now. Awkward Theatre Critic Guy. And you've picked him for Rosa?'

'Well, they have the same job, and he was quite good-looking, and he wasn't *so* bad. Just—you know.'

'Not quite right for you?'

'Yes. And don't say I'm commitment-phobic.' Ani could hear Helen's diplomatic silence.

'Maybe he was just nervous back then. Why didn't it go anywhere?'

'Aside from taking me to the world's worst play and not asking if I wanted a drink? I don't know. I don't think he fancied me. No kiss. So I didn't call him.' Sometimes Ani found it overwhelming, how hard it was to connect with people. Dating was like groping for a foothold on a cliff, and falling again and again. It was hard to imagine how anything could ever work.

'It'll be OK though, won't it?' She could hear the worry in Helen's voice. This would be her first date in years, after all.

'Of course. It'll be…fun.' Even to herself, Ani didn't sound convinced.

'An experiment, anyway.'

'That's right. An experiment.'

'Speaking of which, I better go and set your date up! Marnie's already sent me the email address for mine. Dan someone. Lord knows who she'd pick, he could be anyone.'

'So she didn't pick…you know? Ed?'

Silence down the phone. Then Helen laughed in a strained fashion. 'Ed? Ha ha, no. I don't think he's— I think he's not about at the moment. They're not in touch.'

'And you're really OK with her, after everything?'

'Of course! Ed and I were just friends. Anyway, it was ages ago. Of course I'm OK!'

Ani really wanted to ask who Helen had chosen for her, but they'd all agreed not to give out pre-date information in case it jinxed things. Just because one friend hadn't got on with them, didn't mean the other wouldn't like the guy. 'If you're sure.'

She hung up and went back to worrying about Simon and Rosa, her dear and recently heartbroken friend. It would be OK, surely? It had been years—maybe he'd changed, maybe he was a bit more suave. She called up an email.

Hi Simon! Long time no see, huh? I hope you don't think this is weird but are you single?

\* \* \*

*Helen.*

Helen put down the phone, and scowled at what she'd written.

'*Oi, Moby. MOOOOOOBY.*'

*When I first heard the nickname the cool boys had given me, I thought they meant the singer. Which was mystifying, as I wasn't cool, edgy, or indeed bald. Then I realised they meant a different Moby, one less known for their ambient hits. Moby Dick.*

*'Just ignore them,' said the boy who sat behind me in Computer Camp.*

*'I can't,' I said miserably. 'They're the cool boys.'*

*'They're the cool boys at Computer Camp,' said the boy, pushing his thick glasses up his spotty nose. 'Like duh. None of us are cool.'*

He'd been right, Helen thought. The year was 1997; the location, Reading University Summer Computer Camp. Helen was fifteen, finding way too much meaning in the words of Alanis Morissette songs and, at that point, still four hours away from her first kiss. Nik was small for his age, and had glasses, and spots, and dressed in what looked like his mum's idea of trendy clothes. But who was Helen to talk? She'd had to buy her clothes in Etam, not Tammy Girl, so she was at the Camp disco in a massive pair of denim dungarees. Uncool even at Computer Camp.

Nik had pushed his tongue dutifully around her mouth, hands clamped on her waist (a large area). Helen had moved her tongue too, and so what if her mind kept wandering to the piece of code they'd learned that day, it still counted as her first kiss, and even Marnie, who'd already kissed twelve boys and let one feel under her bra, had been a tiny bit impressed when Helen had rung her from the payphone to tell her. She and Nik had lost touch after Computer Camp, since Helen didn't have a mobile or the internet at home, and, anyway, she'd been a bit preoccupied in the months following it. However, a quick Facebook search threw him up.

Helen scrolled through his profile—articles from *The Economist*, the odd photo, check-ins at various airports round the world. His latest picture showed a man in board shorts, posing on the deck of a boat. A proper grown-up man, with chest hair, who looked to be reasonably handsome. Helen hoped so. She didn't think spotty nerds who knew all the dialogue from *Return of the Jedi* were really Ani's type. But globetrotting business tycoons who hung out on boats—very much Ani's type.

She sent him a message. Dear Nik, how are you these days? You seem to be doing really well. I hope you don't mind me asking this, but do you ever date? Weird request I know!

Helen sent it, then pushed her laptop away and went to her wardrobe. The mirror showed her current self—a woman of thirty-two, size ten-to-twelve, with blonde hair curling round an anxious face—but in her head, sometimes, she was still Moby. Sometimes she wondered if she always would be.

At the back of the wardrobe was a pink box, pasted all over with hearts and stickers. She remembered Marnie making that nail polish smear, back in 1995, the two of them squashed up on Helen's bed. Inside were photos—her and Marnie in their primary-school uniforms, arms round each other's shoulders. Helen had never noticed before, but Marnie was wearing odd socks in the picture, and her jumper had a large hole in it. Something squeezed Helen's heart, looking at that tough little girl, with her fierce expression. It was worth doing this ridiculous project, if it made Marnie happy. And who knew, maybe it would even work out for some of them? Rosa and Ani—yes, and Marnie too—deserved to find lovely boyfriends.

She set it aside and found the picture she was looking for. On the back her mum had scrawled: *Helen takes the*

*prize for World Wide Web design! Computer Camp 1997.*
Helen stroked the red, delighted face of the girl in the picture, clutching her cheap plastic trophy. She'd been so happy
at Computer Camp, with no idea that everything was soon
to fall so spectacularly apart. If she ended up seeing Nik
again—if by some chance he and Ani hit it off—he would
find Helen very much changed as well.

# Chapter 8
## Four Dates and a Social Funeral

*Rosa*

Rosa had spent the day not-writing the rest of her dating article. Not-writing was an activity that could take up vast tracts of time. It mainly involved Googling things, drinking coffee from the horrible machine in the corridor, hiding from Suzanne and, since the split, also hiding from David. Alternated with bouts of weeping in the ladies', and re-applying mascara.

She'd written: *With dating apps such as Tinder and Happn taking the spontaneity out of finding love—promoting the meet, shag, move on approach to dating—more and more women are coming up with their own methods of meeting people.* The 'more and more women' would be her and her friends. She'd also stick in some quotes from a speed-dial psychologist she knew, then she'd monitor the dates. It should be simple, the kind of puff piece she'd done hundreds of times. So why was she stuck on it?

Perhaps because she was terrified, pant-wettingly lunch-losingly terrified, at the thought of her date with Simon, Ani's choice for her. She'd met people at university via the usual channels—six Snakey Bs and a fumble while a pirate copy of *Kill Bill* played on a laptop in the background—then one day she'd sat in a journalism lecture beside a man with a sprinkle of gold in his dark beard and wooden beads twisted round his wrist (Rosa had always had a type), in other words, reeking of gap year. 'Been away?' she'd asked, desperate to make some friends in this vast class.

'In a kibbutz,' said the hunk. Rosa's eyes widened. How could she say it without sounding crass—*hey, I'm Jewish, are you?* 'I'm David,' he whispered, as the class began.

'Rosa,' she said. Adding as an afterthought, 'Rosa Lieberman.'

And just like that, they got each other—family, background, everything. And all through uni they'd been Rosa-and-David, side by side in lectures in matching jeans and Converse, or at house parties topping up each other's plastic cups of cheap red wine. After uni they'd moved in together and both got onto the *Sunday Gazette* grad scheme, while their classmates floundered in trade magazines, regional press and, worst of all, copywriting. Then buying a flat, getting married, opening pensions: all the things you were supposed to do.

And then the universe had decided to punish her for her appalling complacency, and chuck her back out into the howling void of single life. So now she had to go on a date with Simon. Rosa opened a new email and pasted in his address, which Ani had forwarded to her. Part of her had been hoping he'd say no, but according to Ani he'd been slightly bemused but flattered she'd chosen him.

Hi Simon, Rosa typed. Well this is a bit unusual isn't it!? But if you're still on for meeting tonight, where shall we go?

She sent it. Fait accompli. And meanwhile, the love of her life sat just across the room, so close she could almost see the top of his head. Slightly thinning now. The gap year beads were gone too. But still, Rosa couldn't quite believe that the time they'd had together was just erased, and she had less now than she'd started with in that journalism lecture, fourteen years ago.

* * *

Soon it was time to go. She'd changed her clothes in the loos four times, sending panicked selfies to Marnie for her feedback. There was nothing Marnie didn't know about dressing for the event, or about dating. Just be comfortable, Marnie said. But don't dress down too much because then if you really like him you'll be cursing yourself all night. Be comfortable, but feel confident. She'd settled on a floral tea dress and ballet pumps. Was it too casual? Too girly? Oh God. Suzanne was on the phone, shouting at her nanny about flaxseed oil, so Rosa decided she'd sneak out while the going was good.

'Off out?'

Creeping down the corridor, she almost ran into Jason Connell, who was carrying a printout of the next day's front page. He had his sleeves rolled up and looked tired. 'Er, research for the dating piece,' she said shyly.

'Right. Good.' He moved on, and smiled at her over his shoulder. 'Hope he's appreciative.'

What did that mean? Oh God. Comfortable, yet confident, that was Marnie's advice. Rosa wasn't sure she felt confident at all. All the way on the bus she couldn't settle. She decided she'd treat the whole thing like a feature and look for story angles, as she often did with unpleasant tasks. *Seventeen things your gynaecologist shouldn't say when you're in stirrups. How to survive Christmas at your (Jewish) in-laws'. What to do in a four-hour editorial meeting with your boss from hell, who's on a three-day juice cleanse and smells of wheatgrass and molten rage.* (That one had an admittedly niche appeal.) This piece would be called *How to survive your first date in fourteen years.*

*I walked into the bar and saw the collection of retro signs. My palms were sweaty, my stomach in knots, and I wanted to run for the hills...*

She stopped. Felt sick. Among the lumberjack beards and male topknots, a normalish thirty-something man was sitting in a booth, reading a paperback. An actual book, not a Kindle. She squinted at the title, suddenly feeling it was very important to know what he was reading. Was that... *Jane Eyre*? One of her all-time favourites?

He looked up, and saw her, and she froze like a rabbit in the headlights of the number 36 bus. 'Rosa?'

Rosa pasted on a smile, and walked towards him.

\* \* \*

*Ani.*

Nik will meet you at the pub in Victoria at 6.40, Helen had texted. He's travelling for work just now so asked me to set it up, hope that's OK!

Several things annoyed Ani about that message. First, the overly specific time—like he was allocating her a slot. Next, the assumption she'd meet him at Victoria. Of all places—it'd be freezing and full of lost tourists. Also, the message left no wiggle room—and that was the most annoying thing. Ani liked to negotiate. So now she was sitting in the concourse bar, trying to pretend it was romantic rather than busy, cold, and as sterile as an operating theatre—if nowhere near as clean. She was scowling at Helen's text. Nik. Why Nik, not Nick? Was he pretentious? Were his parents Nik Kershaw fans? What had happened to that missing 'c'?

'Ani?' She looked up—just as the clock turned to exactly 6.40—and then she understood.

A man was standing there, dressed as 'busy international businessman'. He was wearing a black suit and leather gloves, and had a wheelie case with a flight tag on it. Dark hair in a cool cut, dark-rimmed glàsses. 'Hello, I'm Nikesh.' Firm handshake.

Ani, who was by now the queen of first date encounters, found herself for once entirely floored. 'Oh—er, hi. Hello. Helen said it was Nik?'

'Oh, of course. That was something I beta-tested at Computer Camp. Trying to fit in, you know. These days I just use Nikesh. I don't want to sound like an eighties pop star, and besides, I'm proud of my heritage.'

'Erm…' Ani was thinking, *Crap, I've anglicised mine since I was ten*, and *God he's assertive*, and also: *Computer Camp*?

Nikesh parked his wheelie case and sat down. 'What about you, is it short for something?'

'Anisha. My family lived in Uganda for ages though before they came here.'

'Interesting, interesting. We're straight from the Punjab, third generation.' He spoke with a strong North London accent. 'So, Anisha—'

'I prefer Ani,' she interrupted.

'Do you? Why do you think that is?' He steepled his fingers and looked at her over them.

'Er…when I was ten I really loved the film.'

'With the little ginger kid?'

'Yes.' Why had she told him that? She could call herself anything she wanted, it was none of his business.

'And you're a solicitor?'

'Family law mostly. Divorces, child access, that sort of thing.'

'And is that hard for you?'

She blinked. No one had ever asked that before. 'Sometimes. It makes it hard to believe in love, I guess, when you see it falling apart in front of you, every single day.'

And again! Ani didn't know what was going on with her mouth. It was just…saying things. That never happened. She charged about £10 per word at work, it wouldn't do to just go around *talking*.

'You've been single for a while then?' He looked at her closely. He hadn't ordered anything to drink.

'For ever, really. I mean nothing's lasted more than a few months.' Ani took a drink of her wine, even though it was warm now, just to stop the weird no-filter talking. He'd thrown her right out of her usual composure.

Luckily, Nikesh decided it was now his turn to talk. He placed an embossed business card on the table, which somewhat surprisingly was a bright yellow colour. 'Well, Helen may have told you—'

'No,' Ani interrupted again. He opened and shut his mouth, as if he wasn't used to it. 'She didn't tell me anything.'

'Oh. So she didn't mention Computer Camp?'

'No. That was all you.'

'Crap,' he muttered, and Ani felt herself warm to him. 'Well, I set up my own company out of uni, and now I have bases here, in Mumbai, and in Silicon Valley. I travel a lot, and I work hard to play hard, so I've not had time to meet anyone special, but now I'm ready to slacken on the reins a bit.' He paused for breath.

Ani drank more wine. It hadn't been nice even when it was cold. 'Did you recite that off your dating profile?' she said. 'Do you also enjoy the outdoors, love your music, and are you just as happy curling up with a DVD and glass of wine as going out for cocktails?'

He looked confused. Ani was too. She seemed to have lost her date-filter. 'No,' he said. 'To be honest, I travel twice a month and when I get home I'm usually so tired I have a bath and watch *The Good Wife.*'

Ani gripped her glass. 'That's my favourite show.'

'Do you imagine yourself as Alicia Florrick?'

'Yes. Only without the cheating husband, of course. If I get married it has to be perfect, you see. I wouldn't bother otherwise.'

'Me too.' In the background, there was the roar of a train. Nikesh blinked. 'I only suggested meeting here because I've just flown back from India and I couldn't think of anywhere nice because I haven't been out in months.'

'I see. And why did you say 6.40?'

'Well, I don't like to be late and I wasn't sure I'd make it for half past. I always think lateness is kind of rude, don't you?'

It was Ani's turn to blink. 'Um…yes. Yes, I do.'

'So do you know anywhere nice?'

Ani turned on her in-built mapping system, which covered bars where you could always find seats, restaurants that didn't play loud music, and hairdressers that could have you in and out in forty-five minutes. 'There's the St James Hotel,' she said. 'Not far. Nice bar.'

'Sounds good…unless you fancy the "buy one, get one meal free for £7.99" deal here.'

'I don't.'

'Didn't think so.' He stood up, grabbing his fussy little case.

Ani remained sitting. She liked assertive men, but you had to push back as well. 'Am I coming with you?'

'Aren't you?'

'Well, you didn't actually ask me.'

'I'm sorry. I'm just used to people doing what I say, I guess.'

'That's OK. But I'm not one of them.'

'I know. Ani, would you like to come somewhere nicer with me?'

She drained her lukewarm wine. 'Yes please, Nikesh, I would love to.'

\* \* \*

*Helen.*

The pub was a let-down. Big, noisy, gloomy, and with a strong smell of stale beer. Why would he choose a place like this? She felt disappointment seep in from the soles of her feet, like spilled booze. Heart pounding, she began to scan the faces of all the men there. Oh God, was that—no, too fat surely. Was that…? Too old, hopefully. She'd heard horror stories of internet dates with ten-year-old out-of-focus pictures. Indeed, she'd fielded a lot of complaints on the subject via the site. What if Dan was the same? Wasn't this project supposed to take such anxieties out of dating? Didn't she trust Marnie? *Don't think about that.*

It had taken ages even to settle on this grotty pub. He'd emailed her first—Marnie had passed on her details, evidently counting on the fact Helen would never make the first move. (True; she'd even thought about seeding in some deliberate spam terms so it would get stuck in his trash folder and she could legitimately claim he'd never replied to her.) Any idea what you'd like to do?

Helen had drawn a blank. What did people do on dates? The drive-in? Theatre? Dinner? She couldn't face anything wacky, like speed-boating on the Thames or learning falconry. (Birds were a major source of communicable diseases and the Thames had failed its last three water purity checks.) We could go for a drink? She remembered Marnie's advice about not getting trapped on a date with a fixed end point, like a play or a film. If you hated them on sight then you'd be stuck there for hours.

OK, said Dan. Where?

Helen was a modern woman. She didn't expect to be swept off her feet. But was it too much to expect him to participate in decision-making? Eventually, he'd suggested this pub. She'd been full of trepidation ever since. Her routines were all upset. She'd even forgotten to change her bed sheets that morning, which would in turn throw off the timings of Wednesday's Dust and Tidy session. Mr Fluffypants wasn't speaking to her because she'd missed his lunchtime treat two days in a row. And tonight she didn't know what she'd end up eating, what time she'd go to bed… It was all a mess.

She told herself to stop it. This was no big deal—NBD, as Marnie would say. Her friends did it all the time. So why did it make her feel sick, armpits sweating and stomach churning like she was going to the guillotine? He was just a man. One her best friend had thought good enough to date. But then that did cover a large swathe of the male population. Was it OK that she was just wearing jeans? Nothing else fitted now—why hadn't she bought new clothes? She couldn't ask Marnie; she'd only get overexcited and give Helen a makeover again, like she had when they were fourteen and Sam Foxton claimed he wanted to snog her behind the bike sheds. She'd turned up in a flowered catsuit, and of course it was all a joke and everyone had laughed and because of the stupid suit Helen hadn't been able to pee for the whole day. Then a few days later, Marnie had been behind there with him herself. Had she known about the prank? *Don't think about that.*

'Helen?' She lurched at the sound of her name, and turned to see a short man—only coming up to her eyebrows—in a large ear-flapped hat, peering at her.

She waited for the thing, which despite her denying its existence she had been hoping to feel. The spark. The click. She felt nothing but anxiety. She cleared her throat. 'Er, yes. Hello.'

'Hi. It's a bit busy.'

'I know. Shall we sit down, maybe?'

Since Dan wasn't reacting, Helen began to move to a table that seemed free, the coats of a twenty-something group draped over the chairs. 'Do you mind if we…'

A disdainful girl with braids and a jumpsuit looked up. 'Some friends might be joining us.'

Helen tried to channel Marnie's charm, and Ani's assertiveness. 'It's just there's nowhere else to sit. We can always move if your friends arrive.'

'Well, all right.' Ungraciously, the girl pushed aside her duffel coat. Dan scuttled over, eyes down.

Helen settled herself. 'So…do you work near here?'

He hadn't met her eyes yet, staring into his lime and soda. She was having a large wine, which had come out of a tap. Helen was no wine connoisseur, not like Ani, who was always going to tastings at her office, but she was pretty sure that wasn't a good sign.

'Yeah. I work on Mercer Street. You know it?'

'Um…no.' She took a gulp of wine. 'I work from home, see.'

'Oh. Do you like it?'

'Yeah. Yeah, I do. You know, I like having my own space, my things around me.' She tailed off. What else could she ask? Why hadn't she written down a list of topics they could talk about? 'Um…what do you do?'

'Didn't Marnie say?' He was still wearing his floppy-eared hat.

'No. We decided it would be more fun not to.' At that precise moment, Helen didn't remember why. The whole idea seemed ridiculous.

'I work in insurance,' he said.

Helen's heart sank. 'Um…what kind?'

'Re-insurance. We, like, sell insurance again.'

'Oh. Is that interesting?'

'Not really.'

A silence fell between them. Helen swallowed more wine, sweet and acidic. Oh God. It wasn't as bad as she'd thought—it was worse. She stared at the floor, where someone had stepped on and squashed a packet of ketchup. 'I work in IT,' she volunteered. 'I run a dating website. It's funny because I don't use them myself. Do you?'

He looked up nervously and then down at his drink. 'I've been on Tinder. I didn't like it. People are so impatient to meet up, I just want to chat a bit first.' Funny then that he didn't want to chat much in real life.

Helen wracked her brains. Family. School. University. Marnie (*no no no*). Work they'd already exhausted. 'Um...' She clutched at the cold stem of her glass. 'Do you have any hobbies?'

One drink later Dan had perked up and was expounding on his LARPing, his video games, and his interest in the fall of Nazi Germany. 'What a lot of people don't realise about Hitler's last days, is, you see...'

After an hour or so, Helen realised she'd stopped holding all her breath in. Maybe it wasn't actually awful? She nodded along as Dan talked about Sim City, her thoughts drifting to Marnie. What if Ed actually came to Marnie's drinks? He wouldn't. All these years she'd been safe, so surely he wouldn't just appear... She realised Dan was looking at her. 'I'm sorry, did you say something?' They had finished their second drinks. Did everyone know about the two-drink test? Who was meant to pull the plug first? If you didn't both say it, did that mean the other person would think you were really into them?

Dan looked nervous. 'I asked if you'd like to get something to eat?'

Oh! He wanted to carry on the date. So it wasn't a total disaster. Helen tried to sound nonchalant. 'Sure, we could do that, if you like.'

She pulled her coat round her, feeling a mild buzz of something that was, if not quite excitement, then a distant cousin to it. It was ages since she'd had even the possibility of romance. Two years was a long time to swear off something. She might actually have a better love life now if she'd gone to prison back then instead.

# Chapter 9
## The Madwoman in the Attic

*Rosa*

'Shall I tell you something really bad?'

'Go on then.'

'I'm not sure I should. It's pretty shocking.'

Simon leaned in to her. 'You can trust me, Rosa.' He smelled nice. Something lemony. She was so out of touch with men's aftershaves—David had worn the same cologne until a month before he left her, when he'd suddenly invested in a fancy bergamot one from Jo Malone. Another sign she'd missed.

But she wasn't going to think about that. She took a sip of her wine—they were sharing a bottle. 'Well, OK, here it is. I always secretly hoped Jane wouldn't go back to Mr Rochester in the end. He was so mean and broody. Always negging her. I reckon she should have just gone to Ireland and been a governess.'

'You're saying you were rooting against one of the greatest romantic endings in literature?'

'Oh come on! What's romantic about locking your mad wife in the attic? And I bet he'd do the same to Jane too, as soon as she did something even slightly batty, like putting the remote control in the fridge.'

'Um, spoiler alert?' Simon looked shocked. 'What mad wife? What attic? What fridge, for that matter?'

'No way. You've read it before, you must have.'

He laughed. 'You got me. This is my fifth time. I love it, though I've never thought of your…unique take on it before.'

'I have more. Tess of the D'Urbervilles, right—she had a pretty good thing going with that dairy. Why didn't she set up her own business selling organic yoghurts? But no, instead she gets ditched by slut-shaming Angel and then heads on back to rapey old Alec. It's rubbish.'

'So you're saying love is what ruins things for all these characters?'

'Maybe. Less love, more cottage industries—that's the key to surviving a Victorian novel.'

Simon laughed, his eyes crinkling. 'So, Rosa, another bottle? Or would you maybe like to get some food? All they do here is those little mini-burger things, and they always remind me of…'

'…the Press Awards drinks reception?'

'Yes! How did you know?'

'That's the same reason I can't eat them. It just makes me think of being horribly drunk on cheap warm wine and trying to hear the speeches over the table from *GQ*.'

'Well then. Let me just visit the facilities, and we'll make tracks?'

'Um…' Rosa toyed with her glass, suddenly shy. 'I'd like to, but before we do, I should probably tell you something.'

He stopped. 'Oh?'

Oh God. She had to tell him. She couldn't. She had to. 'I—I'm getting divorced. My ex and I split up recently.'

'You're married?'

'I'm sorry. I guess I should have said. I'm not really married, exactly—somewhere in between. Are you annoyed?'

Simon gave her a strange look—kind, and sympathetic, and a little sad. 'Rosa. I can hardly be annoyed, when I'm in exactly the same situation.'

She stared at him. 'You are?'

'Yeah. I didn't mention it to Ani when she emailed, because I was a bit ashamed, to be honest. My wife—my ex—urgh, no idea what to call her now—she left me a few months ago. I wasn't sure how to bring it up. This is my first date since.'

'Mine too.'

'Well then. How am I doing?'

'Pretty good, I think.' Rosa was suddenly shy, hiding behind her fringe.

'You too. So, how about that food?'

'Sure. Sounds great.'

'Give me a sec.'

Rosa watched him go, a pleasant glow suffusing her that was only partly to do with the bottle of wine. She'd no idea why she'd been so nervous. What an amazing coincidence, to find someone in the same boat. And Simon was nice. He had a slightly receding hairline, true, compared to David's full head. But she wasn't thinking of him. She was out on an actual date, with a nice, interesting man, and she wasn't going to think about her ex, not-quite-ex husband, for one more second. She only hoped things were going as well for her friends.

* * *

*Ani*.

Nikesh perused the cocktail menu. 'Do you have anything that's really sweet? Like so sweet it might actually push me into a diabetic coma?'

The waiter remained admirably inscrutable. 'Might I suggest a Brandy Alexander, sir? Hopefully coma-free.'

'Great!' He shut the menu with a snap. 'I wish it was socially acceptable to drink Bailey's and hot chocolate in public. It's hard being a captain of industry, you know, Ani. I blame *Mad Men*. Everyone expects you to drink whiskey, even if you'd rather have hot milk with cinnamon in.'

'My mum makes me that.'

'Mine too.' Of course she did. So far they had discovered a list of surprising—and to Ani slightly alarming—similarities.

Nikesh then proceeded to grill her again, asking all about law school, and her current cases. What did she think about elected judges? Did she wish she could wear gowns in family court? What was her opinion on prenups? He seemed interested in everything. At first Ani felt like she was being interrogated, but then she started to bask in his attention. OK, he was somewhat direct and assertive, and possibly a massive nerd—she hadn't forgotten about Computer Camp—and then of course there was the other issue…but… they were in a posh bar, warm with flickering tea lights, and they were drinking fancy frosted cocktails, and it was nice. He'd placed his gold card on the bar: a naff touch, she'd thought, but three strong drinks later, it was quite cool that they were just arriving. And after her long day, Ani felt her tongue loosen. 'So you're like a hot-shot businessman.'

He pushed his glasses up his nose. They were Gucci, Ani

thought. 'I try to be. I've built it up all by myself. I started out with a Saturday job in Computer World in Slough, then learned everything I could about how computers worked.'

Ani licked sugar from the side of her cocktail. 'What are your strengths and weaknesses? Where do you see yourself in five years?'

'Well, I'd say—oh. You're joking.'

'Yes. You sound like you're at a job interview.'

'Maybe. But I think it's important to discuss these things on a first date. You'd just be wasting each other's time if you weren't compatible.'

'It's not a waste of time if it's fun.'

'Is it fun? I mean, do you enjoy dating?'

Ani thought of her experiences—the crier, the guy who kept 'forgetting' his wallet, the borderline racist who went on about her 'exotic colouring'. 'Um…'

'Exactly. I don't want to be negative, but so many people just mess you around. Say they're interested, then you find out they're dating five other people at the same time, or they have a boyfriend already and want some fun on the side, or they're just, you know, totally wrong for you. Racists. People with more than four cats—I'm allergic by the way. Amateur astrologists. Do you know what I mean?'

Ani took a large swallow. 'I might have some idea.'

'You've had bad dates before?'

'Um…maybe. A few.' A few hundred, maybe.

'Right. So I just stopped doing it randomly. Now I only date women whose personalities and goals complement my own, because I'm ready to settle down and get married.'

Ani almost spat out her drink. 'You're saying…you want to *commit*?'

'Yes, of course. Why else would I be dating? I'm thirty-three now, it's a good age to do it.'

'But…you mean you don't want to take time out to work on your stand-up comedy, or retrain as an art therapist, or travel through South America?'

He looked puzzled. 'No. I've sorted out my company now. Of course I work hard, but I'm ready for other things. I'd like to meet a woman and build a life with her.'

'And…you don't feel marriage is a capitalist institution and everyone should be in open relationships, and you're not really looking for a girlfriend, you just want to get out there and have fun?'

'No. I mean, I'd hope we'd have fun. But in a way that's going towards something. Moving forward.'

'Moving forward.' Ani repeated it like a phrase from a foreign language. She'd never met a single man in his thirties who spoke Commitment. 'Sorry. It's just unusual.'

'I'm an unusual guy,' said Nikesh non-ironically, drinking his creamy cocktail. It had an umbrella in it.

Ani suddenly had a thought. 'But you don't know anything about me, do you? How do you know my goals match yours?'

He had a moustache of cream on his upper lip. 'That's why I got Helen to fill in the questionnaire.'

'Questionnaire?'

'I do it for all my dates. It just saves time. You know, background, hobbies, interests, life ambitions, food intolerances, preferred holiday spots, and so on. I'll happily send you one for me too, if you like. To be honest I was really pleased when Helen got in touch—it makes total sense to set a friend up with a pre-tested ex. I think your project is a great idea.'

She was going to kill Helen—she'd hoped the stupid Ex Factor project would remain a closely guarded secret. 'You sent her a questionnaire about me? Is that not…really weird?'

'Why? What do you usually use to choose your dates?'

'Um—pictures. Or we meet in real life.' God, she realised. She mostly just went on looks, and attraction, and their general air of confidence. Nikesh had confidence, but in a nerdy cheerful way she wasn't used to. Where was the flirty banter, the long stares over the table, the hand creeping onto her leg?

'Isn't that inefficient? What if you dated someone for months, only to find out they always want to do extreme sports on holiday, when you'd rather just take a cruise?'

Ani said, 'I'd love to go on a cruise. My parents go every year.'

'Mine too. I went with them last time. Look.' He took out his phone and showed his Facebook shot. In it he was in swimming shorts, smiling from the deck of a ship. Ani couldn't help but notice he was rather buff. 'It was amazing. I had pina coladas every single day.'

She was still struggling. 'So…you think it's best to date people you have things in common with?'

He looked puzzled. 'Of course! How else would you do it?'

Ani thought of Will, who she'd dated just because they'd met in real life and she'd been feeling insecure. Of all the cheapskates and overgrown teenagers and unstable arty types she'd met over the years. 'Um, I don't know. Maybe you're right.'

Nikesh raised his Brandy Alexander and smiled. He had a nice smile. 'Here's to the project, Ani.'

'It's not really a project,' Ani said, trying to sound firm. 'More of an…experiment.' But she lifted her glass and clinked all the same.

* * *

*Helen.*

This was OK. This was nice. Nice food, nice music, nice…decor. OK, maybe the restaurant was a bit empty, being a Wednesday in January, and maybe the lights were a touch glaring, and perhaps there was just the faintest smell of bleach… 'What would you like?' she asked him brightly, looking at the menu. 'I might get a steak. It seems like steak weather, doesn't it?'

Dan's eyes were swivelling round the room, nearly empty except for some bored waiters. 'I'm a vegetarian,' he said.

'Oh. Right. Well, there's cheese…or look, there's some veggie options, or I can ask them what else they have.' *Oh God, Helen, stop mothering him*! The waiter came over. 'Hello,' she said. 'I'll have the *moules frites*, please.' (It seemed insensitive to have steak in front of Dan.) 'And a white wine, please. Large. Very large.'

The waiter looked at Dan, listlessly. 'Sir?'

'I, er… I'm not really that hungry. I'll just have the onion soup. I'm vegetarian.'

'It is made with beef stock, sir.'

'Oh. Um. Well, it doesn't say.'

'Does not say "v" either, sir.'

'No, but you might assume, hello, onions, it's a vegetable.'

The waiter gave him a 'whatcha gonna do' look. Helen said, nervously, 'Do you have a vegetarian option?'

'Goat's cheese tartlet?'

'I'm lactose-intolerant,' said Dan, miserably.

'Risotto?'

'I can't eat white rice.'

The waiter glared at Helen, as if to ask why she'd brought in this difficult man. 'Omelette, sir?'

'I suppose that'll have to do.'

'I'm sorry,' Helen said, as the waiter went. 'If you want we could go somewhere else.'

'Where?' Dan was staring at his cutlery.

'Um…' She didn't know, and the silence once again grew up between them. When her mussels came, Helen realised how stupid this was. They were fiddly, and she was bound to flick him in the eye with the sauce, or offend him by scraping them out of their shells. 'Did you not want a drink?'

'I'll stick to tap water.'

And he'd had soda and lime before—was he a cheapskate? Did he disapprove of drinking? Right on cue, her glass of wine arrived, frosty-cold and full, promising an end to this interminable awkwardness. Helen stared at it longingly, then pushed it away. 'Hey,' she said brightly, when her finger bowl was set down. 'I didn't order the lemon soup, did you?'

'What?'

'The…' She indicated the slice of lemon floating in the bowl. 'Lemon soup.'

He looked confused. 'It's for your fingers. You're not supposed to eat it.'

'I know. It's just—I was joking. It was a joke.' Her dad had once made it, the time he'd taken her and her mother for a fancy Chinese meal, when she was fifteen. She'd thought it was a lovely treat, not realising it was the last time her family would be normal.

They ate their dinners in near-silence. They kept starting topics—where did he live? Did she like the cinema, the theatre, the arts? Did he read? Did she have a lot of friends in London? What were his thoughts on the upcoming Eurovision Song Contest? (She was getting desperate by then.)

After every one, silence opened up again. It was like an inflating balloon, gradually going up and up, pressing out everything else in the restaurant. Eventually, Helen laid down her fork—she'd gone right off her food—and said, 'I'm sorry, but are you all right? You're so quiet. Did I— did I annoy you?'

'No!' He averted his eyes. 'It's just so bright in here. And everyone can hear us. It's freaking me out a bit.'

'I know, but we're eating, we can't exactly sit in silence.' *And it was your idea*, she added mentally.

His head drooped further. Helen waited…and waited. How long could an awkward silence go on for? Approximately one hundred and fifty years, it seemed. Her phone buzzed, and she leaped on it. It would be really great if one of her friends could be in a non-serious accident right about now. Just light scrapes, maybe a bruise or two, but something that required her to leave immediately. She read the text—PPI spam. Damnit. She stood up, knocking her fork to the floor. 'Excuse me.' She fled to the ladies', shoving her phone in her pocket. She debated texting Marnie, asking why the hell she'd picked the world's most tongue-tied man. But no, Marnie was most likely having lots of fun on her date with Tom, probably at a swing-dancing class or a retro sewing night or a tour of the Shard by night. Instead Helen quickly sent an emoji-filled Facebook message to Rosa and Ani. *Please kill me now.* Nothing came back. They must be having good dates.

Helen went out, scraping the bottom of her mental barrel of things to talk about. House prices? Childhood pets? Holidays? But the table was empty. Dan was gone, and so were his Puffa coat and ear-hat. What?

She turned to find the waiter hovering. 'Mees? Your

friend say he have to go. He say to tell you, "Sorry, I cannot do this.'"

She'd been ditched while in the loo. He hadn't even said goodbye.

The waiter set something on the table, discreetly. A note? Perhaps an explanation that Dan been called away, that one of *his* friends had been in a non-serious light scraping accident, or there'd been an insurance-related calamity…

'The bill, mees,' said the waiter. Helen sighed and reached for her wallet. One thought was uppermost in her mind, and not for the first time either. *I am going to kill Marnie*…

\* \* \*

*Marnie.*

'I'm sorry I have to leave early. It's just, I said I'd be at this all-night vigil thing for human rights in, er, China. You know how it is.'

'Sure,' said Tom enthusiastically. 'It's cool to care.'

They had paused at the top of the Jubilee Line escalators in Waterloo, and Marnie realised it was here—the end-of-date awkward kiss-or-no-kiss moment. The one that would decide whether the two of you ended right now, or carried on to marriage, kids, grandkids, and a second home in France. No pressure then.

Tom was hanging back, which was generally a good sign. He was wearing a beanie and tatty jumper, big combat trousers with chains and patches. 'It was cool to hang.'

'Yeah. Such a good idea to sit on the Southbank beach.' Even though it was January, and she was freezing and chilled to the bone. He'd turned up with some beers in his ripped backpack, and she'd got the impression that the bars in that area were out of his price bracket.

'Yeah. It's cool down there.' He paused. She paused. She

tilted her head up—she'd have to stand on tiptoes to kiss him. The pause went on. Neither moved.

She cleared her throat. 'Um, so would you maybe like to come to that party I mentioned, on Friday?'

'Oh! Yeah, maybe. Will Rosa be there?'

'I think so. But I'm sure she won't mind. She set this up, remember!'

'Yeah. Sure. Cool.'

'I'll Facebook you.' Marnie caught sight of the clock over his shoulder. Crap. Still, a quick mysterious exit could sometimes be better than a kiss. She leaned in briefly, pressing her head against his chest. He smelled vaguely of damp dog. 'Bye, Tom. I had a lovely time.'

'Oh. Yeah. Me too. Cool.'

She darted off, turning over her shoulder to smile at him. He smiled back, a touch bashful. A little wave. Good sign. Maybe, just maybe, there was something there, even if she hadn't felt her feet for two hours. She wondered how Helen was getting on with Dan.

It had come as something of a shock to Marnie when she'd had to write her 'how we met' piece for Rosa's paper. She couldn't actually remember how she'd met Dan. Had she been on *that* many dates in her life? It was before everything, before she'd left, she knew that much. And they'd met…online, maybe? And the date was…in a bar? Maybe she'd been drunk. She had vague memories of a fun time, and that he was into computer games, so hopefully he and Helen would have something in common.

Marnie dashed through the concourse and doubled back on herself, arriving at the Bean Counters concession, which stayed open all night. 'You're late again, Marie,' said Barry. 'I need you to clean the toilet, someone's been sick in there.'

'Sure.' She made herself smile. She'd get something better soon. Of course she would. She took out her phone to switch it off, spotting a text from Helen. But before she had a chance to read it, she saw she had another message. A Facebook one. As Marnie clicked on it, standing in the cold, vomit-smelling train station, at almost midnight, a huge genuine smile spread over her face. She couldn't believe it. Amazing.

'*Marie*. The toilet.'

'Yes, OK, sorry, Barry.'

She opened the door to the loo, wrinkling her nose at the stench. 'I think they were eating a kebab,' said Barry, helpfully. 'That looks like chilli sauce to me. At least they didn't buy it here.'

## Chapter 10
## Broccoli in the Bathtub

*Ani*

'Don't come any closer, you goddamned asshole, or I swear to the Almighty I'll cut your Johnson off.' The sound of a loud chop came from the kitchen.

'What was that?' whispered Rosa.

Ani cocked her head at the door. 'A cucumber, I think.'

Rosa had come round after work, to fill Ani in on the date with Simon and hear about Ani's with Nik—or Nikesh, as he turned out to be. They were chatting with their feet up on the sofa, scoffing olives, while Ani's flatmate sliced vegetables in the kitchen, learning lines for an upcoming audition. Ani quite liked living with Gina, an actress who spent most of the day in the bath, shouting out things like, 'You effing bastard, it's not even your baby!' and 'But, Captain, the aliens are on our tail, and all my clothes have inexplicably fallen off!' (She mostly appeared in gritty experimental theatre or low-budget sci-fi films.) But sometimes Ani wished she had her own place, maybe a chic loft apartment or a glass-walled penthouse. Or at least a Victorian town-house that she shared with her handsome stockbroker hus-band. That wasn't too much to ask, was it?

'Yeah, you better run, you spineless cockweasel!' The hall door clicked as Gina went into her room.

'I don't know how you cope.' Rosa shook her head.

'Gina's OK. Though I did once find some broccoli in the bath.'

'Urgh. I'll have to go back to all this. Weird flatshares and dirt in the bathroom—or cruciferous vegetables. I can't face it.'

Ani changed the subject. Rosa hadn't cried once since she'd been there, and that was a record. 'So you saw Simon?' she asked brightly.

'Yeah! It was surprisingly fun. Did you know he was married? Well, getting divorced now. Snap.'

'No, he didn't mention that.' It was hard to imagine it—the Simon she'd met five years ago, married. 'What did you do?'

'Oh, drinks, then went for ramen.'

'Is that still in? I thought we'd reached Peak Ramen in 2014.' Ani suddenly imagined them slurping on noodles, like the scene in *Lady and the Tramp*. 'Do you think you'll see him again?'

'Don't know. There's only been David since I was nine-teen, but he seems fun. He listens. And he's really interested in theatre, obviously.'

Fun, and a good listener—was this really the same Simon who'd struggled to make small talk with Ani, and taken her to that awful play?

'Anyway, what about your Ex Factor date?' Rosa prodded Ani with her toe. 'It sounds like we're all in a cult, planning a mass suicide with poisoned Chardonnay.'

Ani swilled her glass. 'I think this stuff has already been done. Where'd you get it?'

'Your corner shop.'

'God, never do that. I think he makes it out the back in buckets.' Ani winced, though she kept drinking. 'Well, mine was…surprisingly OK too. Not as bad as it could have been. Better than poor Helen's, by the sound of it.'

'I know, it sounded horrific. Is this what Marnie means when she talks about new low standards? When "not awful" becomes your dating baseline?'

Ani toasted her. 'Welcome to the game, kid.'

'Urgh. So it's all good with Nikesh then? Promising?'

Ani made a face. 'Maybe.'

Rosa sighed. 'Aneeee. What's he done now? Called you a "lady"? Ordered a mild curry? Spelled it "definately"?'

'Worse. He's emailed me already.' The email had said: It was really nice to meet you, Ani, and I would very much like to see you again. Regards, Nikesh.

'So that's…bad?' Rosa looked at her friend, puzzled. 'Really awful and terrible? A human rights violation? I'm sorry, you'll have to help me out here.'

'It's a bit keen.'

'But keen is good! Keen means he likes you!'

Ani rolled her eyes. Rosa had no idea how dating worked. You couldn't just go around dating people who were keen on you, for God's sake. 'It means he might be a desperate stalker who hasn't been near a woman since 2003. Never date a man who's too into you. Very important rule. He should have other things going on in his life. Anyway, that's not the only thing that's wrong. He's…Indian.'

'I…' Rosa threw up her hands. 'I don't even know what to say to that.'

'I don't like to date Indian guys, you know that. It just makes it all too serious. Chances are their great-granddad kissed my great-grandma beside some fountain in Amritsar. I wish Helen had told me.'

'You're mental. You don't have to marry him, just go on a second date.' Rosa swallowed more vile wine, then got up. 'Must go to the loo. There better not be vegetables in there. In this place I went to with Simon, they didn't even have loo roll. It was horrific. Luckily, Simon had some tissues.'

Simon, Simon, Simon. He sounded like a different person now. Did he just like Rosa more than her? Think she was prettier? To distract herself, Ani picked up her phone and thumbed through Twitter, curious to see how Marnie had fared on her date with Rosa's ex. Sure enough, she had live-tweeted the whole thing.

@marnieinthecity Excited for my date tonight! #exfactor #datingexperiment

Unnecessary hashtags were number three on Ani's list of Most Annoying Things (after tourists on escalators and people being late). She scrolled on.

@marnieinthecity Kicking things off with a cocktail or three! #southbank #exfactor #datingproject

'It's not a project,' muttered Ani.

@marnieinthecity Mr Hot Hippie has gone to loo. Things are going well guys!! The plan works! #mysterious #london #firstdate #exfactor

@marnieinthecity Just had vv gd convo about the melting ice caps. #notjustsmalltalk #exfactor #guysheisreallycute

@marnieinthecity Off to take a stroll along #southbank now...here's hoping for some—

Ani squinted. What was that? Oh. A hand-holding emoji.

Rosa burst back into the room, buttoning her jeans. 'OMG! Have you seen Marnie's Facebook invite?'

'Er, no, I'm too busy reading her live-tweeted date with Tom. Anyway, were you checking your phone on the loo?'

'It's what people do now. What's all this about welcome-home drinks?'

Ani groaned. 'Marnie's having a party? Last time she did that I lost one of my Jimmy Choos and had to go home with a bin bag round one foot.'

'It's even worse this time. She's only bloody invited Tom!'

\* \* \*

*Helen*.

After the upheavals of the previous few days, Helen's heart had started to beat again. The big return had been accomplished with a minimum of trouble—being embroiled in a ridiculous dating project was so far down the list of Marnie-related chaos that it didn't even make the top ten. Facebook messages indicated that Rosa and Ani had actually liked their selected dates, and Helen didn't mind that she'd had the worst of the lot—it was further excuse not to do it again for another two years. Maybe Helen would never ask Marnie why she'd left, or what she'd been doing for two years. Maybe she'd never tell her what happened with Ed. Maybe they could sweep everything under the carpet, just like Helen's mum and dad would do.

She should have known. You never skipped the rituals—you never stopped the Routine. Because if you did, things happened. Like your phone ringing at 5 a.m.

Helen shot awake, scrabbling for her handset. 'H-hello?' Her first thought was: it's Mum. Finally; well, she'd known this day would come, and three years was a good run… She stuck her finger in her ear, trying to hear. 'Who is it?'

'It's me, silly,' trilled Marnie. 'I'm just calling to remind you about my welcome-home drinks. Are you coming?'

'Oh. I don't know. Is it definitely happening?' She'd been hoping that if she just ignored it, it would go away, much like the mould behind the bathroom door. Marnie must have organised it herself. Helen felt a small stab of guilt, and told herself firmly not to be so stupid.

'Of course it is! You haven't even responded to the Face-book invite.'

Helen avoided Facebook where possible, considering that she had enough reasons to feel bad without being bombarded by other people's exotic holidays, baby scans, and smug coupled-up pictures. 'Well…I guess I'll be there, yes.' Though it would cut into her important plans of eating spaghetti hoops out of the tin while watching her box set of *Sex and the City*.

'Right. Can you bring someone? Only there's a minimum spend to hire the area.'

Hire the area? This was sounding alarming more like a party and less like a few drinks down the pub. 'Who?'

'Well, Dan for example! How did it go? Did you like him?'

Helen rubbed her eyes. She didn't say, *It didn't go that well, actually, seeing as you set me up with the world's most awkward man.* She didn't say, *It might have gone better if you'd taken even a moment to think about what kind of person I'd be interested in.* She didn't say, *It was one of the worst nights of my life, thanks, and I probably won't ever eat mussels again without wanting to peel my skin off in social embarrassment.* Instead, she said, 'Oh, I don't know. What made you pick him for me? I'm not sure we're really compatible.'

'Why not? He's a nice guy. Likes computer games and stuff. I thought he'd be your type.'

Helen thought about this for a second—that her best friend imagined she'd be into tongue-tied insurance-reselling LARPers, rather than hot intellectual hunks, so what did this say about Helen?—and pushed the thought away. Marnie had no idea how similar their taste in men really was. 'Didn't you find him a bit...hard to talk to?'

'Dan? No, he was fine, as far as I can remember. I'm sorry it didn't go well. Do you want me to contact him, see what he thought?'

'No! No, we better just leave it.' Helen was too ashamed to say he'd left her with the bill.

'Well, bring someone else then. I'm inviting everyone.'

'Everyone?'

Marnie ignored the implied question, and Helen was too afraid to push it further. He wouldn't come. He hated parties, and anyway he was probably out of town. 'Yep. So see you then.'

Helen squinted at the time. 'Why are you up at five anyway?'

'Oh, I'm often out late,' said Marnie airily.

Of course. She was probably with Tom, wandering hand in hand, breaking into gardens like in *Notting Hill*, stumbling from cool dive bars to all-night warehouse parties. Whereas Helen had gone to bed at 9 p.m. 'How was your date, by the way?'

'It was pretty good. Did you not see my tweets?'

'You tweeted about your date?'

'Of course. It's a social experiment, after all. The Ex Factor. Anyway, you'll see him at the drinks. He's really cute.'

'You're bringing him to your drinks?' Actually that was good. That meant she would hardly invite Ed as well. 'Um… won't Rosa mind?'

'She set me up with him,' said Marnie. 'Why would she mind?' *Because he's her ex and she might not want to watch while he snogs her friend?* 'It'll be fine, Helz. Anyway, got to run, don't forget to bring someone, byeeeee!' Marnie hung up, and Helen pictured her making her way home through still-dark streets, the fire of a winter sun just touching the sky, probably with some cool music ringing in her ears. In other words, everywhere that fun was. Helen looked round at her own bed, empty for as long as she could remember. She couldn't even get Mr Fluffypants to sleep with her. He'd come in for a brief cuddle but wouldn't stay the night, as he had an early breakfast meeting with his food bowl. Oh God, who could she bring to the drinks?

Awake now, she thumbed into her emails. KARL OLSEN, one said. She squinted at it, wondering why she felt a sudden quickening in her pulse. Anxiety, probably.

Dear Helen, he said, formally. I'm writing to check if your site is still all right. Your boss suggested my kneecaps might be at some risk if there were any more problems, and as I am a keen cyclist I am quite anxious to make sure they remain in their current condition. So let me know if anything goes wrong. Yours, Karl Olsen. In brackets it said (computer guy you didn't offer tea to).

Helen didn't quite understand the thing she did next. Perhaps it was the early hour or the reminder of Marnie's cool life or the aftershocks of the world's worst date or the idea of being the only person at the drinks without a date in tow, but she found herself writing back: Dear Karl, I don't suppose you might be free tomorrow night...?

# Chapter 11
## Drowning in a Vat
## of Rescue Remedy

*Helen*

Deodorant. Make-up. Rescue Remedy. Deodorant. Makeup. Rescue Remedy. Standing on the steps of the bar, Helen knew she had everything she needed in the Doombag, all her charms and potions and talismans. But it didn't seem to be helping. Her stomach was a churning mess and she was already sweating through the three layers of Sure she'd applied. What if Ed was there? What if Karl came? Worse, what if he didn't? Wait, which was worse? She wasn't even sure.

The bar was one of the painfully trendy kind Marnie favoured, called Moon on a Stick. As soon as she entered, Helen was bashed into by a girl in a tight crop top, who shot her a dirty look. Oh Lord, it was a jostling type of place. There was a queue five people deep at the bar. Why couldn't they have had the party in someone's house, where you could control the volume and temperature and there were always enough comfy chairs and the loos weren't questionable?

A quick scan revealed no handsome men with floppy brown hair, and Helen felt her heart slow. She was stupid to worry. Ed was likely thousands of miles away. He'd probably joined a commune or changed his name and become a rock star or was holed up on a tropical island with some stunning model while he wrote songs. She'd looked for him over the years, of course—once a day at least, Googling *Ed Bailey, Ed Bailey, Ed Bailey*, but none of the results was ever her Ed. Not that he'd ever been hers. He never posted on Facebook, and she didn't dare try his old email address. Because what would she say?

She spotted Marnie in the corner with a scared-looking Rosa, who widened her eyes at Helen, code for *thank God you're here*. Rosa nodded subtly to the balding man beside her, and mouthed, 'Simon'. She'd brought her Ex Factor date too?

Helen didn't recognise any of the other people. Marnie was wearing a red halter-neck dress with a full skirt, and bright red lipstick, and had her hair tied up in a scarf. Round her throat was the birthday necklace again. Helen was in jeans and boots, but in a gesture to the occasion had risked going out in a green silk top Marnie had once said was 'a little bit too nineties All Saints, babe'. Her old clothes, more structured than armour, didn't fit any more, but now she was worried that her breasts were trying to escape.

Marnie kissed her. 'You look great! I love that top.'

'I thought you said you didn't like it?'

'I did? No, I'm sure I didn't. Come meet everyone. This is Bill, from my last job, you remember, in the temp agency...

This is Carol from yoga… Asham from my pottery course… Brad from Canberra…' It was a very odd collection of people, souvenirs of Marnie's fractured life, the inordinate amount of jobs and flatshares she'd had over the years, the places she'd travelled.

Helen wished Ani were there—and her wish was granted a moment later when the door opened, letting in frigid air. Ani was dressed in her work clothes, a tailored navy suit, and looked tense. She also looked surprised to see Simon. 'Oh…hi! Um, it's me. Remember?'

'Hi! Ani! Gosh, it's been ages.' Simon got to his feet. Now he and Ani were awkwardly cheek-kissing. Rosa looked like she wanted to drown herself in her drink. Helen still hadn't taken off her coat. Marnie seemed oblivious to all, smiling and doing introductions again. Then she stopped, a wide grin on her face. 'He came. Hey, Rosa, look who it is!'

Rosa began to choke on her lurid yellow cocktail. 'Oh— God. I wish you'd…' Then she was giving a fixed grin to the man who'd just ambled over, leaving the door open so a cold breeze blew in. He had blond dreadlocks and wore a Greenpeace T-shirt and shorts, despite the weather. Rosa said, 'Heyyyy! Oh wow, haven't seen you in…in…well, a long time. Tom, this is my friend Helen, and you remember Ani from uni? How are you?'

'Oh, good, good. Awesome actually. I've been made Head of Protest Banners at my squat.'

'That's…awesome,' Rosa said gamely. Helen wondered if she could get away with not shaking his hand—they probably didn't run to showers in a squat.

'What is it you're protesting about?' Ani asked, taking off her jacket.

'Oh, you know, like…the global capitalist system and

that.' Tom was cut off from further philosophising as Marnie bounded up and kissed him on the cheek, leaving a crimson smear.

'Hey, you came! We had such a nice date, didn't we?' Marnie hitched herself under his arm.

Tom and Simon were shaking hands. 'So how do you…'

'Oh, I came with Rosa, but I know Ani too.'

'Yeah, I know Rosa from uni.'

Helen exchanged a quick panicky glance with Rosa and Ani. Weird, it said. So weird. As weird as all the beards in Communist Russia. And swimming merrily in all the eddies of social confusion, Marnie looked to be thoroughly enjoying herself, talking animatedly to both men.

Rosa extricated herself and came over to Helen and Ani. 'Jesus Christ,' she said, draining her drink. 'Oh, sorry Helen…'

'Honestly, I don't mind—me and the big man are not particularly acquainted.'

'Oh my God. This is mad. I'm sorry, Ani, I cracked and invited Simon. I just wasn't sure I could face seeing Tom otherwise, after all this time, since I'm getting divorced and everything.'

Helen was trying to keep up. 'So, you liked Simon? It actually worked out?'

Rosa said, 'Well, yeah, he's a nice guy. And Ani's date went well too. Apart from his hideous social faux pas in sending her an email the next day.'

'Isn't that good?' asked Helen, confused.

Rosa threw up her arms. 'Well, Helen, you and I might think so. But apparently not!'

Ani sounded defensive. 'It can be a bad sign is all. But Nikesh is all right, actually. He's a bit intense and nerdy—remind me to ask you about this questionnaire business another time by the way—but he's successful, and actually quite handsome.'

'So he doesn't have awful acne? Or milk-bottle glasses?'

'No, his glasses are pretty cool.'

So people did change. 'You mean you…liked him?'

Rosa nudged Ani. 'She did, despite what she says about his outrageous *emailing*. I mean imagine dating a man who *emailed* you and said he *liked* you.'

'All right, all right,' said Ani. 'I actually did like him. We've arranged to go for dinner when he's back from San Francisco.'

'Why didn't you invite him tonight?' asked Helen.

'Because we've only been out once! I want to take it slow.'

'She's afraid that if we all like him then she'll be stuck with him for ever,' Rosa said wisely. 'Commitment-phobic.'

Ani glared at her. 'Who died and made you Dr Freud?'

'Actually, Freud was my great-great-cousin or something like that. And I'm right. Aren't I, Helz?'

'Ummmmmm…maybe I'll go to the bar.' Helen suddenly became very occupied in looking for her purse. *Defleeeeect*.

At that point, thankfully, Simon ambled past. 'Rosa, drink? Red wine? Ani? And, er—sorry, I've forgotten your name.'

'Helen.' She weighed up the bar queue against her anxiety about getting out of step with rounds. 'Thank you. White wine, please.'

'Ani? Gin and tonic, was it, still?'

Ani looked wrong-footed. 'Er… Yes please.'

Simon touched Rosa lightly on the arm. 'Won't be long—or actually, I might be! Just look at that queue.'

Ani stared after him, her face working as if she was try-ing to solve some kind of complex mathematical problem.

'He seems…nice,' said Helen, deeply puzzled as to what was going on. Oh, to be at home with Mr Fluffypants and a box set.

'Come on,' said Rosa, with forced cheer. 'We're all out, for once, and there are nice guys, and Marnie's back. Let's enjoy ourselves.'

'OK,' agreed Helen, thinking, *At least he hasn't turned up…* Then, with his usual devastating timing, a tall, lean man appeared in the door, wrapped in a black wool coat. This time the air seemed not freezing, but blissfully cool. It wasn't him. Was it? It couldn't be.

Jesus Christ on a bike, as Rosa would say. It was Ed. It was really him. He was here.

It took Helen several moments to assimilate it, the fact of him being there, in the same room as her, breathing the same air. He looked a little older, but it suited him—a few strands of grey in his brown hair, a few lines around his eyes. God, the eyes, she had to remember not to look straight at him. His face was still pale and sculpted, and even the shape of his shoulders was so familiar it was like a punch to the stomach. Then she remembered to breathe, and the room came back into focus.

Rosa was saying, '…that guy Marnie was seeing two years ago? She's invited him and Tom too? Jesus Christ! Oh, sorry, Helen…'

* * *

*Rosa.*

Rosa had been doing her best to avoid him, but about an hour into the night she collided with Tom standing by the bar, a fraying tenner in his hand. 'It's so commercialised,' he complained. 'In the squat everyone shares their drinks.'

'You actually live in a squat then?'

'Of course. We've got a common cause, it's important.' He looked her over. 'You look well, Rosa.'

'Thanks. I don't feel it. I'm getting divorced, you see.'

'Oh, are you? That's—well, marriage is a capitalist institution anyway.'

'Maybe,' sighed Rosa. All she knew was she'd had… something, been a thing, and now she wasn't it any more. Now she didn't quite know what she was.

'Are you still working at…?'

'Yes, yes, still a journalist, still propping up the fascist state. I'm the worst kind too—I persuade women they need lipstick, and juice fasts, and really expensive holidays in the Maldives. And yes, before you say it, I know they're almost underwater due to climate change.'

Tom looked surprised. In truth, she was a bit surprised herself. Calling someone out like that was more of an Ani thing to do. 'Well, if you want to do something else, you should.'

'I don't know. I mean, sure, I imagined myself writing a great novel, but I'm good at this, it seems.'

'You can be good at more than one thing,' said Tom, reasonably. 'I remember you telling me all about your book. You seemed so determined.'

'You remember that?'

''Course I do.'

Rosa met his eyes for a moment—one of his best features, a bright startling blue, and for a moment relived the feel of him back then, like going too fast on a bike downhill, their words tumbling over each other, bands they liked, books they'd read, and then the awkward sex, his scrawny body barely out of its teens. Rosa wondered if he knew he'd been her first. But no, she'd not told him. Wanting to seem grown up, not fresh out of school. And then it was so suddenly over.

'Why did it not work out with us?' she blurted. 'I mean—
it was ages ago, I know. I just always wondered. Did I do
something?' The question every woman asks herself at some
point, but no one actually wants answered. *Well, yes, actually, you smell quite faintly of Hula Hoops at all times. Well,
seeing as you ask, you've been mispronouncing 'quinoa' all
your life.* If she'd only worn a slightly different top one night,
or pretended to like Radiohead more than she did, or arrived
five minutes earlier to meet him in the student union, would
she and Tom have stayed together, got married? Now be living together in a charming three-bed squat? *Get a grip*, she
told herself. Tom had been a feckless child who didn't wash
enough and spelled 'whales' wrong on his protest banner, so
it looked like he wanted to save the entire country (at least it
went down well with Hywl, his floormate), and in any case
she'd have ditched him soon enough for David. 'I'm sorry.
Just—you know, divorce-related low self-esteem.'

'Um.' Tom did a head-dip. 'Dunno. You were lovely. I
guess I just didn't want anything serious. I was nineteen.'

'You could have told me. You didn't have to snog another
girl in full view.'

'I know. I was just—it seemed easier.' He was almost
contorted with awkwardness. 'But I felt really bad about it.
I was going to get in touch, a few years back. I always wondered what you were up to. Then I heard you got married…
I always hoped you'd write that book, you know.'

'Well, maybe I will. I'm not exactly rushed off my feet
now I'm a thirty-two-year-old spinster.'

'You're not a spinster if you've been married,' said Tom,
helpfully. 'You'd be a divorcee.'

'Great. That only makes me sound a hundred and five.'

He peered into her face, putting up a hand, brown and

rough, to push her fringe out of the way. The fringe she'd not had back then. Rosa held her breath. 'Nah, you look the same,' he said. 'I'm the one going grey.' He was, a bit. His fair hair was shot through with it, streaks frosting his beard.

'It suits you,' Rosa heard herself say. There was another awkward pause.

'So…you think I should date your mate?' he said.

They both looked over to Marnie, who was chatting animatedly to her ex, Ed, and swirling a piece of hair in her fingertips. What was he even doing here, if Marnie had invited Tom? Was this what everyone did—befriended their exes, achieved closure, simply got over things? Would she and David ever reach that point? 'Marnie? Sure, she's great.'

'Yeah, she's pretty, and she seems fun.' Tom looked at Rosa again. 'Is it not a bit odd for you though?'

'Well. It was a long time ago, you and me. It's just a new thing we're trying, it's…' She used her last, desperate-measure excuse for everything weird she'd ever done. 'It's for a piece.'

'Right. And you're dating that bald guy?'

'He's not bald! Well, not really. We've only been out once.' Rosa was confused. What was this conversation actually about?

Tom said, 'To be honest, I mostly said yes to the date because I wanted to see you again.'

Rosa just stared at him for a moment. Did he mean…?

'I wanted to tell you about the work we're doing,' Tom said. 'The protest movement. People are going to be feeling the effects of the financial crisis for decades to come. You think you'd get into journalism now, without family money behind you?'

'No,' admitted Rosa. 'I was lucky.'

'You should come to our protest tomorrow.' Tom was

fumbling in his pocket. She saw he kept his cash in a plastic sandwich bag, and felt an odd pang of tenderness for him. She remembered how he'd tried to live 'off-grid' for a term, breaking a toe when he refused to put the lights on in his room, not showering until his flatmates held an intervention, and not using computers until he—ironically—almost failed his Environmental Law course. Then she remembered he'd also tried to convince her condoms created unnecessary ocean waste. Hmm. Could people change? He was holding out a smeary flyer, which looked as if it had been printed by a toddler using wooden blocks. We're thirty-two, she thought. We're supposed to have babies and Abel & Cole veg boxes and fixed-rate mortgages. Not this.

'Come,' he said. 'And—I'd invite you anyway, so don't think I'm hustling you—but maybe if you like what we're doing down there, you could write about it.'

Rosa could just imagine how she'd get that one past Suzanne. *Hot fashion tips from the squats. The Occupy diet— is socialism the new Atkins?* 'Um, maybe,' she said, taking the flyer.

'Thanks,' said Tom. Then: 'It's good to see you.'

'And you.' He smiled, and Rosa suddenly struggled to remind herself why it was they'd broken up all those years ago.

* * *

*Marnie.*

*Game face. Get your game face on.* For the first hour or so of the party, Marnie had been having her usual reaction, i.e. realising what a terrible idea it was and wishing she could go home and hide under a duvet. Not that she even had a home. And her duvet she was pretty sure had a dubious past—a strong herbal scent came off it when the heat was on, which actually wasn't that often in the freezing house.

What had she been thinking? Of course it wouldn't be a lovely fun gathering, where she'd move effortlessly through the crowds, smiling and touching people's arms. Instead, it was a reminder that she'd been away for years, and she hardly knew anyone in London now. It was embarrassing, having to invite someone you'd done a yoga class with five years ago. Even more embarrassing that they came.

But Tom had come too, that was something. He must like her, surely. She'd kissed him on the cheek—he was so cute, so serious. This was good. Maybe this could go somewhere. But then, like a bomb under her, like the spanner in her works he had always been, the door had opened, and Ed was there.

Ed. Here. Now. A face she'd been chasing, and running away from, for two years. He came towards her, his hair falling over his pale face. She stared at him, feeling the blood drain from her own cheeks. When he looked at her, it was as if the rest of the room faded out. Everything slowed down, and blurred, and her heart began to race.

'Hi.'

'Hi.'

'It's been…'

'I know.'

He reached out and touched the necklace she wore. 'You still have it.'

'Of course.'

His eyes were fixed on her. 'You look…wow.'

She held his gaze. All kinds of feelings were coursing through her, hitting her bloodstream like champagne. She'd wanted to see him just for closure, just to explain, just to be friends, maybe, but her body seemed to remember the shape of him. It would have been so easy to step back into his arms. She opened her mouth to say something—what, she didn't know—and then couldn't. 'Um…do you want a drink?'

Some time later—ten minutes? Ten hours? She didn't know—they were talking, just as easily and naturally as they always had. What he'd been doing. What she'd been doing—a heavily edited version, of course. Marnie was dimly aware of Tom somewhere in the distance, talking to Rosa, but he seemed to fade away. Ed. Ed. It was all Ed again. Bollocks. Was this what she'd wanted all along? Was this why she'd made so much effort for the party, blown money she didn't have on this stupid dress? But she'd broken up with him, hadn't she?

She had to say something, try to get control of the complicated emotions filling her up. 'Ed—I, um. I was hoping maybe we could talk sometime. About everything that… you know.'

His head dipped. He said nothing for a moment.

'It's just…the way we left things…I need to explain why I did it. And maybe, then…' She tailed off. No idea what the end of that sentence was.

Eventually, after what seemed like a hundred years, he said, 'Yeah. We should talk, of course. Just give me a sec.'

She watched him walk away, across the room. Going to the loo, she assumed, or the bar. But then he realised he was smiling—smiling at someone else. He was walking straight towards Helen.

# Chapter 12
## War and Piss

*Helen*

'Help me,' Rosa hissed. 'I'm having a nightmare.' Helen, glad to get away from the conversation about tax codes she'd been having with the accountant Marnie had invited (why?), fumbled in her bag. Eye drops…hand sanitizer… there. She pulled out the Rescue Remedy and squirted a few drops into Rosa's mouth.

'Thanks,' said her friend, slumping against the wall with its peeling paint. 'This is just so confusing. Simon and I have been getting on fine, but now Tom's here, and he's actually being nice, saying remember first year, remember the time we went on the march against climate change. For God's sake, he just started humming "Closing Time" in my ear. Why?'

Maybe because Marnie had been ignoring him, the skirt of her red dress spread over her legs as she chatted to Ed in a booth. Was she trying to play him and Tom off? Make Tom jealous? Or did she really not care about Ed, did she just see him as an old friend? What the hell was going on? Helen was doing her level best not to look at them. At some point she'd have to say hello. And then what? 'Tom's cute,' she said, distracted.

'Yes, but he's still so self-righteous. "Still working for the media overlords, Rosa?" Yes, I'm sorry we don't all live in the woods and poo in buckets, but I have bills to pay, and I don't exactly earn loads and…'

'But he's cute?'

'Yes,' said Rosa sorrowfully. 'He is so cute. All those muscles and the tan. Argh, it's so confusing.'

'That's what you get from essentially sleeping rough.'

'I know. Believe me, Helen, I know. I knew this at eighteen; it's why I moved on so quickly. I've always made good decisions about men, but now…even Simon, he's sweet, but he's a mess too. And look at me—I brought him here and I've essentially ditched him to reminisce with my ex about how awesome Radiohead used to be. I don't even like Radiohead!'

'Relax,' said Helen, trying to sound calm and soothing. 'Simon's fine, I'm sure. And you've had a terrible time. You're allowed to let your hair down and chat. You deserve this.'

Rosa looked miserable. 'No I don't, I made a total mess of my marriage. I don't even know what I'm doing here.'

'Oh, love, you didn't. David left you.'

'But things were bad for ages, and I didn't do anything about it.'

Helen patted her arm. From the corner of her eye she saw Ed lean towards Marnie. Her stomach squeezed. She heard herself say, 'It's hard to get out of something so long-term.

You've been very brave.' Helen could see the eyeliner Rosa had smudged into the corners of her eyes, and was suddenly filled with admiration for her friend. She'd taken the worst hit imaginable and here she was, dressed up, out and about. So why couldn't Helen just get on with things, instead of brooding over something that happened years ago, which maybe no one else even cared about?

Rosa was saying, 'Your Ex Factor date wasn't great then? I really hoped it might work out.'

Helen sighed. 'It was so bad he left before dessert.'

'God, that's terrible. Why on earth did Marnie pick him?'

'Who knows.' She was doing her best not to think about it. Why would someone's best friend set them up with a man who had no social skills? Or was it all Helen's fault? Was he maybe cool and fun when he wasn't around her? 'At least it doesn't have to go anywhere now.'

'Is that really what you want? Wasn't there a part of you that sort of hoped, you know, maybe he'd be nice?'

'Errrrrr...' Was there? Had she maybe, in some very very distant corner of her mind, been wondering if Marnie would pick her someone good? Help her get out of this oh-so-comfortable rut she'd cosied up in?

'I mean, we have to take risks, don't we? Otherwise we'd never meet anyone.'

Risks were bad. Helen didn't do risks. Except for one time...and look how that had gone. She could still barely stand to be in the same room as him. 'Just have fun,' she said to Rosa, turning her back on the corner where Ed and Marnie sat. 'Tom's probably miffed that Marnie's ignoring him, I mean, errr, he's probably realised what a mistake he made back then, seeing you so fantastic and successful!'

Rosa sighed. 'He did say he wants me to come on a protest. But I wasn't sure if Marnie would mind. Though she did invite her ex! Are you all right about that?'

Helen looked over to where Marnie was playing with her necklace, holding it up to the light. The ache was back, so familiar it was almost comforting. 'Oh, of course. Ed and I were just friends.'

'But I thought that you...'

'More Remedy?'

'No thanks. Can you overdose on that stuff?'

'Dunno. Might put a slug of vodka in and call it a cocktail.'

'Better than most of the concoctions here.' Rosa shook herself. 'Right, I better go rescue Ani. I don't think she was expecting to see Simon tonight.'

As Rosa pushed her way through the crowds, Helen saw someone was coming in the other direction. Right towards her. Ed. For a second she felt every emotion there was— terror, guilt, worry, excitement. He was coming to see her. He wanted to talk. Then she realised she was just standing beside the men's toilets. 'Hiiiiiiiiiii!' Yikes, that hi had at least ten too many letters in it.

Ed approached her with a smile, pushing his brown hair out of his eyes. 'Helen! My God, look at you!'

Helen steeled herself for the awkward hug, the smell of him almost too much to take. Old books and Pears soap. She could feel his heartbeat under his fraying blue shirt. They were almost the same height, so their heads brushed awkwardly, his mouth suddenly too close to bear. 'Wow! You're here!' she said. *Helen Sanderson, stating the obvious since 1982.*

'Yeah, I, well—it was funny really.' God, his voice, the timbre of it vibrating in her bones. 'I was just thinking of coming back to London, and then I got Marn's message. I was really pleased to hear from her—no reason we can't be friends. That's the thing about Marn, she was always cool about stuff. Laid-back.'

Marnie was cool and laid-back, while Helen was not. She just moped about things for two years and practically barricaded herself in her flat. 'Yeah, she just got back.' Helen ground to a halt. So many minefields in every sentence. How to talk to Ed about Marnie, and not mention anything that had happened? The things he knew about, the things he didn't?

Ed was staring at her. 'It's been forever. And you look…' Oh no. She could feel his eyes travel over her newly discovered waist, legs, chest. 'I mean, did you lose…?'

'Yes!' she trilled. 'Big diet last year, ha ha. Managing to keep it off.'

'Well done,' he said sincerely. 'I mean, you always looked fine to me, but now—you must feel so great.'

He was still looking. Helen changed the subject, trying to halt the furious blush that was spreading over her neck and face. 'So, you said you've been away?' That would explain his two-year silence, at least.

'Just in Bristol, you know, with my parents. You remember I'm from there?' So he had been around, he just hadn't contacted her. That made it worse somehow.

'I think so,' said Helen vaguely. She remembered everything about Ed.

'It's such a great city, Helen. So much culture, art. It's been really good for my music.'

*Oh, God, don't say my name, don't say it.* A tidal wave of memory was breaking over Helen's head. 'That's great,

great. So what brings you back?' She knew he must have been doing something cool all this time.

The wrong thing to say. Ed's face fell. 'Things have been a bit tough at home. My dad died, you see.'

'Oh no. What happened? Do you mind if I ask?'

'Cancer. Last month. It's been quite hard—I needed a break. So here I am.'

Ed being noble and sad was more than she could bear. 'I'm so sorry.'

'Thank you.' He forced a smile. 'Hey, Helen, it's really good to see you. I always wondered about you. What you were up to.'

And he reached out, as if he was going to touch her—she wasn't sure where, on her waist or arm or even her cheek, and Helen realised she couldn't take it. The memories of that night were flooding her—his hands on her face, and then her back, the warmth of his mouth and his chilled skin, the sound of his breath in her ear. 'Excuse me,' she blurted, and ducked into the nearby ladies', all peeling paint and dubious smells. She leaned against the dirty basin, taking deep breaths as she looked at her face in the mirror. She did look well. Her skin glowed, her eyes sparkled, a half-smile lifted the corners of her mouth. The Ed effect. She remembered what he'd said—*I mean, you always looked fine to me, but…* Oh bollocks. She felt her heart start to give, like a squashy marshmallow. Not again. She wasn't going down that road again, or she may as well drown herself in a vat of Rescue Remedy.

* * *

*Ani.*

Ani, in fact, did not need rescuing, either real or in a bottle. She was, strangely enough, having a perfectly lovely chat with Simon the Awkward Theatre Critic, because everyone else had vanished. Maybe she should have invited Nikesh after all; she was feeling a bit third-wheelish.

'Cheers,' Simon said, lifting his beer. 'Lovely to see you again.'

She raised an eyebrow. 'I thought you didn't drink?'

'Oh, did I not back then? Yeah, I had some weird ideas about it. To be honest, I once got up at the Press Awards and sang "Copacabana" with a Veuve Clicquot ice bucket on my head. So I was trying to lay off it.'

To her surprise, Ani laughed. 'You didn't!'

'I did. So I quit for a while. But I soon realised that most journalists are like ninety-five per cent booze, so I started up again. So what have you been doing with yourself?'

Wow, he'd actually asked her a question. She didn't think he'd done that once on their date five years ago. 'Well, I'm still a lawyer. Divorce, mostly.'

'Oh.' His face fell. 'Maybe you should give me your card. My wife—I got married, by the way—she's left me.'

'I'm sorry.'

'So me and Rosa had a few stories to swap.'

Ani would never have thought she could feel jealous of Rosa and her current woes, but, just for a second, she almost did. She and Simon had been married. What did Ani have to show for the past five years? Nothing but a string of failed dates, a lot of bitter-hilarious anecdotes, and a growing list of divorces she'd presided over.

'There's a lot of it about,' she said, feeling silly.

'I know. Masha—Maria, that's her name, she's Russian—said she just didn't feel it any more. The passion. She said I was too English for her.'

'I'm sorry,' she said again. 'If it helps, I'm still terminally single. And I recently went on a date with someone who accidentally proposed to me, then burst into tears.'

Simon laughed, a rich generous sound she'd never heard before. 'God, is it really that bad out there?'

'Yep. Be glad I set up you with Rosa.'

'Oh, that. I mean, she's a lovely girl, very pretty, but is it not a bit weird? I said yes because why not, I don't exactly have a lot going on right now, but still.'

'Well, we only dated, what was it, one or two times?'

He held her gaze and she took a slug of gin. 'Just once.'

And then she'd never called him. Why was that again? There must have been a reason. 'Of course. That terrible play we saw—you remember?'

Simon gave a groan. 'I'd forgotten. That awful subBrechtian nonsense. The bit where he weed in a bucket!'

'Then he filled that Super Soaker from it and shot it at the audience, remember?'

'I know! God, what a thing to take you to. What was it called again?'

'I looked it up afterwards,' Ani said. 'I had to be sure it wasn't just a terrible hallucination. *In Your Face*—a challenging and barrier-breaking look at our own prejudices and the impressions we make on others.'

'I was so bloody pretentious then. I just wanted to be in theatre myself, you see.'

'You did? As an actor?'

'Yes. My secret dream. Too bad I was no good. I did a few courses, but I just felt daft, waving my arms around and pretending to be a tree.' He smiled. 'Can you keep a secret, Ani?'

'Sure,' she said. 'Lawyer–client confidentiality.'

'Well, I might take a stab at writing scripts. I was always

decent with words. And it could hardly be worse than that
"wee in a bucket" play.'

'*Gone with the Wee*,' said Ani.

'*War and Piss*.'

She spluttered with laughter, then felt guilty. 'You know,
Rosa is really good at stuff like that. She has a novel hidden
away somewhere, I keep telling her to send it out.'

'Where is she?' Simon looked around, his beer drained.

Good question, thought Ani. Rosa had vanished, which
was most unlike her kind, thoughtful friend. So had Helen,
which was also more the kind of thing you expected from—
Ani looked up and saw it all like a tableau. Helen was coming out of the toilets, where Marnie's ex Ed—and why was
he even here?—was waiting for her, putting his hands on
her arm, as if to calm her. Rosa was in the corner with
Tom. Marnie stood nearby with her hands on the hips of her
OTT dress, staring at Ed, and then at Tom, and biting her
lip. And from the main door, just arrived, a large, bearded,
red-headed man in black combats was advancing on Helen,
who saw him and froze. Ed's hand was still on her arm.
The bearded guy's T-shirt said: *Have you tried turning it
off and on again?*

Simon looked at Ani's face. 'I told you. It's all a bit weird,
isn't it?'

\* \* \*

*Helen.*

It was Karl. Bloody hell, it really was him. He was an
actual person, out in the world, in the same room as her
friends. For a second, seeing his T-shirt, she was sorry she'd
invited him—especially now that Ed was here. But he'd
saved her job, after all. 'Heyyyy,' she said, waving past Ed,
who'd waited by the loo for her (Why? Did this mean he

wanted to talk about what happened? No, better not think about that.) 'How are you?'

'I'm sorry I'm late.' Karl pushed his shaggy hair out of his face. 'Well, I'm not really sorry, I knew I would be. I was at band practice. But I'm told it's acceptable to turn up late to this kind of casual gathering.'

'You're in a band? What are you called?'

'Citation Needed.'

'Like—on Wikipedia?'

'That's correct.'

Helen's mind tried to take this in, and failed. She realised Ed was still there. That was a first—usually in his presence she was attuned to his every move. 'Um…this is my friend Ed.' *And you know, the enduring love of my life.* 'He's into music as well.'

'Oh yes?' said Karl politely. 'What kind?'

'Oh, you wouldn't have heard of it,' said Ed vaguely. He was wrapping a blue scarf around his neck, looking at the door. Was he going? 'Listen, I'll leave you to it, Helen. This kind of bar isn't really my scene. Will you tell Marn I said I'll call her?'

Helen's heart felt like it was being pushed through a sieve. 'Oh, OK. Bye.'

'Nice to meet you.' Karl held out his hand, and the two men shook, awkwardly, and Helen felt her mind reel, as worlds collided. This whole project was dangerous, she realised. Breaking down the barriers everyone had between work and home, between friendship groups, between past you and present you. And Helen liked barriers. Barriers kept you safe. Just ask the characters in *Jurassic Park*.

'Karl,' she said, to distract herself after Ed had walked

off, parting the crowds of hipsters. 'Can I buy you a drink? I definitely owe you one.'

'I'll take something in a sealed bottle that's been opened in front of you, please,' he said. 'I searched for this place online and it failed its last two Environmental Heath checks.'

Helen looked at him and then back after Ed as he went through the door, out of her life again, after two years, and her mind boggled. And then it just went right on boggling for the rest of the night.

# Chapter 13
## Bumhead and Eggface

*Rosa*

'Rosa! You came!'

Tom's message had said to assemble on the Embankment, and she'd gone along, because Saturday afternoons had opened wide up ever since her husband left her, but she was very nervous. 'Yes, hi! What's going to happen now?' Rosa had never been on a protest before. What did people do?

'It's going to be great,' said Tom. 'We're going to march past Parliament and wave banners. It's breaking the law to protest here, you see.'

'Is it? I'm not sure if I can then… You know, my work.'

'Oh, they won't prosecute. We're just trying to show how silly their fascist laws are.' Tom was in protester-chic: ripped jeans, piercings, and a line shaved into his dreadlocked hair. He dressed exactly as he had when they'd kissed in the student union bar, under the romantic darts board. And look at her—sensible haircut, weekly manicure. Her jeans were even from Gap. She pulled her T-shirt down at the back, in case someone tried to set her on fire in an anti-capitalist protest.

She smiled nervously at Tom as they strode along the Embankment, struggling to keep up as he dodged traffic (was getting run over a protest against carbon emissions?) 'So…no Marnie?' Was it OK that Rosa was here? It was just a catch-up with an old friend, wasn't it? Though that might be easier if Marnie wasn't about. And Marnie had invited her ex to the party, so did that mean she and Tom were off anyway?

Apparently not. 'Hi!' A short, red-headed figure was coming at them. 'Sorry I'm late. There was some tube problem.' From the moment they'd met, Rosa had marvelled at Marnie's ability to dress for any occasion. Burlesque party, city brunch, dirty weekend, and now urban protest. She'd drawn slogans with eyeliner on her luminous skin, and wore a patterned scarf round her coppery hair, clashing attractively. She was dressed in paint-stained jeans and a 'No More Page 3' T-shirt. In one ear was a peace symbol, in the other a Solidarity fist. Tom gave her an awkward one-arm hug. 'You made it!'

'Rosa!' Did she imagine it, or had Marnie's eyes narrowed slightly? 'I didn't know you were going to be here.'

'Oh, well, Tom invited me, and I thought, why not live a little—I don't get much real reporting done, stuck in that office recycling press releases about Botox.'

'It's great that you're doing new things. So proud of you.' Marnie gave her a hug, enveloping her in a cloud of patchouli, and Rosa felt ashamed of her bad thoughts. Marnie meant well. It wasn't her fault she was adaptable and likeable and very, very pretty. And a size eight.

'So what are we protesting about?' Rosa asked, as they meandered towards a larger crowd, mostly consisting of tie-dye and anoraks. She was trying to piece together the cause from the various banners. Poverty? Climate change? North Face jackets?

'Oh, you know,' said Tom, extracting a banner from his tatty rucksack. 'The government and stuff.'

'You mean something they did?'

'More just them, generally.'

'Right… We do have to have a government though, right?'

'Do we? I'm not convinced.'

'But who would empty the bins and run the hospitals and build roads, and you know…run the country?'

'We can run it ourselves,' said Marnie, who'd acquired a purple whistle from somewhere. She blew into it, ear-splittingly. 'Woo! Smash the state!'

Rosa tried again. 'I mean, I know a lot of people feel let down, but we do need someone to be in charge, and this is who got in. I just think it's more important to work out who we'll vote for next time round and…'

Tom had stopped walking. His banner drooped. 'You mean, you're planning to *vote* in the next election?'

'Well, um, yes, of course I am. I mean, women literally died so I could.'

'But politicians are all as bad as each other!'

'So shouldn't we try to change that? What are you going to do next time?'

'Picket the polling station and spoil my vote,' said Tom immediately.

Marnie watched them argue, a faint crease puckering her forehead.

'And that achieves what exactly?' said Rosa.

'It sends a message to the agents of oppression!'

'No, it doesn't, it's just a waste of your vote.'

Tom opened his mouth, but she never got to hear his incisive rebuttal because a girl with platinum hair and a whole stapler's worth of metal in her face ran towards them excitedly. 'Everyone! We're being kettled!'

Something told Rosa this did not involve the relaxing cup of tea she was in dire need of. She took out her phone and on impulse texted Simon. In town, don't suppose you're free later?

He got right back. Sure, drink at the Oxbow?

Her favourite bar. Quiet, warm, welcoming, and entirely free of banners. Love it there. 5 p.m.?

Great x.

Tom saw her using her phone. 'You better save your battery,' he said, with relish. 'We're going to be here a loooong time.'

* * *

An hour later, Rosa was sitting disconsolately on a pavement. She was so cold she couldn't feel her feet, she was starving, and she would have given the entire contents of her bank account to be able to have a wee. Her phone had almost run down, so she could no longer send screaming-faced emojis to Ani and Helen. Nearby, Marnie and a group of protesters were chanting, 'Smash the state! Smash the state!' Rosa was close to hysteria. The state built loos and allowed you to make tea! Without it every day would involve sitting out in the cold, desperate to wee! She *loved* the state! Tom was holding up his iPhone, recording a video diary in dramatic tones. 'We've now been in this kettle for forty-eight minutes. The agents of the fascist state are restricting our liberty and right to free association. Worse still, we ran out of Twiglets five minutes ago…'

\* \* \*

Simon was sitting at the bar when she finally got there, sipping a cocktail. She ran past him, waving apologetically. 'Sorry—excuse me!'

Two minutes later she was back, the expression of cross-legged agony gone from her face. Never again would she take plumbing for granted. Or phone chargers, or being indoors, or…

'I got you a Sidecar,' said Simon, passing her a frosty, cloudy drink, clinking gently with ice. 'I remembered you liked them.'

For a moment Rosa was worried she might cry. Then, instead, she leaned over on her bar stool and kissed him. A gentle kiss, mouth closed, but a proper kiss all the same. His hand went up to the back of her head, and his stubble grazed her face. He tasted sweet, and boozy—she broke off and took a massive swallow of her drink, blushing. 'Sorry. I just…'

'Gosh, no, don't apologise. It was…nice.' He cleared his throat. 'Listen, I can't stay out tonight, as I'm reviewing a play, but I have tickets for another on Tuesday. Would you… would you like to come with me?'

If you didn't count the party—where after all she had neglected him most of the night—that would be their third date. And everyone knew what that meant. Time for awk-

ward first-time sex! 'Yes please,' said Rosa shyly. 'That
would be nice.'

For the rest of the time, they just talked, but when she
looked over, Simon was smiling at her slightly, as if they
shared a lovely secret.

* * *

*Ani.*

'Look at you, stupid fat cow. Stuffing your face as usual.'

'At least I'm not bald. You look like an egg inside a stupid tea cosy.'

Ani met the eyes of Louise, the barrister. 'Did you tell
them they really shouldn't talk?'

Louise shrugged. 'You try. They can't be within five feet
of each other without a fight.'

'That'll be fun in court.' Ani swallowed the last bitter
dregs of her coffee.

Across the courthouse café, her client, Mrs Willis, was
howling insults at the opposing side, Mr Willis. He did in
fact look something like an egg, his large bald head nest-
ling in an ill-advised turtleneck. 'Why don't you just go and
*poach yourself* or something?'

'Who's the other barrister?' Ani asked Louise, out of the
side of her mouth. She could already see the opposing solicitor, a middle-aged man in a depressed suit, remonstrat-
ing with his client.

Louise giggled, which was most unlike her. 'Oh, it's Legally Hot again, didn't you know?'

'Eh? Who's that?' Ani did not approve of the lists of hot
male barristers doing the rounds on the internet. She felt it
cheapened the profession.

'You'll see. Anyway, I can only look.' Self-consciously,

Louise pushed back her hair with a hand that sported a giant diamond sparkler.

Ani blinked. Surely she'd only been going out with Jake for like five minutes? 'Oh my God! Congrats!'

'Thanks. Jakey popped the question at the weekend, when we were skiing. It was soooo romantic, the snow, the mountains... He put the ring in my champagne glass.'

Ani had always thought that was quite risky, from a health and safety standpoint. 'Lovely, lovely.'

'So I better research venues, I'm thinking some kind of stately home, Mum's already driving me mad about dresses...then after the wedding I'll cut back on work a bit.'

'What?' Ani had begun to drift off at 'dresses' but snapped back. 'Why?'

'Well, I'll be Mrs Lockhead then. We're thinking of getting a place out of London...'

In her head, Ani began to mouth along with the script:

'You know it's so crowded, no place for a family... And then hopefully the patter of tiny feet...'

Ani shook her head to see if she was hallucinating. Was this really Louise, tough and cynical, with whom she'd shared many a cocktail and bitching session, who'd sworn she'd be single for ever? She tried to say the right thing. 'Wow, that sounds... I mean, it's all quite sudden, isn't it?'

Louise assumed a gooey expression. 'It's just so different when you meet the right person. You know? You want all that stuff. The ring, the house, maybe a dog.' Louise looked at Ani with an expression not far off pity. 'Are you seeing someone? What happened with Will in the end?'

Ani grimaced. 'Well, nothing happened there. But I am seeing someone.' Why had she said that?

Louise clapped her hands. 'Ace! What's his name?'

'Nikesh. He's…interesting.' Why was she mentioning him? They'd only had one date, and she wasn't even sure there'd be another. He'd emailed her diligently and politely since they'd met, and each time he did Ani could feel her own interest leach away.

'We must all go for dinner.' Louise nodded to the door, adding a quick slick of lipstick. 'Look, here's Legally Hot now. I'll go see if we're starting.'

Ani watched her click off in her Pied a Terre heels, thinking: *Another one bites the dust.* Then she saw who was coming in the door. The green eyes, the tall, impressive bearing—she groaned. Of course Adam Robins would be nicknamed Legally Hot. She bet he knew it too. He was wearing a long dark coat and a striped cashmere scarf, carrying a bundle of papers under his arm.

'Hello.' His eyes flicked over her. 'Are you…'

'Opposing solicitor, yes. Ani Singh.'

'I remember.' He didn't tell her his name, and she was annoyed he would assume he was unforgettable. But then, he was, wasn't he?

'We shouldn't really be talking,' he said, arching an eyebrow.

She wondered if her shirt buttons were done up properly. 'Oh, well, the clients are, so why not?'

'Fattie! You're so fat you gave me a slipped disc trying to carry you over the threshold.'

'Well, you're so bald they could send you into space to deflect the sun's rays from the earth.'

Ani felt a laugh bubble up in her, and covered her mouth. 'Sorry. But that was a pretty good burn, you have to admit.'

'She burned him like the ozone layer,' said Legally Hot, deadpan. 'Well, this will be fun. Who've we got?'

'Judge Mental.'

He groaned. 'Ah well, that might go in my favour. He's a bit down on women since his wife left him for the gardener.' He paused. 'Listen, I hope this isn't out of order, Ani, but I hear Louise wants to cut her hours down a bit and—'

Ani made an involuntary noise of disgust and then caught herself. He was looking at her, amused. She tried to cover it up. 'Uh, I believe so, why?'

'I'd love to work with you sometime. Maybe we can grab a drink and chat one night?' Smoothly, he popped a business card out of his suit pocket and proffered it with a blinding smile. 'Get in touch. I think we could be very interesting together.'

She stood there holding it. Was he…hitting on her? Even though she'd been so rude to him the first time? Then Louise came tapping back, clocking Legally Hot and morphing before Ani's eyes from a terrifying legal warrior to a simpering teenager. 'Hello! Louise Hadley, errrr, well, it'll be Lockhead soon. Haaa, I don't know why I said that. You're Adam.'

'Yes, hi. I better go.' He smiled at Ani. 'See you in there. Think about what I said.' He left, in a swoosh of expensive wool.

'OMG!' Louise exclaimed. 'He was totally flirting with you!'

'Don't be daft. He's just trying to get into our heads before court. And we shouldn't let him,' she added pointedly.

'He so was. OMG, you'll have two men fighting over you. That's hot.' Ani had once seen Louise make a global CEO cry on the stand. Was this what love did to you, turned you into a total sap? If so, she wanted none of it.

She watched the clients, who were glaring at each other

and hissing oddly primary-school insults—they were used
to not swearing round their seven-year-old twins, Brad and
Angelina, who'd been born at ruinous IVF expense.

'Bumhead!'

'Eggface!'

They'd likely started out as happy as Louise, babbling
about dresses and venues and cakes. But look at them now.
Look at Rosa and David, one shacked up with a teenager and
the other crying under her desk every day. What would be
the straw that broke Louise and Jake? Her spendy habits and
insistence on calling it 'kitchen sups'? The fact he'd once
described Nick Clegg as 'dangerously Bolshevik'? It could
be anything, but the truth was the spore of it would already
be there, silently germinating as they kissed and held hands
and made their vows, only to sprout and kill things, three
or five or twenty years down the line. And that was why
Ani would only ever settle for something totally perfect.

She shoved Legally Hot's card into the depths of her
handbag and prepared to get another couple divorced.

* * *

*Helen.*

'I'm sorry, Logan. What are you saying?' Helen tried to
make out what her boss was yelling down the phone.

'...another bloody hacking attempt! They're testing the
fences, Helen, just like the bloody raptors!'

'They didn't get in though?'

'Not yet. I've already called that web geek, he's on his
way over.' A sudden nervous warmth spread through Helen's
chest, which lasted for about 0.5 seconds until Logan doused
it again. 'Oh, and I've got those useless PR twonks I'm paying to send out a press release about the site. Try to get some

good publicity in case it all goes to crap. Blood-sucking zombies. Should be in the papers tomorrow.'

'Um, I think technically zombies eat brains, but…'

'And I'm off to Barbados, so any problems are on you. See you.'

'What…but… No! That's not my—Logan!' But the line had gone dead. Frustrated, Helen rang him back.

'Greetings, Cassidy residence, this is Consuela speaking.' Logan's housekeeper was from the Philippines and had learned her English from 1940s war films.

'Hi, Consuela, it's Helen. Is Logan there?'

'Mr Logan has said to tell you he is just popping out. That's right, Mr Logan?' In the background she heard muffled cursing. Consuela sang out, 'Sorry, Miss Helen, he's going into a tunnel!'

'But he's in the house, I just heard him!'

'Bye, Miss Helen, do keep buggering on!'

As the line went dead again, Helen heard the doorbell.

* * *

At least this time she was dressed. Thoroughly dressed. She had on a vest top, a jumper, and a cardigan on top. All the same, having Karl there made her feel nervous. He got straight to work, not mentioning the party or offering any social niceties. 'So, how's it looking?' she asked, nervously, after a while.

He'd colonised her living room again with his hiking boots, his laptop, and his fluorescent bike helmet. 'The firewall I put in seems to be holding, but you're under a pretty sustained attack.'

'Crap. We have to stop it, that personal data can't get out.'

'I'm trying. Your hanging over me isn't helping.'

'Well, I can't do anything else, I'm too anxious.'

'Try counting steps.'

'You mean sheep?'

'That's for sleeping. If you feel anxious, you count your steps. That's what my mum always told me.'

'You're anxious?' He seemed as calm as a cushion, typing away.

'Used to be.' *Tap tap tap.* 'Not any more.' *Tap.* 'Meds.' *Tap.* 'My brain just produces too much of a certain chemical, so I take some other chemicals to balance it out. That way I feel OK, and I can leave the flat without checking twenty-four times that my cooker isn't on. Especially when I haven't used my cooker in sixteen months.'

'You have OCD?' Helen couldn't keep the surprise out of her voice. 'It's just you…erm.' She glanced towards where his glass of water was dripping rings onto her lovely antique coffee table.

'It takes different forms,' he said. 'Anyway…' He looked pointedly at the piles of magazine under her table. 'These are all in date order.'

'That's not weird. You finish one, you put it on top.'

'To the week? For…thirty-seven weeks? This is the tidiest flat I've ever been in.'

'Thanks.'

'Wasn't necessarily a compliment.' *Tap tap tap.* 'There are actual featureless vacuums—redundancy, sorry—which have more mess than this. What's that about?'

Defensively, she said, 'Well, when I was growing up, things were a little…chaotic. I just like my home to be ordered. Tidy. Calm.'

'Calm like an old folks' home. Why do you read *Woman's Weekly?* Isn't that for grannies?'

Helen blushed. 'I like the household tips. It's how I

learned you can get out most stains with baking powder and vinegar, for example. Still looking for a solution to bathroom mould, though. I could clean your laptop for you—how old are some of those crumbs in there? Fragments from the actual Last Supper?'

'Good burn. But look at this.' Karl read out one of the magazine headlines, upside down. *'Evil Plumber Tried to Kill Me With Stopcock.* If you're anxious, does this not make things worse?'

'Actually no, it sort of helps. Makes me see the worst has already happened, only to Deirdre in Huddersfield.' Helen gestured to the magazines. 'How did you count them so quickly anyway?'

'I have an eidetic memory. Oh, and I'm really good at counting. Not maths, you understand. Counting is useful. Maths is…fabric of the universe type stuff. And I don't like that, it makes me get anxious about asteroids and the world and the probability of aliens taking over the planet and the statistical unlikeliness of life on earth.'

'I see. So your medication…?'

'It means I can still count, but I don't need to. Not so much.'

'How many jars are in each row of my spice rack? No peeking.'

'Eight,' he said, without looking up.

'Wow. Didn't realise I had Rainman in my living room.'

'Yeah, I'm amazeballs, as your friend would say. So you better let me get back to fixing the enormous catastrophe that's going to engulf you otherwise.'

'Oh. Of course.' That was odd. For a moment, she'd forgotten to worry, about the site, about Ed, about Marnie, about anything. That never happened.

She decided she'd leave him be and crack on with the Routine. With an angry Mr Fluffypants crouched in the corner of the bathroom—he tended to bite first and ask questions later—she put on her pink Marigolds, feeling a sense of calm defuse the anxiety. She began to scrub the sink with a toothbrush and lemon-scented cleaner, washing away toothpaste stains and face powder. Making everything clean. That way it would all be fine, and neat, and she wouldn't have to think about what Ed might have said to her had Karl not turned up the other night...

'Helen?'

It struck her suddenly—*I like the way he says my name.* 'Yes?'

'I was just having a look in your work folders for anything that could be malware, explain how the hacker got in there, and, well, I opened something.'

Helen froze. Gently, she set down the sponge—in its correct place, there was no need to panic just yet. 'Just shut it down, will you?'

'What's Swipe Out?'

Helen shot out of the bathroom, letting the cleaner spill, followed by an enraged cat. 'YRROOOWWWWL!'

'Oh my God, stop looking at my stuff!'

'I'm sorry, it looked like malware!'

'Well, it isn't, it's just... Give me that!'

'It's a game,' said Karl, surrendering her laptop. 'Isn't it? You're making a computer game based on online dating.'

She cradled the computer to her protectively. 'It's none of your business. It's just something I was playing about with.' Karl was looking at her with new respect. 'What?'

'You're surprising. I thought you were...you know, the

chintz, the—' he sneezed '—the cat, who by the way is staring at me with pure evil from under the sofa.'

'YRROOOOWWWWL.'

'Yes, well, people aren't always what you think.'

'So is the idea of the game that you negotiate the obsta-
cles of dating, with the goal of finding love?'

'I thought it could be more like Monopoly. You know, you
get random rewards and forfeits, like in Community Chest.
Only now it's the mystical free Pret coffee, or there's a tube
strike on the day of your date or something.'

Karl was scribbling on a piece of paper—Helen's TV
guide, she noticed. She tried not to mind. 'So it would look
something like this.' He'd sketched out a rough game board,
with squares containing different symbols.

'Yes.' Helen was amazed. 'That's exactly how I pictured
it.'

'It would be easy to code. And app setup is cheap as chips
nowadays. Could be done in a month, tops.'

'You mean…actually make it?'

'Well, of course. Isn't that what you wanted?'

Was it? Sure, in her sleepless nights and wildest dreams
she sometimes thought of being a game designer. Ditching
Logan and the feelings of shame she had to swallow down
every day she sat at her desk. But she'd never imagined actually doing it. 'Um, I suppose so, but how…'

'I'll do it for you,' he said, casually, scribbling again. 'Is
Wednesday any good?'

'Sure. Sure. That's…that's amazingly kind of you.'

'I can't paint or draw and I'm at best a slightly above average songwriter. I like the idea of putting something new
in the world. Coding lets you do anything, but, best of all,

you can actually *learn* it. You don't need talent. Talent is so…inefficient.'

'Well,' said Helen shyly. 'I had thought that instead of just a game, you could link it to Facebook and use it as a dating app too. You know, for people who like gaming.'

'So you'd play and it wouldn't feel like just swiping through picture after picture?'

She nodded.

'That is—and I don't use this word lightly—genius. Citation Needed are having a week off while Ian gets a gastric band fitted, so I have some time. Let's do it.' He reached over the table and held out his big hand. There was something scrawled on the back. It looked like 'COUNT STEPS'.

Feeling an odd surge of tenderness for him, Helen shook it. It was warm and solid. 'What the hell. I guess it won't hurt to try.'

He held her hand for a few seconds then let go. 'Right. I need to leave. I've fixed your problem, for now.'

One of them, Helen thought. 'OK. Thanks for coming to the party, by the way.'

'I enjoyed it. Your friends are… Was there some kind of strange boyfriend-swap going?'

'What? Er, what makes you say that?'

'Well, your friend with the fringe seemed to be there with your other friend, the lawyer's, ex. And your friend with the red hair was there with fringe-friend's ex. Yes?'

'Yes. It's…well, it's complicated. And I'm not involved.' *Please don't ask about Ed.* She hadn't heard from him since the party and, after he'd gone, Marnie had been glued to Tom for most of the evening. They seemed to be still dating, judging from Marnie's excitable tweets about the protest march they'd gone on. The whole thing was giving Helen a tension headache.

Karl said, 'OK. Well, I must go. It's twenty-one per cent more dangerous to cycle after 5 p.m. Bye, Helen, bye, angry cat.' And, collecting his helmet and high-vis jacket, he was suddenly gone. Without him, the flat seemed oddly silent, and Helen was once again alone with her swirling thoughts.

'Yrrrrrroooowl.' Mr Fluffypants padded at her leg, indicating that it was high time for his mid-afternoon snack.

'Yes, yes, OK, you're such a glutton. If I die, will you wait a day before you start to eat me, for decency's sake?'

'Yroooooooo.'

'Didn't think so.'

# Chapter 14
## Undercover Cheerleader

*Rosa*

The day of her planned third date with Simon, Rosa was clicking peacefully through the news on *Popbitch* and tearing up a blueberry muffin when suddenly all the joy seemed to leach from her, as if a Dementor had just floated past. 'Hi, Suzanne,' she said, without looking round. Luckily, trawling gossip sites was actually part of her job.

Today Suzanne was wearing a Cos shift in bright yellow, making Rosa's eyes throb. She tried to crane round to see her boss's office—if it was a juice cleanse day, she was going to hide under the desk and never come out.

'What's up?' she said, praying that Suzanne's journey to work had been smooth. She was not above bursting into the office and shouting, 'I've had to wait four sodding minutes for a soy latte, give me five hundred words on declining service standards in this country.'

'Affairs,' said Suzanne.

Rosa tried to indicate 'I completely understand what it is you want from me'. 'Um. OK. What?'

'Are they a good idea? Will it save your marriage?'

It hadn't saved Rosa's. 'Um…'

Suzanne clicked her fingers. 'Come on. That sordid little cheating website is trawling for PR again, they've put out some dubious stats. But we'll bite. Is the New Year time to get a new lover? Are cheating couples actually happier? Find one to say they are—French people or something. Then find someone who says it's immoral and this site ought to be shut down. Oh!' She brightened. 'You can do that bit yourself. What it feels like to be the betrayed wife. Waiting at home with your shepherd's pie going cold, your posh lacey knickers on.' Rosa only ever wore cotton briefs—thrush was not a friend to her—and she'd never cooked shepherd's pie in her life. If anything David, who had a more relaxed boss on the Business desk—Attila the Hun was probably a more relaxed boss than Suzanne—used to get home before she did. 'I want a thousand words by the end of the day about what it feels like to be cheated on.'

'But…' Rosa opened her mouth then subsided. Suzanne wouldn't care that she was supposed to be seeing a play with Simon that night. 'I'll need to stay late then—I'm still working on that dating article, and subbing the features pages too.'

'If that's what it takes to write a simple piece. I'm thinking online adultery, is it a new trend, is marriage outmoded in the age of instant internet gratification, blah blah.' She patted the back of Rosa's chair. 'Good job I've got a betrayed wife right here.'

'Yes, it's *super* lucky.' Even as her fingers stumbled, Rosa was opening a new document. All features journos were used to mining their own life for stories, and it would buy her some important credit with Suzanne.

'Get your ex's side too,' said Suzanne, casually.

'What?'

'What's his name again? Daniel? Give him a right to reply. This research shows a lot of people are having affairs, forty per cent or something. Don't want to alienate our core demographic.'

'You want me to…interview David about his affair? You know he left me. For an intern. Who's twenty.'

'Yes, yes, so? He's just over there. Get on with it.'

Amazing. Every time Rosa let herself think that Suzanne might not be a fire-breathing robot in designer clothes, she was surprised once again. 'Oh, and don't slack off on your other work,' said Suzanne. 'Jason wants to see how your dating piece is coming along. And you better not reuse any of the copy.' She checked her Rolex. 'Right, I'm off to my Bikram yoga class, so you'll have to stay here.'

Rosa watched her go, feeling relieved despite this meaning she'd have to sit by the phones all lunchtime. Once, Martine McCutcheon's PR had rung with an exclusive while Rosa was having a root canal, and she'd never been forgiven. At least now she could sit Googling her horoscope and avoiding David.

'Suzanne said you wanted to see me?' said David, popping up beside her.

Rosa turned very slowly, doing a rapid mental inventory of her person. Tights—only one ladder. Shoes—kicked off. Food stains—a bit of this morning's porridge. She took him in from the waist up. His shirt was crumpled. Of course—a twenty-year-old wouldn't own an iron. His brown eyes were tired—too much sex with the Intern? 'Hello. Um, I don't—I mean, it was her idea.' Rosa just couldn't. She'd tell Suzanne he'd said no. As David didn't actually work for her, he was still allowed to keep a few shreds of dignity in his personal life. 'You know her, she gets these mad whims. Don't worry about it.'

'OK.' He was looking at Rosa's desk, a mess of paper and Diet Coke cans. Rosa realised she had 'GET DIVORCE PAPERS' written prominently on a Post-it stuck to her monitor. 'How are you?'

'I'm… Well, you know.' She couldn't bring herself to say 'fine'. 'Fine' was for dull Tuesdays and tax bills, not for when your husband, the love of your life, left you for someone who hadn't even been born in 1994.

'It's tough, I know. Big upheaval for us both.'

'What's so hard for you? Sounded like you were having a wonderful time with Whatsherface.'

'Rosa. Don't be like that. It isn't Daisy's fault, you know that.'

Daisy! Not even a proper name! In her little playsuits, so happy and enthusiastic about working at the paper. Even Suzanne had once remembered her name, instead of referring to her as 'the workie' or 'thing one'. 'Well, everything was OK before she came along,' Rosa muttered.

'It wasn't though, was it? And anyway, you're one to talk, when you're literally writing an article right now about how you're dating other people and—' David stopped himself. 'We shouldn't do this here. But we do need to talk. We'll have to sort the flat, for one thing. I'm still paying for it, but at some point I'll want to buy a new place.'

She stared at his shoes—unpolished, unfeasibly pointy. He meant so he could get a place with the Intern. He wanted to sell their lovely flat, the one they'd bought together, and he wanted to kick her out on the street so he could set up a love nest with Dandelion.

'I mean,' David went on, relentless, 'it was mostly my parents' money for the deposit.'

'I—' Rosa was suddenly remembering a hundred discussions with Ani about why people needed prenups and contracts and difficult conversations. *It doesn't matter how much in love you are. When that goes, it all comes down to cold hard cash.* 'I can't believe you'd do this.' She heard her voice thicken with tears.

'Oh, Rosa,' he said, irritated. 'It's already done.'

She couldn't hide under her desk, as he was beside it, so, Suzanne be damned, Rosa got up and bolted across the newsroom to the corridor.

This was too much. Working alongside David, constantly worried she'd see him in the canteen or on pub trips, or that the Intern would get a proper contract with the paper once she finished uni, and then she'd have to avoid both of them. It was just too much. 'I'm going to have to get a new job,' said Rosa aloud to herself. She'd ducked into a cupboard that usually held the cleaner's mop and the sad plastic tree from the Christmas party, shreds of tinsel clinging to it.

'Not too soon, I hope,' said a voice.

Rosa jumped. Her first thought was that Suzanne had somehow started bugging her, and was listening even now as she bent herself into Dolphin pose, but no, it was a man's voice. She turned, feeling deep in the pit of her stomach this wasn't going to be good. 'H-hello, sir.'

'Please, it's Jason.' His Australian accent sounded strong in the confined space, and his shirt was made of such soft fabric that Rosa had a sudden irrational urge to rub her face over it. Her boss, her boss's boss, editor of the entire paper, was sitting on an upturned bucket, with what looked like a Crunchie bar in his hand.

'Did I disturb you?' she asked. 'What are you…?'

'Oh, I'm just trying that thing you said—what was it, head-desk-space? I thought this might be the next step, quiet meditation zones in the office. All those emails and calls coming in, it's overwhelming.'

'This is the janitor's cupboard,' she pointed out.

'It's quiet. And no one judges me for eating refined sugar.'

'Rice cakes,' sighed Rosa. 'It's all about rice cakes and kale. They used to have snacks at Cookery but now they hide them. The men's pages are all fitness freaks and chuck them in the bin.'

Jason looked sadly at his Crunchie. 'God. And the weather here—I don't think I've seen the sun since I arrived. At *Listbuzz*, the site I set up back in Oz, we were near the beach. So after work we'd all go surfing.'

'Sometimes we go to the pub,' Rosa offered. 'That's if we finish before eleven and people aren't doing Dryanuary or Veganuary or something.'

'What is it about you Brits? Basically the only way to get through the winter months is beer, meat and the love of a good woman. You've nixed the beer and the meat, and as for romance…' He suddenly looked at her with interest. 'You're still doing that dating piece, right? Swapping exes with your mates?'

'Sort of. It's just an experiment. Get us out of our ruts.'

'But all my mates are happily married and in Sydney. I've no one to set up an ex-swap with.'

'Give it time,' said Rosa, a touch bitterly. 'Turns out you might *think* you're happily married, but your husband could be having it off with the work experience girl, and then you might have to keep working with him even though he stomped on your heart like an overripe grape.'

He looked at her, and she felt a blush rise up from the soles of her feet. This was her boss's boss! Informality in a janitor's cupboard didn't mean she should tell him all her secrets! 'Hm,' said Jason. 'Let me make an investigative leap—he's why you need a new job? I won't ask what desk he's on.'

Rosa nodded shakily.

'Well, I hope you don't quit yet,' he said. 'I never had anyone leave at *Listbuzz* and I don't want to start letting the ideas people go. That's two great features I've had from you so far.' His smile was so engaging. Rosa forced herself to remember that you didn't become editor of a national paper at thirty-eight by being genuine. 'Stick with the lifestyle stuff,' he said. 'I think lots of people are in your situation, looking for love, but sick of dating apps. Turning analogue with it.' He even spoke in pitches.

'The pursuit of appiness,' she said absently. He laughed, even though what she'd said was definitely not funny enough to warrant it.

He said, 'Do you know any good things a newbie to London should do? I'm missing my surfboard. Do you guys have an equivalent?'

'Drinking pints, mostly. Or darts? In winter, we just tend to stay in and watch *The X Factor*, to be honest.'

'I was afraid so. I can't handle that, being on the tube every day for an hour, cooped up in the office. I feel like a sardine. I need fresh air.'

'There's some lovely walks in London. Well, you walk a

bit and then you duck into a pub and play Scrabble in front of the fire.'

'That doesn't sound so bad. Anywhere you'd suggest?'

'The Parkland Walk? It's like an old train line you can walk on. Takes you out near Highgate Cemetery, you know the one with all the famous people in.'

'Great. I knew you'd be the right person to ask. How's Sunday?'

'Sunday?' She was puzzled.

'Yeah, lunch, walk, cemetery, Scrabble? I'll warn you though, I'm pretty good. We could meet at, say, 1 p.m.?'

'Umm...um...' Rosa's brain, long-married, did not understand what was happening.

'Oh, are you busy?'

'No, I'm not, but...'

'Bonza. See you then. I better get back to my budget meeting, but let's go out separately. You know how people are.' He stood up, and the winning smile was back. Dammit, he even had a dimple. 'Thank you, Rosa.'

How could he know her name when he had so many staff? Suddenly he was leaning towards her and, for a spilt second, she froze. Doh. He was just reaching for the door. 'Um, you've got...' She pointed at his chin. 'Just a bit of chocolate...'

'Rats. That won't do. Where is it?'

'Just there, no, left...here.' Rosa put her hand up and very quickly wiped her boss's cheek, feeling the gold-tinged stubble graze her skin. 'All gone.'

'Thank you.' He shifted past her. 'Don't stay in too long.' He indicated the forlorn plastic tree. 'It's like a Radiohead song in here. And I've never liked them.'

And he was gone. Rosa stood very still. Had she...had

she just agreed to go on a date with her boss's boss? Had she rubbed Crunchie off his cheek? Had she arranged *another* date before she'd even cancelled on Simon for tonight? Was it even a date? On the plus side, if it all worked out, and they got married, she could probably arrange to have David, the Intern, and Suzanne all fired, or at the very least hired as her own personal minions.

* * *

*Helen.*

Helen was often suspicious when numbers were not recognised by her state-of-the-art caller ID. But it didn't matter that Ed's had changed, because he didn't believe in having fancy phones and was always losing his—she'd know his voice anywhere. Even before he spoke. The intake of breath, the pause, the sound of a smile breaking out on his face. 'Hey, you.'

Her heart began to beat wildly. His voice, deep and rich, had always made something unfurl in her stomach, like a flower opening in the sun. 'Hi! How are you?'

'Oh, you know. I hoped you'd still have the same number. I found it written in the back of this old copy of *Catcher in the Rye*.' That was so Ed. 'It was nice to see you at the party the other night.'

'Nice to see you too. It's been ages.' *Since the night we had sex, in fact!* Helen tried to keep her voice light.

'Who was that guy who came? With the computer T-shirt?'

'Karl? Oh, he helped fix the website I run, that's all. Is everything all right? How's your mum?'

'Well, that's why I was ringing.'

'Oh yes?' Helen sighed a little, then told herself not to be so silly. Of course he was ringing for a favour. What did she think, that beautiful, fascinating Ed was calling her for a chat? Because he'd missed her company for the past two years of zero contact? Daft.

'Well, I have to go down there and move some of Dad's things. Mum's too upset, and she doesn't drive. I'm not sure what to do, and I wondered if you had any ideas. You were always so good at practical things.'

'Well you could…' Helen's little-miss-fix-it mind whirred. 'You could hire a van down there. In Bristol. Catch the train.' Her mind suddenly flipped to another image—the two of them, speeding through the countryside, passing the honeyed spires of Bath, drinking plastic cups of wine, maybe doing the crossword, their heads back laughing… 'Do you… Would you like me to come with you? I mean, only if you think I could help.' She held her breath. What if he said no? What if he wanted to talk about what happened? What if he didn't? Since he hadn't brought it up, Helen was beginning to worry she'd been instantly forgettable, not even a blip on his radar.

'Could you? Helen, that would be so great.' The relief in his voice made warmth spread through her. She'd done that. She'd made it OK for him. 'But you probably have work to do.'

'I work from home!' She almost shouted it, so great was her need to help. 'And my employer owes me about a hundred hours of overtime.'

'So we could make a day of it? Tomorrow maybe?'

What a lovely phrase. Make a day of it. Something her mother used to say, back when she could still enjoy days out without worrying about killer bees or car crashes or kidnap by armed terrorists.

Tomorrow was the day for Karl to come around and work on the game. But Ed needed her, and she couldn't turn her back on him. 'Tomorrow is great.' She could tell Karl she was sick or something. They made the arrangements—well, Helen offered to buy the train tickets and book the van, since Ed was going through such a hard time—and she stood holding the receiver in her hand for a while after he hung up, still hearing the sound of his voice in her ear. Then she put the phone down, the day's work, her plans with Karl, and all worries about Marnie completely forgotten.

\* \* \*

*Ani.*

Simon! Hi! Wondered if you were by any chance free tonight and...

Ani sighed and deleted what she'd written. He'd know, wouldn't he? He'd know she knew Rosa had to bail out of the theatre because of Suzanne being more evil than Doctor Evil, and that Ani was fishing for an invite. And why was she fishing? What kind of person was she, that she'd move in on her friend's date as soon as said friend was called away in the service of great evil?

*Well*, said a nasty little voice in her head, *you did know him first.* And it was true…wasn't it? What was the protocol when you set your friend up with an ex, then realised he was quite nice after all? Was it as if you'd offered her a pair of wedge heels, thinking they gave you blisters and looked way better on her, only to then wonder if the blisters had been so bad after all, and if the heels might in fact go quite well with your new floral maxi-dress? Besides, Rosa wasn't even wearing the wedges. She was off flirting with Australian flip-flops. She'd called earlier to dissect her supply-cupboard encounter with Jason the Surf God.

'What about Simon?' Ani asked. 'If you're dating your boss?'

'He's not my boss. He's my boss's boss. And it's not a date.'

'A walk and a trip to the pub? Sounds like a date to me. And I would know.'

'I'm sure it's not a date. Anyway, I thought you said it was fine to see lots of people at once?'

'Yeah, but it's Simon. You might hurt his feelings. He'll be all alone at the theatre.'

'Ani, you're the one who didn't want to see him again!'

'I know, but—'

'Look, I have to go, I can hear the clack of Suzanne's heels.'

Ani had hung up, feeling slightly miffed. She'd gone to the trouble of finding Rosa someone lovely, only for her to dally in cupboards with tall, hunky Australians. So if Ani took the wedges for another spin—the wedges that had been hers to start with—who would judge?

As she sat brooding, her email dinged. Her heart sank to see it was another message from Nikesh. Hi, Ani, how are you? I'm back from San Fran now, could I take you to dinner tonight? Oh no. She couldn't think about this now.

Feeling guilty, Ani quickly typed back: Hi! Can't do tonight I'm afraid as I'm working late, can we take a raincheck? It was fine. They'd only been out once, and she had well-publicised misgivings, and anyway it wouldn't be a date with Simon. And she really was busy.

She started typing again in the other email. Simon! Hi, hear poor Rosa got held up at work. Just wanted to drop the hint that I've been dying to see that play, in case you're stuck with the tickets!

She thought about it and changed that to *the extra ticket*. No point in it if he offered her both. That was OK, wasn't it? And if she had ever so slightly given the impression that Rosa knew about the email and it was her idea, well, Ani could not be to blame for Simon's interpretation.

He came right back, warm and friendly. Sure, I would love some company, if you can face another theatre trip with me after *War and Piss*.

Alluding to their shared past! Ani felt a warm glow spread in her chest. This was OK. This was fine. She just wanted to catch up, chat a bit more, hear what he'd been doing. Just a friendly evening out. No court of love would convict her.

# Chapter 15
## The Dirtiest Martini

*Rosa*

*Marnie and her date Tom hit it off right away, hanging out on London's trendy Southbank discussing climate change. Soon they were attending protests together, marching in demos, and campaigning for an end to the fascist state. Was passion boiling up inside that kettle?*

Rosa sighed and hit the delete button, rubbing her hands over her tired face. She couldn't write about this objectively—this was her ex and her friend, after all. Marnie had even suggested a photo shoot to go with the piece: 'Me and Tom can handcuff ourselves together, what do you think?' Rosa had copped out and said there was no budget for pictures. Which was true. Most of their articles were illustrated by pictures of Women Laughing at Salad, ever since they replaced the picture editor with an intern and a subscription to Shutterstock.

Was there something wrong with Rosa? Sticking with one

man for fourteen years, and never looking at anyone else,
was that weird and creepy in the modern world? Marnie had
always dated hard and dated deep, with several guys—and
sometimes girls—on the go at any given time. Even now,
she was dating Tom and inviting Ed along to things. Maybe
Rosa had to learn to be the same. But her brief rekindling
of interest in Tom had been a mistake. He hadn't been right
for her at eighteen, and he was even less right now. Rosa
could think of nothing worse than living in a squat, having
to share milk and wait your turn for the no-doubt ecologi-
cally dirty shower. In the meantime there was Simon, who
she was supposed to be out with right now, and after the
earlier cupboard incident maybe there was also…

*Crash.* Rosa heard a noise and looked round the empty
office, startled. Suzanne had swanned off for a facial at
4.59 p.m., after condemning Rosa to a night of working
late. She followed the sound into the corridor, and to Jason's office. The door was open, but there was no sign of
him.

'Hello?' she called, nervously.

'Hi,' came a mournful muffled voice.

Rosa looked around her. The office was empty. 'Um…
where are you?'

'Down here.'

Jason was crammed into the small space under his desk,
his legs squashed up like a giant insect. A giant hot insect.
'What happened?'

'I was trying your desk meditation thing. I guess I'm a
lot bigger than you.'

'Are you stuck?'

'I just can't get my arm… Ow!' Jason dislodged himself, crawling out. His tie was askew and his hair messed

up. Rosa had an urge to stroke it back into place. 'Show me how you do it.'

'Now?'

'Yeah, go on. I'm can't be doing it right, I don't feel relaxed at all.'

'Well, the idea is not to get trapped in there.' Rosa bent down and scooted under his desk. It was more spacious than hers, like a welcoming cave. It was also a lot less dusty. 'See?' She waved from the back, her legs in their skinny jeans tucked up neatly.

'OK. Let me try this.' Jason lay on his stomach and half crawled in, his legs sticking out. He was suddenly very close, the small space filling with the citrus smell of his aftershave. Rosa tried to press herself against the back of the desk. 'Yeah, I see what you mean. Relaxing.'

The space was so small she could almost feel his breath. Her heart was racing. 'Totally relaxing. Yes.'

For a second they just stared at each other, his pupils huge in the dark. Watching her the way a hawk watches a mouse. Rosa opened her mouth to say something. 'Eh… about Sunday. Is it…?'

'Yeah?'

'Did you mean…?'

'Mr Connell! Blimey, wake up!'

Jason gave a startled look as he was suddenly dragged out backwards by the legs. 'No, Bob, Bob! I'm OK!'

Rosa looked out to see Bob, the janitor in whose cupboard they had flirted—was it flirting? Felt like flirting—earlier, turning Jason over and pounding on his chest. 'Don't go into the light, son! Bleeding heck.'

'I'm all right! I'm fine! I was just…meditating.'

Bob gaped. He had a pen stuck behind his ear, and tattoos on each burly forearm. CPR from him must have been quite painful. 'Thought you was 'aving a bleeding 'eart attack, son.'

'No, no, I'm all right.'

Bob spotted her. 'Rosa, love? Whatchew doing in there?'

Oh God. Jason saved the day, standing up and straightening his tie. 'Thanks, Ms Lieberman. I see what you mean now about the Wi-Fi cable.'

Rosa caught on. 'You just need to make sure it's connected, you see.'

'And here was me thinking Wi-Fi meant wireless.'

'Um, not this kind, no. It's very…wire-y.'

'I see, I see.'

She stood up too, smoothing down her top. 'All right then. I'll go and finish my piece.'

'Great. Thanks.'

As she went, she saw Bob staring at her with deep incomprehension.

* * *

*Ani.*

'Astonishingly poor use of exposition, didn't you think? Not to mention the dire *deus ex machina* ending of Act One.'

Ani and Simon had nipped outside in the interval of the play, so he could get a signal to send in his initial copy. Ani rubbed her arms, wishing they were in the warm bar and not this cold, pee-smelling alley beside the theatre. Even if the bar was full of out-of-towners in anoraks moaning about the prices. *'Three pound bloody fifty! I could get three pints for that down t'working man's club!'* Over the previous hour and a half, she had remembered several key facts. First, that the only time she ever enjoyed the theatre was when Andrew Lloyd Webber had written the music for it. (She'd fallen asleep when Rosa had taken her to *Waiting for Godot*. On waking with a start she'd loudly asked, 'Oh bollocks! Did I miss Godot? Where's Godot?') Second, that Simon was *really* into the theatre. Watching it, talking about it, and even writing a review while still on a date— not that this was a date, of course not, no. 'You weren't a fan then?' The lead, a Hollywood actress in her first stage role, would likely never win an Oscar, but she'd done her best with what was a fairly terrible play about female prisoners on death row. Her character fell in love with the journalist who'd been sent to interview her and tried to bribe him with sex to get her out. *Last Writes* was, in Ani's opinion, even worse than *War and Piss*.

'I've eaten yoghurts that made a more vital contribution to culture. It's only getting press because people want to see how badly Sukie Miller screws up. Especially after that drink-driving conviction during her last film. How do you spell "execrable"?' He was typing. '*E...x...c* or *e*?'

'*E*,' said a voice behind them. Throaty, smoky, with a strong Californian drawl. Ani and Simon turned, very slowly, to see a tiny blonde woman leaning against the stage door. She wore leather trousers, a baggy sweatshirt and the full stage make-up they'd seen her in not minutes before. And the face, well, that was unmistakable to anyone who'd read a magazine or paper in the past five years.

'Sukie!' said Simon shakily. 'Um...hi!'

'You hated it, huh?' Sukie stubbed out her cigarette beneath one towering heel.

'Um...' Simon seemed struck dumb. Ani decided to rescue the situation. She was never lost for words. What had Rosa said? Sukie was to be commended for taking a low-budget play over yet another Hollywood blockbuster?

'You were amazing. I can't think how you remember all those lines. And it must be so hard to transition from film.'

Sukie seemed to sag, suddenly looking like the twenty-four-year-old she was behind the make-up. 'I knew it would be hard. But I never knew it would, like, be this hard? The critics here, man, are they *mean*.'

Simon was suddenly very interested in his BlackBerry. 'Sod them,' Ani said. 'What did you get for your last film, ten million dollars or something?'

'Eleven.'

'See? If you can get eleven million for playing a cheer-leader whose clothes all fall off every time there's a stiff breeze, who cares what a bunch of bitter London critics say? You earn more in five minutes than they do in a whole year. You carry on, girl!' Had she really said 'girl'? Ani went on, 'I mean, you're doing really well, Sukie. They're just jeal-ous.' She nudged Simon.

He cleared his throat. 'Er…right. It's just a terrible play, Sukie, really, really bad. You're better than that. I loved you in *Killer Heels* and in *Undercover Cheerleader*—you really conveyed the anxiety that's at the heart of all narcissism.'

Sukie perked up. 'You got that?'

'Of course!'

'Cos, like, I was trying to play it as sort of *Witness* meets *Bring It On*.'

'And you nailed it,' said Simon earnestly. 'So she's right—sod them. Er, us. You can do so much better.'

'All right.' She peeled herself away from the wall, stand-ing up to her entire five feet—plus four inches of heels. And began to walk past them, out the end of the alley. Simon gave Ani a panicked look. 'Er, isn't the stage door that way?'

'No shit, Sherlock,' drawled Sukie.

'So where are you...'

'Doing what you said. I am sodding them.' In her Californian accent, this sounded great. 'I'm off to the Groucho Club for a dirty Martini. Always wondered what makes them so damn dirty.'

'But, what about the second half? What about your contract?' Simon gaped.

She shrugged, one elegant bony shoulder coming out of her sweatshirt. Her shoes were worth more than Ani earned in a month. 'Hon, I can buy the whole theatre and audience if I want. I don't need this.' She glanced back at Ani and Simon. 'Come for a drink if you want, babes. I don't know anyone in this town and I hate getting smashed alone.'

Simon was standing there, making fish-movements with his mouth. 'I can't go, I have to file this copy!'

'Be a better story if you come,' Sukie said laconically. 'Out on the town with notorrrrrious Sukie Miller. Raising some hell. Taking asses and kicking names.'

Simon looked at Ani. 'Oh my God. Should we? Is that mad?'

Ani had court in the morning and she still had to iron a shirt and polish her shoes and read the case notes. But she'd never been to the Groucho Club, or had a dirty Martini. Or gone drinking with a Hollywood star, for that matter. And she wasn't ready to give up on this night with Simon, not just yet. 'Let's go,' she said.

'Are you sure?'

'Yeah, come on. We'll never get this chance again. Think of the story.' Plus, she reflected, as she hotfooted it after Sukie, who was hailing a cab with a jut of the hip and a New-York style whistle, getting in on the Hollywood divorce market was an opportunity she couldn't afford to miss.

*  *  *

Around 2 a.m., things were a little hazy. Ani was leaning on the bar, trying to sober up. Had she really…danced on a table? Had Sukie disappeared to the loos with that guy out of *Downton Abbey*? Simon came over, clutching a whiskey and swaying slightly. At their table, Sukie had her tongue down the throat of the under-butler.

'Crazy, huh?' Ani shouted to Simon.

'I'm not sure it's even real. There's about a year's worth of celebrity gossip columns going on right now in this very room. I wish Rosa could have been here.'

Ani felt a small stab of pain. Her tongue was loosened by what she thought was her sixth…no, seventh…gin and tonic. 'Simon?'

'Yes?' He was distracted by something over her shoulder. 'Is that…Sir Alan Sugar?'

'Simon!' She'd tugged his arm. 'Why did it not work out, with you and me?'

He frowned. 'What?'

'I just want to know. Am I… Is there something I do that means things never work out? That made you not call me?'

'Um…' Simon began to look shifty. 'You didn't call me, actually, Ani.'

'I know. But I thought you didn't like me. There must be a reason. Just tell me. I can take it. Cos it's been five years, and you got married and everything, and look at me. I can't even get past a second date most of the time. So what am I doing wrong?'

'Well, you are a bit…confident. Some people might find that, you know, intimidating.'

'You're saying I'm scary?'

'Only because you're so successful and fabulous and you

know exactly what you want, and make it very clear when someone falls short of that.'

'Do I?'

'Well, yes. You kept asking about my career, remember, and what my plans were—when I've never really had a plan, to be honest. I've only just figured out I want to write plays, and I'm thirty-four.'

'Oh.' Ani suddenly felt like she might cry.

Simon put an awkward arm around her. 'Hey, I didn't mean to upset you. You're great, Ani—funny and cool, and sharp as a tack.'

'Tacks can hurt you.' She sniffed.

'If you're careless.'

'So you and me…it wasn't right?'

'Well, I don't think I was quite what you wanted. And that's probably still the case.' He squeezed her gently. 'Now let's get you home.'

As they limped to a taxi, having said a blurry goodbye to Sukie—had she really invited them to stay in her Malibu beach house?—Ani remembered asking: 'Would you mind not telling Rosa we were out? Only, see, she gets really bad FOMO.'

'FOMO?' Simon was signalling to the taxi driver over her head.

'Fear Of Missing Out, durrrrr. Everyone knows that.' She fell into the cab. 'Oops. Am I being scary again?'

'Just a bit. Come on.'

In the cab, Magic FM playing, she let her head slide onto his shoulder for a second. He smelled of soap, and tweed. He was nice. 'Maybe we can be friends,' she mumbled.

'Of course we can,' Simon said kindly. 'And hey, if we

are, that means at least one good thing came out of the dating project.'

'S'not a project, s'an experiment,' said Ani, and passed out.

\* \* \*

'Ani? ANI?'

Floor. Clothes. Cold. Carpet. Her own floor and carpet. That was good. Ani peeled open one eye to see Gina standing over her, dressed for morning yoga in skintight Lycra, skin glowing, a green juice in her hand. 'Gosh, darling, are you OK?'

'What time is it?'

'It's like 7 a.m., darling. Did you go to the Groucho club? Who with? How?'

Ani struggled up, wincing at the smell of booze coming off her. 'Um…it's kind of a long story.'

There she was, thirty-three years old, and she'd passed out on her own living room floor in all her clothes. She'd more or less thrown herself at someone she didn't even want to go out with five years ago. She'd be late for court. And tonight she had to go out for dinner with Marnie, Helen, and Rosa, who, fingers and toes and everything crossed, didn't know Ani had been drinking till 2 a.m. with her date. She groaned and wondered if it was possible to consume coffee via an intravenous drip.

\* \* \*

*Helen.*

The next day, Ed was standing in Paddington by the statue of the eponymous bear. He looked just as adorable, with his floppy brown hair, and he had on a similar duffel coat. 'Hi!' He pulled her into a squishy hug, and Helen allowed herself to drink him in for a second, the warmth of him, the feel of his narrow chest under the coat. He pulled away. 'Oops, are we squashing something?'

'I got us some train snacks.' Helen waggled an M&S bag.

He smiled. 'Do you still love eclairs? Or have you...you know? Quit?'

Helen felt herself blushing. Though her grey winter coat was voluminous, there was no denying that underneath she was now in possession of a changed body. You couldn't drop from a size twenty to a twelve and hide it—though she'd tried. 'Oh, I still eat them. Just, you know, not four at a time.'

'You're so right,' said Ed earnestly, as they began to walk to the ticket machines and he linked his arm casually through hers. Helen willed herself to keep walking, even though his gloved hand was almost grazing the side of her breast. 'Obesity is such a problem. People pretend it's their metabolism or their bones, but it's not. We buy too much, we eat too much. Supermarkets waste a ton of food every day. It's just greed.'

'Yeah. Greed is the worst.' They passed a Millie's Cookies, and Helen looked longingly at the rows of crisp, oozing biscuits, the hunks of chocolate, the gooey raspberries. *I'm sorry, my loves. We will be together again...one day!* Maybe when she hit forty she'd allow them all back in her life, the creamy eclairs, the Victoria sponges, the salted caramel brownies. She'd fill a bath with custard and soak in it. She'd build furniture out of Cadbury's chocolate fingers.

'At least you're safe from all those awful health problems now,' said Ed, squeezing her arm tight.

But Helen wasn't sure she was safe at all. Not now he was back.

\* \* \*

As the train left London, Helen felt her heart bob up and up, like a helium balloon on a string. OK, the circumstances were sad—going to collect Ed's dead father's things for a charity shop—but he'd allowed her to help. She couldn't reach inside him and fix his aching heart, but she could do this small thing. Be with him. She smiled at him across the table and her heart contracted as he gave a small smile back, dimples appearing in his wan cheeks. 'Hungry?' she asked.

'What did you get?'

'It's quite the picnic.' Helen unpacked the bag, pulling out sandwiches, salt and vinegar crisps, a tub of chopped pineapple, and several boxes of chocolate cakes. 'Sandwich? Those have mayo in, but these don't. I remember you don't like it.'

'Thanks.' He took a ham one. 'Thank you for doing this, Helen. It means so much.' And he smiled at her, and her heart dissolved a little further. 'I'm so glad you're here.' Helen's heart seemed to crack on her ribcage. *You are beautiful*, she thought. Everything. The smudge of highlighter pen on his hand, the dips of the bones in his wrist as he held his sandwich, the way he wrinkled his nose when he needed to sneeze.

Shortly after eating, Ed nodded off. Most people would dribble or gape while sleeping, starting awake as their neck cricked, but he lay still as the carriages rocked and people got on and off. Helen watched him all the way, and when the ticket inspector came she gave him such a fierce glare that he only checked her ticket, and Ed was left like a sleeping prince, waiting for a true love's kiss to wake him.

He was here. Ed was here, within touching distance, something she'd thought would never happen again. She remembered the morning she'd woken up to find him gone, the bed empty and cold. No goodbye. No contact for two years. She'd never had the chance to ask him why—like for her, was the guilt just unbearable? And the nights after that, when she'd lie awake reliving it, and her hands would flex and clench, so sure they would never touch him again. How for months her heart would stop every time she saw a man with brown hair and a wool coat. And it was never him, because he was gone. But here he was, back again, an ordinary miracle. So she would just enjoy this day, this small gift she'd been given. She would just try to be there for him. And then because of Marnie, because of how much it might hurt her, Helen would give him up again. Let him go for another two years, or longer. Just this one day. That was all she asked for.

\* \* \*

'Mum?' Ed called. 'We're here.'

It was the house Marnie used to talk about—the one Helen had imagined visiting so many times. Honey-gold sandstone, set back in a large garden that whispered with birds. The hallway was dark, and cool, and smelled of beeswax polish.

Ed's mother was an upright woman in her sixties, her hair tinted ash blonde. She wore slacks and a twinset, tasteful gold jewellery, heels. Helen was very aware of her own scruffy jeans. 'Hello,' she said nervously.

Ed's mother scrutinised her. 'You brought someone, Edward?'

'It's my friend from London, remember I told you about her?'

'The arty girl?'

Marnie. She meant Marnie.

'No, Mum. This is Helen. My friend.' He smiled at her, and another bit melted and fell off inside her.

'I hope I'm not intruding. Maybe I could help?'

Ed's mum said, 'Oh, no, I'm sure we can manage. Why don't you get her some tea, Edward?'

Helen followed her into the living room, which looked out on the sloping back lawn. She noticed two things: that Ed had called her his friend—was that what she was?—and that his mother did not seem to be that keen on the idea of Marnie.

\* \* \*

'How's it going?'

An hour or so later, Ed reappeared in the drawing room. He and his mother had been upstairs, Helen's offer of help politely but firmly turned down. So she'd sat fiddling with her phone, worrying about all the work she was leaving undone at home.

'Oh, God. It's so hard. All his things. You know, his hankies, his suits… They still smell of him.' Ed screwed up his eyes. 'I'm going to have to stay for a bit, Helen. Mum is…not good. I can't leave her. Sometimes I worry I'll have to stay here for ever.'

*But if you're in Bristol, how can we…* Helen shut down the selfish thought. 'It's always going to be hard at first.'

'But she's just so…dependent. She needs me so much. Is your mum like that?'

Helen dropped her head. 'Errrr, sometimes. She has my dad, I guess.'

'Anyway, I'm sorry. I can drop you at the station.'

'Can I not do anything? Wash up the dishes even?'

'Oh no, the housekeeper does that. Come with me a minute. I want to show you something.' He held out his hand to her. Helen stared at it for a moment, and then she took it, her heart swooping and falling like a swallow in flight. It was warm and strong in hers, calluses on his fingers from playing the guitar.

Ed's room. She was going into Ed's room. The air smelled of books and furniture polish. His childhood things were crammed into the shelves—toy soldiers and tennis balls and a guitar leaning against the window. Helen had imagined this so many times.

Outside the window, a winter sun turned everything in the huge garden crisp and glowing. Helen thought of her parents' semi in Reading. Ed was so different to her, with his floppy hair and expensive jumpers and air of nobility. A war poet in Converse, while Helen was the practical one, making reservations, buying snacks.

Ed took something from a drawer. 'Look what I found.'

In the picture, it was Marnie's birthday. Helen remembered it exactly—Marnie had worn a cream lace dress, and her hair had been loose about her face, fire and amber. It must have been her who'd taken this picture of Ed and Helen. He had his arm round her for the photo, and she could almost feel again the brush of his jumper against her cheek, the smell of his shampoo. The way she hadn't been able to breathe for hours after. And there she was, in a big hoody and cords. Smiling like her face would burst.

'You look so different now!' Ed sat down on the bed, rolling up the sleeves of his old blue shirt. He pulled the guitar to him and started picking out a few chords. 'I could hardly believe it when I saw you at the party. I wouldn't have recognised you from when we first met.'

Helen couldn't quite place the tune he was playing, but it seemed to lodge in her chest, sad and sweet. 'Mmm.'

'Do you still do the night classes?'

'Well, not so much. You know, I've been busy.' Busy turning into a grade-A crazy cat lady, that was.

Ed said, 'We were good friends back then, weren't we? I feel like I'm…sort of restarting a video I paused.'

Helen held her breath. Was it coming? The words piled up in her throat. *Why did you go? Why didn't you contact me?*

'When Marn messaged, it seemed logical to go back to where I left off. I mean, I didn't even get to say goodbye. To you either. When she left, I had so many questions. I bet you did too.'

Helen stared very hard out at the frosty grass. It was so beautiful, so fragile. If you stepped on it, it would break. 'Yeah. It was… Well, I missed you. I mean, both of you.'

Over her shoulder, Ed put the guitar down. 'I'm sorry I just took off back then. I thought about you a lot, I just didn't know what to…and then I saw you at the party, looking so…and I thought, yes. This is where I left off. Do you know what I mean, Helen?'

She had to look up. *Look up, for God's sake.* She could feel his eyes on her. She could almost feel his breath, he was so close. Slow as a flower poking from the soil, Helen turned to Ed. His blue eyes seemed to ask a question. Did he remember everything? She'd never been sure. They'd never talked about it. One moment he'd been there, right within reach, and the next gone without a word. Leaving her heart as frozen and brittle as that grass. Surely he couldn't care about her, when he'd done that. 'I…'

'Edward?' Dammit! His mother was standing in the door, rubbing her arms. 'Could you come and help me, please?'

'Of course. Sorry, Mum.' He scrambled up and went, and Helen was left alone. She drew in a shaky breath. She'd been right—nothing about this was safe.

* * *

Later still, Ed's father's things were bagged up and in the van ready for drop-off, and Helen had been left back to the station.

Ed jumped out of the van to say goodbye. 'I'm glad you came,' he said. 'You made it bearable. Mum is… Well, she has quite strong ideas on what I should be doing with my life. Mostly staying with her.'

'That's OK. I'm glad I was able to help.'

'I'll be back in London soon, I hope. Maybe we can…' He left the sentence unfinished, and Helen found herself nodding blindly. Of course. Whatever he wanted.

He grasped her in a quick awkward hug, her chin hitting his nose, his arms meeting behind her back. 'I can get them all the way round you now,' he said, and he was gone, leaving his smell of old bookshops and rain. Helen stood there, reeling, clutching on for dear life to her Doombag and M&S carrier.

* * *

*Marnie.*

No new messages.

Marnie had clicked and refreshed her messages from Ed at least a hundred times since the party, and they stubbornly refused to change. Maybe she'd scared him off, saying she wanted to talk. She had to admit she'd hoped for something. What, she didn't know. Vague images of the two of them, taking off round the world. Or even getting a place in London. But it wouldn't work—of course it wouldn't work. He must be still angry with her, after she'd just left back then. And then there was Tom—she'd been pleased when he invited her on the demo, and that almost counted as a third date. But he'd invited Rosa too. Nasty doubts had crawled into Marnie's mind then, as she lay awake in her cold little room in the houseshare. He liked Rosa more. He'd only come to the party to see her, not Marnie at all. And Ed—maybe Ed had come to speak to Helen. He hadn't even said goodbye. Maybe neither of them liked her. Maybe no one did.

The door to her room opened, letting in the loud banging sound of drum and bass. It was Cam, her sleazy housemate, a joint hanging out of his mouth. 'All right, Marn? Coming to join the party?'

'Again? You had a party last night.' Which had gone on until 4 a.m., and then she'd had to get up to make coffee at 6.

'We like to party. Make the most out of life. What do you say?'

'No, thanks. I'm having dinner with my friends.'

'After that then. We'll be on it all night long.'

'Um…I'll probably need to sleep, to be honest, or wind down with some Netflix.'

He snorted. 'Jesus, darling, if we wanted to live with an OAP we'd have advertised down the old folks' home.' As he left she saw him eyeing up her underwear, which was drying along the inadequate radiator.

'OAPs don't use Netflix,' she said, to the door. But quietly. There was no lock on her door and she was slightly afraid of Cam. Yet another reason why she had to get out of here, and fast. She clicked and refreshed again. Nothing. Nothing, nothing, nothing. Time for plan B. She messaged Tom. Hi you! So, I have a little proposition for you…

# Chapter 16
## Triple Word Scores

*Helen*

'Sorry I'm late!' She usually tried to get the restaurant early when they met all for dinner, so she could check everything was all right. Marnie had suggested they go to House Prices, an Asian-Mexican fusion place in Dalston, but it had taken Helen a long time to get back from Bristol, and now she was late. Rosa and Marnie were already at the table, and so was…

Marnie wasn't alone, she was with a man. For a moment Helen saw the curve of his shoulders and her heart sank all the way down to her feet. But no, of course it wasn't Ed, he was miles away where she'd left him. Stupid. Those mini-dreds could only belong to Tom. Her eyes flicked nervously to Rosa. 'Hi, Tom! I didn't think you'd be here.'

'What a surprise!' said Rosa, who was smiling fixedly.

'Tom just walked me over,' said Marnie, beaming. She tugged on his sleeve like a child. 'Tell them our big news!'

Helen's heart flipped again. It had only been a few dates, surely they couldn't have got engaged, or worse, was Marnie pregnant? Was Marnie actually over Ed then? And, if she was, and she really wouldn't mind Helen dating an ex of hers, as she'd said, well…

Helen wasn't going to think about that yet.

'We're moving in together!' burst out Marnie, when Tom seemed reluctant to speak. Moving in already? Well, it could be worse. Helen looked but couldn't see if Marnie was still wearing the necklace, under her high-necked poncho jumper.

'Really?' Rosa's voice sounded strained and high. 'That's… soon.'

Marnie waved a hand. 'Oh, my place hasn't really worked out. It's so big and draughty. I get a bit scared, to be honest. So Tom said I can join the squat. Help out with things there. Isn't that brilliant!'

Rosa seemed to have lost the power of speech. Her brows were knitted, as if she was trying to divide 167 by 14. Helen tried to catch her eye. Was it possible the project might actually work out, and one of them could end up with the other's ex? (But no, she still wasn't going to think about that.)

Tom looked awkward. 'Yeah, she needed a place, and we could do with some extra hands, so…'

A pause. 'I'm still seeing Simon,' said Rosa abruptly. 'He asked me to the theatre last night, but I had to work. I'm sure we'll go out again soon though.'

'That's great!' Marnie clapped her hands. 'I'm so glad you all met nice people. I knew this was a better option than Tinder. Oh, but you didn't like Dan, did you, Helz?'

*Of course not, he was so awkward he could hardly de-cide whether to breathe or not.* 'Well, he was a bit hard to talk to.' Not to mention leaving her with the bill.

Marnie bit her lip. 'God, I feel so bad. I guess you can never really know someone.'

*No, because you set me up with someone you probably had one drink with seven years ago.* Everyone else had tried—even she, with hardly any exes to speak of, had dredged up Nikesh, who she'd after all spent an entire summer with learning about JavaScript while they held hands sweatily under the desks. 'I guess it's not your fault,' she said, sounding unconvinced even to her own ears.

'Maybe he was just your pancake man,' said Marnie. Helen met Rosa's eyes across the table. Was this some dating term they were supposed to know about? 'You know how when you make pancakes, the first one is always mis-shapen and holey? You can't fix it, and you just have to flip it and make another. So now you're back in the game, Helz, you can find someone nice. What about that guy you brought to my party?'

Helen blushed. 'Oh, no, he's just…a guy I know through work.'

'Do you like him?'

'I'm not really in the mood for dating at the moment.'

'But don't you want to meet someone?' Marnie gestured round the table. 'I mean, I'm dating, even Rosa's dating again… I hoped this project would show you it's not so scary. Maybe I can find you someone else? What about Ivan, that guy I went out with who became a trapeze art-ist? Or Kevin—you know, the one with all the hamsters.'

Helen stared at the table, trying not to think of Ed. Down in Bristol, she'd almost thought, just for a second, he might kiss her. Stupid. And why couldn't Marnie see that there was only one man Helen wanted? Why had she never been able to see that? 'It's fine, really. Anyway, should we order? Ani says she's running late.'

Marnie was full of chatter as they ordered their food, about how great it was going to be to live in the squat, how she couldn't wait to join in with communal life, how she'd already had her eyes opened to so many issues... She then ordered a £12 cocktail. Tom, meanwhile, continued to look miserable and glance at the menu with fear in his eyes.

'Do you want a drink?' Helen asked him gently, as the waiter hovered.

'I need to shoot off in a minute. Night-time climate protest at City Hall.'

'It's terrible,' said Marnie, who had been known to leave lights on all night because she was afraid of the dark. 'The council won't commit to using green energy sources. Something has to change!'

Ani appeared just then, trailing bags and briefcases and exclaiming about the Central Line: 'I swear, it'll be the death of me— Oh! Hi, Tom. I didn't know you were...' There were only four chairs.

'I'm just going.' He leaped up. 'Please, um, I have to— um, nice to see you.'

'But we can get another chair...'

Tom glanced a kiss off Marnie's cheek, muttering something about 'girls' night', and was gone so fast he practically left a Tom-shaped hole in the wall. Ani took his seat, puzzled. She looked like she'd slept on a floor, Helen thought. 'What was all that about?'

'Marnie and Tom are moving in together,' said Rosa, brightly.

Marnie said, 'And things with Rosa and Simon are going really well.'

'Oh,' said Ani, looking between them. 'But what about your date with Jason?'

Rosa frowned. 'It's not a date.'

'But… OK then.'

Helen had a moment to think how strange it all was. Marnie, dating Rosa's ex. Rosa, dating Ani's ex. And Ani had even hit it off with Helen's old partner-in-nerdiness Nikesh. Had she been wrong all this time—was dating a friend's ex an acceptable, even healthy thing to do?

*Stop thinking about it!*

'Are you seeing Nikesh again?' she asked Ani, trying to distract herself from that line of thinking.

Ani picked up a menu. 'Oh. I'm not sure, really. He's a bit of a nerd—the kind of kid who went to Computer Camp. Oh God, sorry, Helen.'

'It's OK. I was definitely the kind of kid who went to Computer Camp. And it was the most fun of my life, ever.' She thought back wistfully to the simplicities of code. Why couldn't relationships be like that?

Marnie was looking disappointed. 'Oh no! I really hoped all the Ex Factor dates would work out. What's wrong with him, Ani?'

'I don't know. I just…wasn't sure if he was the one.'

Rosa rolled her eyes. 'You only went out once! And you liked him! Why does he need to be the one or not? Maybe he's your pancake man, as Marnie was saying. Pour him in the pan, flip him, move on!'

Ani looked at Helen—pancake man?—and Helen gave a helpless shrug. Ani said, 'I didn't say I was going to flip him, exactly. Just that I wasn't totally sure we're right for each other.'

Rosa said, 'But you had loads in common with him!'

'That's the problem. Wouldn't that get boring, eventually?'

Rosa was shaking her head. 'I don't understand this. Am I *not* supposed to look for a man who's nice and who's similar to me? I should look for one who's horrible and nothing like me at all, is that right?'

'It depends what you're after. I just want—you know. A bit of fire.'

'There's nothing wrong with that,' said Marnie soothingly. 'Everyone wants different things. That's the whole point of the Ex Factor. Look, we're running low on drinks. I'll get us a round.' Off she went, drawing the gaze of the men at the next table, in her tight jeans. Helen watched her go. Was she happy, moving in with Tom? How did she have the money to buy them all drinks? What on earth was going on in that red head?

'She's right,' said Ani gloomily. 'We all need to start getting serious about what we really want. We're never going to meet someone otherwise.'

Rosa sighed. 'What happened to romance? And spontaneity?'

'Those are for people in their twenties with another decade to find someone. Or who live on Scottish islands where there's only one person to fall for anyway.'

'Do you know what you want?' Helen asked. She herself had no idea. It was hard to imagine a man who wasn't exactly like Ed in every way.

'Well,' Ani said, 'I usually just go out with anyone I think is cute and shows an interest—even guys who still live with their parents, or unemployed musicians who don't believe in monogamy, or…'

'That guy with the pet snake,' said Rosa helpfully.

'Oh God, Snakey Steve. I'd forgotten him. And then there was…'

'That guy who turned up to your dinner date in denim cut-offs.'

'Right. Thanks for the rundown. Thing is, I always believed that too, that real romance would just find you. But I've been dating for years and that's clearly not working. So maybe I should only date people who have everything I want.'

'But you can't have *everything*, can you?' said Helen.

'I thought I had it all with David,' said Rosa. 'I should have had "won't sleep with a child named after a weed" in my criteria.' Ani and Helen rubbed her arms automatically, one from each side.

'So what *are* your criteria, Ani?' asked Helen, before Rosa could spiral again.

Ani put down her mojito so she could tick things off on her fingers. 'Well. I guess they'd need to be doing well in a good job. I know that sounds snobby, but I don't want to eat in Nando's or stay in watching illegal downloads of *Breaking Bad* on a laptop. We did all that at uni. And they'd need to have a similar family background. Mine are so overbearing, you know, he'd get sick of me going round there every weekend.'

'Yet you won't date Indian guys,' Rosa pointed out nonchalantly. 'Some might say there was a contradiction in that.'

Ani scowled. 'Hmph. Maybe. I also want someone who's not pretentious. Happy to watch *The Great British Bake Off* with me, and not worry about high culture. I wear my brain

out at work, I just want to relax when I have time off, not
go to boring highbrow plays.'

Rosa frowned. 'When did you last go to a highbrow play?
You told me you'd rather boil your eyes than do that again,
after the *Waiting for Godot* incident.'

Ani stuttered, 'Yeah. No. I would. I'm just…remembering.'

Helen was puzzled. 'But, Ani, this all sounds quite like
Nikesh, no? I thought you said he loved trash TV and going
on cruises, and he has a great job…'

Ani's scowl deepened. 'Oh, I don't know. This is going to
sound shallow, but I sort of want someone cool too. Suave.
Handsome. Who can get tables in restaurants, tip the taxi
driver, know about wine…all that.'

'Nikesh is handsome though, isn't he?' said Helen tim-
idly. 'These days, at least.'

'I guess. But…Computer Camp.'

'Some of your best friends went to Computer Camp, Ani.'

Ani gave her a wonky smile. 'I know. And you're totally cool.'

'Of course I am. Crazy Cat Lady with Boxsets chic is
so a thing now.'

Rosa stabbed a chip with her fork. 'I guess that's why
Simon was no good for you, Ani. He's broke and he's totally pretentious, bless him. But then, so am I.'

Helen was still trying to keep up. 'So…the whole Tom
thing was just…'

'Mistake,' said Rosa quickly. 'Nostalgia-based foolishness. Freezing-cold demos with no loos are definitely not
my scene. This is why we didn't work out to start with.'

'I guess that was Marnie's thinking,' said Helen, looking
over to where her friend was chatting to the barman, lean-

ing in close, throwing her head back to laugh. 'One woman's meat is another woman's…tofu.'

Rosa patted Helen's hand. 'Except for you. Sorry, babe.'

'Yeah, well, it might have worked if Marnie had spent more than ten seconds choosing my date.'

Rosa and Ani exchanged looks. Usually, Helen always defended Marnie. *Oh, she's just impulsive, she struggles with relationships because her dad left, she doesn't like being tied down.* But somehow, she was running out of excuses.

On cue, Marnie came bounding back over. 'Great news, guys, the barman's going to hook us up with a round of mojitos! Oh, and he's single,' she said, turning to Helen. 'So I said you were on the market. He's free tonight—well, after his sketch comedy group finish their rehearsal, that is. Oh and he's not been paid yet so you'd have to get the drinks. He's lovely though!'

Under the table, Helen's hands clenched.

* * *

*Rosa.*

Jason was waiting for her at the entrance to Finsbury Park tube station, as she fought her way through the Sunday morning crowds, a curious city mix of poor immigrant families, church-goers, and hip young Londoners in buttoned coats, sniffing out the latest brunch place, where a croissant would be £4.50 a shout. She'd had another total 'what am I meant to wear OMG' meltdown. She had to look sexy, but not slutty. Approachable, but stylish. Friendly. But also cool. Ready for a date, but not like she thought it was a date, in case it wasn't. In the end, and with more selfie-help from Marnie, she'd gone for flat boots and skinny jeans, and she was glad, because Jason was dressed like he was going to the Arctic. Walking boots, a blue North Face jacket and a beanie hat. She'd only seen him in his sharp suits, tugging at his tie as if it was permanently choking him.

He nodded approvingly at her footwear. 'Glad you're not in heels, it's really muddy down there.'

''Course not,' Rosa said, thinking of the black court shoes she'd taken off at the door in a last-minute funk.

'Let's go,' he said, stamping his feet. 'If I stand too still in this country I'll turn to ice.'

'This is quite mild for January,' she said.

'Not you as well. It's not something to be proud of. Oh, it's not appalling! We haven't all died yet! You're in an abusive relationship with your weather, mate.'

'Ha. Funny.' Rosa saw he was fishing his phone out. 'Are you writing that down?'

He looked slightly sheepish. 'It could work. Seventeen ways the Brits are in a relationship with their weather. I guess you can take the boy out of the lists…'

'How are you finding it?' she asked casually, reminding herself to stay professional. She wished she'd recorded herself saying over and over, *He's your boss, he's your boss, he's your boss*…

They were trudging along the muddy path. It was the route of an old train line to the Alexandra Palace, chock-a-block with middle-class families—'Zara! Don't throw your mango slices into the mud!'—and dog walkers and smug New Year joggers. 'Oh, it's OK,' said Jason. 'I mean some of the business practices are shocking—the web links are too slow to load and most of them are too long for Twitter. It needs to be social media-optimised.'

'Does it?' Rosa frowned. 'It's a newspaper.'

'And when did you last sit down and read a paper cover to cover?'

'Um…' She and David used to buy the Sunday papers, when they were still a smug urban brunching couple. But inevitably she'd saved most of the bits until Wednesday, then put them in the recycling.

'Right. And you're a journalist. Stories get read now in the three seconds while you wait for your mate to turn up in the pub. No one's reading the paper over breakfast in the Home Counties.'

'Actually we have a very high readership in the sixty-plus…'

'Exactly. Your readers are literally dying off. So you need to attract more, and clickbait is the way we do that.'

'Oh,' said Rosa, thinking sadly of those sweet older ladies, clipping out the reader-offer coupons and writing in to complain about immigrants. OK, maybe he had a point.

'Speaking of which,' said Jason. 'Is your dating piece almost done?'

She'd been sitting on it, was the truth—what if David saw it? He was bound to, he read the paper cover to cover every day so he knew who to suck up to in the canteen. Was he even bothered that she was back dating? Rosa heaved a sigh, realising that every date took her further from her old life, and saw Jason looking at her. She put on a weak smile. 'The piece is almost there, yeah.'

'And did any of them work out?'

'Well, one date definitely didn't work.'

She told him Helen's story, and he winced. 'Jesus, that's awful. I once had a date go to the loo in a bar and never come back, but at least I didn't get shafted with the dinner bill.'

'The other three are…ongoing,' she said, feeling suddenly

shy. 'And it's been interesting. My friend had a party the other day and some of the guys came.'

'And?'

'Well, it's funny. I hadn't seen my ex for nearly fifteen years, and suddenly he's there, with my mate. And it was weirdly quite nice to see him.' She didn't say he'd asked her to his protest, and she'd gone. Why? Was it seeing him with Marnie, a resurgence of jealousy all the way from 2001? At least she'd managed to escape the kettle and come to her senses before she did something stupid.

Rosa found she was telling Jason all about it. He laughed at the right points. 'That's brilliant. We could make this a series, what do you say? Looking up exes, seeing what they're doing?'

'Oh, Tom was my only ex, really. I met my—eh—my ex-husband not long after that.'

'Ah. Well, you could do different ways to meet people. You're anti–online dating, that's the angle. But you could meet people on demos, on the tube…'

'God, no one talks on the tube. They'd have me arrested.'

'All the more reason to try it. And then there's the gym, speed-dating…work…'

She fell silent for a moment. The idea of more dating was daunting. With Simon it was all right, because he was in the same boat, but once she started properly she'd have to admit that was it. She was no longer married. She was a single woman again. 'I'll see how the first piece goes.'

'This is great,' he enthused. 'Very cutting edge. We'll be the paper that says no to Tinder, goes back to basics.'

'Suzanne won't like it. She wants all the pieces to be about yoga and how to get your toddler to eat kale.'

'Suzanne. That bogan.' She burst out laughing. 'Sorry,' said Jason. 'Is she like your workplace BFF?'

'Um, not ex-*actly*...' (*He's your boss he's your boss.*)

They had now reached the end of the track and were in Highgate. Jason rubbed his gloved hands together. 'How about warming up in a pub? Something tells me those graves won't have a fire or a branch of Costa.'

'You never know in London. Pop-up graveyard cafés could be the next big thing. But you're probably right.'

Soon they were in a warm pub, on cracked leather sofas by a roaring fire, and he was queuing for cups of tea, and Rosa experienced a brief burst of something...what was it? She hadn't felt it for a while. Jason was coming over with two steaming teas and a plate of caramel shortbread... Oh yes. Happiness. That's what it was. Sundays had been the hardest day when David left her. It was so set up for couples that, left alone, she felt as empty as a scooped-out avocado.

'I got something else,' he said, clinking down the cups and two small glasses of amber liquid. 'Warm us up. I swear this country will turn me into my Irish granddad.'

'Are you... Oh, yes, Connell.'

'Great-Grandpa Brendan got sent Down Under for stealing cattle.' He raised his glass to her. 'Here's looking at you, kid.'

'Is that an Australian toast?'

'Tsk, it's Humphrey Bogart. Tell me one of your family's.'

'Well, we usually just say, "Please God, nothing else will go wrong," or "This will help with your cold." Even if you don't have a cold, you've probably got one coming on. Jewish, see.'

'Oh, right. Lieberman. Could have guessed. Well, *l'chaim*, Rosa.'

She swallowed her whisky and things didn't seem so bad any more. She was in a nice pub, with a nice man, with drinks and cake. The archetypal Sunday, the ones she'd missed, which if she was honest she and David hadn't had for a while. The ones that started with lazy sex, and brunch, and the papers, then later a roast and a film. The only thing that could make it better was…

'How do you feel about Scrabble?' asked Jason.

'Well, I feel I am very, very good at it.'

'Oh really?' He raised an eyebrow. 'I happened to spy a set over there.'

A while later, Rosa was leading by 153 points after getting an extra fifty for 'bedstead' and Jason was claiming that this was a hyphenate.

'It is not,' insisted Rosa. She'd somehow had another three whiskies, even though she usually hated it. 'I'm a glorified sub, don't argue with me. You could try reading your own paper's style guide.'

'Style guide, schmyle guide.'

'And they say standards of subbing are just as high on-line.' The batteries on Rosa's internal tape player had run right down (*he's your boss…he's your boossssss*) and she was having what she dimly recognised as A Nice Time. Different than Simon. There were no war stories, no rueful chat. Just…well, flirting. At least it seemed like flirting. It had been so long she might have confused it with friendliness, or worse, professional politeness. But Jason was leaning so far over the table that his hand—large, strong, the wrist sprinkled with golden hairs—was almost touching hers. Was it deliberate? An attempt to distract her from Scrabble victory? If so, it was possibly working. She looked up and caught his gaze. The steely-grey eyes, and there was that dimple again. Damn. Rosa felt her stomach lurch. 'I...'

'Listen, Rosa...' Jason's phone beeped on the table. He glanced at it quickly and set it down. 'Do you fancy grabbing a bite to eat? There's a pizza place over the road. They have an iPad jukebox. We can pretend we're in the fifties. Well, the fifties with iPads.'

'And without sexism.'

'Don't you worry your pretty head about that.' He winked. 'What do you say?'

'Sure, why not?' She had no food in the flat except a box of stale Oreos, and didn't want the date to end. Had it been a date? It felt like a date.

'Great. Excuse me a minute, then.'

Jason left his phone on the table as he went to the loo and, almost immediately, it buzzed again. Rosa picked it up, automatically—she and David had always answered each other's phones. That was how she'd known, when he'd started hiding his. She set Jason's down right away, horrified at what she'd done, but not before she'd seen the body of the Tinder message he'd received from 'Kara'. *Hope ur boring work thing is over*, it said. *Still on for 2nite?*

He'd described her as a 'boring work thing'? And he had a date later on that day?

She wasn't ready for this, she realised, as she saw him come towards her, all smiles in his rugged jumper. The cut and thrust of dating, competing with some other girl she hadn't even known about—who used text speak!—never sure whether someone liked you or not. How did Ani do it? How could you play a game when you'd no idea what the rules were?

'Ready?' he said.

'I've changed my mind,' said Rosa, her voice sounding cold and tight. 'I'm sure you have lots to do.'

'What? I don't, I've cleared my schedule.'

'Oh. That's big of you.'

'What is this, Rosa?' He swivelled his head. 'How long was I in there?'

She didn't laugh. 'I'm going. I'd hate to keep you out on a boring work thing. Thanks for the drinks.'

# Chapter 17
## The Love Algorithm

*Rosa*

'Make yourself at home. I'll just…'

'Oh! Sure.' Rosa tried not to look awkward as Simon excused himself, no doubt to perform some act of ablution. Their third date had progressed as expected—dumplings in Chinatown, a film at the Prince Charles Cinema. And then after some awkward bus-stop kissing, they had got on the Central Line to go to his flat in Bethnal Green.

She'd never feel at home in this living room. Not even if there was a sudden landslide and she had to spend the next fifty years locked in it. It was decorated mostly in gold and diamanté, with a gold couch. The wallpaper was black with sparkly accents, like a bottle of 'premium vodka' you'd see in the corner of a tacky club. One end of the room was dominated by a huge TV, half the size of the wall, and the other by a gigantic framed wedding shot. Rosa recognised

St Petersburg. The bride had dyed blonde hair and pursed lips slathered in frosted lipstick, something Rosa thought had died out in the nineties, along with Girl Power and mini-disc players. Simon, the groom, was decked out like a seventeenth-century highwayman, in a frock coat and breeches. Even with all the Photoshop, he looked cold and miserable. Around the main shot, several other pictures had been faded in—the bride and groom kissing; the bride leaning against a railing, *Titanic* style, while the groom stared off into the distance; the groom down on one knee and the bride clasping his head to her—quite large—corseted bosom.

Simon came back to find Rosa in front of the picture, entranced. 'Oh dear,' he said. 'I really ought to take it down. It weighs a ton though. They love all that Photoshop stuff in Russia.'

'It makes everything look like it's 1994.'

'I'm sorry. I don't want to make you uncomfortable.'

'It's OK. I just imagined your place would be full of old books.'

'Not allowed, sadly.' Simon pressed a panel on the leather-bound wall and it opened, silently. Inside were shelves, lined top to bottom with paperbacks. Green Penguins and orange ones, tattered spines, the smell of old paper.

'Oh,' she said. 'It's…beautiful.'

Simon put down the bottle of wine he'd been holding and took a few steps towards her. Rosa didn't know whether it was the books, or the drinks, or the heady smell of floor-to-ceiling literature, but suddenly her pulse was racing, her eyes locked into his. Shyly, he put his hand up to her face. The other slid round her waist. 'You're lovely,' he muttered. 'That husband of yours. He must have been crazy.'

'Well, same,' she said, loath to slag off another woman on her home turf. 'It isn't fair you have to keep your books in prison.'

'Do you think they want to get out?' Simon pushed one of the paperbacks, so it toppled out and fell onto the thick carpet with a small flurry of pages.

Rosa looked down. *Madame Bovary.* One of her favourite books. David didn't read at all these days, too busy checking football scores on his iPad. She scrabbled in the case, knocking out a few more books. 'I'm pretty sure they do.'

Simon stared at her, and then they were both laughing, and pulling at books, grabbing handfuls of them, throwing them onto the thick cream carpet, and then Rosa was somehow lying on the pile of paperbacks, with *Wuthering Heights* digging into her side, and Simon was on top of her, kissing her, his check shirt rising up to reveal a surprisingly trim stomach. All the while, Rosa's brain kept up a steady monologue. *Oh my God I'm kissing a man who isn't David. Different chin. Different lips. Wait, I haven't kissed David properly in ages, that's sad...uh, pay attention... OK, my hand is on his stomach—hmm, more hair than David... mmm, it's nice... OK, now a man is unbuttoning my jeans...*

She sat up suddenly, almost bashing him on the head. He stopped, slipping around on the pile of books. 'You OK?'

'Yes, sorry. It was all just going a bit fast.'

'Sure, sure.' Simon looked a little crestfallen. 'Sorry. I got a bit carried away.'

'Me too.' Rosa straightened her bra, which had gone askew. 'It's a long time since that happened.'

'Me too.'

'It was sort of...nice.'

'Yes.' He had a sweet smile, peeking shyly at her. 'But how about we move somewhere more comfortable?'

Rosa removed a book that was sticking into her spine, glancing at the title. *Pride and Prejudice.* Her all-time favourite. 'OK,' she said, gathering up her jeans.

Once in the bedroom—leather, diamond studs, swooshy full-length mirrors, no natural light—their sense of desire seemed to vanish. Simon sat down and took off his socks, then got a tissue out of the (leather) bedside table and blew his nose. Rosa squinted from the doorway. 'Er, it's very dark.'

'Oh yeah. Masha's taste. Any hint of natural light or pastel colours and bam, it had to go.'

Rosa regarded the leather bed, with its heavy purple cover. 'Is this…this is the bed you both slept in?'

'Well, yes. Are you saying you've got all-new furniture at your place since Whatshisname left?'

'Of course not, I can hardly afford to buy shoes after all the legal stuff.'

'Exactly. So don't judge me—please? I'm just like you. Trying to get through this awful time by having some fun, meeting people—and I like you, Rosa. You're pretty and sweet and you have the best laugh.'

Rosa blushed. Maybe she wasn't totally on the scrapheap. But she still wasn't sure how to approach this situation.

'Come here,' said Simon, patting the other half of the bed. His wife's side. *Don't think about that.* She shuffled awkwardly onto the huge bed. Simon was suddenly very close, his pinkish ears, his receding hairline, his kind eyes. *This isn't David! It's all wrong.* Well, it was always going to feel weird the first time. So she closed her eyes and leaned in.

Soon Rosa was staring up at the (leather) ceiling—seriously, had they skinned a whole herd of cows to upholster this place?—while Simon fumbled with the lace of her pants. 'Er, how does this work?'

'Shall I?' She sat up, covering her breasts in her hand—stupid, he'd already seen them—and wriggled out. Simon was down to his boxers, silky black ones she was sure his wife had chosen.

In her head Rosa was already imagining how she'd describe the encounter to her friends. She'd decided the word she would go with was: nice. It was good to feel wanted, to feel his eyes on her when she stepped out of her clothes, hear his intake of breath. And, even if there was no electrical tingle when their skins touched, and he'd accidentally elbowed her twice in the face, and taken five goes to get her bra off, well, maybe that was how things were and she'd been spoiled by David all this time.

*No, don't think about that. This is fine. This is good.* Simon was doing something in the region of her waist. Should she have waxed? God, she wasn't ready for this at all! It was like entering a donkey into the Grand National. Marnie and Ani probably kept themselves groomed and ready to go, and could contort their legs behind their heads and...

'Are you all right?' said Simon, breathlessly.

'Oh! Yes, yes, I'm fine. Just a bit nervous.'

'Me too,' he said. 'Sorry, but I don't think I can...'

Oh. Rosa looked down. Except there was nothing to look at. Another way she'd been spoiled by David. 'Well, I'm sure you're just tired or nervous or...'

'I'm really sorry,' he said miserably.

'Don't worry.' But insecurities began to bubble up. Was it her? Was she not sexy enough? Was there a trick other women knew, and she'd been in the loo or something when they learned it? What if she'd been doing sex wrong her whole life and no one had told her? Simon was now doing…something, and she stared at the ceiling and let him get on with it.

'I think it's working now.' His voice was muffled against her shoulder.

'Oh. Good.'

'Do I need a…'

'Oh! Yes, yes, well I assume so.'

'I think I have some somewhere.'

Then more rummaging and checking of dates, and tearing, and cursing, and Rosa wondering if she could surreptitiously look at her watch—then he was back, with more fumbling.

'Um, shall I?'

'Oh. Yes. I guess so.' This was it. It was time. It was going to happen and—

*Smash!* Something broke near Rosa's head. She screamed. In the doorway stood a bleached-blonde, size-eight woman, in thigh-high boots and a tiny fur jacket. 'Who are you? Get out of my bed, beetch!'

Simon fumbled off, naked except for the condom. 'Jesus Christ, Masha, you can't just barge in like this!'

Masha? Ohhhh no. This was bad. Rosa looked round frantically for her clothes, but they were nowhere in sight. The woman was now in noisy tears, gabbling in what Rosa assumed was Russian—though she was pretty sure she'd heard the word *skanky* in there. 'Um, should I just…'

Simon was holding Masha by the shoulders, also shouting in Russian. He broke back into English to say to Rosa, 'Yes, sorry, would you mind just giving us a moment?'

Her jeans were behind him on the floor. 'Could I just… maybe I could…'

Masha slapped Simon across the face. Naked as the day she was born, Rosa fled to the living room.

\* \* \*

*Ani.*

'So then I thought, aeroplane toilets are so small and gross, why don't they just make little cabins people can pay to have sex in? That way they can join the Mile-High Club and the airline makes money, and the loo is free if people happen to have had a dodgy burrito from the street stall outside the airport and need to get in in a hurry. It's win-win!'

'Uh huh,' said Ani, trying to follow this.

After disgracing herself in front of Simon, she'd decided to take her friends' advice and give Nikesh one more go. Usually, she never had a second date unless the first had been entirely perfect and she had no doubts whatsoever. Which meant she rarely had a second date.

Nikesh put down his drink. 'I was glad you got in touch, Ani. I had a feeling the word "raincheck" meant "until never".'

'Oh no, ha ha, 'course not.'

'Sorry if I seemed a bit keen, I just don't see the point in messing about if I like someone, and I like you.'

Ani blushed into her gin. 'No, no, I just got really busy at work. Sorry.'

'Big case? What was it?'

'Um, divorce. Nasty.'

'Did they go for separation of the assets, shared residence, or spousal maintenance?'

Ani took a sip of gin that was so long she hoped he'd have forgotten his question by the end of it. She'd never factored in dating a man who was interested in, and had researched, her work. 'You seem really up on the law, Nikesh. Is it just from watching *The Good Wife*?'

'Well, that, but also I knew I was meeting you, so I read about it.'

She stared at him. 'You…read up for dates?'

'Of course. I wouldn't go into a business meeting without preparing. Think of the time you'd waste!' He laughed merrily at the idea, taking a slug of his cherry vodka cola float and getting foam all over his top lip. 'Mmm, fruity!'

Ani smiled weakly, thinking of all the times she'd gone on dates only to find out about the girlfriend they hadn't mentioned, or the fairly serious cocaine habit, or the fact they still lived with their parents. 'You mentioned you had a questionnaire. Is that what that's for? I asked Helen but she was cagey.' She'd actually muttered something about 'data harvesting' and then changed the subject by admiring Ani's handbag.

'Oh, it's very simple really. I know you can't have everything in a partner, so I've narrowed it down to a list of things that I really want.'

'You *have*?' Ani sat bolt upright.

'Of course. It makes sense. First of all, my family matter a lot to me, so they'd have to understand that. And not mind that my parents are actually second cousins.'

Ani almost dropped her gin. *'Your parents are second cousins?'*

'Well, yes. It's not weird where they come from, I promise. They're the happiest couple I've ever seen. Sometimes it's hard to live up to that. Like my dad's face still lights up when my mum comes in the room. Every day. You know?'

'Um, yes, I might have *some* idea.'

'But my wife would have to understand my family, and not be freaked out. Do you see? I guess that's why I tend to date Indian girls now.'

'Um, yes, I do see.' *My wife.* Ani didn't think she'd ever heard a single man say that phrase.

'Number two, I'd like someone ambitious. Sometimes I meet girls who—how can I say this—they know what I do and they think they'll never have to work again if we get together. My last girlfriend, Jen—I found out she'd given notice at her job because she thought I was about to propose. I only wanted to tell her I'd found a limited-edition copy of the first Word program. On a floppy, imagine!'

'Imagine,' murmured Ani, her brain fizzing like his drink.

'So, I need someone who has a job they love, a passion. Who's independent and strong. Who'll push back a bit. I know I can be kind of overenthusiastic, so I'd want someone who could tell me when I was being an arse. Number three, someone who can relax. I work and travel so much, sometimes I just want to stay in and...'

'Watch *The Good Wife*?'

'Yes! How did you know?'

'Um, a wild hunch. So is there a number four?' Ani gripped her glass, feeling the beads of cold beneath her hand. She suddenly very much wanted it to be an in-depth knowledge of plot lines on *Ally McBeal*, or how to make a perfect Aperol spritz, or the finer points of UK family law.

'Oh, it's simple really. I just want someone who's nice and kind. I get enough aggro at work. I know you're supposed to play games when you date, but it seems like such a waste of time.' He pushed his glasses up his nose. 'I just want someone who won't judge me. Who I can be myself around. Who'll always be honest with me—I hate being misled. You know, someone who isn't bothered about looking cool. Who has time for that?'

Ani asked her next question carefully. 'And…Helen said I'd meet those criteria?'

'Of course. That's why I wanted to meet you. If you make sure you both want the same things, dating is quite straight-forward really.'

Dating. Straightforward. Two words she had never thought about in the same sentence. She said, 'So does it work, the questionnaire?'

'Well, a lot of people find it weird and "strange autistic behaviour"—' he did air quotes '—which strikes me as an oxymoron, but there you go. I just think it's so important that it's worth taking seriously. I mean people spend more time researching where to get their hair cut than what they want in a partner. I want to make sure I get it right.' Nikesh's phone began to buzz in his pocket. He fished it out and frowned at it. 'San Fran on the line. Would you excuse me for just a mo-ment, Ani? This might be important. I'm sorry to be so rude.'

Ani blinked as he went, thinking of the dates she'd been on with men who'd sat on their phones all evening. And this ques-tionnaire—if he'd sent it to her she'd likely have run a mile, before forwarding it to Rosa as a possible feature idea on the nutjobs you met while dating. But could it be that he was right?

Ani got her own phone out of her bag, only to see ten messages from her mother, aunt, and cousin about Mani-sha's upcoming wedding.

Top-secret shoe info.

V important rule about make-up.

Ani—I hope you haven't got your hair trimmed.

And then: Are you bringing a plus one?

'Ouch! Sorry.' Nikesh was coming back, tripping on another table and apologising. 'Shouldn't drink with jet lag, but I like to live on the edge—and it's just a lot of fun being out with you.' He pushed his dark hair out of his face, smiling at her.

'Nikesh,' she heard herself say. He wouldn't be free anyway, she told herself. He'd be jetting off somewhere. 'I don't suppose you're doing anything on the thirteenth…?'

\* \* \*

*Helen.*

*'The person you've been chatting to for a month suddenly stops replying when you suggest meeting up. You dig a little and find out they're using a stock photo and don't actually exist. Sit out three turns of the game due to losing all faith in love, life, and humanity.'*

'Catfishing?' Karl's hands hovered over the keyboard. 'Does that happen?'

'God, yeah. I get messages all the time from angry people who've found out the stunning blonde they've been chatting to is a fifty-something dinner lady from Hull.'

'Talk about the dark side of the internet. I can't stand lying. It sort of…corrupts my internal hard drive. Why not just tell the truth?'

Helen felt a stab of guilt—Karl had brought over a pack of Lemsip when he came, as she'd told him she was ill when in fact she was in Bristol with Ed. He'd also brought several sheets of notes and his heavy-duty laptop, and now he was sitting in her chintzy living room as she talked him through her ideas for the game. Mr Fluffypants, incredibly, was lying on Karl's enormous feet, emitting a noise that could almost have been considered purring. Helen remembered the last time a man had been in her flat—an ill-advised fling while trying to distract herself from Ed, which of course just made everything worse. Mr FP had expressed his disapproval by pooping in the guy's shoes. 'You never online dated?'

'Not me. I had a girlfriend for years.'

'You did?' She tried not to sound surprised.

'Eleanor. She's a Goth. We met at Comicon.'

'Comicon?'

'Comicon, yes. It's sort of like…well, the canteen scene from *Star Wars* crossed with the library in *Buffy*. You should go. I've already got my Chewbacca costume for this year's— February thirteenth. It's going to be a protest at the continuing exploitation of the *Star Wars* franchise.'

'I hope that won't turn out to be a "Wookiee" mistake.' *You should go*—was that the same as *you should come*? Was he asking her out? To Comicon? Helen's head was spinning. All this time she'd been imagining nerds stuck at home like her, their only relationships via World of Warcraft, but then arch-nerd Karl turned out to have had a girlfriend? 'So what happened with Eleanor?'

'Oh, she's quite into the Goth polyamory scene, and I'm not, to be honest. It's a lot of admin more than anything else. We tried using Google calendars but it didn't quite fix the problem of finding long-haired elves in her bedroom when I went round.'

'Polyamory? As in, dating more than one person at once?'

'Being in a relationship with multiple people. She left me for a guy called Steve. And a girl called Bethany. She met them doing LARPing in Devon. We still game together sometimes online.' He sounded quite sanguine about it. Almost as if things could end without you spending the next two years moping round your flat.

'LARPing?' asked Helen. She felt like she'd suddenly lost the ability to speak English. Dan had also mentioned this, but she wasn't really listening.

'Live Action Role Playing. Like when you dress up as warriors and go into the woods. Not my thing—I feel the cold, and in summer my hay fever is so bad I have to wear a medical alert bracelet.'

'Oh,' said Helen again, weakly. She didn't feel she was doing much to hold up this conversation.

'So are these stories based on real life? This for example.' He read from her game notes: '*You have a great first date with someone and you're sure it's going somewhere. Then they get ill on the day of the second date and you think they're blowing you off and you never meet up again. Game over.*'

'All true—horror stories from the front line of dating. Um—my friends I mean. Not me.' Wait, was it worse if he thought she dated everyone, like Marnie, or if he knew she hadn't been near a man in years? 'I mean, some are mine,' she lied.

Karl looked thoughtful: it was something she hadn't seen before. He was very sure of himself, which you didn't expect in a man wearing a *Star Trek* T-shirt. 'Is it really this hard to get things off the ground?'

Helen nodded. 'So often you'll have a brilliant time, then for some reason it just loses momentum, and you never see them again.' Or you see them two years later and they don't even mention that you slept together *and why not why?*

Karl was typing something. 'So dating momentum equals interest divided by, what, time available?'

'Yeah, and also who else you're dating. And how much you both want a relationship. Some people just want to play around, so they date you once, then ghost you. It's worse than a horror film.' She'd seen it time and time again—Marnie gushing over some guy, hitting them with the neutrino bomb of her interest, only to have them retreat, the texts slowing down, concrete plans becoming vague, and often then a total silence descending.

'I always thought it was just a case of…finding the person who tessellates with you. Like Tetris.'

'Or Velcro,' she said. 'I don't know. It seems nearly impossible for things to work out.' She thought again of Ed, who hadn't been in touch since Bristol. Of Ani, so hard to please, who would cut a guy off for the slightest infringement of her rules. And of Marnie, living it up in the squat, no doubt, sewing banners out of hemp and sharing a bong.

'But we're going to change all that.'

'We are?'

Karl turned around his laptop. 'I wish I had a massive blackboard I could scribble on like in films about NASA but this'll have to do. Ta da!'

Helen saw a long list of numbers. 'What is it?'

'It's a love algorithm,' he said proudly. 'For our app. It's going to actually *work*, unlike all the other ones. Help people find the right date, not just the one they think they want. The person who is actually available, not just the one they'd like to be. It'll input all the variables—not just whether you fancy someone, but how much you want to meet up, how much time you have, who else you're seeing, and so on. We're going to make love…*get logical*!'

'I can see the billboards now. Sounds like a dating site for Vulcans.'

'I wish. I bet Mr Spock never catfished or ghosted anyone. So what do you say?'

Logical. Was this the answer? Not pining over someone you couldn't have, for years and years? Instead, just making lists, and swapping exes, and inputting numbers? Helen liked numbers. With numbers, one plus one always equalled two, and not nothing. Or three. Or seventeen. She smiled at Karl, who was tickling Mr Fluffypants casually on the belly, something that usually caused the tickler to require an immediate tetanus shot and possibly stitches. 'I say... may the odds be ever in our favour.'

\* \* \*

*Marnie*.

*Bang. Bang. Bang*. Marnie flinched as she sat in the bath, trying to read a copy of *Cosmo* by the fading light of her phone battery. 'Just a minute!' she called.

Outside, a muffled girl's voice. Posh. Angry. 'You've been in there for like an hour! I need to wash the henna out of my hair!'

One bathroom for ten people. No electricity since it got cut off two days ago. No heat, only vegan food and, worst of all, no chocolate. How would anyone think this was a good idea? Why had she? 'All right, keep your Rigby & Peller knickers on,' she muttered, dragging herself out. She was dry and fully clothed. There was no hot water, and the bath was just a convenient place to hide when yet another argument about global capitalism sprang up over the organic mung beans.

She went out past the knocking girl, with her nose in the air. Fenella, or whatever her name was, always looked beautiful despite having nowhere to wash and making her own cosmetics from baking soda. Her long hair was as shiny as honey—and who knew that wasn't considered vegan, for God's sake? Marnie went upstairs to find Tom, who was sitting on the sagging mattress they shared, painstakingly drawing an aeroplane onto his Stop the War banner. Which war, he wasn't clear on. It looked like drawings the boys used to do in primary school. 'Hi.' She began going through her clothes to see if there was any way she could fit another layer on without rolling down the stairs like a ball.

Tom looked up. 'Fen's upset.'

'Fen's always bloody upset. If it's not the plight of the bees it's the fact someone moved her coconut oil.'

'Was that you?'

'Um, noooo.'

He sighed. 'You've got to start pulling your weight, Marnie. You've hardly made any banners since you've been here.'

'Yes, well, I failed primary school art.'

'And you don't cook, or clean. You don't even make coffee!'

Marnie shuddered. 'I get plenty of that at work, thanks.'

He looked sombre. 'And that's another thing. We feel that it's not ideal, you working for a big evil corporation like Bean Counters. They haven't even committed to fair trade beans!'

'We? Who's we?'

'Oh, you know, Fen and me, and so on.'

*Fen and me.* Marnie knew what that meant. She swallowed down the ache that had opened up in her stomach, the familiar feeling of rejection. Tom didn't want her, not really. They shared a room, but they may as well have been friends for all that happened. Ed didn't want her—he hadn't even been in touch since that one moment at her party. He'd seen her with Tom and been briefly interested, but once she'd made it clear she was still keen, off he went. Typical.

And why did she even care? She'd broken up with him. Or so everyone thought. So why would she want him back? Was she that stupid?

Tom carried on painting, his tongue poking out with the effort. He'd thoroughly embraced squat living, to the point where he hadn't cleaned his teeth in five days. Marnie made a decision. She stood up again. 'Where you going?' he asked, not looking up.

'Out,' she said, with as much dignity as she could pull together. 'Oh, and by the way, that's not how you spell "disarmament".'

# Chapter 18
## The Leather Ceiling

*Rosa*

An hour later, Simon, Masha, and all Rosa's clothes were still locked in the bedroom, weeping and shouting in Russian—well, the clothes were silent—and Rosa was starting to get a bit bored. She sat gingerly on the sofa—it didn't seem right to be naked on someone else's furniture—and picked up *Pride and Prejudice*. After all, there was only so long you could feel guilty and upset before it started to get dull.

*It is a truth universally acknowledged, that a single man, in possession of a large fortune, must be in want of a wife...*

Yeah right, thought Rosa. She was up to the point where Mr Darcy shuns Lizzy at the dance when the door opened. She quickly shut the book and wiped the smile from her face. Masha was standing there. 'Hello.'

'Er, hi. Where's Simon?' Had she killed him?

'He shower.' She jerked her head. 'I am sorry I throw picture. You are hurt?'

'No, no, I'm fine. But the wall might be scuffed.'

'Is no matter. I am sorry to lose temper. I just come and you are here…naked…'

'I'm so sorry. I thought you'd gone. And I—I'm getting divorced myself. Simon and I were just keeping each other company.'

Masha bit her lip and fresh tears came out. 'I say I leave him, he is so English and repressed and always obsessed with making the cups of tea and the country walks, but I miss him too much. I am missing his bald head and the blowing of the nose and the stupid Radio 4 programmes about farms, so boring, but I miss!'

'Oh, Masha, I'm sure he misses you too, he talks about you all the time.' Rosa felt tears in her own eyes. 'I'm sorry. I don't know what I'm doing here. I—my husband left me, you see. I was just…lost. And so was Simon.'

Masha wiped her eyes. 'He tell me I break his heart when I go. I hurt him so much! And here you are, so pretty.' She waved a hand over Rosa's (still naked) body.

'Um, thanks. But so are you. And if you think there's a chance for you two…well, you should take it. If you're married, it's supposed to mean something.' She stood up, using Jane Austen to shield some of her modesty (not enough). 'I should go. Can I get my clothes?'

Masha nodded gracefully. 'Please. Use things in bathroom if you need.'

In the bedroom, she encountered Simon coming out of the en suite in just a towel. A slap mark was visible on his cheek. Rosa got into her clothes in record time, avoiding his eye.

'I'm sorry,' he said, in a low voice. 'I'd no idea she'd come back.'

'So what's going to happen now?'

'I… Rosa, I have no idea. I'm so sorry. I…' He shook his head. 'I really liked you.'

Past tense. Rosa realised, all in a rush, that here was the phenomenon Ani and Marnie talked about. Three dates, a promising romance, and suddenly: game over. Do not pass Go. Do not collect two hundred dollars. She pulled herself up, determined to at least leave with dignity. 'OK, well, I think you should talk. I'm just going to go.'

On the way out, Masha gave her a hug, nearly impaling Rosa on her huge necklace, and gabbled something about coming to dinner another time.

'Yes, maybe!' Rosa would have said anything to escape. 'Bye now, bye, bye! Good luck!'

As she reached the street outside, her clothes still in disarray, she felt the first prickings of tears behind her eyes. Game over. Back to square one.

\* \* \*

*Helen.*

'YRRROOOOOWL!'

Helen turned around from making tea to see Karl and the cat apparently engaged in a staring competition. She warned, 'Watch it, he sometimes goes for the face.'

'We have an understanding, don't we, Mr Cat? Does he have a human name, by the way? You've never told me.'

'Um. Yes, of course.'

'That's the bit where you tell me what it is,' said Karl helpfully.

'Um…' Helen muttered something inaudible.

Karl rubbed his ear. 'Oh no, I must have sudden-onset

hearing loss. That's a symptom of many things. Could be a brain tumour, or ear parasites.'

Helen mumbled, 'Mr Fluffypants.'

'MR FLUFFYPANTS!'

'Yrooooowl!'

Karl shook his head at the cat. 'I know! I can't believe she called you that. Cats are very dignified creatures, Helen. I think he deserves something more…majestic.'

'Well, as a kitten he was sort of fluffy and sweet. For about five minutes.'

He narrowed his eyes. 'You know, with that spot on his face, if you squint, he kind of looks like…'

'I know, I know. I have a cat who looks like Hitler, who I named Mr Fluffypants. I'm aware of the irony.'

'At the very least he should be a sir. How's that? Sir Fluffypants? Is that his second or first name by the way? You didn't do that thing where you gave him your last name, did you?'

'No,' said Helen quickly, making a mental note to delete the Facebook profile she'd set up in the name of Mr Fluffypants Sanderson. 'Anyway, should we get back to this? We were discussing whether people would honestly rate how much they wanted a relationship.'

'How about Lord?' said Karl. 'Lord Fluffypants. Heir to the ancestral seat of Fluffyington Towers. How's the inheritance tax on that place, my lord?'

'Yrrooooowl.'

He nodded gravely. 'I see. Well, I expect you'll be voting for a Conservative government then next time around.'

'Would you like some tea?' Helen tried again to change the subject.

'After 5 p.m.? No chance. You should see what caffeine

does to the brain synapses. It would be illegal if our drugs policy was at all evidence based.'

'I have herbal.'

'That's just water with flowery bits in. Think of that next time you're paying £2.50 in a fancy coffee shop.'

'OK, well, do you want anything at all? Anything?'

He glanced away from the cat, who was now rubbing shamelessly against him like the sweetest kitty in the world. 'Will it make you feel more socially comfortable if I drink some kind of liquid?'

'Yes.'

'I'll have an expensive and pointless flower water then, please.'

'On its way.'

She'd always liked the smell of chamomile tea. It meant things would be OK. That her mother would calm down, and stop panicking, and Helen could do her homework or watch *Grange Hill* in peace and her dad would come home and it would be a normal evening. Making it, Helen experienced something in her chest. A lifting, like a boat raised up by a swelling tide. A warmth, like steam rising off a cup of expensive herbal tea. Karl was here, and it was raining and cold outside, and he was playing with her cat and they were having fun and she wasn't even thinking about Ed and…was she *happy*? Was this what that was like?

'Karl,' she heard herself say, with no idea what the end of the sentence might be. And that was new. It was even… exciting. 'Do you…?'

Karl held up a massive hand. 'Do you feel something, Helen?' he said.

Her heart raced. 'Um, wow, that's just what I was going to…'

'Vibrations. Thought so.' Karl nodded and went back to typing. 'Someone's coming down your path.'

\* \* \*

Tom wasn't the first person Marnie had moved in with in eyebrow-raising haste. There was Carlos, who she'd met while teaching English in Madrid post-uni. Except he was macho and suspicious and went through her phone while she was in the shower and eventually kicked her out when he uncovered what he considered to be overly flirty messages to her language-swap partner—in fairness, she had actually been swapping other things with Javier too. There was Dina, the Dutch girl who let Marnie move into her vegetarian houseshare, only to boot her out when she discovered Marnie was not only eating bacon on the sly, but also snogging the guy in the butcher's. And of course there was Brian, who had a sensible job in insurance and a three-bed semi in Surrey. With him, Marnie had spent a disastrous month in suburbia back in 2010, before he proposed and Marnie legged it to New York.

So since Marnie and Tom moved in, Helen had been waiting. Despite all the relative calm, she had the sense of a gathering storm. It couldn't last. And it hadn't.

When the doorbell went, despite Karl's spider senses prewarning her, Helen jumped, spilling some herbal tea, which would mean she'd have to bring forward her midweek sinkwipe. It was late, much later than Karl usually stayed. Helen had been trying not to think about why that was. 'Are you not going to answer?' said Karl, still typing.

'Um. Yes. Yes, I am.' She opened the security chain and peered out into the dark wet night. 'Hello?'

A gulping sob. 'He—Helen?'

Of course it was Marnie. Who else would turn up at this

time without calling? She stood there with her red hair in sodden, yet somehow still artfully touching, ringlets. Her denim jacket—woefully inadequate for the weather—was dripping onto Helen's doormat, which ironically said *Lovely to See You!* If only she could have found one that said *Please go away, I am about to have a potentially important moment with a ginger man who used to date a polyamorous role-playing Goth.*

'You're wet,' Karl said, pointlessly, to Marnie. 'Do you feel like you might be getting a cold?'

'Who are you?' Marnie shivered.

'Karl. Since you asked, I'll assume social convention dictates I should remind you we met at your drinks party. Marnie, yes?'

Even though she was soaked in tears and rain, Marnie narrowed her eyes slightly. On guard. To flirt, to flee, or to fight, as needed. 'Yes. Helen's best friend.'

'I've always wondered how women quantified those things. I mean do you rank friends in order? How often do you revisit it? Can people get knocked off the top slot, like in the Tour de France?'

Helen realised she should say something. 'Um, sorry, Karl, I guess Marnie probably needs to talk to me.'

He didn't budge. 'I guess she needs to dry off first and maybe take some pre-emptive Cold and Flu Remedy. Getting wet lowers your immunity by an estimated thirty-five per cent.'

Marnie looked from Helen to him. 'How come you're here this late?'

Helen said hastily, 'He's helping me with some work. I'm sorry, Karl, but I really need to talk to Marnie alone.'

'OK.' He kept typing.

'Um, so that means…alone?'

Karl slowly looked up, puzzled. 'Do you mean you want me to go?'

'I'm sorry, no, that's not…'

'You want me to stay?'

'Um, no.'

'Right. Why don't you just say it?'

'Well… Because it sounds rude I guess.'

'And this doesn't?' He started gathering up his things. 'I've told you, Helen. If you need me to do something you have to tell me. I can't deal with unclear inputs.'

'I'm sorry,' said Helen wretchedly.

'I'm so cold,' said Marnie, sniffing pointedly. 'Do you have a towel or something?'

'See,' said Karl, nodding to her. 'That's much clearer. I'll go. Bye, Helen. Bye, hostile damp friend-of-Helen.'

Marnie watched him go. 'Are you *dating* him? Why didn't you tell me?'

'Karl? No, no, course not.' Some chance. The mention of Comicon was the nearest he'd got to asking her out. 'Look, let's get you dry, you look wet through.'

Helen brought Marnie in and gave her a towel for her hair—out of rotation, which would knock off her wash cycle—made some tea, and sat her down. 'Is it Tom?' she asked, afraid to hear the answer.

Marnie gulped dolefully. 'Oh, it's that stupid squat. I couldn't even text you or tweet. There's no power half the time, so my phone's dead. Everyone lives off lentils and it's damp and freezing and they just talk about climate change and social justice and helping people all the time.'

'Idiots,' muttered Helen, ashamedly. 'So, you've left? You're not going back?'

'I can't. I had a big row with this girl called Fennel or something ridiculous about who used the last of her coconut oil—I mean, hello, I needed it, my hair's really dry because it's so bloody arctic in there. And no one liked her stupid vegan carrot cake anyway.' She sniffed, pushing back her hair—which did indeed look quite shiny for someone who'd been living in a squat. 'I think Tom's into her. He kept taking her side every time she had a go at me. Oh, Helz, it was horrible. It's just so cold and uncomfortable. You remember that camping trip to Wales in year six?'

'As cold as that?'

'Colder. Only with slightly fewer cows.'

'You and Tom broke up then?'

Marnie nodded, sniffing. 'I don't know if we were ever really together. I guess I came on too strong, moving in and everything. I just… I thought he liked me.'

'I know. I'm sorry.' Helen knew she should be more sympathetic. But she'd seen this so many times. She'd mopped up Marnie's tears so many times. So. Many. Times. She tried again. 'So, you think you'll go back to the guardianship thing?'

'I can't do that either. There was an issue with the heating bills. I didn't know we weren't meant to have it on. It was arctic in there too.' Marnie had always loved the heat, seeking the sun like a cat.

A familiar sense was settling over Helen. An ache in the pit of her stomach, like she'd eaten too much. The sense of having to shoulder a responsibility you never asked for. Solve a problem that wasn't yours. She tried, 'But you have work, right? Weren't you doing that drama thing? So you could rent a place, at least.'

Marnie gave a wry smile behind her tears. 'Oh, right, the

*drama* thing. No, I don't earn enough to cover rent at the moment. I'm on a zero-hours contract.'

'Oh.'

A silence began to grow. Marnie sniffed, staring down at her cold hands. Damnit, she knew Helen couldn't stand a silence that lasted more than five seconds. One. Two. Three. Four. F— 'Well, you can stay here for a bit,' Helen began.

Marnie looked up. 'Until I find somewhere?'

That sounded a bit longer than 'for tonight'. One. Two. Three. 'Of course,' said Helen, resignedly. 'Stay as long as you need to. There's nowhere really to sleep though so…'

Instantly, Marnie's face brightened, like the sun coming through a rain shower. 'Thank you! Oh God, thank you, you're a lifesaver. I don't know what else to do, I honestly wouldn't have come if I'd anything else… I promise it won't be for long. And it might be fun!' Helen did not want fun in her home. She wanted calm, and order, and tidiness. Marnie flung her arms round her. She smelled of the rain, and pilfered coconut oil. 'Thank you, Helz. I'll be your best friend.'

Helen hugged back, but inside she was thinking: *Why didn't I buy a single bed?*

## Chapter 19
## Bling the Merciless

*Rosa*

'Busy, Rosa?'

Suzanne's chiropractor had banned her from wearing heels for a fortnight, and her newly silent approach was making things rather fraught for Rosa. All she wanted to do was mope about her failed romance with Simon—had he even liked her at all? Would she ever have non-awkward sex again?—and stare covertly at Jason as he strode about the office, ignoring her. She snapped out of her fug. 'Yes?'

'Shelve whatever time-wasting puff piece it is you're working on and write me something on how you discovered an affair by going through your husband's phone. That cheating website's been hacked! No wonder they were chucking out so much PR. Must have got wind someone had it in for them.'

'Um, but I didn't go through…'

'We've also been offered some pap shots of Sukie Miller snogging that guy off *Downton Abbey* on a night out last week. That'll do for a celeb-cheating angle. See if you can contact that himbo she's been dating for a comment.'

'Um, but…'

'Oh and you'll have to work with Business on this. Some-one from there is doing the boring investigative side.'

The Business desk was where David worked. 'But I can't…'

'Hi, Suzanne,' said David, faux-chummy, materialising. 'You're looking well.' Why was he sucking up? He used to call Suzanne 'Bling the Merciless'. Back when he'd still been on Rosa's side, that was.

Suzanne gave him a cursory glance. 'Oh, Daniel, it's you.'

'David.'

'Whatever. Get me the names of those company directors, will you? Off you go. Rosa, why are you gawping at me?'

She watched David hurry off. 'I can't… I mean, you can't expect me to work with David.'

Suzanne sighed. 'Honestly, why must you make every-thing so difficult? Marriage isn't *hard*. Look what my Kyle just bought me. Twenty years together.' She flashed a huge cocktail ring under Rosa's nose. A pale amethyst, beautiful.

'It's lovely.'

'Hugely expensive too.' She held it up to the light. 'Hon-estly, I don't know what's wrong with all these people, and you too. Letting your marriages get in such a state. You just work together. Be a team. It's simple.'

Rosa nodded into her keyboard, glad that David had gone back to his desk. They would never make twenty years now. Nearly fifteen together, and it was all gone via one girl who'd been in primary school when they met. Game over.

Start again, find someone new, jump through all the hoops of first date and tenth date and meeting the parents and the first time he hears you pee.

Rosa opened her emails, looking for the pap shots of Sukie Miller, and waited for them to download. Sukie had been in the Groucho Club last week, snapped with her tongue irrefutably down the throat of some D-list actor. Two other people seemed to be with her, chatting with their heads close together. The man had a receding hairline. The woman had a neat bob. That was strange. It almost looked like…

'CHRIST ON A BIKE!' Rosa shouted.

'Er, do you mind?' said the religious affairs editor, who was passing.

'Sorry. Sorry.' Rosa stared at the screen, with some very un-Christian thoughts on her mind. Ani and Simon were in the picture. Simon and Ani. So that was why she'd blown hot and cold with Nikesh—she'd been sneaking in on Simon! While Rosa had been trapped in the office, Ani had usurped her date! Rosa gritted her teeth together. She was going to hit something. Or someone…

'Rosa,' said David, from somewhere near her ear.

'Oh, great! Why are you still here?'

'What's wrong?'

*Aside from you leaving me for a kid and finding out my best friend is moving in on my date?* 'Look, I've got to get a piece done. If this is about the flat or whatever it'll have to wait.'

'It's not. I just wanted to check you were all right. I can't believe your friend would do that!'

Rosa said, without thinking, 'I know, but don't tell Suzanne it's Ani, or she'll make me write something about…'

'Ani? What about her? I was talking about Helen. It's her who's been running the cheating site.'

\* \* \*

*Helen.*

*Crash.* The front door slammed on its hinges, and the noise of tinny dance music filled the small flat. At her desk, Helen winced. Marnie was home.

True to form, Marnie had quickly bounced back from her break-up with Tom, and was her usual whirlwind self. She seemed to be in the flat all day long, painting her toe-nails or updating her blog, then at 8 p.m. suddenly getting texts to go to parties in Crouch End, or have coffee in underground shipping containers in Shoreditch. Helen found herself sitting alone in front of the box set of the day (she watched a different one each day of the week: currently *Mad Men*, *Sex and the City*, *Breaking Bad*, *Game of Thrones* and *The Walking Dead*, refusing to give in to the temptation of binge-watching a whole series). Sometimes she could only keep track of Marnie through Twitter, which was all:

@marnieinthecity hanging out @housepricesbar, supercool tunes and #cocktails!

@marnieinthecity about to eat these amazing healthy huevos rancheros #nom #nom #eatclean.

@marnieinthecity Out with some awesome friends at a gig! #music #london #fun.

She had a key, but even if Helen tried to go to bed she'd be lying awake, listening for the scrape of the key in the lock—missing it several times—and cataloguing each movement

Marnie made around the flat. Whoosh—she was filling the kettle, flicking it on. Clatter—she'd taken off her stupidly high heels and dropped them on the floor, where Helen would fall over them in the morning. Rustle—she was going through the cupboards, looking for anything edible. The next day the kitchen would be littered in crumbs, the butter and milk left out to sour, the toaster plugged with burning bread, the whole living room full of glasses and plates and clothes and Marnie asleep on the floor in a giant hamster-ball of quilts. It was as if a hurricane had picked up every single thing in the flat and dropped it somewhere else. Only the hurricane was made of make-up and crumbs and shed red hairs all over the place. Odd bits of tissue. Discarded, laddered tights. And worst of all, the box set DVDs left out of order. Helen still didn't know what happened in series six of *Grey's Anatomy*. She hadn't heard from Karl since Marnie had turned up, she was behind on her site maintenance, and she'd run out of milk three days in a row. Mr Fluffypants was so traumatised he'd actually stayed out all night twice. Now it was day four—four! When would it end?—and Marnie had rolled in at 10 a.m. Helen got up from her desk and went into the living room.

'Morning, lovely!' said Marnie. She ripped her headphones out but left the music on, so it leaked out. 'I got us some croissants. Bit sick of all that eat clean stuff, to be honest.'

Helen found herself staring at the headphones. Why did she always throw them on the table? They'd been in her ears! Why didn't she roll them up? Then she might be able to find them when leaving the flat without turning the place upside down. 'Don't you have work?' At least while Marnie had a job there was a chance of her moving out soon.

'Oh, I don't know if I'll do that any more. It's not really what I wanted.' Marnie was rummaging in cupboards, distracted. She'd taken off her red suede ankle boots and left them in a heap by the door. Helen bent to pick up a discarded piece of clothing. She smoothed it out, stared at it. Her silk top—the one from the party, the one Marnie had said she didn't like, until she'd seen Helen looking good in it. Worn, then tossed onto the floor like a rag. Because that was what she did, wasn't it? With Ed. With Sam Foxton at school. Maybe she'd even make a play for Karl if he came around again. As long as Helen had it, it was fair game, whether Marnie even liked it or not.

Marnie was still gabbling. 'I guess I'll audition for a few things. Or do some blogging. Or do you fancy doing a circus skills workshop with me? I just saw one on Twitter.'

Helen could not think of anything worse than a circus skills workshop. 'Marnie,' she said, girding all her meagre reserves of assertiveness. Thinking of Karl. Of Ed. Of the damn silk top.

'Umm?' Marnie had taken the croissants out of their paper bag, so flakes fell on the floor Helen had just brushed. 'These smell amazing, don't they? So buttery.'

'We need to talk.'

\* \* \*

Several minutes later, Marnie was still yelling. 'I can't believe you! You won't even let me stay with you for a few bloody days!' Her emerald eyes were quivering with tears.

'I never said you couldn't stay—I just need space! I'm sorry!'

'No one needs this much space, Helen. Look!' She waved a hand round the room. 'You and your cat and your box sets. Getting upset if someone moves a cup. It's no way to live. When was the last time you even let a man near you? I mean, what *happened* to you? Why are you like this? You used to be much more fun than this, you used to have hobbies and nights out and even dates! You wouldn't have got upset before if there was, like, a *speck* of food on the floor.'

Helen couldn't bear it. Marnie had no idea. All those years of keeping quiet, of hiding her own broken heart, and her so-called best friend had never even noticed. 'In case you didn't notice, there actually *was* a man here. Only you scared him off.'

'That geeky guy?'

'Karl is his name.'

'Oh yeah? Did you ask him out? Or do anything at all about it?'

'No, but…'

'See? You're happy to waste your life away in this flat. I hate to say this, Helz, but you're turning out…'

*Don't say it. Don't say it.*

'…exactly like your mum. I'm sorry, but it's true.'

Helen tried to bite it back, like she always did. Like she'd been doing for the past thirty-odd years. Couldn't. 'Yeah, well, you know what, Marn? *You're* turning out just like your dad. Buggering off abroad for years, then coming back and expecting us all to be there for you. When are you going to grow up, and stop being so selfish?'

Marnie stared at her for a moment, white-faced. 'I thought we were friends. Best friends.'

'We *were* best friends. Before you took off two years ago without even a backward glance. Look, I know I'm not like you, always hopping off to exotic places, but this is my life and I like it. I don't like to date, and I hate adventure sports, and yes I gave my cat my surname, but I like being at home, I like TV, and I like…cushions and stuff. Maybe you should find yourself some cooler friends.'

'Exotic places.' Marnie almost laughed. 'That's what you think, is it? Fine.' She shouldered her bag, chucked in her shoes and make-up and clothes. 'I'll leave then. You won't have to worry about me moving your precious DVDs any more.' And she went, slamming the door.

Helen stood there for a moment, tears catching in her throat. Oh God. Oh God. She sank down onto one of her lovely armchairs, shaking. Around her, the silence of the flat seemed to echo. As she sat there, rocking to and fro, she heard the buzz as an email arrived in her inbox. Then another. Then another, and another, and another. Helen felt the familiar lurch in her stomach: *something is wrong*.

# Chapter 20
## My Miniature Heart

*Ani*

'And then for favours, we're going to have miniature tubes of Love Hearts, only with our names printed on them!'

'Sounds lovely,' said Ani absently. Louise had been talking about her wedding all day in between court sessions. The shoes. The bridesmaids. The hen do. It was interminable.

'It's going to be fab. You must bring your new fella. Or is it too soon for that?'

'Well, actually, I invited him to my cousin's wedding.'

'You did?' Louise squeezed her arm playfully. 'Little miss independent here, with a plus one?'

'Well, it doesn't mean I'm not independent, I guess, if I date someone. Does it?'

'I hope not. I still want to be able to make grown men cry on the stand once I'm married, after all. What's your guy's name again?'

'Nikesh. I'm seeing him tonight actually, and—'

'Ani?' said a voice.

'Nikesh!' Ani turned, flustered—the man himself was standing on the steps of the court, as if she'd summoned him in a puff of smoke. 'Hi! What are you…? Did we say we'd meet here?' She liked that he was always on time, but being five hours early was a bit much even by her standards.

'No. I need a word with you, Ani. I'm sorry to just turn up, but I remembered you said you were here today.'

'How romantic!' Louise held out her hand. 'Hi, I'm Louise Lockhead-to-be!'

He shook it politely. 'Nikesh Desai.'

'I've heard sooo much about you, you must come to my wedding! 'Scuse me a minute, must ring the caterer, there's some massive celeriac emergency in progress!' She moved off, waving her manicured hand.

'Sorry,' said Ani. 'She's a bit wedding-mad at the moment. What's going on?'

Nikesh looked different. He wasn't wearing his usual enthusiastic, go-get-'em smile. 'Er, well. I don't know how to say this really.'

Oh God. Ani felt a familiar bottoming out in her stomach. Was he about to *dump* her? That wasn't right! He liked her! She was the one who'd not been sure! She tried to sound nonchalant. 'What's up?'

Nikesh was holding the day's paper. 'I don't even read this usually, but I got stuck on the tube with no phone battery.'

'That's Rosa's paper. You know, my friend.' She looked at the page he'd been reading, spotting the headline. *Sukie Miller out on the town. Starlet abandons audience to cheat on boyfriend.* Her stomach fell even further. There was a shot of Sukie in the Groucho Club, and in the corner, face pressed near to Simon's was…

'It's you,' said Nikesh. 'Isn't it?'

'Ehhh…'

'Isn't that the night you told me you were working late? Why would you say that if you were going to the theatre?'

'Uh…' Ani, who was never lost for words, waited for her defence to come. Waited for the excuses and explanations. And found that she had none.

Nik looked from Ani to the paper a few times. Then he blinked and straightened up. 'I'm sorry. I must have totally misread what's going on here. I thought, because you asked me to your cousin's wedding, this must be something serious. I know everyone dates loads of people now, but I'm not like that. I only wanted to date you.'

'But…'

'I mean, I thought you liked me too. But then you wouldn't have lied to me and gone out with someone else if you did, so…' He shook his head. 'I guess I'm going to have to re-read the dating books again. I don't know what I did wrong.'

And what had he done? Just been nice, just remembered things, just booked tables, just been interested. Everything Ani always wished the other guys would do. The ones who didn't call, who instantly forgot whatever she told them, who sometimes couldn't remember her name in the morning. 'I…'

Nikesh was looking sad. 'I know I can be a bit geeky and weird, but I'm a good guy, Ani. I promise I wouldn't have messed you about. You should have just said if you weren't that keen on me.'

'I know! I did like you! I do! I just… I'm sorry, I wasn't sure for a while, but I do like you, honest! I just didn't want to rush into things—you know, I worry about it going wrong, and—'

'That guy in the paper there, wasn't he the one you set your friend up with? And you went to the theatre with him?'

Of course, Nikesh always remembered things. 'Er…'

He was still shaking his head. 'This isn't going to work, Ani. When Helen filled in the questionnaire she wrote that you were kind and honest, which is non-negotiable for me as I said. Maybe if you'd told me there was someone else, but…you see, I get lied to and messed around in my business. I want to be with someone who's on my side.'

'But…' Ani realised there was nothing she could say that would stop this happening. She had no counter-argument. No chance to cross-examine.

He straightened his shoulders. 'I don't think, in the circumstances, I should come to that wedding. Either wedding. Maybe you'd make my apologies. Goodbye, Ani.'

'Goodbye,' she said, in a small miserable voice.

As Ani stood on the steps of the courtroom, watching him walk away, hands in the pockets of his coat, the first drops of rain began to fall. And, along with them, she felt tears start somewhere deep inside her. Game over. Game bloody over, yet again, because of her stupidity. Because she didn't know a good thing when she had it. Because she insisted on everything being perfect, all the time.

'You look like you could use a drink,' said a laconic voice behind her.

Ani turned to see someone watching her. Legally Hot.

\* \* \*

*Rosa.*

*Hi, you've reached the voicemail for Helen Sanderson and Mr Fluffypants Sanderson…*

'Oh come on, Helz, pick up, pick up!' Under her desk, clutching her phone, Rosa groaned. No answer. She had to speak to Helen, get the truth before her friend's name was plastered all over the paper. The afternoon editions, with Ani's picture in, had already gone out. Ani's phone was also off, so she must be in court. Anyway, Rosa wasn't sure she could stand to speak to her right now. Her best friend, going behind her back with Simon? And Helen—had she kept this website a secret? All this time? When Rosa was weeping to her about David's betrayal, when she couldn't breathe for crying…all that time Helen had been running a site for internet cheaters? This, on top of Ani's lies. Rosa dialled the number again.

*Hi, you've reached the voicemail for Helen Sanderson…*

A pair of gladiator sandals materialised by Rosa's desk. 'You're not still doing that stupid desk meditation thing? I thought it didn't even exist?'

Rosa crawled out, coughing on dust. 'Um, sorry, Suzanne. Just, er, dropped my contact lens.' Not that she wore them.

'Whatevs. That girl who runs the "pay to stray" site— you know her, right?'

'Um, noooo, I don't.'

'Whatshisface, your ex, he says you're best mates.'

She was going to kill David. 'Um, yes, *maybe* I know her, but she doesn't…'

'Good. I want an interview. Put her side of it across. What it's like knowing you're ruining other women's lives. She's single, isn't she?'

'Um, yes, but…'

'Great. That's the angle. Bitter spinster defends right to play away. On the chubby side too, isn't she? I got some photos off your Facebook page, David suggested it. I must say, he's shown some chops on this one. I thought he was a general waste of space before. So put that in too. Does being overweight make you more of a bitch?'

'She's lost a lot of weight actually.'

'Christ, what was she like before then? So get me her story.'

'That's not what I… No! I can't do that.'

Suzanne examined her cuticles. 'I think you'll find you can, Rosa.'

'But she won't agree to an interview.'

'Oh, she will. Otherwise we'll name her.'

'We can't do that!'

'Again, I think you'll find that we can. Or rather, you can.'

Rosa felt the world tilt. She was talking to someone, she realised, who had no morals at all. But Helen was her dear, dear friend. Even if she did run this horrible site. 'No,' she said, surprised to hear her own voice sound so firm. 'We're not doing that.'

'I beg your pardon?'

'We're not doing it. If you threaten to name her, I'll advise her to get an injunction.'

Suzanne's voice got very low and reasonable. 'You do realise that this is your job?'

Rosa took a deep breath. 'Well, actually, Suzanne, it isn't. You employ me as a sub-editor. I write features for you on the side, and you save on your freelance budget.'

'Refusing an order,' said Suzanne, almost kindly. 'I've fired people for less.'

'I'm sure you have.'

'I could fire you too.'

'I'm sure you could.'

'You don't care about your job? About journalism?'

'I care about my friends more. Also, this isn't journalism. It's just…crap.'

There was a dangerous silence. Rosa opened her mouth to break it, plead for mercy, then thought, *What if I don't? What if I just…don't?*

Suzanne narrowed her eyes. 'Jason won't be happy. He already said you were on thin ice when we discussed you the other day.'

'What?'

'Oh yes. He's wanted you out for ages, but I said you weren't that bad.' Suzanne shook her head sadly. 'Looks like I was wrong.'

That would explain his cold silence. But screw him. Rosa deserved a whole date to herself, and she deserved a job that didn't ask her to rat out her friends. However badly said friends had behaved. 'I'm not doing it,' she said, her voice wobbling. 'I don't care if you fire me.'

'Rosa,' said Suzanne. She could almost have been sad behind the Botox. 'Please clear out your desk.'

Rosa stood up. 'No need. All that's in it is some kirby grips and forty-seven mini Mars bars. You can have those, you look like you could do with a decent snack.'

\* \* \*

*Helen*.

'You have to let me in sometime,' said Karl through the letterbox. 'You've not even offered me a cup of tea yet. What if I die from dehydration?'

Helen didn't answer. She couldn't, and she hadn't been able to for the past half hour since Karl had turned up at her door. Her worst nightmares were coming true. The hacker was back. All the personal details had been taken off the site, and published on an anonymous blog. Her phone had rung almost continuously for the past hour, until the battery wore down and it died. Her email had 1,456 messages in it. Twitter and Facebook were erupting. And all Helen could do was sit, and stare at nothing.

'I really need the loo,' said Karl mournfully, through the door. 'So it would be great if you could let me in.'

'Yrroooowwl!'

'Is that Mr Fluffypants? See, he agrees.'

'YRRRWOOOOWL.'

'Sorry, sorry, *Sir* Fluffypants.'

Helen managed to stir herself from her torpor and stand up. One foot, then the other. Reach for the handle. Turn it. Open.

Karl stood there, in his combats and a Pac-Man T-shirt. 'I don't really need the loo, that was just a cunning ruse. Are you all right? I saw the paper.'

She opened her mouth, then just raised her shoulders in a helpless gesture. Of course she wasn't all right.

'OK. I can see you're not. What can we do? What does Logan say?'

'I can't reach him,' said Helen, in despair, finding her voice in the depths of her feet. 'His phone's switched off and I can't get through to his office. Plus he's emptied out the work folders. I think maybe…' She couldn't bring herself to say it. All that time worrying about her job, all those sleepless nights with the awareness of Logan's vague dodginess flitting past the corners of her eyes. Trying to manage it with chanting, Rescue Remedy, affirmations. And now it was actually happening. She'd lose her job and her name was all over the news. OH GOD. She couldn't feel her feet.

'And Marnie's gone too. We had a fight. I—I don't know where she is.'

'Well, she's a grown-up, I'm sure she's fine. Doesn't she go off-radar a lot?'

'Y-yes, but…'

'There you go. Worry about one thing at a time. Now, what's happening with Logan?'

'It's even worse. Karl, the game notes. For Swipe Out. It was all in that folder. It's gone.'

He only paused for a second. 'It must be somewhere. Let's think.' Karl spoke so calmly. It was hard to imagine him being anything other than calm, and it cut through her raging anxiety like a gentle stream of water. 'So he's not answering emails or phones. What's another way to find him?'

'I don't know!'

'Yes, you do. What?'

'Go to his house, I guess, but I can't…'

'Do that then.'

'I can't!'

'Why not?'

'Um…' Helen's mind went blank. 'I don't know where it is.'

'The address will be registered at Companies House,' said Karl, calmly again. 'It's a legal requirement.'

'Well, I don't have a car. It's in Essex, I think.'

'I'm pretty sure they have public transport in Essex. I haven't owned a car in all my life and I never intend to. It's one of the most dangerous, not to mention environmentally damaging, things you can do.'

'So…'

'Break it down into steps,' said Karl. His voice was gentle. 'You can do it, Helen. One thing at a time. Small steps.'

'OK, so I need to…um, go to the station.' Oh God, she couldn't. Panic was spinning her into a vortex.

'Smaller than that,' he said. 'What's first?'

'Put my shoes on. Find my coat and bag. Make sure I have my debit card.'

'Good. Then what?'

'Bring my phone and stuff, get the tube to, I don't know, Liverpool Street…'

'Then?' he prompted.

'Get the first train to near where Logan lives.'

'Then?'

'Find a taxi and ask it to take me there. But I'll need cash for that, I don't know if I have enough.'

'You'll get some in the train station. And a chamomile tea, to calm you down, even if it's basically paying for hot water and flowers. Then you'll get on the train and practise what you're going to say to him.'

'And what am I…?'

'Well, you're going to tell him he's behaved very badly, letting you take the flak for something you have no responsibility for, and you're going to say you want the notes for our game back, and a severance payment, and then you'll say no more about it, and you can part ways.'

'But people know my name now,' Helen said, miserably. 'In the paper they said I was…the fat girl who ruins other people's marriages.' Oh God. Oh God. She began to shake. 'They even have pictures of me. Rosa must have printed them. She must be mad at me. For running the site. Her husband cheated on her too and—Oh God. Oh God.'

'Helen.' Karl placed himself in front of her. Gently, he took hold of her shoulders. 'Are you overweight?'

'I don't know, I used to be big…'

'What clothes size do you wear?'

'Um, a twelve, maybe, but sometimes…'

'Is that considered fat, by normal people?'

'You don't understand! Here! This is what I used to look like!' Helen grabbed a picture from her bookshelf and shoved it at him. Teenaged her, smiling so proudly with her stupid Golden Keyboard award.

Karl gave it a cursory glance. 'You look the same to me.'

'What?'

'Oh, I guess you're probably a bit—' he made vague hand gestures '—you probably wear different-sized clothes now, but this was years ago, wasn't it? I mean I know Reading is backward but this is sometime in the nineties, surely? And your eyes, your—well, your *you*—it's the same. So what does it matter? It's all a part of you, Helen. Every cell in your body is part of who you are. That's just…science. So who cares if there used to be more of you? Now, are you currently considered to be fat?'

'N-no.'

'Right. So some evil people in the media have chosen you to bear the brunt of all this. It'll be forgotten in a few days.'

She tried to breathe. In. Out. In. Out. It wasn't going away. This was happening. This was real. Irrational panic was far behind her. The worst was here.

But so was he. She could smell him—soap, and bike oil. He met her gaze, steady. 'That's better. Eye contact. Breathing. Your body is having a physical response, but you're still in control of it.'

Helen gasped for breath. 'Is this a panic attack?'

'Do you feel like you're going to have heart failure and die and like you can't breathe?'

'Y-yes.'

'That's the badger then. It'll pass. Walk a bit.' He rubbed her back like she was a colicky baby.

'My career,' she said, when she could draw enough air into her tight chest. 'I'm finished. No one will hire me now. Every time they Google me this will come up.'

'So what? You didn't like working for Logan, did you?'

'N-no, but…'

'So go freelance.'

'I can't,' she gasped. Panic gripped her again, and she stumbled.

Karl grasped her under the arm. 'Come on, keep pacing. Count the steps. It helps.'

One. Two. Three. Four. Helen walked. Even Mr Fluffy-pants was watching, uncharacteristically subdued, from the top of the bookcase. She wouldn't be able to afford to feed him now. She'd lose her flat, everything she'd built up, have to move—OH GOD. She gave out a little whimper.

'Helen,' he said, urgently. 'Talk to me. Why can't you go freelance?'

'Too…unstable,' she wheezed. 'Not enough…money. Need to pay…mortgage.'

'Sure, it's a bit less stable, but you'd never have to answer to idiots again. And, once you build it up, it's actually *more* stable. Lots of sources of income, not just one awful one who might ditch you at any minute…pretty sure you can get an employment lawyer on him, b-t-dubs…'

'What?'

'Cool acronym the kids are using for "by the way".'

Helen felt some breath get into her chest. That did sound like an actually sensible argument. 'But I don't know where to start,' she said in a tiny strained voice, like a squeezed balloon.

'Well, that's OK,' he said. 'I'll help you. I've been freelance for ages, and I've not starved. Come on.' He put his arm around her in a brusque hug. She felt how strong he was, how solid. The fabric of his T-shirt was soft against her face. 'You'll be OK. Now, where are we going?'

'We?' She looked up at him, as her brain began to crawl towards the idea that maybe, possibly, if she tried hard enough, she might be able to put her shoes on.

'Well, yeah. I'm coming with you. Did you think I'd let you go on your own?'

# Chapter 21
## Jurassic Garden Centre

*Rosa*

'So, as you can see, projections for future readership are pretty much off a cliff. That's why we need to focus on engaging with the twenty-to-thirty age bracket, probably via clickbait content and enhanced SEO rankings…' Jason was standing at the head of the conference-room table, attempting to take the board members—combined age four hundred and seventy-three—through the intricacies of the digital age.

'Clickbait,' said the Head of Reviews. 'You're suggesting we write about fishing? I know the angling column's got a very loyal following but…'

'Um, no, that's not what clickbait—'

'Don't bother explaining, they don't have a clue,' said Rosa, from the doorway.

Jason looked up. His golden curls had been cut too short.

A shorn Surf God, not made for this world of strip lighting and grey carpets. 'Rosa! What are you doing?'

Bill, the MD of the company, squinted at her through his bifocals. 'One of Suzanne's girls, isn't it?'

Rosa sniffed. 'Well, not any more, she's just fired me. And I'm not a girl, sir, I'm in my thirties.'

'She's fired you?' said Jason.

'Yeah, and it was your idea, I hear. Well, I just wanted to say, don't worry, I've had enough of working at this excuse for a newspaper anyway. Writing pieces about Kim Kardashian's arse, making women feel their ear lobes are fat or their nostrils are too far apart or whatever.'

'What's a Kardashian?' muttered a desiccated board member, peering with interest at Rosa's own posterior in her skinny jeans.

'I don't know,' said another, adjusting his hearing aid. 'I believe it's a republic in the Caucasus.'

Jason moved towards her, lowering his voice. 'Rosa, I don't know what you're talking about, and it's not really appropriate for you to be here. This is a very important work thing.'

'Yeah, yeah, I know how you feel about *boring work things*. So boring you have to arrange another date for the same day.'

'What are you…bloody hell, is that why you went off like a badger with a hedgehog up its arse? You looked at my messages?'

'A hedgehog up its…? That's not even a… Never mind. I know what you said about me—it came up on your bloody phone. And I want to let you know, I don't care if you fire me, or you don't want to date me, or whatever you think. I quit anyway. Or I would have if I hadn't already been fired. So there.'

'So you've come in and interrupted my very important meeting just to tell me you don't care.'

'Exactly.'

'You've been fired?' said Bill, who was struggling to keep up.

Rosa turned to him. 'Just because I wouldn't perpetrate an act of great injustice! Sir, you should know what's going on in your paper. Something is rotten in the state of the *Gazette*!'

Rosa had a brief vision of the board members applauding—though several of them might need immediate treatment for fractured wrists—and then marching her in, shoulder-high, to fire Suzanne and make Rosa features editor. This pleasant image was quickly quashed when Bill said, 'That's good, Jason, we can knock her salary off the budget forecast.'

Jason was looking at her with a strange expression. 'Rosa, this isn't a good time. The projections—we're in serious talks right now.'

'Fine. I'm going anyway. God, you stand up there like you know so much about business, like you're Christian bloody Grey or somebody, with your suits and your whizzy graphs, when really you're just like every other man. You're such a…cliché. I bet your Facebook profile picture is of you topless and holding a surfboard.'

'Rosa!'

'Oh, I'm going. Hope *Kara* is doing well, by the way.' It was a childish dig, she knew, but as a person whose husband had recently left her for someone born in the nineties, she refused to feel guilty for it.

* * *

*Helen.*

Somehow—she could never remember how—Helen got herself dressed, and out the door, and onto the tube. Karl

kept up a soothing monologue near her ear. 'Now just swipe
your Oyster card…now just press the door button…now just
sit down there…'

She took breaths, feeling seasick when there wasn't any
sea. What if they didn't find Logan? What if they did? What
on earth would she say to him? At Liverpool Street, Karl
negotiated her up the escalators. He stood on the one below,
so for once their eyes were level. His looked kind. 'It's going
to be OK, you know.'

'How is it?'

'Because what's the absolute worst, most terrible conse-
quence of all the things that could happen?'

'I don't want to think about that!'

'Well, your brain is doing it anyway. So let's talk about
it. Pull it out into the light.'

Helen delved into the twisted mass of images her brain
was throwing up. 'Um, well, I lose my job.'

'OK. I hate to tell you this, but that may be a given.'

*'What*? How is that helpful?'

'No point hiding from it. If it's real, you can face it. So
what if that does happen?'

'Well, I'll have no money, obviously.'

'I bet you have savings. You even have a little novelty
jar in your living room for spare change. Cat-shaped.' He
guided her off the escalator and onto the platform, where a
tube was coming in.

Over the rumble Helen managed to say, 'Yeah, Mr Fluffypants hates it. He tried to eat it when I first bought it.'

Karl laughed. 'You know, I do kind of admire that cat.
Not a single crap is given. So you have savings?'

Helen nodded reluctantly. She did, of course. Salted away

over years of not buying clothes or dating or ever really
leaving the flat.

'So, you'd be fine for a while. And you have a really
marketable skill with web design. Honestly. You would not
believe the questions I get. Can you make this website red?
Does that cost extra? Think of all those idiots, Helen, just
waiting for you to help them put a site up on the "World
Wide Web".' He was taking up nearly all the tube seat they'd
squeezed themselves into. Her leg was pressed up against his
combats—it was unavoidable. He was very warm. 'What's
the absolute, worst-ever thing you can imagine? The thing
you think about when you're awake at three in the morning?'

'Um…moving in with my parents,' said Helen in a tiny voice.

Karl shot her a sympathetic look. 'That bad, huh?'

'I…I can't go into it right now. But it's not an option.'

'Well, at least you know what rock bottom is. And now
you can do your damn best to stay above it.'

'I need some of Spider-Man's webs,' said Helen, sniffing. 'Keep me up.'

Karl rolled his eyes. 'Don't even get me started on that dire
and derivative remake. It totally fails to grasp the subtleties
of the Marvel universe. Look, we're here.'

It was unusual, Helen thought, as she gathered her things
and attempted to gather her wits (harder). Finding a man who
didn't mind at all if you had a total anxiety meltdown on him
and forgot how to put on your shoes, but couldn't bear a bad
remake of a film he liked. It was…sort of refreshing.

* * *

'Which one is it?'

'Guess.' The taxi had stopped.

'The hideously vulgar one with the Tudor frontage on
what is clearly Georgian cornicing, built for cheap in 1995?'

'That's the…what did you say? That's the badger.'

'Honestly. It's like these people don't even try to have a grasp of architectural cohesion. Cornicing wasn't invented until the 1700s, why would it be on a Tudor house?'

Helen was still taking deep yogic breaths. She was pretty sure the taxi driver thought she was having an asthma attack. 'You all right, love?'

'F-fine.'

'Hay fever, is it? Bit early for that.'

Karl handed over cash. 'She's just feeling a bit poorly. Thank you very much.'

At the last minute Helen tried to barricade herself in the car, like Mr Fluffypants going to the vet's. 'I can't.'

'You have to. We can't detain this nice taxi driver any longer.'

Damn him. He seemed to have figured out that her 'be nice to people' trigger was even stronger than her anxiety. She crawled out, crab-like. 'How do you know so much about panic attacks?'

'Oh, I was a big walking one till I was twenty-five. Captain Panic, that was me. Like a superhero.'

'What were your superpowers?' They were approaching the huge pile of a house, on a cul-de-sac of similar monstrosities, all gated to keep out undesirables like hawkers, thieves, and people on less than £100k a year.

'I had the power to imagine the worst possible scenario in every situation, in the blink of an eye.'

'Me too. Do we have to do this?'

'He might not be there. Let's just see.'

But the gates were open, and swung silently back. Helen looked at Karl in wordless fear.

He said, 'Come on. Let's ring the doorbell.'

They crunched up the gravel drive. The garden, more manicured than the nails of a footballer's wife, was peppered with stone statues—surreally, Helen saw that instead of gnomes, they were dinosaurs.

Karl shook his head. 'It's like Jurassic Garden Centre. The low-budget sequel no one wanted. Look, that one has a fishing rod. Everyone knows it was only later mammals who learned to use tools, duh. How could they go fishing when they don't have opposable thumbs?'

'Shh. They might hear us.' Because the door was also ajar. Very odd, in this area of neighbourhood watches and crime terror—even though the actual crime was being done by the tax-dodging residents of the houses. 'Hello?' Helen pushed the door. 'Logan? It's me, Helen.' No answer.

'We should go in,' Karl stage-whispered.

'You don't think it's rude? Why's the door open?'

'They might have been robbed.'

'So, you want to stop a robbery?'

'No, but I really want to see this dinosaur statue you told me about.'

They opened the door into a gloomy marble lobby, their footsteps the only sound. In unison, they stared up. And up.

'Wow,' said Karl, in a small voice. 'I don't care what else he's done. That is magnificent.'

The T-Rex model, in full 3D glory, was the same height as the double staircase that led up to the first floor. Its tiny hands reared up, its mouth open in silent rage.

'And it's the actual one from the film?' They were still whispering.

'So he says.'

Karl regarded it critically. 'If I had to say, I'd guess it

was from *Lost World*. Which is obviously a bit more shit. But still *amazing*.'

'OK.' Helen tried to impress on him the gravity of the situation. 'But it's not time for dinosaurs now.'

'I know. It hasn't been for sixty-five million years.'

She called again. 'Hello? Logan?'

There was a noise from the kitchen. It sounded like breaking glass.

'Go!' Karl gestured. 'I'll take up the rear.' He adopted a crouching stance, covering her. 'If only I had my paintball gun.'

'You've got your own paintball gun?'

'You don't?'

'Hello?' Her voice wavered. 'It's Helen.'

They rounded into the huge open kitchen, which was thankfully flooded with light from patio doors, looking out onto the painfully tidy garden. A woman was standing there, holding a jagged broken bottle in each hand.

'Aarrrgh!' Helen screamed.

# Chapter 22
## Suggestive Topiary

*Rosa*

*Five ways to quit your job in style. The time I told my boss to stuff some mini-Mars bars up her bleached... What to do if you've told your hot editor-in-chief he's a cliché and probably poses topless on Facebook.*

It was fine. It was all going to be fine. So, she'd been fired, and both Helen and Ani, her dearest friends, had been lying to her, and Simon had gone back to his wife and David had left her and she'd been rude to Jason—her boss's boss!—in front of the entire board. But that was fine. Maybe she'd get an amusing think piece out of it.

Oh God. Rosa sank to the floor of the supplies cupboard—had it really been just last week that she'd flirted with Jason in here?—hands covering her face. It wasn't going to be fine! She'd lose the flat. She'd be single, and homeless, and jobless, at thirty-two.

She sat there for a few minutes, letting it all sink in, when she heard the door handle turn. For a second her heart leaped—maybe it was Jason, coming to tell her everything was fine, he was sorry about Kara, and of course she wasn't fired…

She jumped up. 'What the *bloody hell* do you want?'

'What are you doing in here?' David frowned.

'I'm hiding because I've just been fired. Obviously. Thanks to you sucking up to bloody Suzanne. What made you do it?'

He shut the door behind him. 'Listen, I know you've been a bit distracted recently at work…'

'Um, and whose fault is that?'

'Listen! Things aren't good with the paper, Rosa. Circulation is way down. It's all online these days. They're looking for redundancies. I was trying to help you out. This online cheating thing is a big story, and you had the perfect angle. If you'd just done what Suzanne asked, you'd be safe now.'

Rosa couldn't think about that. Currently, she had one principle left after ten years in journalism, and that was: don't screw over your friends. 'I can't. It's Helen! None of this is fair, she didn't do anything wrong.'

'She's been running a cheating website, Rosa. She must have expected something like this to happen.'

'You're not going to preach to me about cheating, are you? Because I warn you, that mop isn't far enough from my hand if you are.'

'No, no, I just… I'm concerned about you is all. What will you do for money?'

'What's it to you? If you're worried you'll have to support me, then don't be. We can sell the flat, and both take out what we put in. The thing is, a lot of things I thought about myself have changed. I'm not your wife, or I won't be soon. I don't work at the *Gazette*. I'm single and unemployed in my thirties.' She gulped. Out loud, it sounded a hundred times worse. 'But I know one thing about me, and it's that I care about my friends. So even if Helen let me down, it doesn't mean I have to do the same back to her. If you came to change my mind, you should just go.' A rush of freedom went to Rosa's head. She didn't need him. Not really. Not any more.

David didn't move. 'That's not why I… I just… Look, we need to talk.'

'I know, we need to get lawyers, and sign things, and divide it all up, I just couldn't face it, OK? Can you try to understand? You obviously had longer to get used to the idea than I did, but I thought this was us for life, and that was our home, and I wasn't really ready to give it all up.'

'I know. I thought that too.'

'What, until you accidentally fell on top of Dandelion?'

'Rosa,' he sighed. 'Please.'

Rosa felt very tired. 'All right. Daisy then. Why don't you just go to her? Why are you even here?'

'Well, because…' David heaved another sigh. 'Oh, Rosa. I don't know what's going on any more. How did we end up here?'

For a moment, Rosa's brain couldn't process it. 'What? In the janitor's cupboard?'

'I don't know why I thought it would work. For God's sake, I'm fourteen years older than her. She's never even heard of Britpop. She was born *after* Blur got to number one with "Country House", Rosa!'

'Yeah, I know. I did try to tell you this when you left.'

'And all her friends…they all have these stupid made-

up names like Twinkie or Jemoma, and they want to quib-
ble over every restaurant bill and see who had extra bread,
and they haven't the first idea how to wash dishes or clean
a loo.' He shuddered. 'You wouldn't believe the dirt in that
bathroom.'

'I would. I did also mention this, in fact.'

'Well, maybe you were right.'

Rosa stood very still. The bristles of the sad plastic
Christmas tree were pressing into her back. 'What exactly
are you trying to say?'

He rubbed his face. 'Daisy and I had a fight. And now—
well, I'm staying at Mum and Dad's. I can hardly live in
that disgusting pile of Rizlas those students call a house,
can I. Besides, Daisy threw my Halston messenger bag out
on the street and tried to set fire to it. Lucky quality leather
doesn't burn.'

'Lucky.' Rosa's brain couldn't catch up to her mouth.
'Um, David, are you saying you…'

'Oh, I don't know what I'm saying. But are we doing the
right thing here? Ending this? I mean, we had something.
We were Rosa and David. Weren't we?'

Her eyes took him in. Once, not so long ago, he was so
familiar to her she barely saw him. A part of the furniture,
like her shabby-chic chest of drawers or her antique lamp.
Now she saw him as he was. Thirty-four. Designer stubble.
Bags under his eyes. Yellow jeans and a check shirt. Too
young for him. He looked…stupid. And tired. She snapped,
'Are you listening to yourself? In case you've forgotten, you
left me, quite brutally and out of the blue, for some child
who was working in our office.'

'She's twenty.'

'Whatever! What was the fight about, by the way?'

He had the grace to look ashamed. 'Um, the chances of One Direction splitting up.'

'Exactly. And you did nothing to soften the blow, and now you're asking are we doing the right thing? This was all your idea, and I'm just starting to get used to it and you're…'

'But I thought you wanted me back.'

'Er, why?'

'I don't know, the five hundred begging emails and voicemails you sent me? Daisy suggested I get a restraining order.'

*Keep calm, keep calm. Don't smash the toilet cleaner over his smug and slightly square head.* 'I was your wife. I was entitled to try to understand why you'd broken your marriage vows. Remember them?'

He rolled his eyes. 'Oh, come on. As if you kept yours.'

Rosa swelled in rage. 'Are you suggesting I cheated on you?'

'No, but there are other vows. About cherishing. About supporting. Do you think I felt either of those things when you were working till 4 a.m., then falling asleep in all your clothes? Or refusing to come to my cousin's wedding so you could go into the office on a bank holiday? Or forgetting our anniversary two years in a row?'

Rosa opened her mouth. 'But I had to work. You know what Suzanne's like…'

'You could have worked somewhere else. It was just an excuse, and you know it. You didn't want to face up to the fact we'd fallen out of love.'

Rosa felt her nose burn with unshed tears. 'It's not fair. You left me. That's not the same thing as me working hard.'

'But we had fallen out of love, hadn't we? I didn't make this up. Did I?' She shook her head, afraid to speak. His voice had softened. He sounded more like the old David, the one she'd fallen for all those years ago, in the space of one lecture on Copyright Law. 'The thing with Daisy—I know I hurt you, but it was more like a cry for help. I didn't know how to make you see.'

'Well, it worked. I see now.'

'OK. That's good. So maybe we could…' She looked up at him. His face was no longer smug, but strained. 'Maybe we should give it another go, now we've both admitted we did something wrong.'

'Er, did you actually admit this? Because I don't think I heard it if so. Did you even say sorry, for leaving me like, out of the blue?'

'I am sorry. You know that.'

'I don't, actually. And you can't equate me working too hard—trying to pay for our bloody flat!—with you shagging someone who was born in 1995. For God's sake, David. I get that you weren't happy, but we're in our thirties! You go to Relate, or you drink too much Merlot and have a row— you don't run off with a teenager.'

David flinched. 'So what now?'

She shrugged. 'Well, now I'm different. I can see we weren't working. I don't need you any more.'

His face fell. 'There's someone else, is that it?'

Rosa thought of Simon, reconciled with Masha. Of Tom, never the one for her. And fleetingly of Jason, Jason with his dimples and ruthless eyes. Game over. 'No,' she said truthfully. 'There isn't anyone right now. And that's OK. There might be in future—in fact, I'm sure there will be at some point. I'm only thirty-two after all. I have my whole life. But for now, it's just…me.'

'And you'd prefer that to being married to me? You'd rather be all on your own?'

Rosa considered it. 'You know what, David? I honestly would.'

* * *

*Helen.*

The woman with the broken bottles looked unperturbed. 'Who the bleeding heck are you?'

'I'm Helen. I work—I worked for Logan. His web designer.'

'Oh, it's you.' She put down the bottles and held out her hand. It was smeared with red. 'Amanda. I'm his wife. For my sins.' She saw Helen glancing at her hands and laughed. 'Don't worry, I've not offed him. I'm just chucking out his wine cellar.'

She indicated a large ceramic sink behind her, which was filled with broken glass and no doubt priceless red wine glugging away down the drain. Karl looked at it with interest. 'How much would one of these bottles be worth?'

'Oh, Logy paid five grand for that one at auction. Belonged to some old French king. Can't stand the stuff myself, prefer a rum and Coke.'

'I see. So you're throwing them away to get revenge. You didn't think you could sell them instead and buy yourself something nice? Rum and Coke if you wish? Approximately a thousand of them?'

'Bloody hell, Einstein, that's not a bad thought. Couple of top nights out, that'd be.' Amanda was around forty-five, Helen guessed—though bits of her were younger. She wore tight white jeans and a white stretchy top and heels so high they must have been giving her altitude sickness. All of it was splashed with red, like a blingy not-quite-a-Lady

Macbeth. She stopped breaking the bottles and extracted a packet of cigarettes from her pocket. 'Smoke?'

'No thank you,' said Karl politely. 'I can't get past the lung cancer stats myself.'

She nodded, lighting up. 'What you two doing here then?'

Helen said, 'Well, I've been trying to call Logan all day. The site's been exposed.'

Amanda coughed. 'The site's the least of our woes, darling. His whole bloody empire's gone bust. This hacking, it's only the start. Someone got at his restaurant—sixteen diners are in hospital with the runs after their prawn cocktail starters had a bit more cock in them than you'd hope for—and one of his planes went down in Sussex.'

'Oh my God!'

'Calm down, darling, it hadn't got up more than ten feet. Like its bloody owner.'

'So, it's industrial espionage,' said Karl. 'I thought so.'

'And now there's debts, and the investors are getting spooked and calling him on it, and he's bloody skipped town.'

Helen felt her head spin. 'He's gone?'

''Course he bloody is. Why do you think I'm here making expensive sangria? He's left me, the bastard. Taken the rest of the cash and the private plane and done a runner. Worse, he's taken bloody Consuela too.'

'The housekeeper?'

'His bit of stuff, more like. Well, she's welcome to him. I just want to know who's gonna do my ironing? No one can get a seam crisp like Consuela.'

'So what are you planning to do?' asked Karl.

'I'm gonna leg it too, that's what. Still got my little run-around. Just looking for anything I can flog before the bloody bailiffs get here.'

'I haven't been paid in two months,' Helen said awkwardly.

'Sorry about that, darling, but there ain't no money left. You're welcome to lift something if you think it'll fetch much down Cash Converters.' Amanda indicated what looked like a Picasso drawing on the wall. 'That old thing if you want, never liked it. Why can't he draw straight, eh? No one wants to look at wonky boobies when they're having their wheatgrass smoothie of a morning, do they.'

'No indeed,' said Karl, raising his eyes at Helen.

She shook her head. She couldn't do that. 'I was just hoping to speak to him,' she said. 'You see, Karl and I—this is Karl, by the way.'

'Charmed,' said Amanda, putting her fag in his mouth to shake his hand.

'We'd been working on some ideas—outside of work time, of course—and I'd stored the document in the shared folder. But it seems Logan has cleared the lot out. It's very important. You don't know where it might be?'

Amanda shrugged. 'Wouldn't know it if I saw it. His laptop's over there, if you want to have a poke.'

Helen glanced at Karl, and went to the MacBook. What would his password be? Jurassicpark? Ilovedinos? Helenisfatandiwillripheroff? Tentatively, she touched a key and it sprang to life.

Karl came over. 'He didn't have a code? Honestly, his attitude to digital security really is…'

'Wotcha, darling.'

Helen yelped, darting backwards into Karl. She had time to register how big and warm he was. Logan was on the screen of the laptop, his overly tanned, hair-plugged face peering out at her. 'What… How?'

'I knew you'd turn up,' he said, tinnily. 'Skype, innnit.'

Oh. Right. Of course it was. Not a surveillance camera. She was an idiot.

'Is that him?' Amanda shouted. 'You bloody bastard, Logy! You said you'd never leave me short!'

'Calm down, Mandy, it's all still there. I just had to hide it, didn't I. Case the pigs turn up.'

'What'll I do, Logy?'

'Go to your mother's. Empty the safe—the code is—'

'I already worked that out, do you think I'm daft?'

Logan chuckled. 'Good girl. Consuela says your dry-cleaning tickets are in the box by the bed, by the way.'

'How long's that been going on, then?'

'Coupla months.'

'Thought so.' Amanda nodded. 'Guess you know about me and Darren what does the garden, do ya?'

'Some of his topiary leaves little to the imagination, babe.'

'Fair enough. We're quits then?'

'We're quits, babe. Good luck to ya.'

Helen and Karl were looking between them, like baffled spectators at a very odd tennis match. 'Um, sorry,' said Helen. 'I really need to talk to you, Logan.'

'Oh yeah. Shoot.' His manner changed from gruff affection back to shark-like businessman.

'I had some documents on the work drive, and I need to get them back. They weren't anything to do with the job.'

'Personal stuff, was it?'

'Yes, that's right. Very, very personal. So I need…'

'Personal stuff in work time? Think you'll find that's in

breach of your contract, Helen, babe. Means I'm entitled to hold on to your pay.'

Helen felt sick.

'It's just some documents,' Karl said, turning the laptop to him.

'Who the bleeding hell are you?'

'I'm Karl, the web guy. Helen and I wrote a game together. The notes for it have all vanished, most of the coding, everything. Can we have it back, please?'

On screen, Logan scratched his head. The light looked brighter, tropical. Had he fled the country? 'Any work in them folders belongs to me, mate. Check the contract.'

'But it's our idea! It's all our work!'

'Good work it is too. I'll be talking to developers. My dating empire will rise from the ashes! No such thing as bad publicity, is there.'

Helen felt herself slide into panic. Waited for it to stop, checked by reality. It wasn't stopping. This was happening. 'But, Logan, it's not fair! We did the work!'

'Life ain't fair, princess. That's what contracts are for. Now, I'll give you all your pay, as a goodwill gesture, but you signed away the rights to that game when you put it in the work folder. Soz.'

'That's well harsh, Logy,' tutted Amanda. 'Poor girl.'

'Life's harsh, babe,' he said. 'See ya!'

And the screen went black.

'No!' Helen seized it. 'Come back! Come back!' A flicker, and a face appeared. Not Logan, but a beautiful Filipina woman in a fifties-style swimsuit and huge sunglasses. 'Consuela?'

'Hello, Miss Helen, is that you?'

'Yes, it's me. Please, can you help us? We just really need a document off Logan, but he won't…'

Consuela strained away from the screen. 'I must go, Miss Helen. Nice to talk to you on the videophone. Logan says shut down the bloody laptop bloody quick.'

'But—wait!'

'Bye bye!' She waved cheerily, and Skype went dead.

'Oh well,' said Amanda stoically. 'Least he left the cash. He's not a total bastard.'

From the look on Karl's face, Helen could see he didn't quite agree.

\* \* \*

'I'm sorry.'

Karl hadn't spoken all the way through the journey to the station—Amanda had kindly driven them, a fag dangling from her mouth and Magic FM on the radio—or while waiting for the train back to London, or while on it. They were now at Liverpool Street, which they'd left only a few hours before, surrounded by the rush and hurry of London. Helen stopped, miserably, at the tube gate. She knew he'd be going one way, and she'd be going another. 'I'm really, really sorry. I had no idea this would happen.'

He cleared his throat. 'Why did you save all your documents on that drive?'

'I thought… I thought it would be safer. It's all backed up remotely. I was scared of losing data if my laptop crashed.'

'You didn't read the contract where it said he owned all of it?'

She shook her head. That was the worst bit. She was the world's most cautious person, checking everything twice, and she'd missed this. 'It was so long,' she said in a small voice. 'A hundred and four pages. I skimmed it, but…'

'It wasn't enough.'

'No.'

Karl wiped a hand over his face. 'I put so much work into that.'

'I know. I know you did. Maybe we can...'

'No point imagining. It's gone, and we just have to accept that.'

Helen nodded, staring at her feet. 'Which way are you going?'

'North. I have band practice.'

'I suppose I better go home.'

'Bye.' He started off, striding down the ticket hall in his big boots.

'Karl!' she shouted. She darted through, fumbling out her Oyster, chasing him. 'Wait! Stop!'

He turned.

'Will I...' She didn't know what to say. 'Will I see you again?'

'I don't know. We have no obvious thing to bring us together now.'

'But maybe you could come and see me sometime. I mean...you know where I live.'

'I know where lots of people live.'

There was a brief pause. 'Please,' said Helen, in a rush. 'Come and see me. I'd like that. Tomorrow, even. I—We should talk about what happened.'

Karl gave a brief nod and turned, walked off without looking back. Helen watched him go, the biggest person in the corridor by miles, a sinking sense of misery spreading through her. *Game over.*

# Chapter 23
## The Awkward Makeover

*Rosa*

*How to tell your boss, who just fired you, that she has to stop using pictures of your friend in a national newspaper, because if she doesn't your friend will never speak to you again. How to explain to your friend why the paper you work for has stolen pictures of her off Facebook. What to do when your soon-to-be ex-husband decides he maybe wants to be your current husband again.*

Oh God. Basically, there was no way to turn her current predicament into copy. Rosa took a deep breath outside Suzanne's door and burst in, her speech all prepared. What would Ani do? She'd be assertive, and professional, and definitely not break down into snotty rage-tears or beg for her job back. 'Suzanne, I'm here to tell you that it's very much not OK that you—Oh my God. Are you OK?'

Suzanne was slumped over her desk. Usually she sat

ramrod straight—she did Pilates every day before work. And her face actually seemed to have an expression on it—was that...*sadness*? Rosa blinked. Beside her boss's hand, on the desk, sat what looked for all the world like a full-fat chocolate muffin.

'Suzanne! That has refined sugar in it!'

'Sod the refined sugar,' mumbled Suzanne. She had bits of chocolate in her teeth.

Rosa's hands flew to her mouth. 'What's the matter? Has someone...?' Oh God. Someone must have died. That was the only explanation.

'It's Kyle,' Suzanne muttered, through the muffin.

'Your husband? Oh my God, I'm so sorry.' Rosa wondered what would kill a hedge fund manager. Heart attack? Choking on the steak at J Sheekey's?

'That...*bastard*.' The word tore from Suzanne's mouth.

Rosa paused in her consolatory crossing of the room. 'Wait—is he all right?'

'I'm sure he's fine. The total arsewipe.'

'But what...'

'That stupid site. I went on that hacker's blog to look at the user details. Guess who was on there?'

Oh no. 'Not Kyle...'

Suzanne began reading something out from the screen of her Mac, in a monotone. '*Hey there. Work in finance but not boring...maybe you and me could add up to something fun? Forty-something*—lying bastard, he's fifty-two—*trim, all my own hair*—yeah, in his NOSTRILS maybe—*married to a...a*—' a sob ripped from her '—*Melanie Griffiths lookalike who'd rather eat kale than me...seeks Penelope Cruz type for discreet afternoons. You bring the stockings, I'll bring my Gold Amex.*'

'Oh my God,' said Rosa. 'I am so, so, sorry, Suzanne. That's horrible.'

Suzanne was crying now. It was very unnerving, given that her face still wasn't moving. 'How do you cope, Rosa? How can you go on? I just feel so…humiliated. Imagining him with some younger woman, who doesn't have stretch marks and a Caesarean scar, laughing about me.'

'Oh, I'm sure they aren't…'

'Your husband. He ran off with that little chit of an intern, didn't he?'

'Yep.' *Which is why I've been falling apart for months, not that you made me any allowances.* Rosa rooted in her pockets for a tissue. Where was Helen when you needed her (and were speaking to her)? She'd have tissues, Rescue Remedy, eye gel and a spare copy of *The Female Eunuch*. 'It was awful. But, you know, it was for the best, I think. David and I weren't really happy. In a way, it set me free that he left.'

Suzanne sighed. 'That's all very well for you, Rosa. You're what, thirty?'

'Thirty-two.'

'And you're very pretty.'

'Oh, than—'

'It's just a fact. I'm forty-five and I have twin toddlers. What am I going to do?'

'Did Kyle actually meet someone?'

'He says no. He was going to though. Isn't that just as bad?'

'I don't know,' said Rosa. And she honestly didn't. She looked on, helpless, as her boss slid into another bout of silent, unmoving weeping. It was like watching a crying statue. She asked herself, what would Helen do? If only her friend was around, with her bag of tricks, her comfort, her lack of judgement. And yet her work had done this, wrought so much damage. She took a deep breath. She would simply have to be her own Helen. 'Come on,' she said to Suzanne, firmly. 'Let's get you cleaned up. Then you're going home to talk to him. Maybe this is just…' What had David called it? 'A cry for help.'

Suzanne sobbed. 'I did everything for him. Four hundred kegels a day. No carbs since 2002. I had his bloody children, and it knackered me. And all for what?'

'I know. I know. But, trust me, you'll feel better with some make-up on.'

She might not have Helen's bag of tricks, but she did know where there was a beauty cupboard she could raid.

\* \* \*

'There,' said Rosa, stepping back to look at her handiwork. 'Isn't that better?' She'd helped Suzanne cleanse and moisturise her face, then chivvied one of the stylists into washing her boss's hair over the sink and blow-drying it straight. All the while Suzanne, face immobile, kept up a steady weeping, occasionally punctuated with 'that bastard' and 'that's the last time I'm pushing anything out of my vagina for a man, I swear'.

Suzanne looked in the mirror at her clean and de-puffed face. Working on the women's pages at least meant you had access to the most expensive skincare known to humanity. 'I suppose. What's in that cream?'

'Essence of unicorn tears, I think, based on the price.'

'Hmph.' She patted her hair down. 'I do feel a bit better.'

'My mum always says a blow-dry cures any ills. Apart from, I guess, alopecia? She didn't cover that one.'

Suzanne glared at Rosa in the mirror. 'Why are you help-ing me?'

'I suppose because I've been there. Recently.' Rosa viv-idly remembered the day she'd come to work after David had left her, and Suzanne had sent her out on the freezing November streets to take vox pops about whether shoppers would be spending more or less on their partners this Christ-mas. She felt a small glow of self-righteousness.

'But I fired you.'

'Yeah, I know.'

She sniffed. 'I suppose I should offer you your job back now, like in a sappy rom-com.'

'That's OK. I think it was time for me to move on. If you're feeling kind though, perhaps you could stop using those photos of my friend? You know, the ones you nicked off my Facebook page?'

'The beached whale? Oh, I suppose. We'll probably get sued anyway once she gets a handle on everything. I'll tell the printers to take them out.'

'That's very kind of you,' Rosa lied. 'Shall we put some make-up on now? Look, here's a nice foundation.'

'Oh Christ, not Clinique, Rosa, I'm not about to start shopping in *Poundland*. I'm not *totally* humiliated. Use the good stuff.' Rosa complied. After a moment, Suzanne— eyes closed, waiting to be anointed like a burial mask—said, 'Oh, by the way. Jason didn't want you fired.'

'What?'

'I just said it. I don't know why I said it.'

'Maybe to make me feel bad?' suggested Rosa, feel-ing she'd earned a little leeway after she'd helped Suzanne tweeze her moustache.

Suzanne sniffed vaguely. 'Hmph. I don't know. Anyway

he was quite annoyed I'd earmarked you for redundancy. He wanted *me* out, in fact, but I have something of an in with Bill. That's a secret, by the way.'

Rosa tried to look suitably surprised. 'So, you were saying about Jason?'

'Oh, him. Kicked up quite the fuss about how we were losing all our best staff and had no relevance to the under thirty-fives—the cheek! I did a piece just last week on ten ways to fire your nanny—anyway, the upshot is, he's quite a fan of yours.' Suzanne's beady eyes flicked open. 'Why? Fancy him, do you?'

Rosa stood still, Touche Éclat in hand. 'Erm, maybe I do?'

'Don't blame you. I would. And he probably likes you, to get so wound-up about it. Anyone would think he hadn't read my piece on stress management for thirty-something men.'

Rosa was amazed—a lovely bonding moment with Suzanne! Maybe the older woman could become a mentor, giving her advice about love and access to great vintage fashion, and…

Suzanne grabbed the eyeliner Rosa was holding. 'I'll do my own eye make-up, thanks. You always look like someone punched a panda in the face.'

Oh well, maybe not. She began edging towards the door. 'Well, if you can take it from here, I might just…'

'Run and tell Jason you're an idiot and you made a huge mistake, before it's too late?'

'Something like that.'

Suzanne stabbed the pencil towards her eyes. 'Better go quick, if your running is anything like as slow as your typing.'

\* \* \*

Rosa was panting down the corridor. She had to find Jason, tell him she was sorry…

His door was open. She dashed up. No time to even knock. 'Jason…' She stopped. Jason's Mac was gone from the desk. Bob the janitor was hoovering the same square of carpet over and over while listening to football on the radio.

'All right, love?'

'Hi, Bob. I was just looking for Jason—Mr Connell.'

'He's gone, love. Offski.' Bob drew a hand across his throat.

'He's *gone*?'

Bob spread his arms, eloquently taking in the emptiness of the room. Nothing personal, except for the framed surfing poster on the wall. It was as if he'd never been there. 'Unless he's 'iding in the filing cabinet, love. Word is he got quite the strop on with the MD about some reporter getting fired. Told him to stick his job up his you-know-what. Got the 'ump and stormed out half an hour back.'

She'd missed him. While she'd been rubbing cold cream into Suzanne's Botoxed jowls, she'd missed him.

'You're looking a bit peaky, petal. Is it that husband of yours? Want me to give him a kicking one night when he's getting on his poncey pushbike?'

'No, no, that's OK, I'm…' Rosa shook her head. 'There's no point. It doesn't matter any more.'

\* \* \*

*Ani.*

Ani woke to the smell of coffee, and an empty bed. She turned over, blinking in a shocking white light. There appeared to be no curtains on the floor-to-ceiling windows that surrounded her. Of course—she'd come back to Legally

Hot's place. Rosa wasn't answering her phone, Nikesh was gone—what else was there to do? There'd been the journey up in the silent steel lift, pressed against the side, hardly able to look at him. Then his flat, all polished wood floors and views over the city. She remembered him opening a bottle of brandy, hooking his fingers in two cut-glass tumblers, jazz seeping out from the stereo, and then…

A door which Ani hadn't known was there opened, and the man himself came out in clouds of scented steam, a towel round his narrow hips. Ani felt herself blush at the sight of his lean tanned torso. He even had those little dints of muscle over his hips. She pulled the sheet up over her cellulite. She was body-confident, of course she was, but she was also thirty-three and she'd started taking a size fourteen trouser in certain brands. You could tell Legally Hot worked out every day and hadn't been near a carb in five years.

'Morning,' he said.

'Hi,' she mumbled. 'Can I…?'

'Yes, do shower. There are some toothbrushes in there too.'

He didn't touch her or come to cuddle up in the tangle of bedsheets. She had a small flashback to the night before, him lowering her down on the bed, kissing all the way down her stomach—while she held her breath in until she was in serious danger of passing out. But it seemed she'd had her wake-up call. She scuttled up, struggling to snatch her shirt off the floor and drape it round herself. Not that he was looking. He was applying moisturiser from one of the many bottles that appeared, silently, in a drawer that came out when he pressed a bit of the wall.

In the bathroom—marble and chrome, clean as a hotel—she opened the mirrored cabinet to find a stack of toothbrushes in pristine packaging. On the shelf below, make-up wipes and what looked like mini hair straighteners. Of course. For guests. On the one hand it was thoughtful. Ani had lost count of the number of times she'd had to use someone's scabby toothbrush with the bristles falling out, or take off her mascara using the edge of some crusty towel, last washed when people still thought Ed Sheeran was cool. But… She counted the toothbrushes. There were six. Was that how many he got through in an average week? Everything was so choreographed. The brandy, the clean sheets, the view. The efficient morning turnaround. And Ani realised that, hot as he was, part of her just felt tired, and used. She remembered being out with Nikesh. How he'd offered to get her any drink she liked. How he'd asked after her day.

By contrast, when she went downstairs, with crumpled clothes and wet hair—she was damned if she was availing herself of the facilities—Adam was already wearing his coat and holding out a glass of smoothie. 'All I have in, I'm afraid. There's a café downstairs if you're hungry.' He glanced at her. 'And there's a shirt shop nearby if you need a fresh one.'

Ani looked down. 'Um. OK.'

He looked at his watch—a Tag Heuer one, of course—and began to rinse his own smoothie glass. 'Have you finished? I don't like to leave it all day, it stains.'

And someone else would perhaps be coming home with him tonight. Ani looked at the green gloop and swallowed it in one. Almost before she'd put it down he'd taken it from her to wash in the gleaming sink. The brandy glasses from last night were clean on the rack, the bed had been made while she was in the shower, and now he was wiping down the counters, picking up his gym bag. 'Need to get in an hour of cardio before court. Your shoes are by the door.'

'Oh. Thanks.'

He ushered her to the lift—'You didn't forget anything did you? I have something of a problem with women leaving things here'—and the doors slid back. It was the opposite of last night's journey up, the sexual tension at breaking point. He was now looking at his watch and straightening his tie in the mirror. When they reached the ground he buzzed her out. 'Well, bye. See you in court, eh?' Was that a wink?

'Wait! Um, did you want to discuss that work stuff still?'

'Oh that. I might need to take a raincheck on that. Crazy busy right now.'

A raincheck. The knell of doom for any burgeoning flirtation. A word that didn't mean *I'm genuinely busy but let's meet tomorrow or next Thursday.* A raincheck meant, *Never in a million years, sucker.* A raincheck meant, *I've met someone new but I am too chicken to tell you.* Or worse, *I just can't be bothered to leave my sofa and* Homes Under the Hammer *is more appealing than another night in your company.* Ani knew that better than anyone.

She blinked. 'Oh, OK. Um, listen, should we…'

He paused. So did she. A small, hollowed-out space opened up in her stomach. Briefly, he pushed back a lock of her damp, unstyled hair. The gesture hurt more than nothing at all. 'Take care, Anna.'

*Anna*? He didn't even remember her name? She opened her mouth to complain, but then he was gone, bounding into the road to hail a cab. Ani watched him go. So that was a real one-night stand. Not even a nod to the usual morning-after clichés—let's do this again, I'll call you—just wham, bam, don't leave anything behind you, ma'am.

She felt drips slide down her back from her wet hair, and realised she'd put her shirt on inside out. This wasn't right. At this moment, they were meant to be lying in bed, poking each other and laughing and stopping to kiss again, morning breath be damned. Or maybe siting in a steamed-up café, eating pancakes, with maple syrup running down their chins. She couldn't help but think it might have been that way with Nikesh.

As Ani tried to find her way to the bus stop, she felt her nose begin to ache. If she didn't pull herself together, she'd be that girl crying on the bus with last night's shirt on inside out, old mascara making her tears sooty, at 7.32 a.m. in the morning. One-night stands, she decided, as the bus drove past her, soaking her laddered tights, really really sucked.

\* \* \*

*Helen.*

'Yrooooowl!'

Helen paused in her frantic scrubbing of the kitchen floor, to see a subdued Mr Fluffypants sitting by the front door. 'I'm sorry, Fluffs. I don't know if he's coming. Ever again.' Marnie would never have let this happen. She'd have asked Karl out ages ago, told him plainly that she dug his computer T-shirts and his reflective cycling tabard. And now it might be too late. She'd hardly slept a wink that night. To fight the rising tide of panic, she took the kettle off the hob and began searching in her cupboards for white vinegar. Why hadn't she descaled it sooner? All this time she'd been making tea, and bits of limescale could have been dropping into it! Why had she let the Routine slide? She felt her heart rate rise, and her breath catch in her throat, and scrubbed harder. If she could make things clean—brush under the sofa, dust the top of the bookcase, change the sheets, bleach the cups with baking soda—everything would be OK and it wouldn't matter that her job had ceased to exist or her employer absconded with all her work or that Karl… Oh God. Karl. What if she never saw him again? For a moment felt she might choke, her ears and eyes and throat full of water, drowning her. She held on to the cooker handle to steady herself. What if… *Riiiiing.*

The doorbell was ringing. Or was it? It was possible she was hallucinating, she so desperately wanted to hear it. Helen cocked her head. Mr Fluffypants did the same.

*Rinnnnng.*

Helen dropped the wire wool she was holding and sprinted for the door, pulling it open without even using the security chain. 'I'm so glad you…'

'Hi.' She stopped. Leaning against her wall, as if standing up was too much effort, was a long lean figure in fraying cords and a jumper with a hole in the elbow. Ed.

\* \* \*

'Do you want tea? I'll boil the kettle. Oh no, wait, it has vinegar in it.'

'I don't want tea. Helen…'

'Juice? Water? I don't have anything else, but I could—'

'Helen!' She stopped and looked at him, trembling. His hair was wet. Just like that night two years ago. He said, 'I came to talk to you. I'm sorry I didn't sooner. I was just—I needed to think things through.'

'Oh, that's OK.'

'I saw you in the paper.' Helen froze with the kettle in her hand. This just got better and better. 'Those horrible pictures!'

'Oh.'

'I came to tell you—well, do you remember that night? After Marnie left? The one where we…you know?'

So he did remember. Helen stood in the kitchen with her back to him, staring at her hopefully now scale-less kettle. If only the magazine tips covered removing the scales from people's eyes. She didn't turn around. She couldn't. But she felt the air move in the room, and realised he was behind her. She could almost feel his rain-chilled skin, his warm breath on her neck. Her pulse seemed to slow right down. Was it possible to die of fancying someone? She'd better Google that later…

'Helen? When I saw you in the paper, the things they said about you… I mean, you used to be big, yes. But it was so cruel to print them. So I thought I'd come and tell you you're beautiful now. Tell you I'm sorry I never saw it before—how much I needed you. You were always there to help me. I want that again, Helen. I want you back in my life.' She felt his hands sliding round her waist, and instinctively sucked in her stomach. His hands were so delicate, so pale. 'Turn around,' he said huskily. Helen was an obliging person, always had been. So—ignoring the flashes of guilt when she thought of Marnie, and of Karl—she did.

Kissing Ed. She was kissing him, after all these years. The kisses she'd spent two years reliving, stolen in the dark. And now here he was in her kitchen, his warm lips pressed on hers, his arms round her waist…and she remembered what he'd said in the train station. *I can get my arms all the way round you now!* And: *you used to be big, yes.* And: *you're beautiful…now.*

'Yrwoooooloo00!'

'Ouch!' Ed jumped back, yelping. 'Your cat just bit me on the ankle!'

'Sorry, he doesn't really like people.' Except Karl. He liked Karl…who was…standing in the front door.

Helen leaped away from Ed, who was cursing and rubbing his ankle. 'Oh God, it hurts! What if it gets infected?'

Karl bent distractedly to stroke Mr Fluffypants, who was purring around his legs. Helen saw Karl was carrying a bunch of carnations with a Tesco discount sticker on, and a DVD of *The Hobbit*, extended edition. He looked confused. 'Um, you said I should come around. Did you mean that in a metaphorical sense?'

'No, no…oh God.'

'So, how come this guy is here—your door isn't shut properly, by the way, I do know it's not proper etiquette to just come in—and you seem to be kissing him? Isn't he the man from your friend's party?'

'Um, yes, but it's not…'

'Marnie's ex-boyfriend, no?'

'Yes, but…'

A slow frown of realisation spread over his face. 'Is that the reason you cancelled on me before? You were with him?'

'Um, I…'

Karl shook his head a few times, as if trying to clear it. 'I'm sorry. I don't understand anything about this situation.'

Helen didn't say: *I'm sorry, I never in two years thought I had a chance with Ed, and then he turned up on my doorstep, because people called me fat and I'm not fat any more, and I don't know, the factual inaccuracy upset him or something.* She didn't say: *Oh and he always thought I was huge, apparently, whereas as you just looked at my pictures and said you couldn't tell the difference.* She didn't say: *Actually, I've been wanting* you *to kiss me for ages, but you never did.* She didn't say anything, because the look on Karl's face struck her dumb with misery.

He spoke slowly. 'I think, in the circumstances, the social convention would be for me to go? If that's not right, tell me.' She opened her mouth, and again nothing came out, and Karl nodded. 'All right. Goodbye, Helen. Goodbye, Sir Fluff. Oh, and goodbye, ex-boyfriend of Helen's friend, who was kissing Helen for some reason I don't understand. You're right not to take chances with an animal bite, you know. If it gets infected you could lose the foot.'

'God, I hope I don't need a tetanus shot,' said Ed, oblivious as always to anyone else. 'Do you have any TCP, Helen? I need a plaster, and some disinfectant, and...'

'He didn't even bite through the denim,' Helen said, irritably. She was staring at the door, hearing Karl's heavy footsteps walk away, and her own voice sounded like a stranger's, cold and mechanical. 'You're fine.'

'That cat's dangerous!'

'No, he just doesn't like people who call me fat.' Helen bent and picked up Mr Fluffypants, feeling his heavy warmth, the whirr of his heart under his soft white fur. He laid his head over her shoulder. What was so wrong with being a crazy cat lady anyway? Maybe she'd get some more. Knit them jumpers. Call them her babies.

'I didn't call you fat. I said you'd lost weight.' Ed's confused expression, the one he put on when you suggested he might have done something wrong—Helen used to find it unbearable. She used to long to make it better, with back rubs and sympathy, with hot drinks and blankets, with reassurances and solutions and endless support.

Once, she would have given anything to have him talk to her like this. Now she just felt annoyed. 'I know I used to be big. I don't need to be told that, or that I'm beautiful *now*. I just need someone who thinks I'm good enough for them.'

'But I do think you're good enough!' He dropped his trouser leg and took her hands. His were still cold from the rain. 'That's why I'm here, silly! That's what I'm telling you. You and me—I can see it now. We should be together, Helen.'

The words she'd been dying to hear for so long. She'd put her whole life on hold for him, convinced she would never find anyone she loved as much. She'd been alone for two years, never risking her heart again, waiting for his kiss. And now here he was, offering himself. And she was…not going to accept it. Like a ghostly Greek chorus, she could almost hear her friends in her head. Ani: *Helz, he's an unemployed musician who lives with his mum. That's breaking at least three rules.* Rosa: *Tell him he needs to read* Fat is a Feminist Issue. *And to give those cords a good wash.* Marnie…

But no. She couldn't imagine what Marnie would say about this.

Helen dropped his hands. 'You only think I'm good enough now I'm thinner. You never did before. Remember, you cut off all contact rather than have to date me. You never even said goodbye! How do you think I felt, waking up to find you gone, and my best friend too, and wondering if it was all my fault? I could never even tell her what happened—I've had to lie to her for two years!'

He put his hands on her arms. 'Listen. It wasn't your fault. Marnie's impossible. You know she is. And it was her who left me, remember.'

'Maybe. But you just ghosted me, and you broke my heart, and I've blamed myself all this time.'

'I broke your heart?' The puzzled look was back.

'Ed, you must know I was in love with you.' How could he not have known? She'd never have put up with him otherwise.

'Right, so here I am. I'm sorry I left back then, but I was a real mess after Marnie. I had to get away. And it's—well, you saw what my mum is like, she's so clingy, she needs me so much. I couldn't take that in a girlfriend too. I just—panicked. But I'm here now. We can be together now.'

Helen was shaking her head. 'I need someone who really wants me, as I am. Who doesn't care what size I am. Who'd have been with me back then, even though I was bigger.'

Ed looked bewildered. 'I don't understand. Why did you lose weight if you didn't think you were fat?'

Briefly, Helen closed her eyes. But then, Ed always had been very good at missing the obvious point. 'You need to go,' she said. 'I've got to sort some things out.'

Ed was incredulous. 'You haven't even given me a plaster!'

'There's a shop round the corner. I'm sure you'll manage.'

* * *

Once he'd gone, Helen took out her phone. She typed in: We need to talk. Meet at the usual place in an hour? Please. Really important.

She hoped this would work. Otherwise, she couldn't begin to imagine what she'd do.

# Chapter 24
## The Final Showdown

*Ani*

Ani turned her key in the lock. She was soaking wet, both from rain and tears, and her shirt had now gone see-through. She'd had to go home early, she looked such a mess, and she'd done so little work that day she'd have to make it up over the weekend. And all for what? A brief fling with a hot barrister. It hadn't even been that good. She'd spent the whole time wishing it was possible to have sex with your Spanx still on. And she'd ruined everything with Nikesh. All she wanted to do was get in the bath and have a self-pitying cry.

'You'll never take me alive, Zog, even if all my clothes have fallen off and… Oh, hi, Ani.' Gina reverted from an American twang to her own private-school drawl. She was pacing the living room, wearing shorts and a vest. Her long slender limbs were the same colour as her smooth caramel hair. 'Did you not come home last night?'

Ani took off her coat and shook the rain from it. 'No. There was a certain…attractive barrister involved.'

'But wait, I thought you were dating the nice Indian man?'

'I was. It's complicated. And not in a good way.'

Gina sighed. 'Tell me about it. I'm auditioning to play a four-thousand-year-old alien in this terrible sci-fi film, *Revenge of Zog 4*. I mean do I really look like I come from a planet that's mostly made of slime?' She presented her pore-free cheeks.

'No. You look beautiful,' said Ani truthfully. 'You just work in an insane job.'

Gina put down the script and peered at herself in the living room mirror. 'I don't know what I'm doing, Ani. I'm nearly thirty—*thirty*! And I still haven't broken through. Maybe I should give it all up and marry a millionaire. Anything's better than this. I don't know how much longer I can keep doing it.' She looked at Ani. 'Oh my goodness! Are you OK?'

Ani sniffed. 'I don't know. It's just…all I do is date. And nothing ever works out. And then I do meet someone nice, someone who actually likes me and wants to hear about my life, and I…mess it up. I get so afraid of something not being perfect that I push him away, and go for the cool, suave man who doesn't give a toss about me.' Ani wiped a hand across her face. 'With the acting—are you ever tempted to give up?'

'Only every day. But if I give up, then it definitely won't happen, will it?'

'I suppose not.'

'So we have to keep on trying?'

Ani nodded wearily. 'I suppose so. I just—I need to re-think things. Work out what I really want.'

Gina picked up her script again. 'You'll be OK, darling. You're fabulous, just as you are. Where was I. Oh yes—*I'll always love you, Dwayne, but you need to save the planet now! The fate of the slime people is in your hands!*'

Ani decided she'd get in the bath, put on an Adele CD—she was in her thirties and had been double-dumped after all—and eat ice cream. Then she'd think about how to apologise to Rosa, assuming her friend would even take her calls. God, she wished Rosa was here right now, with wine and hugs and promises to write an exposé on love rats in the legal profession. Or Helen, with DVDs and eye cream and dodgy herbal supplements. Or even Marnie, who'd pep her up and suggest getting drunk or doing guided meditation or taking up unicycling. 'Do we have any Ben & Jerry's left?'

'Oh yah, it's behind my home-made carrot pops. Frozen apple juice and veg, delish!'

Ani gave a small shudder and moved towards the freezer. In her bag, her phone dinged. Rosa, telling her what an awful friend she was? Nikesh, saying he'd changed his mind? Legally Hot, saying sorry he'd kicked her out without so much as a hug?

She read the message and thought for a moment. Bath, ice cream, and wallowing was so very tempting just now... She sighed. 'G, I've got to pop out again for a bit. Good luck with your audition.'

'*Die, Zog, you evil tyrant*... Oh, thanks, Ani, bye, darling!'

\* \* \*

*Rosa.*

*Bookish girl-about-town seeks*... Gah, that made her sound like a librarian rolling down her support stockings.

*Have you got wit, charm, and a bulging bookcase…* No no no. That made her sound sex-crazed and desperate.

Rosa sighed and rested her head briefly on the cool metal of her laptop. How did she end up here? Aged thirty-two, sitting alone in a flat she'd soon have to sell, holes in her socks with unpainted toenails poking through, unemployed to boot, and setting up an online dating profile? And, worse, apparently unable to write a sentence of coherent English. She tried again. *Hello, I am newly single and find the whole of this entirely terrifying. If you are nice and funny and like to read, maybe drop me a line and say hi. Thanks.*

She was just contemplating some of the bewildering matching questions on the site—was her personality sparky, or quiet, or laid-back? Was her body type average, or slim, or more to love? Compared to what?—when there was a knock on the door. This being London, Rosa froze. People sometimes came to the door, but only ever in the day, and then it was usually Amazon deliveries or pizza for the hipsters downstairs who could never hear their doorbell over their own rockin' beats. Was she being burgled? No, burglars probably didn't knock.

'Hello?' She tried to imbue the one word with a strong sense of knowing ju-jitsu. The top of a head bobbed up in the peephole—the person was too small to be seen through it.

'Hi!' came a squeaky little voice. Rosa recognised that squeal. She also recognised the butterfly wrist tattoo and Minnie Mouse hairslides. 'Can I come in?' said Daisy.

\* \* \*

'It's a lovely flat.'

*Stop looking at it!* Rosa felt the girl's eyes swarm over every surface, the pictures of her and David, the mementoes, things they'd chosen together. 'You never…saw it before?'

Daisy looked puzzled. 'No, I… Oh! No. God, of course not.'

Well, that was something. At least David hadn't cheated on Rosa in her own home. 'What do you want?' Rosa crossed her arms, wishing she'd washed her hair and was wearing something fancier than pyjama bottoms with dogs on.

Daisy heaved a sigh, which made her foolishly large chest rise and fall. She didn't seem to be wearing a bra under her She-Ra T-shirt. She wasn't even old enough to remember She-Ra, surely. 'I thought maybe he was here.'

'David? Well, no, he's not. Haven't you seen him?'

She shook her head, dislodging one of the Minnie Mouse clips. 'Um, no. He just…like, he just left.'

'Yes, he told me you'd had a row.' She tried not to gloat, though it was very tempting. Rosa was a nice person, but there were limits.

Daisy's big blue eyes filled with tears. 'Just a silly one. I can't stand it, Rosa—look, I know we hurt you, and I'm so sorry. But I just fell in love.'

'With someone else's husband.'

'Yes. I never thought he'd look at me. He's so brilliant and wise, and I'm just…this little stupid girl.'

David? Brilliant and wise? The man who'd once tried to boil noodles in a kettle and couldn't wash jumpers without turning them doll-size? Maybe Rosa was long past seeing the good in her husband. But Daisy had. And maybe everyone deserved that—a hint of what she'd felt with Simon, and Jason for a day, and even Tom, after so long. Admiration. Appreciation.

Daisy sniffed. 'I'm so sorry I stole him. My mum told me if he left you, he'd leave me too one day. I guess she'd know—my dad did a runner when I was six. And yes, I know, daddy issues, hello. But I really, really love David.'

And Rosa realised it—she really, really didn't. 'You didn't steal him,' she said, impatiently. 'I guess he just needed a way out.' The girl's head drooped. Rosa sighed again, cursing her own forgiving nature. She could just imagine Ani rolling her eyes. 'And, you know, I'm sure he loves you too.'

'But—he left me!' Daisy's chest was heaving again. She was dangerously close to a full-on crying jag, and Rosa, however nice she was, couldn't face comforting the almost-teenager who'd shagged her husband.

'Why don't you talk to him? I think David is just feeling a bit lost right now.'

'I don't know where he is. He won't even answer my Snapchats!'

Rosa rolled her eyes slightly. 'Wait there.' She pulled some paper off the magnetic pad on the fridge, which still held her last shopping list from before her world had fallen apart. *Milk. Kitchen roll. New husband.* She found a pen in a drawer and scribbled something. 'He's probably there.'

Daisy seized the paper. 'Golders Green—is that…?'

'Yeah. Don't let his mum make you her lasagne, it's disgusting.'

Daisy bit her lip and, to avoid an awkward hugging situation, Rosa opened the door. 'Go on. And, Daisy, it's really OK. Well, it's not that OK, you did shag my husband, but I'll get over it I'm sure.'

'I…'

'Bye!' Rosa shut the door. She took a long, shaky breath. Then before she could change her mind, she went to the laptop, clicked on the draft page, and pressed CREATE PROFILE. After all, once you'd lost the love of your life, you might as well just have fun looking for the love of your week, or month, or even of your next five years.

Rosa saw she had an email. She frowned at the sender. What did *she* have to say for herself? No, she didn't want to meet up. She was in her pyjamas already. It was pouring outside. And she was still really, really mad, and… *Dammit.* She pulled on her jeans and coat, and picked up her bag, and went out.

\* \* \*

*Marnie.*

'Just one ticket, love?'

She nodded, not trusting herself to speak. It was humiliating. Having to go back where she'd come from only weeks ago. Failing at London. Failing with Tom, and with Ed, and even her best friend unable to stand her company.

'What time?'

'Um…' Marnie looked behind her at the long queue. 'I'm sorry, could I just have a minute? I'll be back.' She pushed out, ignoring the tuts and sighs. She just had to try one more thing, one last-ditch attempt before she gave up and left.

She took out her phone and dialled the number. *Please answer, please answer.* She heard the click of the line and her heart leaped. 'It's me.'

Silence on the other end. The familiar intake of breath.

'I'm sorry. I know you don't want to. But I really, really need to…' She felt tears rise in her throat, choking her, and swallowed them down. 'I really need to talk.'

\* \* \*

*Helen.*

Helen sat in the restaurant, nervously staring at the door. For once she wasn't worried about where the table was, or if the waiter was annoyed she hadn't ordered yet, or who would sit where. She was only worried no one would come. And what then?

The door dinged. She looked up.

'Hi,' said Rosa. She was wearing a belted mac, her hair down and wet with rain.

'Hi,' said Helen.

A few seconds of awkward silence ticked by.

'Should we…'

'Do you think anyone else will…'

'I'm here,' said Ani, appearing at the table. She was shaking off a polka-dot umbrella, and wore tracksuit bottoms and a hoody instead of her usual work suits. She looked at the empty fourth seat. 'Will she come?'

Helen followed her gaze. 'I don't know. Maybe we should start.' She laid her hands on the table. 'Rosa. I guess you're mad at me because of what I do—did—for a living. I want to explain.'

Rosa frowned. 'Explain why you've been running a site for cheaters? You knew how devastated I was by what David did.'

'I know. And believe me, that wasn't the job I applied for. You know how things can just…slide and slide, and, before you realise it, everything is really bad, and you're kind of just desperately ignoring it? Like mould in the bathroom?'

Rosa sighed. 'I might have some idea, yes.'

'So I sort of got stuck in it. And it was good money and I couldn't face going for job interviews and I guess, by the time I realised what sort of site it was, I was too afraid to quit. I'm sorry, I truly am. But I have to ask—why did you let your paper print pictures of me? Did I really deserve that?'

'I didn't let them. Suzanne fired me.'

'But, they're from your Facebook account.'

'Yeah, well, we've got David to thank for that. It wasn't

me. I promise. I tried to stop Suzanne naming you, but…
well, like I said, I don't exactly work there any more.'

'Oh. A similar thing happened to me, funnily enough.'
Helen gave an awkward smile. 'Maybe we can sign on together.'

Ani cleared her throat. 'I haven't been fired, though I
might be after the performance I turned in today. Rosa, I
take it you know about the Simon thing.'

Rosa said, without looking at her friend, 'Well, I saw
the pictures. It's a weird day at work when not one but *two*
of your friends are papped in your own paper. Ex-paper.'

'I'm really, really sorry I went out with him.'

Rosa said nothing for a moment. 'Was it a date?'

'No! No, it was just… I don't know. I thought you were
messing him about. Keen one minute, the next one flirting
with your boss in a stationery cupboard.'

'It was a supplies closet, actually. And how is that any
different from the way you've treated Nikesh? Or any other
guy you've dated who's dared to be nice to you? Anyway,
you actually said it was fine to date more than one person!'

'I know, but it was Simon. I guess I felt—protective.'

'Protective! Ani, you seem to forget you didn't actually
*want* Simon. You never called him, and you made it very
clear you didn't think he was up to scratch. And now he
shows me a flicker of interest, and you're out with him behind my back! I mean my husband just left me—am I not
allowed a tiny little bit of male attention, when my self-
esteem's in the bin?'

Ani rolled her eyes. Just a fraction, but both Helen and
Rosa saw it. Helen tensed. 'I know your husband left you.
You remind us about ten times a day. But at least you've
been married. How do you think I felt, all those years when

you and David were off on mini-breaks and putting cosy selfies on Facebook? I can't make anything last past a couple of dates.'

'Because you never give them a chance.'

'I was trying! I thought maybe I'd written Simon off too quickly, and you didn't know if you wanted him or not, and…' Ani stopped, put her head in her hands. 'Look, I'm sorry, Rosa. I didn't mean to hurt you. I can't believe we're even having this conversation. Simon belongs five years ago—why am I fighting with my best friend because of him? When did everything get so messed up?'

Helen knew the answer to that. 'Since Marnie came back. It's all because of that bloody project.'

A voice said, 'That's nice. Blaming it all on me as usual.'

The three of them turned.

* * *

'I can't believe you, Helen.' Marnie's face was like a cartoon— huge green eyes with a film of tears. Chalk pale face, and around it her crop of fox-red hair. She wore her cape again, beads of rain shining on the fabric. 'I spoke to Ed. I know what happened.'

Helen felt her heart fail for probably the twentieth time that week. Which was she talking about—the kiss, the trip to Bristol, or what happened two years ago? 'Er, what…'

'You went to Bristol with him! You didn't even tell me!'

'I know, but he—he needed my help and he's my friend too, and I…'

'He's my ex-boyfriend!' Marnie put her hands on her hips. 'Honestly, Helen, I'm just amazed at you. You go on and on about how you hate dating and your friends are more important than any guy, and then you won't even let me stay with you for a measly week without making me feel like a

*leper* or something. And now you're lying to me, going behind my back, and all for a man.'

'I—' No sound came out of Helen's mouth. As if she had
years of home truths piling up in a roadblock in her mouth,
while they poured out of Marnie's in a relentless stream. 'I
didn't lie.' But she had, hadn't she? For years and years now.

'I want to know why,' Marnie was now demanding. 'Why
are you seeing Ed? Do you like him, is that it?'

'I don't…'

Marnie's face was wet with tears now, as she spat out the
words. 'I never got over him. All those guys—Ed's always
been the one. I tried so hard to move on—even with Tom, I
tried to make it work, but nothing ever does. It just fails and
fails. Everything since Ed. So I thought maybe this could be
our chance. Maybe I could go back and find out what went
wrong. Only you had to stuff it all up for me. He says—he
says you were always special to him, only he couldn't see
it. He says I don't have any right to keep you apart, when I
broke up with him.' Marnie's voice seemed to shatter with
pain. 'I thought you were my best friend. I thought you'd
always choose me over a guy. I want to know: why?'

'Because, for God's sake, she's been in love with him for
years,' Ani snapped. 'Rosa and I could see that the moment
she mentioned his name. You'd have to be blind not to, or
just deeply, deeply self-involved. You're the one who said
we should date exes! And if no one else is going to go there,
let me be the one to just say hi there to the elephant in the
room—you've got no right to preach to anyone, Marnie. If
anything, you stole him from Helen in the first place.'

'I *what*?'

Ani fiddled with her bag. 'Look, I came here to talk to

Rosa, that's all, though she clearly doesn't want to hear it. I don't want to get into this.'

'Then don't bring it up!' There it was, a flash of the white-hot rage that lay beneath Marnie's cute little kitten act. The one Helen had been glad of, when Marnie had thrown Lilt over the hair of the class bullies, when she'd Tippexed the girl who'd laughed at Helen for still wearing a crop top at fourteen. (Her mum wouldn't buy her a bra because she'd decided they caused cancer.) When anyone at all hurt Helen.

Anyone but Marnie herself, that was.

Marnie's arms were folded. Surreally, her print dress was covered in little penguins. It was like being attacked by Attila the Hun crossed with a kids' TV presenter. 'Is someone going to tell me what this is about? Rosa?'

Rosa was scarlet. 'Don't know.'

'Ani? What do you mean, I stole Ed from Helen? How? She didn't even like him back then.'

'I did,' said Helen, finally finding her voice. As if she would forget. She could remember every detail about meeting Ed—the first moment in the reception of the dingy adult-education college, where she'd signed up to a course on furniture repair—ironically, hoping to get out of the house more.

'Hi,' said a deep, thrilling voice, and she'd looked up to see Ed. The shock of his pale, sculpted face, the grey-blue eyes that seemed to punch through her.

'H-hi,' she'd mumbled.

'I don't suppose you understand this map? I can't really make it out.' Ed held out the piece of paper, a smile on his beautiful face. 'I'm looking for the furniture class. Thought I'd have a go at the old self-sufficiency lark.'

Helen knew immediately she had to help this beautiful

man. That was her role, to find the room, to make sure he had his pincushion and paintbrush, to remind him about the homework, to finish up his for him when he'd been too busy with his music.

She remembered the feeling of excitement, of anticipation. Gradually dressing up more and more for each class, doing her make-up nicely, heart hammering in case he didn't turn up, then flooding with joy when he came in the door, late. Inviting him to her birthday, which fell conveniently after the end of class. She hadn't told her friends she liked him—they would only try to make her ask him out—but she was proud all the same, the idea that she'd be at her birthday with this handsome, arty man, whose hands wrapped so deftly around the wood they worked with.

She remembered how she'd sprayed on too much Jo Malone perfume, how she'd dressed in her new jeans and loose silk top. Found her way to the nice quiet bar she'd chosen, where there was plenty of room to hear yourself think and lots of seats to sit down on. Feeling so happy, surrounded by Ani and Rosa and Marnie, and then more happiness almost exploding inside her when the door went and there was Ed, clutching a volume of poems, tattily wrapped in silver paper.

She remembered Marnie saying, 'Who's that?'

And her saying back: 'Oh, it's Ed. The guy from my furniture class.'

But she remembered most of all the feeling of coming back from a lengthy bar queue and seeing Ed kissing Marnie, his sensitive hands around her tiny waist. Feeling the moisture from the pints she'd bought them drip onto her wrists. Then thinking what an idiot she'd been. Of course he hadn't wanted her. Of course he'd want slim, fascinating Marnie.

'I did,' she said, louder. 'I asked him to my birthday because I really liked him. And then you kissed him. Right in front of me.'

'See?' said Ani. 'So don't start moaning about how Helen's been bad to you, Marnie. She's kept you going all these years and you know it.'

Rosa was looking supremely uncomfortable. 'Maybe she didn't realise Helen liked him.'

'She just doesn't care.' Ani got up. 'I'm going. I can't take this today.'

Marnie exploded. 'You're such bloody hypocrites! Ani, you're telling me off, when you tried to steal Rosa's date? Your best friend! And Rosa! You're in a mood with Ani, when you did exactly the same thing! You arranged to meet Tom on that stupid demo, after you knew I liked him! Didn't you?'

'Well, no, because I…' Rosa bit her lip. 'Maybe. But I didn't think it was… Oh, I don't know. I'm so confused.'

'You're all as bad as each other. Well, guess what? Your precious Helen here, goody-two-shoes Helen, she slept with Ed two years ago! What do you think about that? Not that she ever told me, no, I had to find out from him just now!'

Oh God. Helen felt the blood drain from her head.

Rosa was staring at her, white-faced. 'Is that true?'

'I…' Helen couldn't speak. She dropped her head. 'They'd just broken up and she'd left and I…I honestly didn't mean to. It just…happened.'

'That's what everyone says,' said Rosa faintly.

Ani put her head in her hands. 'For God's sake, Marnie. This is why we didn't want to do your stupid dating project in the first place! I knew it would end up like this. But you forced it, just like you always force us into your mad ideas. And now look—everything's all messed up.'

Marnie had gone white as bone. She said, 'None of you have the slightest idea what I've been going through this past year. I came back because I thought you were my friends. I thought you'd support me. And you're no different to me, for all your fancy jobs and flats. You're all totally lost, and you all want to meet someone as much as I do. You just can't admit it. So stop pretending you're better than me. Oh and don't worry about my "mad ideas" in future, because I'm going, and you won't ever have to see me again.' She paused for one final jab at Helen. 'You can have Ed, if he's more important to you than my friendship. I hope you're happy.'

Helen wanted to shout after her: *But I don't want him! But I'm not happy, not at all! I've lost Karl and now I've lost you too!* But she found that, once again, she couldn't say anything.

# Chapter 25
## The Incident

*Helen*

*Two years ago*

Helen got used to the pain of loving Ed. You could do that, like walking around on a broken ankle. Eventually it was second nature—the brief blankness when she woke, and the sense of a weight settling back on her as she remembered—*I'm in love with my best friend's boyfriend*. She kept going. She worked hard in her job at an IT firm, and did unobtrusively well—computers were the only thing that made sense now, seeing as Ed had nothing to do with that world of codes and order and certainty. She watched him and Marnie tear each other apart with blazing rows, tears and screaming from her, brooding silence from him. The week-long absences when Ed would turn his phone off and disappear. Marnie in tears on Helen's floor, listening to Joni Mitchell on a loop until the woman next door, who only liked German techno and went jogging at 5 a.m., banged irritably on the wall. The endless dissections—were they right for each other? Did he really love her?—and not just from Marnie. Ed too started leaning on Helen, calling her up for coffee, sending long emails. Why was Marnie so flaky, always late, always lost, always changing her job and her hobbies and her hair colour? Why couldn't she support Ed with his music? Why wasn't she nicer to his mother? Maybe she wasn't serious about a relationship after all. At the end of these chats Ed would turn to Helen—sometimes squeezing her hand, or even patting her head, like an adoring pet—and say: 'You're so relaxing to be with, Helz. Peaceful.' Which was, she knew very well, just another word for boring.

* * *

Marnie and Ed had dated for a year, and during that time Helen could remember every day she'd spent with him—the seconds slowed down when he was there, like breathing underwater. Missing him was something to be rationed one piece at a time, like a chocolate so rich and dark it almost choked you. There was the day they sat in Regent's Park until it got dark, the air cooling on her skin, Ed on her left side, his leg sometimes grazing her foot, while she held her breath in case he noticed. The evening in the pub, with his arm pushed against Helen's as they perused the quiz picture round. Marnie's birthday, when he'd presented her with the necklace that was as green as her eyes, wrapped in tissue paper. Marnie loved it. It was a theme she returned to often in the endless discussions of Ed's behaviour, lying head to foot on Helen's sofa.

'But he picked me that lovely necklace.' Her finger on it, as it never left her neck. 'I mean, he must care about me if he chose that. It's exactly what I'd pick for myself. Don't you think it must mean something?'

Helen didn't say—*Actually I picked it, and I can't tell you because I wouldn't take this away from you.* Helen didn't say—*Actually Ed complains about you all the time to me and I don't know what to do.* She didn't say—*I don't think you two are right together at all and I never did.* She said instead, 'Of course. I'm sure he loves you. He's just—special.'

She got used to being the go-between in Marnie and Ed's fractured relationship. Brokering meetings between them, then melting out of sight when they fell into each other's arms. She was the mutual friend who jollied them both along, the terminally single pal who highlighted their love for each other.

And she said nothing. She never did, of course. Until one night—a rainy night in February, cold and miserable—there was a knock on Helen's door.

She was in bed, in her sheep-patterned pyjamas, watching her DVD of *Pride and Prejudice*. Outside the door, a wet and shaking Ed. 'Oh my God! Come in!'

'She's gone.' He was shivering like a dog. She realised some of the wet on his face was tears, not rain. 'I'm sorry. I didn't know who else to talk to.'

'What do you mean? Where's Marnie?'

'She's *gone*.'

'What do you mean, gone?' Helen couldn't take it in.

'We had a big fight, and I told her—I can't cope with it. She's just so flighty, Helen. Never there when I need her. Changing her mind all the time, saying she won't move in with me even though I asked her to.' And he started to sob. 'So she left. She's gone.'

Helen was practical. She took him in, offered him a

jumper—trying not to look at his pale, freckled torso, the line of hair down his stomach, the curves of his muscles—made tea, gave him a towel for his hair. And she put her arms around him and let him cry, then fall asleep in her bed, covering him with her kitten-print duvet (Helen didn't have a lot of sex at this point) and curling up on top of the covers, trying her best not to touch him.

There was plenty of time to feel guilty later—when she realised Marnie had left the country without saying good-bye. When she realised Ed wasn't going to contact her again after that night. And many times in the intervening years, when Helen would remind herself she'd slept with her best friend's boyfriend. Ex-boyfriend, technically, at that point, but she knew enough to realise it made little difference.

But back then, several hours into the endless and yet far too short night, rain drumming off the roof, when he reached for Helen and drew her under the covers with him, both of them blindly pulling at each other's clothes to get to the comfort of skin, and suddenly, with no words, they were closer than breath—well, she didn't feel guilty at all. Not even for a second. Because all she could feel was him.

# Chapter 26
## The Dating Dessert Buffet

*Ani*

In the centre of their families, Manisha and her new husband spun, laughing, arms reaching out for each other. And Ani stood by the dessert buffet in her beautiful sari, her arms clanking with bracelets, and for the first time in her life she felt totally alone. Nothing had worked out. Not Simon, not Will the disappointed fiancé, not Nikesh, not Legally Hot. Not any of the forty-odd dates she'd been on in the last year alone. She was tired, and she wasn't speaking to any of her friends. What if she just never met anyone? What if there wasn't someone out there for her? What if this was really it?

She heard a rustle of silk—her mother had come up behind her. 'You look sad, darling.'

'Oh, I'm all right. It's just...' She indicated the room around her, the laughing people, the husbands and wives, the aunties and uncles. Slotting together like bricks in a wall that couldn't be knocked down. 'Everyone has someone,' she said. 'I want someone.'

Her mother was quiet for a moment. 'Anisha, do you want Daddy and I to look into a match for you?'

'Errr, I don't know. What would it involve?'

'Nothing set in stone. Not even an arranged thing, really. We'd just ask around, introduce you to some people. Think of it as just like your online dating, but run by the people who love you most in the world, and want only the best for you.'

Ani thought about it. Put that way, it didn't seem so bad. And it wasn't as if she was doing a good job by herself. 'Would they even want me, Mum? I mean I'm thirty-three, and I'm terrifying to men, apparently.'

'Not want my clever, successful daughter? Darling, if a man is scared of your confidence, he's not the right one for you anyway. Is he?'

'I suppose not,' she mumbled.

'So just meet a few boys, see what you think of them.' Her mother peered at her in the dark, coloured lights sweeping over her face. 'Are you nodding, Anisha?'

'Yes. I'm nodding.'

'Come here.'

Ani hugged her, pressing into her mother's silk-clad shoulder. 'Oh, Mum. I'm lonely sometimes, that's all. All this trying and trying, and nothing ever works. How do you do it?'

'You just do,' said her mother. 'You pick something, and you stick with it. That way, there'll always be problems in life, and you'll always have to work at it, but you can do it with someone at your side. Like Daddy and I.'

'That's different. You and Dad are special, you're meant to be. I might never find that.'

Her mother laughed. 'Meant to be? You should have seen us the first year. I almost divorced him at least once a month. The snoring! And he'd never washed a dish in his life. But we worked it out.' She passed Ani a syrupy cake from the buffet, dusted with sugar. 'Your problem is you never liked to choose, my darling. What job to take, what boy to love. Always so many options, you wanted everything. Like when you were little at the sweetshop. Afraid to make the wrong choice, and regret it. You just have to pick something. Otherwise you'll be here for ever, waiting.'

Ani stared at the array of cakes in front of her. All so tempting in their own ways, sticky with sugar, oozing with cream, glinting with nuts. How could she decide on only one? She eyed the dessert buffet, and she decided it probably made sense to choose the cake that would choose her back.

She fished out her phone and texted. Hey. I don't know if actually said this, but I am really sorry about Simon. I was just being jealous and horrible because he liked you, and I feel like no one ever likes me.

After a moment, Rosa texted back. Except for Nikesh and about a hundred other guys I could name right now. Snakey Steve. Blubbing Ben. Mansplainer Max...

OK. Fair point. I really am sorry.

Me too. I guess I did go back and forth a bit too. It kind of sucks, dating in the non-married world, huh? So many options. How do you choose?

Ani came right back with a screaming-faced emoji. No idea. Think I just agreed to let my mum set me up on some dates.

Cool. Would make a good feature, that.

Yeah, you can have first dibs on the story of how I married my third cousin in a dress the colour of Chewits.

Rosa sent back a thumbs-up emoji. Then one of a bride. Then one of a smiling poo.

Ani smiled. Whatever else happened, she'd never be truly alone. Because when you have real friends, there's not an awful lot you can ever do to shake them off.

\* \* \*

*Rosa.*

'So then your father said he'd never have served white wine with that fish, and I just couldn't believe it, the cheek of him! I was like Oh, Em, Gee!'

Rosa rued the day she had ever taught her mother what internet acronyms meant. 'Uh huh. Sounds awful.' She smiled at her phone, glad things were better with Ani. The world just didn't make sense without her.

'And then you'll never guess what he had to say about my tiramisu?'

'Yeah, I can't believe it. What a disaster.'

'Are you listening, Rosa?'

'He never! OMG indeed.'

'What is it, darling?' Rosa realised her mother had actually stopped talking about her father's shortcomings, and asked her a question. She was peering at Rosa over the coffee table, which she'd already pointed out needed a good polish. 'What's wrong?'

'Um, you mean apart from the fact I've been fired and I'm getting divorced and I had a falling-out with all my friends? You want a new, different wrong thing? OK then, if you insist. David tried to come back.'

'*What*? What did he say?' Her mother's eyes boggled. 'I mean only if you want to tell me. You don't have to.'

'All right. I won't then.'

Her mother made a small noise, like she was about to pop. Rosa half smiled.

'Oh, he said maybe he'd made a mistake and we could give it another go. I think she'd kicked him out, to be honest. Then she turned up as well.'

'Valerie did say something about there being trouble.' Rosa's mum and David's mum often bumped into each other in Finchley Road Waitrose. 'I didn't want to tell you, you know I hate to gossip. So what did you do?'

'I told them they should give it a chance. I've been thinking, see. I was so upset about losing David, and the job, but it turns out I didn't actually like either of those things all that much. I just felt like I should have them—a husband, a stable career—but I didn't feel happy while doing them. I mean not *doing*, er...'

Her mother barrelled through the possible awkwardness. 'Well, sweetheart, it seems there's not much point in being sad about things you didn't really want in the first place.'

'But aren't you disappointed that your daughter's divorced and unemployed? Won't your friends stay stuff about me?'

Her mother shrugged. 'Who cares what those old biddies think. Rivka's grandson got expelled from school for smoking drugs, she's one to talk.'

'Mum? Did you actually…like David?'

A small pause. 'I liked that you liked him. And he was—well, his parents are very similar to us, and that makes things a bit easier. But I didn't like the way he spoke to you. Telling you you were stupid to try to write a book, and making fun of what you did at the paper, that kind of thing.'

'It was quite silly, I suppose. All those juice cleanses and celebrity nip slips.'

'What's a nip slip?'

'Never mind.' Her mother's internet education clearly hadn't got that far yet.

'And who's he to judge? If people didn't want to read it, you wouldn't write it.'

Was her mother always this wise? Rosa sniffed. 'Thanks, Mum. I guess I'll be OK. I'll probably have to sell this place though.'

'Ah well, I always suspected this building had asbestos anyway, you know.'

'Cheers. That's…fortunate.'

'You'll be OK, Rosie-rose. You're strong. And you have Daddy and I behind you.'

'Do you still love Dad, Mum? I mean, you bicker all the time.'

'Your father?' She considered it. 'Well, of course I do. He's a thorn in my side, that man, but he's *my* thorn. He's like breathing to me. And he can still make me laugh, after all this time. You want my advice, Rosa, marry a man who makes you laugh. Who believes you can do anything, be anything. Who still cares enough to fight with you.'

Rosa paused. 'Right. You couldn't have told me this before I married David?'

'Well, we'd already booked the hotel when I realised. And the shop I got my hat in doesn't do refunds.'

Rosa grimaced. 'I see. I'll be OK. Really.'

'All right. Then this might be a good time to tell you you urgently need a haircut. Split ends aren't on trend, darling.'

Rosa leaned forward and hugged her mother, smelling Chanel. 'Love you, Mum.'

'I love you too, darling. Now remember—get it cut.' Her mother mimed snipping actions at her own perfectly set and coloured hair. 'At the moment it all looks a bit hashtag Zooey Deschanel-wannabe, IYKWIM?'

Rosa's phone beeped with an email. 'Sorry, this might be about some freelance work I pitched for. I'm going to need it now I've been fired.'

'That's OK, I need to update my Twitter anyway.' She put on her glasses and peered at her own phone. 'What does "DTF" mean?'

'Er, it means Don't Talk…um, Foolishness.'

'That's very useful. I'll be using that next time your father tries to wine-shame me.'

Rosa's email was from Suzanne. She clicked into it, puzzled. Rosa, it said. Owe you for the patch-up job. K and I are working things through tho still think he is utter bastard. Thought you'd like to know a certain surfing ex-editor is in the office today. Last time. Go quick. I know it takes you hours to do the simplest of tasks but surely even you can manage this. Love, S. x.

'Mum,' said Rosa. 'Do you mind if I run out and do something that's potentially really stupid?'

'Not at all, darling. As long as it's not getting a—what do

they call it—undercut. I know lesbian chic is very "now" but I don't think it would suit your bone structure. Hashtag truth bomb. Sorry, darling.'

\* \* \*

*Helen.*

The house was horribly, awfully, unchanged. The same gnomes in the garden, fishing round the ornamental pond. The same shonky guttering. The same pebbledash. Helen found she was having to remind herself she was not the same. She was not that overweight, sad girl, cringing on the doorstep, terrified of what she might find when she got inside. Would it be a good day, one where her mother had baked a cake and would sit down with her and ask how school was? Or a bad day, when the breakfast dishes would be sitting unwashed, the post not even picked up, the whole house sinking under a sour, frightening funk?

Or it might even be a too-good day, which was the worst kind. When the cat would be wearing a bonnet and her mother would have re-wallpapered the hallway on a whim. On those days, Helen would sit very quietly doing her home-work until her father came home, waiting for his outburst. *Jesus Christ, Susan, not again. We're not made of money!* And there'd be angry voices, and the door slamming, and the noise of the car leaving as he went back to the office. Safer there. And Helen would long to rush after him, throw herself on the car and say, *Please, Dad, please don't go, don't leave me with Mum*, and feel the slow corroding atmosphere of panic. Of knowing you, at fifteen, were the only sane person in the house, and you'd better start getting your own dinner and ironing your own shirts and maybe even pay-ing a few bills, because no one else would and pretty soon they were going to start shutting things off.

She swallowed. She'd have to go in. There was no other way. She'd made the journey all the way up to Reading for this and there was just nowhere else she could think of to look for Marnie. Even her tweets had fallen silent this time. She was really gone.

The doorbell was the same too. *Bingly-bongly.* A sound Helen had come to dread as a teenager, because it meant the doctor or the social workers or even one time the police were coming round, and possibly Mummy was going to have to go away for a long time.

Manic depression, they called it now. Some people said it helped to have a name, to know what to call it, the thing that had shredded your childhood. Helen had never found it so.

The door was opened by a man. In her head he used to be the best man in the world, who could scoop you up if you fell over, fix your bike, know all the words to all the songs on the radio and all the capitals of all the countries of the world. A giant of a man. She blinked, and saw he wasn't that at all. He wasn't even tall—five foot nine at best, in slacks and a polo shirt and old-man bifocals, over which he was peering at her. 'Is it…you?' he said. As if he wasn't even sure.

'Yes,' said Helen. 'It's me. Hi, Dad.'

\* \* \*

Inside, more of the same. The pictures on the wall—the wedding shot of her parents, the same crack in the glass where her mother had once thrown it across the room. Why on earth hadn't they replaced it? The TV was on in the lounge, playing *Cash in the Attic.* On the coffee table, a set of glasses, the crossword, tea in a World's Best Dad mug.

Helen turned away. 'Where is she?' In bed, perhaps. Or

worse, gone inside again. Like when Helen was fifteen and her father had her mother sectioned.

'She's doing the garden,' her father said, bemused. 'We weren't expecting to see you, Helen.'

Helen ignored that. 'What do you mean, doing the garden?'

'Oh, she's quite into it now. We like to go to the garden centre, have a bit of lunch, get some bedding plants.'

Maybe she was in a manic phase then. Uprooting everything, thinking it was weeds. Mowing the lawn into odd strips. Building a fence from flat-pack in twenty minutes. 'Is she…all right?'

'Is she… Oh. Yes, love. She's fine.'

'Fine?'

'Look.' He paused. 'It's hard to explain. But she's been on these new pills a while now and… Why don't you go out and see her?'

Helen braced herself, moving towards the open back door out of the kitchen. What would she find? She blinked. The garden looked… 'It looks great,' she said, astounded.

'Not bad, is it? I help out a bit, did that trellising over there. We like doing it together.'

Helen gave him a suspicious look, moving further out. The garden of the small semi was a riot of colour—clematis climbing over the walls, the shed painted a cheerful blue, the lawn green and neat. At the bottom a figure was kneeling on a little gardening mat, using a trowel and humming to herself.

'Susan?' Her father cleared his throat. 'Look who's come to see us, love.'

Her mother stood up, slowly, hand on her lower back. She was nearly sixty-five, after all. But she looked well. Her hair was tinted light brown, and she wore jeans and a loose pink top. She fumbled for her glasses, on a string round her neck, and peeled off her garden gloves. Helen waited to hear the voice. She could always tell how things were from the voice—loud and high, or quiet and used up.

'Helen? Is that you, love?'

She sounded…totally normal. Like a normal mum. Helen was going to answer, but for a moment she found she couldn't, because her throat had closed up with tears.

\* \* \*

'This is a lovely surprise,' said her mum for the third time, once they'd fussed about with tea, and a jam sponge that her father had supposedly made: 'He does like that Mary Berry, don't you, Bill? How are you anyway, love?'

'Oh, I'm…' How to sum up two years of life? When Ed left, Helen had gone to ground. Quit her job. Stopped dating. And more or less stopped seeing her parents. There was just too much potential for chaos, and chaos was something she couldn't handle any more. Helen had never told them exactly what she did for work (too ashamed), and she could hardly go into the tangle of exes and dates she'd been embroiled in. She said, 'Well, the cat's doing well. And the flat is fine.'

'Wise investment,' her dad said, nodding. 'Property prices must be booming where you are.'

'Oh they are, they are.' It was like chatting to strangers at a cocktail party.

'What brings you to town, love?' asked her mother.

Helen sipped her tea to hide her face. 'I'm looking for Marnie. I thought maybe she'd come back here. We had a bit of a falling-out and she's gone AWOL. You haven't seen her about? Her mum's still round the corner, is she?'

Helen's mother shook her head. 'Oh, Karen's still here,

but she didn't mention anything about Marnie being back. Think she didn't get on with the last boyfriend.'

'The *last* boyfriend? It's over?'

'Oh, yes, thank goodness. Think he was a bit of *racist*, you know, darling. Karen's stepping out with a nice man from the library now. You should tell Marnie that Karen misses her. You don't know where she is then?'

'No,' said Helen, ashamed to admit it. 'She just took off. It was my fault.'

'I'm sure it wasn't,' said her dad soothingly.

'What would you know about it? You barely knew Marnie, you were never here when we were kids.' Helen bit the inside of her mouth. It was as if, after years of keeping everything in, the words were suddenly unstoppable. They wouldn't stay inside any more.

'I know that,' said her dad, looking sad. 'But you always blamed yourself for things that weren't your fault. Like your mum and me and our…difficulties.'

Helen stared at the table. 'You don't understand. It's definitely my fault. I did something, and she went away, and now I can't find her.'

But her mum was nodding. 'He's right, Helen. I know you're fond of Marnie, but she was always a flibbertigibbet. Same as that dad of hers, disappearing off for months on end.'

'He wasn't the only dad who wasn't about,' Helen mumbled.

Helen's mum and dad exchanged significant looks. Her mum put down her cup and reached for Helen's hand. 'Love,' she said. 'Your dad and I…we know things were difficult at times.'

'If you call Dad working every hour of the day, and you having a nervous breakdown because he didn't notice how ill you were, and the police coming round after they found you walking down the M4 in your nightie and then him having you sectioned for two months *difficult*,' Helen said. Then realised she'd said it out loud. That was unusual. 'Um. Sorry. But, that's what happened.'

'We know,' said her dad. 'And I wish I could take all those times back, love, I really do. But things were very hard back then. Very hard indeed. Your mum…she knows I love her, love her like my life, but—well. I didn't always understand her condition. I just… I couldn't always cope with it.' His voice faltered, and he looked down. 'And we needed the money. We tried to keep it from you, but I nearly lost my job so many times. Having to rush home, you see, in the middle of the day and that, it didn't help my promotion chances.'

'Why didn't you help? Why didn't you see how bad she was getting?'

'I did, love. That's why I…got her into the hospital.'

'Only when it was too late. And she was never right again after you put her inside.'

'I can hear you, love,' said her mother, mildly. 'And it wasn't too late. Look at me now! We've found our way back. That's what you do when you love people.'

'But he hurt you,' said Helen, hearing her own voice break. She sniffed back the tears that were suddenly in her nose. 'He sent you away.'

'It was the best place for me, love. I needed the help. I was hurting him, and it hurt you, too.'

Helen looked away, wiping at her eyes. (Luckily she never wore mascara.) She knew she should deny it, say no, it was all fine, she was doing great, but it wasn't true. There was a reason she'd worked so hard for her own place—flatmates being too much of a risk—and had security chains on her door, and obsessively checked every medical symptom, and scoured her house clean, and did her best not to meet new people. Why she'd had to give up her office job, when it all got too much, and why she hadn't dated since Ed left her with a broken heart. Growing up with the suffocating crush of her mother's anxiety—about everything from spray deodorants to overseas travel to mould in the bathroom—had taken its toll.

She looked around the garden, blinking back tears. So many memories here. Her dad, teaching her to play mini-golf on the lawn. Her mum, bringing glasses of Tango and Rocky bars arranged on a plate, as she watched *Saved By the Bell* in the lounge. And every memory had Marnie in the corner of it, making her dad laugh, eating her mum's cakes, persuading Helen to dress up as Agnetha so they could pretend to be in ABBA and perform concerts with hairbrush mikes. There was even a patch of grass that had never grown back after Marnie accidentally set it on fire trying to smoke coffee grounds rolled up in a Rizla. When Marnie was there, the terrifying wolf of fear that stalked the house seemed to lie down, content. And, Helen realised, there was no way she could have got through her teenage years without Marnie. Everything was just brighter when she was around.

And now she was gone.

Her mother was still holding her hand. Sympathy on her face. 'It's OK, love. You're doing your best. That's all any of us can do.'

Awkwardly, Helen said, 'I've hurt her now. Marnie.'

'Well, I'm sure it can be fixed. Look at your dad and me. There's always another chance.' She leaned forward and squeezed Helen's hand. 'Can I give you a bit of advice, love, from someone who knows? Don't hide away from life. I know you like your flat and your work and that, but…don't hide. Because you'll regret it, once you've run out of time. You have to let people in.'

'But…' Helen thought about Marnie, what they'd done to each other over the years. About Ani, and Rosa. About Karl. About all the people we hurt in our lives, all the people who hurt us, and most of us don't even mean to.

'What date is it?' she asked suddenly.

Her dad looked puzzled. 'It's the thirteenth, love. But why…?'

Helen jumped up, wiping her eyes and sniffing. 'I have to be somewhere. I'm sorry.'

'Oh.' Her mother couldn't hide her disappointment. 'All right, love. It was good to see you. Will you come a bit sooner, maybe, next time?'

Helen swallowed hard. 'I promise I'll come back again, very soon. I just…have to go and see about a Wookiee. Dad, will you drive me to the station?'

'Of course, love, but…'

'Thanks.' As Helen gathered her things, she heard her dad ask her mum if a Wookiee was some kind of new dating thing the kids were doing.

\* \* \*

1.36 p.m. Her phone told her there'd be a train to London in five minutes. Helen scrabbled with the car door.

'Will you come again?' her dad asked. 'I know things weren't exactly ideal when you were little—that's an understatement—but I always loved you, Helen. And I always loved your mum.'

Helen looked out the window. 'But if you loved her, Dad,

how could ignore things for so long? Work all the time and leave me with her?'

'I…' He shrugged. 'I can't explain, love. Sometimes we don't want to look a thing right in the face, so we let it get worse and worse, until it's nearly too late to fix.'

Helen sighed. 'Like mould in the bathroom.'

'You've got mould? Damp, they are, those London houses.'

'Sadly, yes.' Helen considered it. 'Any ideas how to solve it?'

'Strip out the sealant and redo it,' he said immediately. 'Stanley knife. Easy job. I could…I could do that for you, love. If you wanted me to, that is.'

'That would be great,' said Helen shyly. 'Why don't you come down one time. Both of you.' She looked at her phone. 'I better run, Dad. But thanks for the lift. And—tell Mum that I'm sorry, and that I understand. At least, I think I do.'

# Chapter 27
## How Voldemort met Chewbacca

*Helen*

'Excuse me,' said the Klingon.

'Oh, sorry.' Helen moved back to let him through—his fins didn't really allow for much freedom of movement. So this was Comicon. And how was she supposed to find one geek in a whole convention of them? She was the only person not in a costume. There she was among the aliens and hobbits and superheroes, in her jeans and M&S jumper. Was she mad? He wouldn't want to see her, would he, after what Logan had done? After Ed? What was it he'd said—*I can't stand lying. It sort of...corrupts my internal hard drive.* Helen felt panic claw at her throat. She'd raced back from Reading, buying a pass on the door from a bossy man dressed appropriately enough as a Stormtrooper. Would she even be able to find Karl? Frantically, she looked around her. Captain Kirk... Thor (with a papier-mâché hammer)...Black Widow...there!

Chewbacca! She fought her way past a stall selling comics, falling over a group of hobbits with clanking pans tied to their knapsacks—apparently you could get North Face in Middle Earth. 'Karl!' she shouted. Several people looked over. Of course, this place was probably a Karl haven.

She struggled over, tugging on Chewbacca's fur as he passed. 'It's me. Karl!'

Chewbacca took off his head to reveal a strapping black man. 'Whatchew want?' he said, in a strong American accent.

'Oh God, sorry, I thought you were... Are there other Chewies about?'

'We all look the same to you, huh?'

'Wookiees? Um, yes?'

'Fair enough, the costume hire place had a sale on, there's about six of us. I blame the damn prequels. First Jar Jar Binks and now this.'

'I know, I'm terribly sorry, excuse me.'

'I mean, they should call him George Loo-cas. Get it?'

'I get it, but I have to...'

'Hey, you'd look good in Leia's bikini, I got it as a rental deal.' Helen fled. On and on she quested, through over-heated, packed rooms full of comic enthusiasts. Past stalls selling weapons and costumes and games and novelty *Lord of the Rings* themed deodorant ('Isen-Right Guard'). Where was he? Helen felt like she was starring in her very own, really bad episode of *Scooby Doo*. Would she have to tear the head off every costume in the room?

'Helen? Is that you?'

Hearing the muffled voice, Helen turned to see a figure dressed all in black, with a terrifying white mask of a face. 'V...Voldemort?' she said faintly.

'Don't say his name!' Beside Voldemort was a slight,

pretty girl with pale hair, dressed as Daenerys Targaryen. Voldermort took off his mask, revealing as he did so his tufty hair. Apparently, he had left his ear-flap hat at home today.

Helen gasped. 'Dan? What…' She almost asked what he was doing there, and then realised the answer to that was a hundred per cent obvious. 'Hi! Eh…how are you?'

'Great, great. This is Rachel, by the way.' Daenerys narrowed her eyes at Helen. Dan said, 'Listen, Helen, I'm glad I ran into you. I wanted to apologise for our date.'

Helen began to blush and gabble. 'It's fine, it's fine, it was my fault, I was super-awkward, I can see that now.'

'Well, I was more awkward. And I ran out on you!'

'I'm sure you had your reasons!' She scanned the crowd desperately. Was she going to be alone at Comicon, while even her terrible date had a girlfriend?

'I'm really sorry. The truth is, I had a massive panic attack and I just had to get out of there. I didn't realise till after that I hadn't paid, and then, well—to be honest I was too embarrassed to get in touch. You see, I quit drinking last year. I was developing a bit of a problem. It was my first date since I stopped. And you just seemed to hate me.'

'I didn't hate you. It's just… It was my first date in ages too.'

'So you were nervous as well?'

'So nervous I almost had to go on an intravenous drip.'

Dan smiled. Helen had never seen that before. 'Me too. It made me realise I had to learn to socialise without alcohol, or I'd never meet anyone. And not long afterwards I got up the courage to ask out Rachel—we'd been chatting on World of Warcraft for ages, but I'd no idea if she was even a girl or not!'

'I am though,' said Rachel, in a somewhat pointed way. 'Sun and stars, we'll be late for the band.'

'OK. Listen, Helen, it was good to see you. I'm sorry

again. Send me your bank details and I promise I'll pay you back.' He lowered his mask again and went off through the crowd, cannoning into a group of Dothraki warriors, who were stripped to the waist.

Helen stood blinking after them. So he hadn't been awful after all? And he hadn't not fancied her, or thought she was boring? He'd had his own issues going on the whole time? That was…kind of a revolutionary thought. She was going to have to ponder it a bit just as soon as she'd found…

'Helen?'

She turned, slowly, adopting a nonchalant tone. 'Oh, hi, Karl. Funny meeting you here! What a coincidence.'

'Well, I invited you along, so it's not funny at all, no.' Karl was standing in front of her, holding a guitar, and dressed in normal clothes—well, for him a Doctor Who T-shirt was normal.

'Oh yeah. I…forgot.'

He frowned. 'Were you looking for me?'

'Oh, no, no.'

'Are you sure? Because I heard you shout "Karl".'

'Oh. Maybe I was then.'

'So why did you say it was a coincidence?' His forehead puckered in confusion.

'I don't know.' Once again Helen felt the conversation slide away from her. What had he said? *I can't deal with unclear inputs.*

She took a deep breath. 'Um, I wanted to see you, but I thought you'd be angry with me.'

'You mean because your boss stole all my game ideas and ran off with them?'

'Er, yes. Are you angry?'

Karl looked as if he hadn't considered it. 'I'm not sure.

If I were, would I be grinding my teeth when I think about you, and having lots of shouty imaginary conversations with you, and shaking my fist in the air?'

'Um, yes.'

'Oh, right then. I am angry, yes.'

'I'm sorry. I honestly had no idea it was in my contract. He said it was standard and I was too afraid to look at it properly.'

'What a berk.'

'I know. I hope he gets eaten by a load of velociraptors.'

'That's very unlikely because…'

'I know. I know. Karl. I'm very sorry this happened. I knew nothing about it. I swear. And—' she took a breath '—I'm also sorry about what happened with…you know.'

'Your inviting me round and then being there with some other bloke's tongue down your throat?'

God, did he have to be so literal? 'Um. Yes, that.'

Karl scratched his chin. 'You know, I'm not good at reading these things. I get it wrong a lot. But I was assured, by people who know—well, Ian the bassist—that your inviting me round, and not to fix your computer or install your Wi-Fi, was code for a sexual or romantic encounter.'

She stuttered, 'Well maybe not *sex*.'

He looked perplexed. 'You didn't have a romantic and/or sexual interest in me?'

Helen felt miserable. 'Yes then. I did.'

'Which? Romantic or sexual?' This came from what appeared to be a girl dressed as Frodo, who was listening in to their conversation along with the mixed crowd of Ghostbusters, Stormtroopers, Klingons, and warriors who had gathered around them.

'Um…both?'

Karl nodded. 'So I was right, then. But that means you had the other guy there to—hurt my feelings?'

'No! Honestly, no no no. He just turned up. And he's… well, he's the…' Helen glanced round at the crowd. 'OK. You know that bit in *Doctor Who* where Billie Piper gets stuck in an alternative dimension and her and the Doctor can't reach each other?'

'Of course,' said Thor, nodding. 'Doomsday. Part two of the episode "Army of Ghosts".'

'Right. Well, Ed is—was—my Rose Tyler. That's how I always felt about him, at least. Like I could never reach him.'

'You know her character's name?' said Karl.

'Of course.' She smiled at him weakly. 'In case you haven't figured it out by now, I too am a massive geek. I made a mistake, Karl. I should never have lied to you. That guy—he's gone now. I haven't even heard from him since. And I'd like to say, just so we can be a hundred per cent clear, I wish we were still hanging out, working on the game, watching *Lord of the Rings*, all that.'

'The extended editions?'

She nodded. 'Plus DVD extras.'

Karl regarded her for a long time, as if trying to solve a difficult algorithm. Then he said, 'Director's commentary?'

'What?'

'Would you watch the director's commentary of *Lord of the Rings* with me?'

'Yes, yes, I would watch anything with you, Karl. Do you not see what I'm trying to say?'

'I'm not sure. Are you trying to say you still have an A) romantic, or B) sexual, interest in me?'

Helen looked round at the crowd of hobbits and Smurfs and Ewoks. 'C,' she said. 'Both of the above.'

'Well, Helen, I think I have that same interest in you.'

'You do?'

The tannoy crackled and a nasal voice said, 'Will Karl please come to the stage area, that's Karl to the stage area. Citation Needed are waiting to start their set and Nigel says they can't lift the amp without you.'

His head turned. 'I better go.'

'But wait!' Helen watched, disbelieving, as he turned and strode through the crowd. The Wookiees and Ewoks and superheroes parted to let him past. 'Wait…Karl!' Helen chased after him, the laces of her Converse getting caught in the wheels of a Dalek.

'Exterminate! Watch where you're going!'

Karl had made it through to the main hall, in which a stage had been erected. Several Karl-like guys were on it, staring out from under long hair and picking at guitars and drums. Karl was now climbing up, adjusting the microphone to his six foot four frame. Helen fought her way to the front, aware that her hair was three times normal size from the heat, her shirt was unironed and sweaty, and her skin hadn't been ex-foliated in weeks. This was what happened when you let the Routine slide. This was what happened when you let people disrupt your life. When Marnie came back.

'Hi there,' said Karl, in his normal voice, booming out of the microphone. 'We're called Citation Needed…'

'Open bracket Citation Needed close bracket!' chanted the crowed. This seemed to be a thing. Helen was surprised. Did Karl's band have actual fans?

'Thanks. We're going to do a song I wrote recently for someone I met. I don't know if I like her any more, or if she likes me, but it's a good song, so we thought we'd play

it all the same. It's called "Ms Not-American Pi". That's
*p-i*, folks.'

The drummer, who was twenty stone and balanced pre-
cariously on a tiny stool, counted *one two three four* and
they launched into the song. Karl belted out the lyrics.

'I met you when I fixed your website
It needed much better security oversight
I came to like you quite a bit
Even though you still had a Wii Fit
But now there's trouble with your boss
And that makes me really quite cross
But then I realised love's a bug
That I can't get out of my site's code…
Woah, woah, my, my, Ms not-American Pi…'

And the other band members started chanting numbers:
'3.14…'

Helen gaped. It was about her! The song was about her.
The Comicon crowd was going wild. Chanting all the dig-
its of pi, whooping at Karl's every slight shuffle, as if he
were Geek Elvis. As the song ended, something hit him in
the face. A pair of Superman-logo pants.

'Thank you,' said Karl, removing them. 'I hope these
were clean because the risk of communicable disease from
underwear is actually quite high. I'll be back once I've applied some hand sanitiser. Rock on!'

And Helen realised, in the way that sometimes a thing
has to slap you in the face to be seen, that she loved him.
This was her Velcro. Not Ed with his dreamy eyes and angst
and expensively tousled hair. This man, who was so honest as to be almost rude, and as straightforward as a line of

code. She ran to the side of the stage, where Karl was indeed cleaning his hands. 'The song?'

'Oh hello,' he said, as if he'd forgotten she was there.

'I didn't know that you…'

'I like you, Helen. I know you're supposed to play games and not say that, but I must say it seems a highly inefficient way of doing things. However, as previously discussed, you had some other bloke's tongue down your throat, which suggests you don't like me back.'

'But I do! I do like you, I do, in fact I might lo—um. The thing is, I didn't understand how it all worked. I was looking for—romance, and angst, and someone I could help. I didn't realise things could be just…straightforward.'

'I don't need help. I know to cook and clean and look after myself. I don't need anything at all from you.'

She stared at him. 'But then how would it work?'

He gave her an exasperated look. 'I'd heard women could be cray cray, but I always thought that was just part of the patriarchal hegemony. However I must say I'm finding this *very* confusing.'

'Oh, me too. It's a whole big situation I won't go into now, but which involves me feeling I have to do things for the people I like, take care of them, make them happy. And also that unless I do that I'm no good to them and they might be secretly angry with me. I won't go into it all but I think that's the basic psychological situation we're dealing with here.'

'I don't work like that. If I'm annoyed, I make an error report. If not you can assume all systems are running fine.'

'That sounds very—restful.'

The guitarist was tuning up. 'I have to go,' said Karl. 'The crowd will go mad if we don't play our biggest number, "Dr

Whom". It's about grammar. And time travel.' He paused. 'If you want, you can stay here and watch.'

'Great. I can hold your hand sanitiser, if you like.'

Karl smiled at her. 'Thank you. That would be helpful.'

So Helen was helpful, and she waited till the end of their set, and she didn't feel worried about a thing. Everything was exactly the way it was supposed to be.

Well, she was slightly worried that the drummer might break his stool or someone might trip on a lead and be electrocuted or that several members of the crowd would suffocate inside their costumes. But perhaps it was possible, she reflected, as she watched Karl rock out to the adoring crowd, to be happy and relaxed while also paying the correct amount of attention to health and safety.

\* \* \*

*Ani.*

'Don't be nervous, now.'

'I'm not nervous. I've been on loads of dates.' Ani dodged her mother's hand, which was on its way to rearrange her hair. 'Stop fussing, Mum!'

'OK, OK. Are you sure jeans…'

'Yes, I'm sure jeans. What do you want me to wear, an off-the-shoulder cocktail dress? It's either this or my court suits. I don't want to scare the poor man off. What does he do anyway?'

'Oh, something in computers. His uncle plays golf with your father. They're a nice family.'

Of course he was in IT. Like every single other boy her parents had lined up. Ani had secretly been hoping for a surgeon, noble and caring. But then, you'd never know where his hands had been. She smoothed down the lock of hair her mother had been aiming for. She'd agreed to having it pinned up, and let her cousin Pria slather her in make-up, but she'd insisted on wearing jeans and a basic white top. Simple. Casual. Anything to detract attention from the fact she was about to go on a date in her parents' living room, with her parents, the guy's parents, and possibly Pria if she didn't bugger off soon. She was hovering around, casting covetous looks at Ani's Mac make-up.

'Is he loaded? If he's loaded and you get married, will you buy me an iPad?'

'No. Why are you still here?'

'Pleeeeease.'

'No, it'll stunt your brain. Anyway I don't need a man to be loaded, I've got my own money, duh.'

'But what if you want to stop work and have babies and get coffee in Starbucks all day long?'

Ani was shocked—was this what girls nowadays aspired to? 'Instead of an iPad, I'm buying you a copy of *The Female Eunuch*.'

'The female unicorn?'

Ani rolled her eyes. 'Seriously, P, go home. If you're here when he arrives, I swear I'm telling your sister you offered to tag her wedding photos on Facebook. All 2,745 of them.'

'Allllll right. God, like, take a chill pill. He's not gonna want a drama llama for a wife, is he.'

'We're not getting married! It's just…casual drinks. With a family friend. In our living room. With Mum and Dad there. And also his mum and dad.'

Ani's father mounted the stairs, looking stricken. 'The Desais are here,' he hissed. 'And my tzatziki's curdling! We won't have enough to go with the breadsticks!'

'Oh no!' Ani's mother disappeared after him, with one last instruction to her daughter. 'Get downstairs. And smile! And don't talk about divorce law!'

Pria fiddled with a lipstick. 'Ani? Can I ask you something?'

Ani poked at her eyebrows in the mirror. Maybe she should have had them threaded? 'OK, as long as it's not about my love life.'

'You know if a boy is kind of mean to you, and ignores you, and laughs when you walk past—does that mean he likes you?' Pria's pretty face was a study in pretend nonchalance. Suddenly Ani wanted to hug her smart little cousin.

'Well. Sometimes it might. But shall I tell you something I've realised recently, P? The boys who really like you, who don't have anything to prove? They'll just be nice to you. You won't have to work out if they like you, because they'll just tell you.'

'Tell you? Weirdos!'

'I know, it sounds mad. But trust me. It's actually pretty refreshing.' Ani felt a stab of loss. If only she'd figured this out a bit sooner. 'And if you do find one of those nice boys, hang on to him, OK?'

Pria tossed her long hair. 'Maybe. I don't care what stupid Andrew McKinley thinks anyway. He keeps singing Bollywood songs when I go past.'

'Sounds like he fancies you then. But what matters more is whether you fancy him. And if he makes you feel happy, OK?'

'OK. Whatevs. You better go, your future husband's in the lounge.'

*I am actually in a Jane Austen novel*, Ani thought to herself as she went downstairs. *Soon someone will fall off a horse and a man I don't like will send me a piano.* Rosa would love it. She had another brief pang, as she had approximately five times an hour since she'd last seen Nikesh. She'd never have had to pretend to like highbrow culture around him.

She pushed open the door with a bright smile pasted

on, pausing only to propel Pria out the front door from where she was lurking by the coats. 'Hiiii…!' She trailed off, speechless. 'Oh my… What are you doing here?'

The man by the fireplace was smartly dressed in a suit, and his hair had been recently cut. He looked nervous too— almost a mirror of her expression, and his surprise was the same too. He frowned. 'Ani? What the hell's going on?'

'Language,' scolded his mother, who was wearing a cream trouser suit and lots of make-up.

Ani's mother came in. 'Now, here we are, isn't this lovely! Anyone for dip? Anisha, don't just stand there, say hello!'

But Ani and Nikesh ignored their parents, and continued to stare at each other from across the room.

\* \* \*

*Rosa.*

'Hey! Rosa.' Jason greeted her cautiously as she knocked on his door, winded from rushing into the office. 'Just to check, are you planning to shout at me again?'

'No,' she panted.

'Not much point without all the senior members of the board present, huh.'

'Um, I guess not.' She looked at his office. Bare of all personal possessions. His framed surfing poster was propped up against the chair. 'You're out too, eh?'

'It turns out print isn't really for me. I need things to be faster, more…you know.' He clicked his fingers. 'Just… more. I only came in for the last issue. Got to at least go out in style.'

'And I hear you're off to run a list site again. Congratulations.'

'Thank you. It's just a small one, but it's growing fast. I have big plans. And you?'

'Who knows. Just can't do this any more. Maybe I'll dig out that novel. Though no doubt you'd say that was a dead art form.'

'Oh, I don't know about that.' Jason pushed his hair out of his eyes. It had grown back, and he was once again in his surf dude clothes of jeans and flip-flops (despite it being February)—the shirt and tie had never really been him, hot as he'd looked in them. Rosa felt fragile beside him, peering up sheepishly from under her fringe.

'I just wanted to say, good luck, and, you know, I'm sorry for how I acted that time.'

'Which time? When you stormed off and left me in the pub, or when you shouted at me in front of the entire board?'

'Er, both? Both.'

'OK.' His gaze was impenetrable, steely grey. 'You're sorry.'

'I'm really sorry!' she said. 'I never dated. I didn't realise it was OK to have lots of things going at the same time. I guess a relationship to me is like…a novel. You only read one, until it's finished. But I know now for most people it's like flicking through YouTube videos or something.'

'I've been known to read a book now and again,' he said. 'I'm not a functional illiterate. I am a former editor of a national newspaper.'

'I bet you always have more than book one on the go, though.'

'Sometimes. Unless it's a really, really good one.' She was suddenly very aware of him, the shift of muscles in his arms, the stillness of his face as he watched her. He said, 'Rosa. Here's the thing. I would like you to write for me at the new place I'm working.'

'Oh, that's…'

'But I'm also quite keen to date you. Once you're over

your divorce and you've spent your own time back in the game, seen a few other people.'

'But I don't want...'

'You do. You just don't know it yet. Trust me, you'll get to the point of being ready.'

'So, what does that mean? I honestly don't think I'm cut out for all that, Tinder and multiple people, and yes, setting up dates while you're out with someone else. I know that's normal now and apparently not incredibly rude after all, but it's not me. I just can't do it.'

Jason said, 'I broke off an engagement last year. I'm not ready for, you know, *War and Peace*. Not just yet.'

'Well, it doesn't have to be...'

'It would be though. With you.'

'So...' Rosa risked looking up from her ballet pumps. 'What happens now then?'

Jason picked up his framed poster, which made his arms ripple in a quite distracting way. 'How about you write for me, and we'll see about the rest. We can bookmark it. For now.'

'But, how will I find you?'

'Well, as you know, I'm on Tinder.' He smiled. 'Why don't you find me on Facebook? I'll be the guy who's topless and holding a surfboard.'

'Ha. Um, OK then.'

'Bonza.' He moved past her.

'Jason?' she called. 'What makes you think we'd be, you know, *War and Peace*?'

'Oh, I don't know. Call it a journalistic hunch.' And he was gone, with a wink. Well, how about that, Rosa thought. There was always another story to tell.

# Chapter 28
## Bean Counting

*Helen*

What with all the upheaval of recent months—Karl, and the website, and the Ex Factor, and everyone falling out with each other, and Marnie's disappearance—Helen had really got behind with the Routine. It'd been weeks since she'd cleaned behind the armchairs, for example, and she didn't even want to think about the effect on her pores of not cleansing and toning properly. Staying at Karl's flat had its advantages, but access to a full range of skincare was definitely not one of them. So one day, about three weeks into their burgeoning relationship—relationship! Her!—Karl was busy with the band, who were laying down some cool new tracks about parabolas, so Helen decided to have a big clear-out. And it was satisfying, snapping on her yellow Marigolds and getting out her little carry-case of cleaning products. Maybe she would have to ease off on the Routine a little—having a six-foot-four hairy man around did not lend itself to domestic immaculacy—but she could give the place a damn good scrubbing now.

Watched by a disdainful Mr Fluffypants—who behaved much better when Karl was around to reason with him: 'Now come on, Sir Fluff, it really is a bit off of you to eat the computer wire, can we compromise on this fishy treat instead?'—she pulled out the chairs and magazine rack and prepared to give everything a once-over with the hoover.

But what was that? Helen prided herself on being the one person in the world who didn't have rogue crumbs, coins, or bits of rubbish under her furniture. Yet there was something lying on the floor. Paper. She bent down and unfolded it. Marnie's name. Of course, she was forever leaving things scattered about, tissues, lip balms, articles she'd ripped out of the paper when she'd decided she could become a potter and then forgotten all about it, etc., etc. It looked like a boarding pass. Helen squinted at it. *Miss Marina Jones, Flight BE265 from Glasgow to London Gatwick, 12 January 2015.* Glasgow. Glasgow? But…she'd been in Argentina, hadn't she? With a suspicious lack of tan and no apparent knowledge of the country. Hmm.

Feeling like a snooper—though why had Marnie dropped it so carelessly if it was important?—Helen picked up the next piece of paper. A P45, also in the name of Miss Marina Jones. Bean Counters. Helen knew the name—a chain of coffee shops, including one in Covent Garden. And they had a black uniform with a small red logo on it. Just like Marnie had been wearing that day when she had to rush off after lunch. The pay was pitifully small once you took out tax and National Insurance and…was that 'uniform charge'? For that horrible nylon top? It seemed to add insult to injury.

The next thing was a letter from Glasgow Social Services. *Dear Miss Jones, we are writing to address your complaint about the treatment of Mr Frank Jones.* Who was…but then, Helen remembered. Years ago. Marnie's mum, crying into the phone, while Helen froze in Marnie's living room playing with My Little Ponies. 'Please, Frank. Please come home. Please don't leave me. She doesn't love you like I do! I'll do anything.' Marnie raising her voice and starting to sing, drowning it out. Bryan Adams, "Everything I Do, I Do It For You". Their favourite song back in 1993. Helen had no idea Marnie was even in touch with her absent father, who appeared to be in a care home in Glasgow.

Glasgow. It all fell into place suddenly. Marnie's pallor when she'd come back. Her wardrobe of thick jumpers and coats. Her sudden penchant for fried things. She'd been in Scotland all that time, not South America. And all of a sudden Helen knew exactly where to find her best friend.

\* \* \*

Helen was not, absolutely not, the kind of person who bought her train tickets at the station. She always booked well in advance, saving up to a third and selecting a quiet carriage and a table seat facing forward with a plug socket. But what would Marnie do? She would just go, and worry about the cost later. So Helen would try that. Because being Helen had got her nowhere in her life, just a shut-in world of cat and box sets and very, very clean floors.

When she reached King's Cross, there was a train in ten minutes to Glasgow. She wanted to be on it before she had time to rethink her decision. She gulped at the cost—had she got it wrong? No, that was just the price you paid for not being organised. For letting your best friend get lost in the first place, so that you had to go and find her. She tapped in the details, and took out her debit card, and then, once the tickets had whirred out, grabbed them and dashed to the platform. As she jumped on with minutes to spare, breathless, and the train began to pull away before she'd even stowed her bag or bought a coffee or found her seat, Helen found she had a smile spread all over her face. Who cared about the cost or the lack of organisation? Just for a change, it was fun to do something impulsive.

Glasgow was five hours from London. Enough for it to be just about worth going there on a whim, but not enough to prevent you having time for a serious rethink. What if she was wrong, and Marnie wasn't there at all? What if Marnie was furious, and gave her short shrift? What if she'd shacked up with an angry Scottish man who would hound Helen from the door with a claymore? (No, that was *Highlander* she was thinking of.) Karl liked *Highlander*. Karl would have helped her pass the journey, asking her a series of riddles to distract her, or engaging in impassioned debate, with bullet points and charts, about who was the best Doctor Who. Then he would have refused to eat anything from the buffet without seeing written proof of its hygiene rating. As it was, Helen had not left herself time to visit Pret, so she had to make do with mini cheddars and tepid tea, while London melted away into green, and the miles and miles of country that wasn't the capital. It was hard to remember that sometimes, when you were stuck there among the rush and anxiety. That the country was full of people who never used dating apps, or worried about getting into the latest bar, and never ever rode the tube, but instead just got on with their lives. Who met other people, and liked them, and just accepted the happiness that was offered. As she settled back into her seat, Helen wondered what that might be like.

She thought of how it was with other friends, how you all paddled in the same river, and people got swept away over the years, however tightly you held their hand. But with Marnie, sometimes, so many times, she'd thought her gone, only to look up and see her behind or in front, paddling the same way. Sometimes Helen wasn't sure which of them was following the other. She could only hope that this time she hadn't lost sight of her for ever.

* * *

'Aye?' A beautiful girl dressed in scrubs greeted Helen in the reception of the nursing home. She had dyed black hair, rings her nose and ears, and a tattoo sleeve.

This was a daft idea. Would Marnie even be here? 'Um, hi. I'm looking for a Frank Jones, is he staying here?'

'Aye, he is. You want to see him, that it?'

'I was actually looking for his daughter. I'm a friend of hers. I don't suppose you might…know where I can find her?'

The girl stared for a moment, looking Helen up and down. Eventually she said, in neutral tones: 'Helen.'

'Yes! How did you…?'

The girl sighed. Helen saw her name badge said *Elspeth*. 'She's in there. But I'm not at all sure she'll be glad to see you, you know.'

* * *

The big room smelled of boiled cabbage and sickness. Old people sat shrunk into chairs, while daytime TV showed the results of an on-air paternity test. Helen spotted her immediately, her skin glowing white and luminous among all this age and infirmity. She was bending over the man in the chair—who Helen knew was not even seventy yet, but looked eighty—and holding a plastic cup for him to sip from. As Helen watched, he batted it away, annoyed. 'Don' want tha' shite.' His voice was slurred.

'Dad, you have to drink water. Look what happened last time, they said your kidneys nearly packed up.' Marnie was wearing jeans and a plain grey hoody, no make-up. She looked beautiful. Helen could see she was about to turn. Every instinct in her body told her to run, avoid the coming confrontation. But she stood there, waiting, as Marnie straightened up. And saw her.

Marnie was not one to avoid confrontation. Or anything. While Helen hid from life, she'd always been the one to march in with her chin held up. And that's what she did now, seeing her best friend, her former best friend, standing in a Glasgow care home. She stared for a moment, her eyes blazing, then she set the cup down and marched over to Helen and past her, jerking her head at the patio doors. Helen followed her out to the cold lawn. Marnie had her arms folded over her body. 'What the hell?'

'Um…hi.'

'How did you…?'

'You left your letters and things. It was under the chair. Were you… Were you here all the time?'

'I did go to Argentina, but I had to come back after a week. Dad had a stroke. He can't really talk or feed himself or anything.'

'I'm sorry.'

Marnie bit her lip, for a second looking twelve years old and vulnerable, and then the tigerish expression was back. 'So now you know. Pissing rain instead of sunny beaches. Arguing with social services instead of snorkelling. Serving coffee to wankers in suits instead of snogging Latin hunks. Dad didn't really want me here—you know what he's like, so damn stubborn and independent—so I came back to London, but they weren't looking after him properly in that other home. I need to be here. So, you were right. Life isn't exciting and amazing and hashtag-blessed. It actually kind of sucks.'

'Why didn't you tell me?'

'Oh, I was embarrassed. I always try to be so positive, and look where I end up. No proper job, no money, staying in my dad's crap council house. I should have been like you, and opened a pension, and flossed regularly, and never dated anyone.'

'I'm dating someone,' said Helen, staring at the gutter.

'What? Who?' Marnie narrowed her eyes, and Helen knew what she was thinking.

'It's Karl,' she said quickly. 'You know, the guy from your party.'

'That nerdy one?'

'He's actually lovely. Really, really lovely.'

'Well, that's good, I suppose.'

Helen swallowed. 'You know, I did want you around, Marn. I've missed you so much. I was just—I hate having people stay with me, you know that. It's my whole tidy-anxiety thing. That'll have to change now I'm basically dating a nerdy Viking. And after the Ex Factor, I guess I was cross you matched me with Dan. We had the world's most awkward date. I felt like you'd just set me up with someone you met once ten years ago.'

Marnie tutted. 'Honestly, he was fine when I met him. He was really fun. And I thought, since you like computers and gaming and that, you'd maybe get on with him. If anything he was a bit too fun for me. I was absolutely hammered on our date.'

'He was still drinking then?' Helen thought about it, and everything began to make sense. Poor Dan. She sighed. 'I'm sorry. I'm just…well, like you said, I'm as bad as my mum. Although she's doing better. And so is yours—apparently she has some nice librarian boyfriend. She'd like to see you.'

'Hmph. Maybe. If she's really ditched the racist.'

'And, I'm sorry I didn't tell you about Ed and me. About all of it. I'm so sorry, Marnie. I did a terrible thing.'

Marnie tutted again, tossed her head. 'And is it true what Ani said? That you've always been in love with him?'

'Um, yes. I was, anyway.' As she said it, Helen realised the terrible yearning had gone. It was like waking up pain-free after a decade of really bad toothache.

'Even when you introduced us?'

Helen nodded uncomfortably.

'Wow.' Marnie threw up her hands. 'I'd no idea. I just thought you were happy being single. I thought you'd be one of those people who falls in love standing in the bus queue or something.'

'I sort of was, I guess. Well, with the guy who fixed my website.'

'Why do you never *say* anything, Helen? Why don't you ever just tell me, *Oh by the way, Marnie, I'm really into that guy I just introduced you to*, or *Hey, Marn, I really need my own space, could you find a flat*, or *Hey, Marnie, it's annoying when you leave your stuff lying about or date people all the time and then it doesn't work out and you tell me all about it*?'

'It's not annoying,' said Helen, unconvincingly.

'How am I supposed to know otherwise? If you don't tell me you're cross, I'll just assume everything is cool.'

'I do the complete opposite of that. I assume everything is bad unless I'm told otherwise.'

'Sounds bloody knackering.'

'It is. I'm going to work on it.'

Marnie sighed. 'Why are you here, Helen? I can't hack it in London. I thought it would be cool if I came back, and I missed you guys, but it's too big and scary. I can't afford restaurants and cocktails and things like that. I was just pretending—I didn't want to tell you I'd no money. And you'd lost all the weight. I mean, you look great, but I guess I wasn't expecting it, and you didn't seem to want me around as much as before. You had your life so sorted. Nice flat, great job...'

Helen snorted. 'I'm practically married to my cat, I'd hardly left the house in two years, and I was working for a cut-throat lunatic. I'm not sorted, Marn. You're the one with the cool amazing life.'

Marnie looked ironically back at the care home. 'Yep, look how cool and amazing it is. Then the thing with Tom—I did like him, but I guess part of me was sort of hoping Ed would see me with someone else, realise he wanted me back. It's stupid, I know. There's just this part of me that always has to have a guy interested. If I don't, I don't know—I feel like I won't exist or something. And yes, I'm aware this is not unconnected to the fact my dad wouldn't stay and my mum can't live without a man.'

Helen said nothing. Sometimes, that was the right response.

'You know, when everything happened and I left...' Helen winced at the memory '...my life just seemed to go off track. All this travelling, meeting guys, dating—and nothing ever sticking. I thought if I came back, if you were around, and Ed too, maybe I could get myself sorted. Go back to the last time my life actually worked.'

It was the same thing Ed had said. All three of them, spending the last two years lost and wandering. What a waste. 'Why did you go, Marnie? I never knew. Why did you break up with him?'

She screwed up her eyes. 'Oh, I just couldn't take it any more. Ed is so—he was always chipping away at me. Why didn't I get a proper job. Why didn't I read more serious literature. Why didn't I dress differently. And always hinting he might be about to leave me, then when I got closer, pulling away again. Asking me to move in, then hinting he was going to go travelling or move to New York. And his bloody music—has he ever actually done anything with it, after ten years going on about it? It was such a headwreck. But I hadn't the strength to break up with him and stay. I just had to run.'

Helen realised he'd done the same to her. Asked her to Bristol once he'd seen her with Karl at the party, then when she'd come running, dropped off the radar again. Keeping her on the hook, never quite saying he wasn't interested, but never committing either. Criticising one minute, complimenting the next. 'What about now? You and him?'

Marnie rolled her eyes. 'Oh. He asked to see me, before I left.'

'He did?'

'Yeah. Maybe we should give it a go again. That he'd change, blah blah.'

'And were you tempted?'

'Tempted? Of course. I mean, he's Ed. You know.' Helen

nodded. She did know. 'But once I found out you were in love with him—I couldn't do that to you. I think he's caused enough damage.'

'And now?'

Marnie shook her head. 'Oh, he's still texting, but he'll stop. I guess the thing about Ed is, he likes to have you as an option. Once he thinks you might be moving on, back he comes. But he'll always leave again. Won't he?'

'Yeah. I think so.' Helen smiled. 'And when you think about it, he's actually exactly the kind of unemployed musician who lives with his mum that Ani would warn us against.'

'Talking about me?' said a voice. Helen and Marnie stared at each other, as around the corner came Ani, struggling in her heels on the muddy grass, and Rosa, waving her phone in the air. 'Is there a plug socket? I need to tweet about this. It'd make a story for my new writing gig. *How I went to Glasgow on ten minutes' notice and I didn't even have time to charge my phone.*'

'Guys!' Helen gaped at them. 'What are you…?'

Ani wiped her shoes with distate. 'Brand new bloody Manolos, these. Oh, Karl told us where you went, and we decided we all needed to be here.'

'You came to Glasgow?' Marnie was gaping too.

'Yes, and it's freezing. I literally don't know how people survive up here.'

'Do you think they have Wi-Fi?' said Rosa, still swinging her iPhone. 'Oh, sorry. I forgot. Come here.' And she gathered Helen and Marnie in a big hug, which Ani joined in on, though carefully, so as not to damage her shoes. 'I'm so sorry about your dad, Marn. You poor thing. Want me to write an exposé of the care home system?'

'Or we could sue them,' said Ani. 'Are you OK, love?'

Marnie looked at them. 'I guess. Guys—the things I said—I'm sorry—'

'We're all sorry,' said Rosa. 'We're a pack of eejits, as Jason would say.'

'Oh, it's *Jason* again, is it?' asked Helen.

Rosa blushed. 'Maybe. Time will tell. Marn, is your dad going to be OK?'

She shrugged. 'Whatever OK means. He'll get better, I'm told, but slowly. Anyway, I'm fine here for now. I'm tired of moving on all the time, plus it's a good excuse to keep Ed away. There's no way he'd ever slum it in Scotland.'

'It's over then,' Ani asked, looking between them. 'For both of you?'

'It is for me,' said Helen, shyly. 'I have a certain web programmer slash singer-songwriter to think of now.'

'It's over for me too,' said Marnie. A familiar smile crossed her face—the one that said, *Well, we've had a rubbish time of things, but there are always more adventures to be had*. The one that said, *Let's get our game faces on, and enjoy life*. The one that said, *You know what would be a great idea, Helz? Let's dye our hair blue!* 'I might be sort of off men for now, anyway.'

Rosa's well-groomed eyebrows shot up. 'Really?'

'Yeah.' Marnie nodded to the window, where inside the beautiful tattooed girl was hanging out cups of tea. 'That's Elspeth. Me and her are—well, she's pretty cool. She plays bass guitar and does street art in her spare time. She's just—I don't have to try with her. I can be myself. I don't have to be that cool laid-back girl who never asks for anything.'

Ani smiled. 'Ah. That's great.'

'Thanks. Maybe you can meet her. Are you staying to-night?'

Ani looked at Helen, who shrugged. She hadn't even thought about it, and she'd forgotten the Doombag to boot. Little Miss Fix-It was away from home without so much as a clean pair of pants. 'Don't worry, I'm on it.' Ani snapped out her BlackBerry. 'Rosa, get on TripAdvisor. I'll do Airbnb. Whatsapp me if you find anything and Snapchat me some pictures. I'll get us an Uber too.' The two moved off across the lawn, typing and emoticon-ing and organising away. Helen realised that, this time, she could leave it all to some-one else.

She turned to her friend again. 'I meant it. You can stay with me anytime, of course you can.'

Marnie shrugged. 'Thanks. I'm OK for now. There's El-speth. And Dad, he actually needs me. I know he wasn't there when I was growing up, but sometimes it's easier to love people when they need you, rather than the other way round.'

Helen bowed her head. 'If I can do anything…'

Marnie gave her an amused, irritated look.

'OK, OK. I have to stop helping people. But in this case it seems polite to at least ask.'

'We're OK. I don't know how long Dad has, and it'll be tough, but you can't protect me from things. It just makes me feel you think I can't cope.'

'But I have to protect you,' said Helen awkwardly. 'It's how it works.'

'Like the time Cath Johnson said your mum was mad, and I kicked her in the boobs during PE? Or the time Sam Foxton tricked you into going behind the bike sheds? Don't you remember, I made out with him so I could tell everyone he kissed like a fish and tasted of eggs, and no one would go out with him for the whole of middle school? I protect you back, Helz. That's how it *actually* works.'

It was true. Helen didn't know how she'd have got through that year without Marnie. Fighting back to the bullies and gossips. Keeping their heads held high and their game faces on, in true Marnie style. 'I'm sorry. I didn't mean it. Any of it. If you could just forgive me, if we could be friends again…'

Marnie made a face. 'We still are friends, you numptie. We're just having a tiff. That's how people are. You can be yourself, and you can mess up, and we can have fights, and I'll still be your friend. You dumbass.'

'I see. Are we still having it, the tiff?'

Marnie squinted. 'Wee while longer. I'm still cross you never owned up about Ed, and told Ani and Rosa stuff you didn't tell me. I feel left out sometimes, you know. The three of you are so close.'

'Are you kidding? I feel left out all the time. It's so easy for you. You have charm. Everyone likes you.'

Marnie waved a hand. 'I'm like…pulled pork. Exciting for five minutes, then it's everywhere and you're sick of it. You're bread. Nice bread, I mean. Sourdough or something. You hold things together.'

'And lots of people won't eat it because they might get fat.'

'Yeah well, they're numpties too.'

'Is this a Scottish word? I kind of like it.'

'Useful up here.' Marnie cast an ironic look about her. 'Anyway, you don't need to worry about me. I'm all right. I don't need you.'

Helen sagged. 'Oh. OK. I'll just… I guess I'll go back then.'

Marnie held the patio door open, then called back over her shoulder. 'Helz? Just because I don't need you around, it doesn't mean I don't *want* you.'

'Will you come back to London some time? Please?'

'Maybe.' It was back, the vague Marnie head-toss. The one that implied she had millions of other places to be. And that even if those were, in reality, the neurological ward of Glasgow Royal Infirmary, and this shabby sad care home, they would somehow be made cooler by Marnie's mere presence. 'I'll have to see.'

'I'll be your best friend,' Helen called.

Marnie smiled. 'You already are my best friend.'

# Epilogue

*What happens when four women decide to date each other's exes? Off-liste's very own dating columnist Rosa Lieberman gives us the round-up, three months on.*

\* \* \*

I've learned a lot in the six months since my husband left me for a teenager (OK, she was twenty, but I think I've earned the right to some hyperbole). Things like: falling for your best friend's ex can lead to jealousy and treachery. Things like: dating a man who isn't divorced yet can lead to items being thrown, and accidental nudity in a stranger's living room. And things like: never date a man who keeps six spare toothbrushes in his bathroom. So what's become of our heroines now?

My friend H is still dating the Geek Rock God. The good news is they got their game ideas back—Consuela smuggled the document out of Spain on a USB shortly before Logan was extradited for tax fraud and breaches of the Data Protection Act. Consuela, Amanda, and Darren the gardener are now happily living in the Cayman Islands off what they siphoned from Logan's accounts before his arrest. Amanda's clothes are very well ironed and, as Consuela would say, everything is spiffing. H reports that she is adapting well to having her first-ever boyfriend. Even her cat seems to like the new arrangement, and has not bitten anyone since an unfortunate incident with an Amazon delivery man a month ago. H has done some work designing the best list-based site around (clue: you're reading it) and their game idea has been bought by the internet mogul behind this very site. Watch out for Swipe Out, coming to the apps store next month.

My friend A is dating Rich IT Man, much to the delight of both their families, and this will soon be her longest-ever relationship. They enjoy watching box sets of *The Good Wife* together while debating the finer points of divorce law. A reports that she is very glad not to have been on a first date in several months, or to have been accidentally proposed to in a restaurant with wipe-clean menus.

M is still out of town caring for her dad, but he's getting better, and she's started talking about how awesome it would be to go to Thailand with her girlfriend and learn Buddhist meditation, or maybe take up jewellery-making or hike the Himalayas. Neither she nor H have any contact with Hot Angsty Man, who reports suggest has finally left home and is now part of the hip electronic-music scene in Berlin.

The Theatre Critic is back with his wife, and they have just renewed their vows in a lavish ceremony on a Thames barge, which was of course extensively photographed. She has now allowed him to keep a maximum of ten books on display at any given time, and is learning to love Earl Grey. Protest Boy got 'married' to one of his squatmates, in a touching but non-official ceremony held under a tree in the New Forest. As the tree was due to be cut down, the bride and groom then shackled themselves around the trunk. The fire brigade had to saw them free after a badger swallowed the handcuffs key, but it made the papers and the new couple were said to be very happy about the publicity achieved.

The police did eventually find the hacker behind the Bit on the Side scandal, which saw marriages implode, end, and, in some cases, get better all across the country. The computer genius behind it, despite the predictions of Geek Rock God (hashtag-not all hackers), was in fact a sixteen-year-old girl from Wolverhampton, whose parents were splitting up because both of them had been using the site. Despite coordinating a countrywide campaign of industrial espionage, she got away with a caution because of her age, and has already been offered a place at MIT to study Computing. A film version of the story, *Love Hack*, will be released next year, starring Sukie Miller. Following a spell in an Indian ashram, Sukie found her zen, ditched her himbo boyfriend, who'd leaked naked pictures of her to the press, and is now tipped for an Oscar in her upcoming role. She's also rumoured to be dating Jake Gyllenhaal, who plays the hunky yet troubled police officer who tracks down the hacker (don't worry, she's been aged up to twenty in the film). A's flatmate, the actress, has been offered the role of the hacker's mother in the film, thanks to a few contacts A made on one whirlwind night out. Despite only being eight years older than Sukie, Gina is very pleased and will soon be moving to LA. This is handy for yours truly, as it means I'll be moving in with my best friend, where we plan to drink terrible wine, gossip, and never freeze cruciferous vegetables.

What about me, I hear you cry? Well, I'm happily writing freelance. My divorce is going through, and my ex-husband is back with the almost-teen he left me for. I wish them well, or as well as I can anyway. I've been on a few dates since joining an online dating site, as readers of this site will know, but for now I'm hanging up my romance gloves and taking some time out. Because here's the main thing I have learned in our bizarre dating project. I'll leave it to my friend M— who I'm pleased to announce will be taking over as our hobbies columnist as of next week—to explain it.

'The thing you must remember in life is this: it's not all about you. Dating, jobs, even your parents—everyone brings their own issues that are nothing to do with the other person. It's like you're having a picnic with someone. You might bring baguettes and ham and remember the napkins, but they might bring ice cream and it might melt all over the place and then you're attacked by ants. Similarly, they might bring the crippling self-esteem issues and the total lack of manners. It's not your fault. You brought what you could to the table. Or rug, whatever.

'So don't be disheartened. Sometimes, the biggest favour a person can do you is to dump you. And sometimes you have to get rid of old things to make way for the new.'

I'd like to thank my friend M for that metaphor, and tell her that, wherever she is, London will always miss her.

\* \* \*

—comment left by SurfDudeJase

Ms Lieberman, if you're going to write about your love life, I think you should be honest with your public and tell them that you're going on a date tonight with your incredibly handsome and very good at Scrabble editor.

-reply from RosaL

Dear SurfDude, please do not distract me, I am about to start reading a very important book. *War and Peace*. Have you heard of it?

-reply from SurfDudeJase
Ms L, we are very much on the same page.

-reply from SuzanneYogaQueen
Stop flirting online, you two, and for God's sake get on with
it, my Twitter feed is awash with your romantic babblings
and quite frankly it's making me want to puke up my kale
smoothie. Love, S. x

* * * * *

I'd like to thank Diana Beaumont, Anna Baggaley, and Angela Clarke, who each helped enormously in making this a better book.

Thank you to all my friends for supporting me during the writing, and sharing their stories of romantic disaster. Thank you to Beth Mason for letting me steal her job for the book. Special thanks to Scott Bramley for not being like any of the terrible men in this book. I should point out that the things I say about online dating are (mostly) for dramatic purposes only. It's not so bad really.

Thanks also to everyone who read *The Thirty List* and told me they liked it– if you'd like to get in touch I'm on @inkstainsclaire and would love to hear from you.

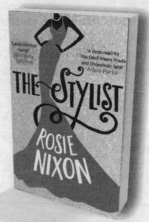